BEEP!

Beyond the Frogpond and Back

BEEP!

Beyond the Frogpond and Back

A NOVEL

by

Stewart Parks

Plowshare Media
LA JOLLA, CALIFORNIA

Library of Congress Control Number: 2008936789
Parks, Stewart
Beep! : Beyond the Frogpond and Back

ISBN: 978-0-9821145-3-7 (paperback edition)
ISBN: 978-0-9821145-4-4 (E-book edition)

Cover image: Richard Gallegos

PUBLISHER'S NOTE

For information about permission
to reproduce selections of this book, write to:
Permissions, Plowshare Media, P.O. Box 278, La Jolla, CA 92038
or visit PLOWSHAREMEDIA.COM
and email us directly.

ACKNOWLEDGEMENTS

FOR THE IDEA, P.D. OUSPENSKY

FOR THE METHOD, REINHARD LETTAU, FRANZ KAFKA & BERTOLT BRECHT

FOR THE MEANS, EVERY TEACHER I EVER HAD

FOR THE INSPIRATION, BOB DYLAN & KURT VONNEGUT

FOR THE PURPOSE, YEVGENY YEVTUSHENKO

FOR HER LOVE AND SUPPORT, MY WIFE MARIA

TABLE OF CONTENTS

Fundamental notions like order and structure condition our thinking unconsciously, and new kinds of theories depend on new kinds of order.... One of the reasons for doing science is the extension of perception and not of current knowledge. We are constantly coming into contact with reality better and better. — David Bohm

A Fork in the Path

It is early morning, still quite dark. Bob Pilhaus opens his eyes, awakening from a fitful dream. Close in his view is the ceiling of a Eurorail car. He is in a private sleeping compartment. The rhythmic vibration of steel wheels rolling on rails penetrates through his back as he lies in the Pullman berth. An occasional sway of the car testifies that the dual rails are not always set perfectly level on their wood ties and gravel bed.

"I've dreamt it then," he mutters to himself, as he recognizes his surroundings. The rather pleasant (and slightly erotic) content of his dream is brutally erased from his consciousness, replaced by the hard facts of waking reality. The more depressing, lonelier aspects of his current situation sink back into his brain with the crushing immediacy of a cannonball obliterating a butterfly.

Rolling over, he reaches out to part the heavy curtains covering the window. The small reading lamp is still burning overhead, so all he sees is his own reflection, pale and hollow-eyed. By switching off the lamp and darkening the compartment, he is able to distinguish some of the passing scenery outside, bathed in moonlight. It looks like farmland—flat fields, pasture, some trees, a fence line running close beside the track.

"We must be in France by now," he computes, checking his watch. "I need some help. I feel terrible!" He has a splitting headache, his stomach is growling, his ears are ringing painfully with the noise of the train, his nose is stuffy, and his eyes feel as though they have been lightly sandblasted.

Wincing as he flips the light back on, he surveys the disarray of his belongings strewn about the tiny compartment. Sitting up and reaching across to his backpack, he retrieves a folded, wrinkled postal envelope from one of its side pockets. Opening it carefully, the small paper bindle containing his last gram of Peruvian cocaine is revealed. He spoons out a couple of grains of the chunky, crystalline powder and begins chopping it methodically.

The tools for this job are close at hand, since he never bothered to put them away after the last twenty-hour binge. A single-edged razor blade and his government-surplus emergency signaling mirror make short work of pulverizing the chunks.

As he works, he sings to himself a folksong he had first heard performed a long time ago by Dave Van Ronk. It has somehow stuck with him, recurring every time he finds himself in this situation: "Cocaine is for horses, not for men. They tell me it will kill me but they won't say when..."

"I may be dying, but I'm gonna have a good time doing it," he says to himself, with conflicting tinges of determination and desperation. A dollar bill rolled up into a tube helps him funnel half the pile up each nostril, after dividing it into two short, white lines. Almost immediately he begins to wake up and overcome the symptoms of his hangover.

"I must have finished that whole liter of wine last night, 'cause there's the empty bottle. And over half that gram is gone so I must've whiffed it, unless I just got sloppy and spilled it somewhere." Such a mishap has been known to occur before.

He is briefly upset with himself, since he had intended to conserve his stash more carefully, but the exhilaration of his latest indulgence quickly asserts itself. All nagging symptoms of discomfort are driven out of his mind by the temporary, electric buzz of cocaine euphoria. He busies himself with packing up his belongings, tidying up the compartment. Getting dressed is no problem, as he had passed out the night before still wearing all his clothes.

Stumbling out into the gently rocking corridor of the train, he makes his way forward to the dining car. He wants some coffee and a cigarette first, then perhaps some food, if his rebellious stomach feels up to the task. By midday, the train should be pulling into Paris, then a short layover and transfer, and he will be on his way to Biarritz. His spirits are buoyed by the prospect that he will soon be surfing on the Basque coast. He is still slightly chagrinned about having fled his friend Dominic's home in Rome the morning before, with only the briefest explanation of "I've gotta get wet, Nic," but the coke quickly washes away that embarrassing memory.

There are few of his fellow passengers in the dining car at this early hour. He seats himself and orders coffee when the waiter comes around. He lights a cigarette and checks out the other occupants of the car. At the far end, in the very last dinette, is a curiously-dressed young woman sitting alone, facing him. She catches his eye immediately as he looks her way, and he is excited to see her offer him a brief but warm smile in acknowledgement. Even at a distance he can tell that she is strikingly attractive, with long, brown hair rolling off her shoulder and cascading down over her red dress, which appears to be a cross between an evening gown and a robe. It is low-cut in the front, displaying a bountiful bosom, but full-length, covering her legs in folds and draping to the floor, with a large hood attached at the shoulders.

"What a dish!" he thinks. "I wonder if she's alone?" He watches her until his coffee arrives, and since no one has joined her, he picks it up, screws up his courage, and shuffles down the aisle, stopping in front of her table.

"May I join you? Are you alone? Do you speak English? I hope you don't think I'm being too forward, but I couldn't help it—you look very familiar to me. Have we met? Are you an American?"

"'Those are very many questions for one breath," the woman replies calmly, "but yes, you may join me if you wish. I do speak English, and I suppose I am also 'American,' if you include the entire North American continent in that definition. I am Canadian by birth." She smiles up at him.

He slides into the seat opposite her, drinking in the vision of alluring, familiar femininity she presents. Though obviously a few years older than himself, she is still within his range, he figures. Her smile is dazzling, her teeth even and white. Her eyes are the clearest, most intense color of green he has ever seen. They absolutely sparkle. "God, she is even more beautiful than I dreamed," he notes to himself in awe, "but what's with this outfit she has on? Man, would I like to see what she's got under that thing...."

He becomes so engrossed in lustful images involving lifting the rich, red velvet fabric of her robe and burying his face in the curvital softness within, that he fails to notice she has not answered all his questions. Worse yet, he does not recognize the truth that he speaks inwardly—he has dreamed of this woman often, and as recently as last night.

With his eyes drooping low-liddedly to the luscious valley of her exposed cleavage, he introduces himself. "My name is Bob, but my friends call me BP, or just Beep, for short. Those are my initials—my last name is Pilhaus."

"My name is Esmeralda," replies the woman, bringing her hands up from her sides and rummaging through the copious folds of material mounded in her lap, "and I am not exactly traveling alone. This is my cat, Abraxus."

Standing up in her lap and flashing onto his screen, like a preview of a bad movie, is a large, black cat, staring back at him with another colder, wilder, feline pair of green eyes. Except for a certain glazed trace of cruelty and selfishness, and a slightly elongated, almond shape to the black pupils, they could be the same irises as Esmeralda's. The shade of green is identical, the luminosity equivalent.

BP is startled by this turn of events but tries to maintain his casual demeanor. "Y-you have a cat?" he stutters, trying to think of why this fact is so disturbing to him. "D-don't cats have to r-ride in cages in the baggage car or s-something? How did you get to keep him with you?" He is beginning to shake, visibly trembling. His cup rattles in its saucer as he squeaks out his words while setting it down.

"Abraxus is a she, actually," explains Esmeralda serenely. "She hates being in a cage and she is very cooperative, so I usually just carry her in my bag on trips like this." As she speaks, she reaches into the voluminous, woven straw handbag at her side and brings out a small, antique, wood-framed hourglass. Shaking it to empty one side of the glass, she turns it over and sets it deliberately on the table between them. The fine, white sand trapped in the upper chamber begins to flow to the one below.

"What are you doing?" BP is beginning to lose his composure as he follows her words and movements, which seem to him to be strangely disconnected. "Is this how much time you're giving me to talk to you? Are you playing some kind of game with me?" He fidgets in his seat, eyes downcast, paranoia creeping into his brain through every pore in his skin. The cocaine is a catalyst for this reaction, and it proceeds rapidly.

"My friend, Bob, don't be afraid," says Esmeralda soothingly, "I'm just trying to help you remember."

"Remember what? You're trying to make me blow it—lose my cool—aren't you? You probably love to play practical jokes on the men who approach you, right? Or else this is some kind of plot against me—is that it? You're playing with my brain, here! Who sent you? They put some kind of drug in my coffee, didn't they? Does this have anything to do with all the weird things that have been happening to me lately?" BP is clenching the edge of the table with his hands, knuckles turning white, ready to use this extra leverage to bolt upright and flee, if necessary. He looks around from side to side quickly, gauging escape routes, checking for any accomplices who might be bearing down on him at this very moment. He sees one of the waiters approaching their table. Is he in on the scheme? Part of her plot?

"No one is after you, Bob," Esmeralda assures him, "and this is not a joke. Please calm down and pay attention. There is no gigantic conspiracy against you, except for the one that you have constructed yourself. If you recall, it was you who found me! It would be a poor conspiracy, indeed, which depended so heavily for its success on the actions of the victim, don't you think? As for your theory about drugs, I'm sure that whatever you've taken was ingested voluntarily."

BP ceases his cowering as her words sink in. He straightens up in his chair and clears his throat, trying to control his racing heartbeat. The waiter arrives, takes their breakfast order politely and leaves. "I'm sorry," he apologizes, calming himself. "I must be in pretty poor shape to be so paranoid. As a matter of fact, I did do a couple of lines of coke when I got up this morning. Things have been going badly for me lately, and I guess I've been trying to make myself feel better with a little of the ol' laughing powder. 'Better living through modern chemistry,' that's my motto," he quips, trying to be glib.

"That's unfortunate," replies Esmeralda without a trace of humor, "because I believe that drugs may be a large part of your problem. Take cocaine, for instance—it can make you feel so good that you can forget things that are very important for your physical health, like eating and sleeping, for days on end. Or perhaps you might be forgetting something much more important, something essential for your mental health, for even longer."

"You're probably right. I've been getting awfully stoned lately, and I often have feelings that I'm forgetting something. But what does that have to do with this hourglass? Why are you timing me?"

"The hourglass is an instrument for measuring the passage of time, to be sure, but I'm using it here as a prompt, a symbol to jog your memory. I was hoping you would be able to remember where we've met before. Tell me, Bob, do you dream much when you sleep?"

"No, I don't think so," answers BP, defensively. "I mean, I don't know how much other people dream, so how am I supposed to compare myself? Anyway, when I do dream, I don't remember it for very long after I wake up." Her question puzzles him, as does her reference to having met him before.

"Do you try?" asks Esmeralda. "Never mind. Try for me now, will you? Look at the hourglass, relax, watch the sand running through its waist, and try to remember if you had a dream last night. What was it about?"

BP is confused and distracted, but he looks at the hourglass and tries to think, thankful for this small respite. "What's going on here?" he wonders. "Is this woman crazy? Am I? Should I get my butt out of here while the getting's good? Why is she playing with my mind like this? God, she's such a fine-looking lady! I'd really like to get next to her, but she scares the shit out of me...." Her physical attractiveness is overpowering. He has lost the drift of their conversation, and brushed past her question entirely, busying himself instead with preparing strategies for improving his position in her eyes. He can think of nothing else but finding a way to insinuate himself further into her sphere of attention, perhaps even to what must certainly be the sublime center—the creamy, nougat core....

He is drifting mightily, but is perceptive enough to realize that in his short experience of her, she has not been easily dominated, so he rejects the application of a forceful, macho image, his usual approach. Unfortunately, the only other alternative in his limited bag of tricks is to whine, and hope that she might want to be his naughty little nurse for awhile.

"I must really be cracking up," he says, finally getting back on track, managing to fashion his face into a limp and twisted half-smile (which he hopes is suitably endearing and pitiable). "I've been burning my candle at both ends for too long now. I must've burnt out some mighty important brain cells, 'cause I can't, for the life of me, figure out where we've met before, and I don't see how I could forget someone as beautiful as you. I mean, you are incredibly good-looking, and unusual as can be—what with the cat, the robe, the hourglass and all! You do look familiar to me, but I'll just have to throw myself on the mercy of the court, your Honor. I plead 'terminally burned synapses.' That's sort of like nolo contendere, I think." He leans back to assess the impact of his ploy. It doesn't seem to be having the intended effect. Instead of melting, she seems to have iced up considerably.

"Perhaps you aren't the man I thought you were," Esmeralda says coldly. "I could be mistaken."

BP plunges into depression as a somewhat stony silence builds up between them. Just when he decides that he has blown it, and is considering getting up and moving on, she speaks again: "Perhaps you can tell me something about yourself and we can discover our mistake."

He is so relieved at this opportunity to reinstate relations on a new basis that he attacks the assignment with the vigor of a capitalist ambassador in a developing nation.

His nausea disappears with the change of subject, and when their breakfast is served he eats mechanically, though he has little appetite for the food. By the time they are finished with their meal, he has delivered a virtual soliloquy detailing his life history (with the standard social editing to render it suitable for breakfast conversation), covering his youth in southern California, how good it was and how bad it went, his move to Hawaii, how much better it was and how much worse it went, and so on....

Throughout his speech, Esmeralda listens quietly and eats, nodding occasionally, acknowledging his words without judgment or declaration [though it is difficult for her to keep from wincing at the regularity with which tragedy has befallen our hero]. Phrases such as "I wish I could have...," "If only I had known that...," "I would have liked to...," "How could I have guessed...," are liberally laced into a fabric of bad breaks, rotten luck and missed opportunities, which make up the shabby clothing of BP's life, as he weaves it.

Nonetheless, she contains her disgust politely and listens carefully, until he has trudged his circular path back to the present and ends his story thusly: "So now my whole life has fallen apart and I don't know where to begin to pick up the pieces. If only I could start all over, I'd do it right the next time. I wouldn't be in the mess I'm in today."

"Everything can be retrieved, but that would not necessarily change anything," says Esmeralda firmly, startling BP with her first statement in twenty minutes. "In truth, you knew it all before."

"Wh-what? I don't think I understand you. How can you bring back something that has already happened? That's impossible!" BP is incredulous.

"That which is beyond one's comprehension always appears impossible. That is the nature of perceptual dependence. What cannot be seen cannot be believed, right? Unfortunately it's our dependence upon perception which creates the illusion of 'time,' the very commodity you feel you have squandered so thoughtlessly, and wish so desperately to have back. Well, my friend, 'time' such as that does not exist, not as you understand it. If you understood the true nature of time, you would realize that you are in a much bigger mess than you can even imagine at this moment, and you would remember where we have met before."

BP is beginning to wish he had not eaten so much—his stomach is starting to churn again. What she is saying sounds terribly ominous, almost threatening, yet he can't help but feel there is something germane, something horribly pertinent to his situation in her words. "I don't think I'm following you. Could you explain that to me again?"

"I'll try, but when speaking of the unspeakable, words are poor approximations of reality. What I'm trying to say is that giving order to our experience is only one aspect of the nature of time. Our perceptual processes are the means by which our human body interacts with the electromagnetic array that confronts us constantly, in our normal waking state. These processes filter, divide and code the radiation they receive so that the incoming information can be processed, transmitted, and stored, by means of the electrochemical conduit we call our 'nervous system,' and ultimately be transformed by our brains into outgoing responses to our environment. Without knowing which signal came first and which came second, we would be lost."

"OK," says BP, slowly. "I think I get that part. I know what all those words mean—I went to college—but what're you driving at?"

"The problem is that an organism's first priority is to survive. It deals with the input necessary for survival first, almost constantly, in our 'normal' state of consciousness. But the regime of perception exacts a price, a prerequisite, so to speak, a structure—what you call 'time'—within which it can function."

"Of course it does. Time is a constant. Everyone knows that." BP's mind is reeling from the esoteric, metaphysical twist their discussion has taken. He's extremely curious about where she's going with this.

"Time might not be exactly what you think it is," continues Esmeralda. "It's the baseline of our ordinary reality, our normal waking consciousness, and it's within this background that each moment comes and goes—but what happens when you sleep? Are you aware of time in the same way? Where does each moment go when it has passed? Is it destroyed? Is it lost? No! It still exists. It's just no longer available to us in fullness, in our normal state of consciousness, although we are connected to it partially by our memories. If one knows how to look, all things can be seen—past, present and future—but they are not seen with the eyes, as one usually sees. When reality is beheld in an altered state of consciousness, the world is transformed. The universe is a different place. You've taken enough mind-altering drugs to know that, certainly."

"Maybe I have, but you're talking craziness, here—hallucinations!" protests BP. "That's just a bunch of occult mumbo-jumbo. It's superstitious nonsense!"

"Believe what you will, I'm merely telling you what you asked to hear, I can't force you to accept what I say. It's very difficult to comprehend anything which doesn't resemble one's previous knowledge—isn't framed in the same format, or the same categories and hierarchies."

"But I wanted to know how you could bring back the past. That's what you said, isn't it—everything can be brought back? If I had only known then what I know now, I wouldn't have made such a mess of my life. I would've been able to see how things were going to turn out, and I would've been able to avoid all my silly mistakes and failures—really made something of my life—made the world a better place for myself and for everyone around me!"

"Well, Bob, explaining the mechanism by which such a change could take place is even more difficult and abstract than what I've already told you, which you don't seem to accept anyway. Why confuse you more? Suffice it to say that by altering your consciousness, it would be possible to project your essence, with memory intact, back into the past to witness your life again, but it would be naive of you to believe that you could change anything by doing so. If you were capable of accomplishing such a feat by your own effort, you would also be capable of understanding the total perfection of your past experience, and how needless of change it is. It has brought you here, and for that, alone, you are fortunate, indeed! I wouldn't push my luck if I were you. I would leave the past behind and concentrate on the present in order to gain more control over your future." Esmeralda's voice has taken on a tinge of impatience.

"You're just trying to weasel out of what you said, and I'm calling your bluff—if it's possible, then show me! I'd love to go back and live my life over and remember everything I've experienced up to now. If you truly can, then do it. Talk is cheap, I want action!" He feels fairly confident, at this juncture, that he might have her absurd argument fairly well countered.

"Such a wish should not be made frivolously, Bob," warns Esmeralda. "These are very serious matters we are discussing here, and not without dangerous aspects." She pauses, choosing her words carefully. "It so happens that you are making this request of one of the few people within your realm of experience capable of fulfilling it. I could direct your consciousness into your past even though you are not prepared for the experience, and may not be able to deal effectively with the change. I could send you back in time to any point in your life that you might choose, and your present memory and knowledge would remain intact, for as long as you wished them to do so, but I am warning you that with your current level of understanding, you would find it difficult to accomplish any but the most minor changes in yourself or the world."

"You're saying you could actually do that?" BP gulps in amazement. "What are you, some kind of witch?"

"That's a poor choice of words. I am certainly not a witch, whatever you think that may be. I prefer to think of myself as an 'evolved' human being. But whatever you call me, the answer to your question is 'yes,' it is possible—I could do it, but it would not make things any better."

"Not make things any better! How can you say that? Why if I could only..."

"Enough!" Esmeralda cuts him off shortly, to save herself some dreary repetition. "Where did all your problems begin, Bob? Think back and tell me, quickly, and I will send you there. But be sure you get to the root, the very beginning of your troubles—be sure to go far enough back. You only have this one chance!"

BP is astonished. An intense adrenaline rush is building in his body, and it is not due to the effects of the cocaine, which have already dissipated. He leans back in the small dinette, heart pounding madly. He feels compelled to answer but he must calm down enough to think about the question clearly, to try to grasp where this bizarre situation is headed. "Where did it all begin," he wonders, "where did I first go wrong? Was it all the time I wasted when I was younger? Was it the rebellion against authority at home and at school that cut me off from other people? That must be it—I always felt I was so different from others—so much smarter, so much stronger and more righteous, that I could just make my own rules and ignore all their silly beliefs, their stupid laws, the conventional morality. It was easier to condemn it all. Why couldn't I simply embrace authority and become like other people? Where did it all start...?"

"The Bears," he blurts out, finally, as it comes to him, "when I was in Little League—that was the name of our team. I was only twelve years old, so young and innocent, without any notion of where my path might lead, and yet I did things, stupid and arrogant things, which ended up having a tremendous effect on my life. There was this one game we had with the Elks, when the coach busted me for showing off on the field and not hustling. If only I could go back to that game and know what I know now—everything would be different. I could make it all right, if I had another chance!"

"If you have decided, then," says Esmeralda, "you will go back as you wish and remember everything, as long as you do not choose to forget! Do you agree?"

"Sure!" BP nods assent, still disbelieving, wondering how she will recover from this sham, this hoax.

Esmeralda rustles through her straw bag, as if she were searching for something. BP waits, following her movements, finding them curious and distracting. He wonders what she might pull out of the bag this time.

Just then, Abraxus the cat jumps up on the table between them and walks closer, stretching leisurely along the way, slinking finally into his lap, purring, brushing his chest with both ears, turning around in a full circle while leaning heavily against him, before curling up roundly.

BP looks down at the cat in his lap. She raises her head and gazes back at him with green eyes glowing. In the distance, he hears the faint music of chimes over the railway noise—a growing crescendo of pealing bells in a seemingly random but grand harmony. Something like a flashbulb suddenly bursts alight in his brain, right behind his eyes, blinding him, as the music of a thousand carillons ringing in unison rushes towards him madly.

AT THE GAME

It is a warm, summer, southern California day in mid-1960, featuring a Little League baseball field in a sunny suburb of San Diego. Two teams of small, uniformed figures occupy a dirt diamond. A chain-link backstop and outfield fencing delineates the dusty space, with parents in rickety wooden grandstands built behind home plate and down each baseline looking on.

Bobby Pilhaus jerks awake. On his perceptual screen is a view of the field from the third base dugout, through the wire fencing. Panning down, he spies his own, small, rubber-cleated feet, a pair of short, skinny, twelve-year-old legs, wrapped in a gray uniform with purple trim, and an enormous-looking leather baseball glove folded in his lap, where a black cat had been in the previous moment.

His mouth is wide open, his eyes bulging out: "What is going *on* here! Where *am* I?" His thoughts virtually scream into his brain, laden with fear, invoking panic. "Am I dreaming? Is this real? Am I awake?" Sitting straight up and struggling for breath, he stares out at the commotion on the field, as the batter hits a long ball to the outfield and players run about.

"It's so *real* looking, this is not like a dream at all." He pinches himself hard. It only hurts. "I must be awake, but it's just not possible, I'm a little *kid*! I mean, I'm *myself*, but this is not *now*, this is twelve years ago!" The possibilities for confusion are endless.

He snatches a glance left and right, studying the details of the scene around him for any signs of fogging or fading, any flaw in the reproduction. Everything appears to be normal. A chill runs down his spine.

"I was on the train with Esmeralda—I know I was! Is it possible? There was the cat—it was just here—or was I just there? What in the world is happening? Am I going to wake up soon? Did she put me here?" He leans back rigidly on the bench, trying to relax, attempting to remain calm. He feels like a fugitive, an imposter, some kind of a felonious voyeur, watching and waiting for the sound of sirens to come wailing up from the distance. But nothing so radical occurs. The game goes on. He seems to be engaged in his normal, waking consciousness.

"This is unreal, it's just lasting so long—usually I wake right up when I realize I'm dreaming. What's strange is this is the very place I was thinking of a minute ago. How could she make me dream about *this*? And worse than that, if this is *not* a dream, how did I *get* here? And how do I get back?"

BP is still sitting open-mouthed at the end of the bench as the third out of the inning is made and his teammates troop out onto the field past him, chiding him playfully. "Hey Beep, did you snooze out, huh? Grabbing a little nap, Sluggo? C'mon, look sharp, we gotta hold 'em." He doesn't know what to do, how to react. He is still questioning the reality of everything before him.

His decision is made for him as the coach, Mr. Miller, walks up, a hairy wrist pushing his cap back on his head to mop his sweaty brow, his voice tinged with exasperation: "Look, Bob, I don't care how much of a hotshot you think you are, or how much you think this team can't do without you—if you don't show a little hustle and go out there and stick to good fundamentals, I'm going to jerk you right out of the game. Do you understand? Now get out there! Let's go!"

BP looks up, glassy-eyed, groping for a way to explain that he is not prepared for this, that it is all just a dream, a radical hallucination that has gripped him. But the glowering figure of his coach is extremely lifelike, completely compelling, and will not admit its illusion to his frenzied stare.

"I better go along with him," he thinks, trying to remain calm. "I need some time to sort things out." Without saying anything, he pushes himself shakily off the bench and stumbles out onto the field to assume his position at shortstop automatically, exactly as he had done so many times before, so many years ago. It comes easily to him once he starts.

Luckily, the kinetics of playing the game, the unexamined involvement of his body in the process, eases his consciousness of the contradictions which lurk explosively beneath each moment's thin veneer of reality. The enforced activity allows him to buffer his brain from the stream of questions his inner voice is insisting on presenting (in ever shriller and more strident tones) concerning the dangerous, absurd, and utterly insane situation he is confronting. He manages to survive this first crisis by just becoming a twelve-year-old boy again, simply warming up for another inning of Little League baseball on a hot, July afternoon.

The first-baseman throws a bouncing ball towards him and his body moves to field it, timing the hops unconsciously, snagging it with his glove and throwing it back to first, in the usual warm-up ritual. The demands of the immediate task, requiring his perceptual awareness and complete attention to direct a complex physical response, give him respite from the fragmented clamor of his rational mind.

"Coming down," yells the catcher. BP moves towards second base fluidly, spears the practice pick-off throw from the catcher and flips it under-handed to Donny Miller, the coach's son, who is playing second base and backing him up on the play. As long as he is absorbed in the flow of the game, the task of the moment, he is able to forget that only a short time ago he had been a 24-year-old fugitive on a train to Biarritz, and that he is currently experiencing something he had always assumed was impossible—something miraculous, to say the least. It is in the lulls, the lapses in the action, where that agitated inner voice comes creeping back.

"Batter up," yells the umpire. As the batter settles into the box and the pitcher checks the sign from the catcher, BP crouches down, bending his knees, spreading his legs, dropping his hands close to the ground, in position to field the ball if it is hit. As the pitcher winds up and delivers, BP is creeping forward on the balls of his feet, concentrating intently on the pitch as it arrives at the plate, ready to react instantaneously to any contact. On each pitch this ritual is repeated, and after five pitches, the count is three balls, two strikes. The batter has not yet taken a swing.

BP's attention begins to lag slightly when the batter strikes out on the next pitch. After throwing the ball around the infield, there is a short break in the action and his mind wanders. Strange thoughts fill his head, driving a wedge in his concentration on the game. Disturbing questions and even more pro-vocative memories—memories of his own *future*—flood in through the crack.

He is standing straight up, flat-footed, stunned by these remembrances, when the next batter steps to the plate and hits the first pitch to the hole be-tween third and shortstop. Caught off-balance and making a late start, he just manages to field the slow grounder with a backhand stab and throw across the diamond to first base, forcing the runner out, but the play is needlessly close.

Coach Miller is standing up in the dugout, shouting at him: "Get down and get a jump on those, Bob! Get 'em right in front of you and charge 'em— how many times do I have to tell you? C'mon—play good fundamentals now!"

BP blinks and shuffles back into position. He knows the coach is right. He knows he had plenty of time to get in front of that ball, but it had surprised him. He had been distracted, thinking about things he had known as an adult—about sex, about politics, about surfing, about drugs—and he thinks now that this game of baseball and this frail, little boy's body he inhabits are so absurd and out of place that he will soon break out laughing, or crying, or wake up from this nightmare.

But then the next batter hits another grounder to the same spot, even slower than the first. BP is so late getting to it that the runner beats his throw to first base and is safe.

Coach Miller immediately calls a time-out and walks out onto the field, straight up to BP. "Listen, kid, I don't know what has gotten into you," he says, speaking through clenched teeth, "but I told you I was going to do it and I am. You're out of here! Go sit on the bench."

BP is dumbfounded and embarrassed, but he obeys. There is little else he can do. His mind is in turmoil, attempting to straddle two worlds.

The enforced inactivity of sitting on the bench turns out to be the very worst therapy for him at the moment. He alternates between feelings of in-volvement and feelings of separateness, his peculiar schizophrenia raging.

On the one hand, he is a small boy who has been disgraced in the presence of his peers. Feelings of frustration, of unfair punishment, well up in his breast and are focused into hatred of Coach Miller, whom he holds responsible for his plight. His pride is injured, for he feels he is easily as good a player as any boy on the team, even better than most.

On the other hand, his adult persona knows that he bears full responsibility for his situation, and that his problems extend far beyond this game. He attempts to break his situation down into sensible, cause-and-effect patterns that can be analyzed and manipulated to his benefit, in order to chart a clear course through a very treacherous sea. He feels like a convicted murderer on Death Row, a man who is totally innocent, yet trapped by insane circumstances into certain execution. Between violent bouts of hatred for his prosecutor, his judge, his jury, the guards, the warden, and society-at-large (for ignoring his plight), he works deliriously on his legal appeals, as his own attorney (self-taught).

His internal dialogue at this point is tragi-comedy of epic proportions: "What the hell is going on here? This can't be happening to me. This can't happen to anyone. It's against the laws of physics! How can I be here? How can I be twelve years old again? What has that witch done to me? If I'm here, then who is with my 24-year-old body that I left on the train? Is it going along without me? Is the twelve-year-old mind that used to be in *here* running *that* show now? If *this* is real, then did I just *dream* a whole half of my life in a nap? And if I am still on the train, then is *this* a dream?" BP is close to tears. Logic does not seem to be a very helpful tool in this situation.

"Maybe I'm still on the train and Esmeralda has just hypnotized me, or drugged me and I'm just hallucinating all this." This thought has some comforting aspects so he hangs onto it, while trying to assemble additional plausible scenarios.

"It'll wear off, whatever it is, or she'll bring me out of it, I hope. All I have to do is wait—but it's lasting so long! Maybe I caught some exotic fever and I'm just delirious in my bunk.... Maybe I died and this is...." This last possibility strikes BP with chilling severity. "No, the possibility that Hell consists of living half your life over again must be pretty small. And I've never heard of anyone claiming to have been reincarnated into the *same life* again either, especially halfway through!"

Unfortunately, as time wears on and his immediate reality shows no signs of changing, or wearing off, he is forced to abandon the more comfortable hypothetical positions.

"I guess if she hypnotized me, it could last for a long time—she wouldn't have to bring me out of it for days, I suppose, maybe weeks! But what would she do with my *body*? Have me hospitalized? Feed me intravenously? Could I be in this trance and still functioning as a human being on the train? This is all too bizarre!" BP is starting to become very afraid.

"What if she really did what she said? What if she was not kidding, or tricking me? What if I am stuck here? She didn't tell me how to get back! And I *asked* for it. How could I be so stupid? What am I going to do here? Look at this puny little body. My voice is so high it could break glass. Who's going to believe anything I say? I've got no credibility. I'm no prodigy with a Ph.D., although I guess I could be one now, if I wanted to....

"What should I do? Write a letter to the President? Lemme see, now. Kennedy is running against Nixon this year, so I could say: 'Dear Jack, I'm writing to you because yesterday I was living in 1972. You are going to kick Nixon's ass this fall, but he will make a comeback later on, unfortunately. Please think twice about sending any more troops over to Vietnam—that's really going to be a much bigger mess than you think. And watch out when you go to Dallas in '63—someone is going to shoot you! I can't tell you who, exactly, because they're still arguing about that.' Shit, there'd be F.B.I. and Secret Service agents swarming all over my house—until they find out I'm only twelve and probably don't know what I'm doing.

"Maybe I could make a fortune in the stock market—buy a bunch of Polaroid and Xerox and IBM. But where am I going to get the money to invest? My allowance? Who's going to put up thousands of dollars on the advice of a pre-pubescent punk? Oh, man, I really fucked-up! Why did I ever want to come back here? It was bad then and it's bad now. What did I think I could accomplish by becoming a little boy again?"

Before he can explore this line of thought far enough to remember his exact intention in coming back to this point in his life, it is too late. While he is sitting on the bench, leaning forward, with his face buried in his hands, on the verge of emotional collapse, Donny Miller walks by him in the dugout. Donny is watching the action on the field rather than where he is going, and his elbow accidentally collides, rather smartly, with the side of BP's head.

BP is startled and angry, his eyes watering, and he lashes out at Donny, shoving him against the wire front wall of the dugout and cursing him. Donny overcomes his initial surprise and responds with a shove of his own. In a matter of seconds the two boys are rolling on the ground, grappling for an advantage, fists flying.

BP channels all his pent-up frustration, anger and fear into the struggle and quickly turns it into a massacre, locking his arm around Donny's neck and flailing at him with the other fist.

Their teammates try to pull them apart, shouting. BP notices through a haze of fury that Donny has a very bloody face. This perception is quite sobering. He lets Donny go and slumps back.

He closes his eyes and has a vivid vision of himself, strapped to an electric chair in an empty room, while behind a glass partition the smiling warden is closing the switch that will send fifty thousand volts of deadly electric current coursing through his body.

Beep Is Rude

BP sits on his knees on the corduroy-covered sofa under the living room window, stomach against the backrest, hands spreading the blades of the venetian-blind window shades, watery red eyes peering out to the driveway where his mother and father are backing out in their 1954 DeSoto station wagon. He has been crying uncontrollably most of the afternoon.

The late summer sun is still shining weakly outside as it sets, but BP is already dressed for bed in cowboy-print pajamas. He feels very sorry for himself and is frequently washed in fresh waves of self-pity, which bring more tears to his eyes.

The events of the day line up and flash newsreel-style through his consciousness in varying shades of conspiratorial hostility. Everything seems so unfair to him—getting jerked out of the game; getting into the fight with Donny; and now his parents are going off to a dinner engagement, leaving him in the care of a babysitter, with strict orders that he is to be sent to bed early, leaving the issue of his further punishment for the day's transgressions wide open. He is beset by the nagging fear of what his father might do to him later. He chastises himself for his lack of self-control.

His mood of persecution and melancholy is interrupted by the voice of the babysitter behind him: "Well, Bobby, if you want to pick out one of your favorite books, you can read a story or two before bedtime."

Her words startle BP and irritate him, though they are spoken quietly and without malice. "How can she bother me at a time like this?" he wonders to himself, as he watches the DeSoto disappear down the street. He turns from the window and sits down, shoulders hunched forward, eyes lowered in silent suffering and self-righteous indignation.

"Would you like to play a game, then? We have time for a game of cards or checkers or something if you'd rather do that." She is trying to be patient and sensitive, since she understands that BP has been having some discipline problems lately.

BP does not answer. He feels his chest tightening, a buzzing in his ears. "She has no idea what it's like in here," he mutters to himself, "I wish I could tell her where to get off!" He clamps his mouth shut.

"Well, Bobby," she continues, after a swollen silence, "maybe the best thing we could do right now would just be to go to bed and get some sleep and wake up to a fresh start in the morning, huh?" She extends her hand to help him up from the sofa. BP has other ideas, though.

"Get away from me, you slimy bitch!" he shrieks. "Whaddya mean 'we,' you skanky whore!?!? I'm not a baby. Don't talk down to me. You don't care one fucking bit about *my* problems! You don't really want to read any damn stories or play any shit-ass games, you just want me out of your way so you can raid the refrigerator and feed your fat, ugly face!" The words pour out of his mouth like vomit, involuntarily flushing poison out of his system, leaving him weak in the aftermath.

The babysitter stands for a moment in shocked silence, rocking slowly back on her heels. Her eyebrows raise as her eyes widen, glaze slightly, and roll up briefly in their sockets. But she recovers quickly, grabbing BP by the ear and herding him down the hallway into his bedroom, speaking only as she is closing the door: "I don't know where you learned those words, young man, but I don't deserve to hear them from you! If I had my way, I would wash your mouth right out with soap, but I'll leave that up to your parents when they get home, after I tell them about this!"

With that she closes the door, leaving BP alone in guilt, shame, and fear. Although he does vaguely remember where he learned all those words, he cannot think of why in the world he ever uttered them aloud, especially at a time like this.

No Requiem for a Lightweight

BP is remembering again. He slouches on his bed in total darkness and picks his way through the minefield of his confused consciousness for several hours. By willing himself to do so, he is able to enforce his adult persona, but it is a thoroughly traumatic experience, not the helpful, reassuring and powerful ability he had assumed it would be at all.

"I've got to slow things down and get this figured out," he thinks, finally accepting the permanence of his situation. "Everything is happening too fast. I'm just not ready for it and I keep lapsing back into being a little boy again. I've got to watch myself! I should be able to handle this—it's child's play compared to what comes later! What a fine start I've made on my new life. How am I going to be able to change anything if I keep blowing it like this?

"That witch *tricked* me, though! She knew I would never be able to remember everything all the time, especially in this little boy's body. Christ! I forgot all about how fucking *small* you are when you're a kid—look at me! I must be all of 5'4" and 90 pounds. I never should have come this far back! But she *told* me to—was that one of her tricks? And I fell for it like a chump—I *begged* her to send me back here. But I didn't think she could really *do* it. I thought it was just an idle boast, a little cocktail conversation, you know, a hitchhiking story. Shit! I had no idea she was talking stark, raving truth.

"Everything has happened today just as it did twelve years ago—at least, with the same result. Even though my thoughts and intentions might have been different this time, I wasn't able to actually *do* anything differently, just as she said I wouldn't. And I know what will happen now. I can remember it all perfectly. My dad is going to come home and give me a licking with a coat hanger because he is so mad and so disappointed with me. And I'm going to get kicked off the All-Star team for breaking Donny's nose, and this is the year our team goes all the way to Williamsport for the World Series. I could have gone with them if I hadn't screwed up. Heck, I'm the best shortstop in the league by a long shot, but they won't pick me now because I'm not a good sport. There goes my childhood dream of being a professional baseball player, down the tubes. Shit! This is the same road to ruin I went down last time. I've got to get myself together and change things, before it's too late.

"But I remember even back then, I was always telling myself that I had to change and I never could. Oh Esmeralda, I didn't *mean* it! I didn't know what this would be like. I don't want to be here anymore, I want to be my old self again. Please, bring me back." No answer to his whimpering prayer comes, and he realizes there is no easy way out.

"Jeez, I need a joint," he concludes, unexpectedly. "I wonder if I've got any weed?" This compulsion drives him up and out of the bed. He switches on the light, crosses over to the oak chest sitting against the opposite wall, opens the top drawer, and absentmindedly begins sifting through the contents. There are underwear, socks, a bag of marbles, two yo-yos, some bottle caps, baseball cards, a cheap magnifying glass, a piggybank—the usual accoutrements of a twelve-year-old's lifestyle. He is suddenly horrified to realize that he is committing another action that is entirely inappropriate for his situation.

"What am I doing? I'm blowing it again! There's not going to be any stash in here. I'm only twelve, I don't even smoke pot yet. What am I thinking? I've got to get a better grip on myself! Every move I make right now could be a *crucial* one, this is no time to get confused."

His self-recrimination is interrupted by the sound of a car turning into the driveway. Involuntary glandular secretions begin in his body, inducing anxiety and fear, as he realizes his parents are returning. His little-boy persona is invited back to share the misery.

Leaping across the room, he shuts out the light and dives back into his bed, hiding under the covers, heart pounding. His knowledge of the coming scenario is no great help to him now. He cannot think of anything he can do to stop, or reverse, the inexorable flow of events. He hears his parent's voices outside, drifting in on the still, night air. His schizophrenia rages.

"I tell you, honey, I saw his light on in there when we drove up," he hears his father say. "I don't know why that sitter has let him stay up this late, but since she has, we might as well talk to him about it tonight."

"Now, dear, why don't you wait until the morning? Give yourself a chance to calm down."

"No, this is serious. He attacked that boy and broke his nose. He has to learn that such behavior is unacceptable!"

BP hears the front door open and hushed voices in conference in the living room. "Oh shit! She's telling on me. I'm really in for it now." The sheer panic of a boy facing a beating takes hold of him. "I've got to get out of here!"

He jumps out of bed and rushes over to the window, loosens the catch and opens it. He climbs out, dropping down to the dewy lawn on his bare feet. "I've got to hide," he thinks, feeling particularly vulnerable out in the backyard in his cotton pajamas. "Where should I go?" His eyes fall on the ramshackle abode of Bones, his pet Labrador retriever, a sorry excuse for a doghouse that he had built himself (with a little help from his father) only the year before, out of some scraps of wood and a few rusty nails. "Yeah, that's it. Good old Boney! He'll let me in." He crosses the yard and crawls into the doghouse.

Bones, who has been sleeping peacefully, does not resent the intrusion. He rolls over and licks BP on the face, happy for the company. "Good boy, Bones, you're a good boy," he whispers, petting the dog's head and scratching him behind the ears. "You still love me, don't you Boney? It doesn't matter what

I do, you'll still be my friend, won't you?" Bones affirms his suspicions with another big lick and a low whimper. "OK, boy, I love you too, but just be quiet now, don't give me away. I don't want them to find me out here."

BP listens carefully to the sounds coming from the house. Doors are opening and closing. He thinks he can hear his name being called. He knows that it is futile to try to escape his punishment, that ultimately he will be found, but he refuses to think about when that might be, choosing to postpone the inevitable as long as possible.

Unfortunately, as time passes, he begins to receive nagging messages from his bladder about the necessity of relieving himself. This unforeseen circumstance proves to be his downfall. He crawls out of the doghouse and runs to the back fence, hoping to take care of this business and sneak back without being discovered. Just as he is finishing, his father, who has begun to search outside, catches him in the beam of a flashlight—pants down, puny little pecker in his hand, a golden stream arcing into the bushes.

"So there you are," his father's voice booms out. "Where have you been, young man? What are you doing? Your mother and I have been worried sick!"

"I just went out to pee," squeaks BP, half-truthfully.

"If you needed to pee, you could have gone in the bathroom, like civilized folks," says his father, taking him firmly by the arm and leading him back to the house. "I don't know what has gotten into you, son, hiding out here like this. First you get into a fight with your own teammate, then you call the babysitter horrible names, and on top of that, you run away and hide, then lie about it when we find you. You can't be allowed to do things like that! How many times have I told you that you mustn't fight, you mustn't swear, and you mustn't lie?" This mobile lecture is taking place as BP is being jerked back to his room by the elbow, his feet rarely touching the ground. When they arrive at his bedroom, his father repeats the question, rattling his entire body by shaking his arm. "Answer me, son, how many times am I going to have to tell you?"

"About a jillion, I guess," mumbles BP, in capitulation.

"Don't get smart with me," warns his father. "I hope this is the last time I ever have to tell you, and to help you remember, I'm going to do something I've never had to do before, and I hope I never have to do again."

Going over to the closet, his father takes out a flat, wooden coat hanger, walks back over to BP and sits beside him on the bed. "This is going to hurt me more than it is going to hurt you," he explains. "Lay over my knees."

As BP submits to his punishment, just before the first thin red welt begins to rise on his tender bottom, his father utters the last in this series of statements, which surely must have been responsible for BP's lifelong hatred of clichés: "This is for your own good, son."

ASLEEP AT THE WHEEL

Before the next day dawns, BP has made a radical psychic adjustment. The mechanism for this change has less to do with logic and reason than it does with intuition and pure instinct for survival.

In its essence, the change consists of BP deciding (though by no rational means) that the personality of an adult is not appropriate for promoting the survival of the boy's body which he inhabits. It is a difficult decision to make, even a torturous one, but he is forced into it, finally, after an agonizing night of total schizophrenia, of complete unreality.

His older, more experienced awareness rages against extinction. As the hours pass darkly, tossing and turning in his bed, he presents himself once more with every conceivable, logical explanation for the phenomena he has experienced. He examines, filters, analyzes and discards them all, one by one.

He attempts to formulate plans for action, bold scenarios designed to underscore the importance of remembering everything, to take advantage of this opportunity to change himself, and possibly even history. He summons up troubling images, minutely detailed reminiscences of his own future, to support each argument, to illustrate the depth of his former failures and the urgent necessity for change.

As it turns out, however, every argument, every explanation, each illustration he contrives, is much more shocking, disturbing, and profoundly unacceptable than it is comforting or illuminating.

To his tired, scared, sore, 12-year-old body [on which his adult awareness is dependent for every basic input—all forms of sustenance, both mental and physical], such stringent self-examination and conceptualization of possible future actions comes as a total assault, an attack on his ability to survive. He is beset by cravings for sex, surf, drugs, alcohol and exotic experiences of all sorts, which are impossible for his boy-persona to satisfy.

In the end, he does the only thing he can do, the very thing that he is sure Esmeralda *knew* he would do—*he wishes to forget!* As he finally drops off into a fitful sleep, his brain begins the necessary electrochemical transformations to wall off and isolate the offending, adult long-term memory cells and synapses. When he awakens the next morning, he goes forward, untroubled (or at least less so), with the business at hand, which is being a young boy again. His adult persona and memories are abandoned and abolished from his brain, permanently and irrevocably, conforming precisely with the condition that Esmeralda had placed on his recall of them, and which he had accepted thoughtlessly on the train, in a moment of doubt and disbelief. A deal is a deal, and he made the bargain himself. There is no one else to blame.

Summertime Blues

BP is bored.

Although he has fallen easily back into his pre-teen existence, this is not to say that he is the same boy he was then. In order to put some distance between himself and the psychic chaos he has experienced, many small changes are necessary, some conscious, some unconscious.

He dismisses his recent turmoil as "bad dreams" and cannot recall the slightest detail from them. As time passes, this task is facilitated by cultivating several personality traits toward which he is predisposed. He becomes a very concrete sort of person, giving the most credence to the visible, sensible, material side of his reality, discounting the importance of his dreams and his subconscious mind. Thus, he becomes a very self-centered person, as his rigid preference for ordinary perception leads him inescapably to the conclusion that he is totally separate from every other human being, and totally alone.

He adopts a number of strategies based on this selfishness. He lacks trust and avoids one-to-one contact with other people as much as possible. He is very quiet and shy, preferring to observe rather than act in many situations. He perfects reclusiveness and laziness to absolute faults.

He has just one close friend, Donny Miller, with whom he is as tight as only little boys who have tried to kill each other can be. But even in this relationship, as well as in his relationship with his parents, BP does not really extend himself, believing that he, himself, is the only one responsible for his own happiness, the only one with any control over his future. Which is not to say that he contemplates his future frequently, for quite the contrary is true—he is extremely fatalistic. He perceives himself as being buffeted about in a chaotic universe, which invites nothing but pessimism and nihilism, attitudes quite unbecoming in a child. He has trouble developing enthusiasm for anything and welcomes each new moment like a rock which might be hiding a snake underneath.

After the Little League season is over and he is omitted from the All-Star team, as he had expected, there is not much for him to do, and he takes up the job with a passion. He loves to work at nothing all day. There are six weeks left of summer, and BP needs every minute of it to halfway heal his wounded psyche, to become "normal" again, before the enforced socialization of school once again encroaches on his freedom.

He spends most of his days cruising the neighborhood on his bicycle, just watching stuff. Invariably he ends up down at the beach, the western border of his neighborhood, because it is obvious to him that this is the most beautiful and interesting part of his urban environment.

The complexion of the coastline changes from day to day with the weather, the tide, the day of the week (weekends are always more crowded), helping to alleviate his melancholy boredom for short periods. He loves to watch the animals that live in this zone and are so accessible—the squirrels who live in burrows in the sandstone bluffs and are tame enough to eat from his hand, the white gulls that soar above the bluffs, the gray whales migrating outside the kelp beds, the brown pelicans skimming low over the surf, the porpoises cavorting within it.

The edge of the land is like a magnet for other people, too, and though he hesitates to interact with them, BP loves to watch people. When the weather is fair, as it is most days, they come from all over the inland metropolis for a myriad of reasons, and he applies his powers of observation to them all, trying to deduce as much as possible about who they are, where they came from, and what their lives are like, from their outward appearances and activities.

He can pass endless hours observing the natural phenomena that surround him with great concentration, always maintaining an inner dialogue, a sort of mental commentary of a personal, idiosyncratic nature. This keeps the subconscious part of his brain from entering his awareness, which is essential during this period. Anything which might remind him of the insane, twisted experiences of his recent, unreal past (it was all just a dream) has been banished and repressed. He has forgotten it all completely, and has no desire to bring it back.

Anyone observing him at these times (though no one pays him any attention, to his overwhelming relief) would see a quiet but intense, curious but seemingly preoccupied, healthy young boy on a bike, who likes to watch the ocean and keeps to himself.

At night he takes refuge in books. His mother will not allow a television set in their house (on the grounds that such an undemanding media is anti-intellectual) so he is denied that form of escapism, which has already become so very popular that his family is considered an oddity, even by their own relatives, for refusing to "plug in" to this modern medium. Reading books, however, is encouraged constantly. His mother has always taken him on special trips to the local library almost any time he wants, even though it is just a short bike ride away, and when she is unavailable, he peddles there by himself, checking out and returning volumes by the gross.

He reads books like some people eat, compulsively and without restraint, so that the contrivances of the author will entertain, involve and occupy him, allowing the story to capture his interest and attention, to become so captivating, that its plot, its imagery, its characters, its golden thread will follow him even into his sleep—weaving its way into his dreams to shield him from the unconscious part of his brain, the side that might still remember.

AT THE BEACH

BP makes the adjustment to his new [old] life automatically. He goes about in a haze, head in the ozone, taking it easy, day by day, meal by meal, hour by hour. He has a charmed life to lead, really—no responsibilities, a comfortable home in the suburbs, little supervision and tons of free time, so what's so tough? He deals with boredom by a simple search for outside input. No problem....

BP's daily pilgrimages to the beach begin to take on a certain pattern without much willful direction on his part. He usually sets out right after breakfast, riding his bike west and south to the bluffs overlooking the beach at Loring Street, where the elevation is sufficient to give a panoramic view of the coast, from Sun Gold Point to the Mission Beach jetties, with the 875'-long, linear jut of Crystal Pier as the centerpiece.

From here he can check out the beach action and decide which way to go. He's looking for stimulation, for visual and aural interest, and there is one group of people who frequent the coast who grab his attention unfailingly—the surfers. They are by far the most colorful, active, flamboyant inhabitants of the coastal zone, never failing to offer him some unique, vicarious entertainment, and he loves to watch them.

They are a group of fluctuating size and identity, some living in the surrounding neighborhoods, others driving in from many miles away. BP checks out the waterscape daily to determine where they will be found in the greatest concentration. Depending on the tide, wind and swell, the best waves may be happening at several different spots along the coast, and BP knows that wherever the waves are breaking best will be where the surfers are congregating.

When he spots which area is sporting the biggest crew, he rides down and parks his bike nearby. Walking around casually, he tries to insinuate himself anonymously among the fringes of their groups, eavesdropping on their conversations, studying their strange style—their clothes, their boards, their cars, their bizarre language, and most of all, their sport—their incredible, unpredictable interaction with the ocean which is the lodestone of their subculture.

It is immediately apparent to BP that this is as radical, fanatic and creative a group as he has ever encountered. It is composed of mostly young men in their teens and early twenties (though he has seen some older men and even some women riding waves competently), who are uniformly fit, healthy, energetic and enthusiastic, to the point of boisterousness. Their entire waking consciousness, he observes, seems to be focused on the experience of riding waves. Even when they are resting on the beach, sunning themselves, their attention never strays far from the action out in the water, where rhythmic sets of waves shift and peak over the sandbars and reefs, and their compatriots rise and dance. They seem to observe every ride and talk about each one in a mysterious slang which confuses BP. It takes him many weeks of constant observation to begin to penetrate their code, to be able to correlate their descriptions with the activity in the water.

By late August his wounded psyche has almost healed itself. He has succeeded in becoming a young boy again by virtue of the power of the moment and a masterful job of repressing his subconscious mind. By the time his friend Donny returns from his trip to Williamsport with their league's All-Star team (oh, how secretly and selfishly glad BP is to hear that they had been eliminated before the final round of games—at least they had not been on TV without him), it has occurred to him that he might be able to do more than just watch these surfers. He realizes that he might be able to become a surfer himself!

This idea appeals to him immensely, once it strikes. He is certain that surfing must be a very exciting and fulfilling endeavor. Though he has been swimming in the ocean since the age of seven, bodysurfing and playing on and around the waves with a number of rudimentary vehicles, including old innertubes, inflatable air mattresses, and Styrofoam bellyboards, gaining some understanding of the dynamics of a breaking wave and a certain degree of comfortableness in the water from these early experiences, he does not consider this real surfing. That category is reserved for the graceful, stand-up, longboard variety only, and he is impatient to move on to the next phase, the real thing. He discounts the preparation, the amount of dues-paying he has already done, and scolds himself for not being more bold.

BP has trouble conveying his sense of urgency to anyone, even Donny, who becomes his occasional partner on his daily sorties to the beach. One day, when they have been sharing an old air mattress in the surf, grabbing short rides on their stomachs in the whitewater of broken waves, Donny makes an innocent and spontaneous expression of boyish joy that BP finds particularly irritating.

"Jeez, isn't this neat-o, Beep? I could do this all day."

"Sheeit, man, this is nothing! I'm bored!" snaps BP. "What we have to do is get a real surfboard, so we can ride like those guys out there." He jerks his head over his shoulder, indicating the surfers sitting offshore. "Those guys have it made. They can stand up and ride so much faster and farther than we can, and they can catch the wave before it breaks and ride the green water, not just catch the fuckin' soup like us!" (The casual insertion of obscenities in their private speech pattern makes both boys feel more grown up, though they are very practiced at code-switching in front of their parents, or any authority figure who might require a clean mouth.)

"But those are older guys, Beep," Donny whines sheepishly, suddenly realizing that he is not supposed to be having so much fun, that perhaps it's not cool to be so ecstatic over riding a surf mat.

"They aren't that much older than us! I've hung around and watched those guys a lot. I know we could do it if we just had a board."

"How are we going to get a board? They cost a lot of money, don't they?"

"About a hundred bucks for a new one, I think, but we could probably get an OK, used one for forty, maybe."

"Where are we going to get forty bucks, Beep? Shit, that's a lot of money."

"Maybe we don't have to buy one. Maybe we could borrow one?" BP is sure he has stumbled onto the solution, but Donny is not so certain.

"I don't know, Beep, those guys are all pretty crazy. You think one of 'em might loan us his board? I bet they'd just beat the crap out of us if we even asked them."

"Nah, they wouldn't do that...I don't think," says BP, considering this possibility. "It's not cool to beat up on littler guys...I'm pretty sure..."

"Well, you ask them, then, if you're not too chicken."

This is the sort of challenge from which BP cannot back down, so he studies the nearest groups of surfers and picks out the smallest, friendliest-looking bunch. "OK, I will."

They exit the water and leave their mat high and dry in the sand. BP heads straight for his chosen mark, with Donny lagging behind cautiously. "Can I borrow your board for a little while?" he asks in a loud voice as he approaches the first surfer in the group.

"Well, what do we have here?" asks the surfer, condescendingly. "A little gremmie trying to leech a board?"

"I'm not a gremmie, I just don't have a board and I want to go surfing," says BP, trying to control his quavering voice.

"Me too!" chimes in Donny, moving up closer when he sees that BP is not immediately punched-out.

"Jesus, there's two little gremlins. Go on, you little rats, get out of here!" Donny backs off a step at the harshness of his tone, but BP holds his sand.

One of the other surfers who has witnessed this exchange intervenes. "Quit pulling hard on those guys, Cosgrove—lend them your board."

"My ass! I'm not going to let some kook take my new board out and ding it all up. Why don't you give 'em your stick? We don't need any more kooks around here."

"Who's the kook, Cosgrove? You almost ran me over twice out there this morning, you were so out of control. How do you think anyone learns to surf? By being a kook like you, that's how, so leave those guys alone. C'mon over here, kid."

BP shuffles over to stand in front of the second surfer, who has been his advocate in a touchy situation.

"What's your name, kid?"

"Bob. What's yours?"

"I'm Mike Devlin. Listen, I'll loan you my board but you've gotta be really careful with it, OK? Stay out of everyone's way and don't get hurt. Bring it back in an hour or so—I want to catch the evening glass-off, all right?"

BP nods assent, not quite believing this good fortune. He and Donny pounce eagerly on Mike's board and begin to half-drag, half-carry it up the beach. After fifteen yards or so, they reorganize more efficiently, each carrying an end under his arm. They set it down in shallow water, well away from anyone else.

"I don't know where you get them, Beep," says Donny with admiration, "but sometimes you have really good ideas."

As he studies the huge board, BP is not so sure. Like every idea, every theory, the practical details of implementation can be a bit burdensome and quite sobering. The board is over ten feet long and about two feet wide. Neither one of them can get their arm all the way around it at mid-girth. It weighs more than thirty pounds and is singularly hard and unwieldy, not at all like their soft, light, forgiving air mattress.

"What do we do now?" asks Donny.

BP is at a loss. He thinks he knows what to do, but he is not sure if he is physically equipped to pull it off. "Let's push it out," he suggests, finally.

The two boys flank the board and guide it out, splashing through the shallows at first, slowing as the water becomes deeper and the walls of soup bearing down on them intermittently become higher. As each surge of whitewater hits them, the board bucks up in the air wildly and tries to thrash them. It is all they can do just to hang onto it, especially when their feet begin to lose contact with the bottom.

"This is far enough," decides BP. "Let's turn it around." They barely succeed in getting the nose pointed toward the beach as the next line of whitewater approaches. "Jump on, and hold on tight!"

Donny scrambles onto the middle of the board on his belly, BP right behind him. The roar of the soup is upon them instantly and BP squeezes his eyes shut, holding his breath, clutching the rails of the board as they are enveloped in foamy, wet whiteness and noise. The board accelerates jerkily, weaving from side to side and bouncing up and down, gaining speed, until they scoot out in front of the turbulence, into smoother water.

BP opens his eyes and relaxes his grip, enjoying the end of their ride as the energy dissipates in the shallows. The fin of the board finally catches the sandy bottom, bringing them to a grinding halt in ankle-deep water.

Donny is stoked. "That was great! We really did it, we rode that sucker."

BP's excitement is fading rapidly, however, replaced by feelings of inadequacy and disappointment, verging on anger. "We didn't really do anything we haven't already done with the mat, though, dummy! We're supposed to stand up on the board, for crying out loud, and we're supposed to catch the wave before it breaks."

"Oh yeah." Donny's enthusiasm deflates slightly at Beep's insult. "This surfing shit's tougher than it looks, I guess."

"Let's try it again," says BP, with a surge of determination. "It can't be that hard. All those other guys learned, didn't they?"

In a little more than an hour, Mike comes to retrieve his board, since they have shown no sign of tiring and returning it to him. They have managed only a few microseconds apiece of actual stand-up riding, having spent most of the time either pushing or paddling the board out, riding it in on their knees or bellies, or falling off when they try to stand, but they are two tired and stoked little kids.

For the rest of the summer, the boys spend all their free time at the beach, trying to borrow a board and learn how to ride it. Their luck varies, but no one beats them up for trying.

Sometimes the waves are so perfect that there is not an extra board on the beach. They must content themselves with patrolling the shoreline, retrieving loose boards and dragging them back out to the fallen rider, who is swimming in for it, hoping to ingratiate themselves, perhaps incurring enough favor and recognition from the owner to allow them to borrow it from him later.

On the smaller, junkier days, they have more success, sometimes each acquiring a board, with a minimum of persuasion, and practicing for hours. The smaller surf is a more equal match for their young bodies, so they can make more progress. Nevertheless, it is a long and tedious, trial and error process to learn to stand up and ride on an unstable plank in a dynamic, ocean environment. It is quite a bit more difficult to master than learning how to ride a bicycle, or play any other sport they have encountered, but they persist, doggedly.

Although Donny enjoys their summer beach sessions, BP is beyond that—he is ecstatic, to the point of obsession. The physical exertion involved is a perfect outlet for his boundless, youthful energy, and the challenge of learning to surf requires great concentration and focus, a certain totality of his attention, that BP finds comforting. When he is in the water, mindful of nothing but the immediate task at hand, trying to walk on water, his other cares melt away. There is something so soothing to his spirit, so intriguing, about trying to integrate himself with the waves, that he is almost instantly addicted to the sport. It just feels so right to him, so familiar. He is convinced that there are great truths to be learned and deep mysteries to be revealed from this endeavor, and he approaches it with the gusto of a glutton sitting down to a 12-course meal.

Back to School

In mid-September, BP's lifestyle undergoes a drastic change, much to his regret. For six hours a day, Monday through Friday, he is required to attend Pacific Beach Junior High School with hundreds of other unwitting, young people.

He is in the seventh grade and finds the proceedings dull and uninteresting, even ugly at times. The work is supremely easy for him; he is a good reader, a proficient writer, and very facile with figures. As his teachers remark on his first report card of the year, however, he "seems to lack motivation and discipline in his study habits," which means he is lazy, ill-prepared, and unforthcoming in class, and he "needs to improve his social skills," which means he is rude, surly, uncooperative, and reclusive. Such claims might have elements of truth to them.

He heartily resents being confined to such an uninspiring environment for such a large part of every day and endlessly drilled in such subjects as elementary spelling, mathematics, reading, writing, history, etc. He is able to review and absorb the course matter very quickly from the textbooks supplied at the beginning of the semester, and it often seems to him as if he already knows everything the teacher presents—there is rarely anything new and challenging in the lessons.

He considers his fellow students to be absolute cretins (or worse) for submitting (often willingly!) to this drivel, and to the oppressive yoke of attendance, attention, and obedience. He figures that the teacher must proceed at a pace determined by the lowest common denominator of understanding present in the class of over thirty students, so he assumes, unjustifiably, that some of his peers must be quite stupid.

He is determined to show his good sense, superior intelligence, and independent, unharnessed spirit by totally rebelling against every aspect of this dreary, regimented experience. He works only hard enough to obtain a good grade, always procrastinating until the last moment on papers, projects and preparing for tests. He never volunteers an answer in class, preferring to wait to be called upon, to be forced to perform. Luckily for him, he usually knows the answer when singled out, and he is able to pull off such behavior without flunking.

Socially, he refuses to have any interactions at all with his classmates, although some of the girls have begun to interest him—especially the ones whose bodies have begun the tantalizing transformation of adolescence. His only good buddy, Donny, does not share any of his classes, so he sees him only at recesses and lunchtime, when they usually make plans for heading to the beach after school.

The only notable exception to his general "bad attitude" takes place during the mandatory (and politically controversial) unit of personal hygiene and sex education required by the state to be included in the curriculum.

During this unit, BP's inattentiveness and frequent absences (caused by vague and short-lived illnesses) disappear. His teacher is surprised to find him asking some very discerning questions and actually participating in class discussions freely.

BP is grateful for the opportunity to clear up some of the details regarding the human reproductive process (and equipment) that have eluded him. Though he may use profanities in his speech, feigning maturity by imitating older men, he is not at all sure of the precise definitions of some of these words, and their relationship to the act of sex or the process of making babies [since all his previous knowledge and recollections of such adult matters have been suitably repressed]. He has had to deduce most of what he knows through self-education and intuition, since such subjects are essentially taboo in his home life.

His mother takes pride in her liberal political, social and religious views. She is an exemplary and loving mother, had dutifully breastfed BP, and never denied him exposure to her naked body during his formative years, according to the very latest theories of good child rearing. She is, nevertheless, as unprepared as BP to deal with the sexual aspects of his approaching puberty.

BP's father is a product of the Great Depression and participates little in BP's upbringing. He works constantly to achieve the American Dream and provide a comfortable life for his family. He is rarely at home, and even when present, he is not the most nurturing or approachable person. He is a pragmatist and an atheist (or at least an agnostic). His religion, if he has one, is science, and BP cannot remember ever seeing his father naked. It has not yet occurred to him to speak to his son about "the birds and the bees."

Thus, BP is left to his own devices to unravel and interpret the powerful, primal forces at work in his body as he begins a monumental adolescent transformation. He has been taught to seek the rational explanation for phenomena, according to the prevailing scientific world-view. He will not rest until he has wrestled the truth out of his predicament, like a good little scientist should.

One aspect of hanging out at the beach which has begun to intrigue BP more and more, lately, are the women. They flock to the beach on sunny days and peel their clothes off shamelessly, down to scanty two-piece suits, to tan their hard, young bodies. Though BP is much too shy and unsteady to actually talk to any of them, he cannot help staring at them, especially when he is sure they do not notice him. The most devastatingly beautiful of them, the most divinely endowed, cause strange stirrings in his lower parts, which disturb him in a strange new way.

It is while he is laying in the sand, after school, on a hot, sunny, autumn afternoon, watching three young women sunbathing next to him, that his complacent routine is shattered. The three are several years older than he, perhaps sixteen or seventeen, which at his tender age is a chasm in maturity the size of the Grand Canyon. They totally ignore his skinny, ragged, little, tangle-haired presence with an air of haughty superiority. He might as well have been a lump of seaweed on the beach.

He has been dividing his time between watching the surf and examining, in detail, how the various parts of the female anatomy are joined together into such an exquisite whole. The girls are lying on their stomachs, as is he, and they have loosened the straps on the top of their suits to avoid unsightly shade lines in their tans. He is engrossed in scrutinizing that particular area under their upper arms where the straps have fallen, and the outer orbits of their nubile breasts (pressed softly into the sand) swell out profoundly, curving gently back inward to meet their ribs.

He can think of no words to describe such a shape, such a place; no way to analyze its creation from the texture of warm skin stretched over underlying bone, muscle, and fat. He is content to let it simply be, to appreciate it, and he drifts off into an unconscious and very erotic fantasy.

He is drawn out of his reverie by a wondrous and unfamiliar warmth growing unbearably urgent in his groin. He wakes up and rolls over immediately, thinking that the warm sand is the source of his discomfort, and discovers the truth. He is experiencing the first, genuine, sexual arousal of his young life and is sporting a very credible and embarrassing erection. The front of his swimming trunks is bulging noticeably, so he rolls back over on his stomach and buries his head in his hands to hide his blush.

"What is happening to me?" he shrieks to himself, totally unsettled. He grinds his hips tentatively into the sand, trying to determine the astounding dimensions of this once trivial and ignored appendage, which has so unexpectedly taken on a life of its own. It seems to reach right up to his navel! "Omigod! Is it gonna bust out of my trunks?" He steals a quick glance towards the three women to see if they have noticed anything, but is relieved to see that they remain totally oblivious to his existence.

He lies stock still in the sand for a seemingly interminable amount of time until the wayward swelling subsides, then jumps on his bike, and rides straight home. It is by the most fortuitous of coincidences that the next day at school, the aforementioned subject of sex education begins, and he starts to collect some hard data and facts. It is the first time that school has seemed like a blessing to him.

His dreams continue to plague him, however. They are a disease-in-the-night, creeping into his consciousness from beyond while he sleeps, even though they are almost always exciting and stimulating, becoming increasingly more erotic. He doesn't have a category for this kind of stimulation. It is totally new to him and very scary. When he is awakened in the middle of the night from one of these delicious dreams, the reality of his twelve-year-old body with a sturdy little woodie is frightening, and it soon shrinks away in a barrage of doubt and fear.

"How do these things come to me?" he wonders. "How can my dreams seem so real, and then just fade away and disappear? Why do I feel so differently in them than I do when I wake up?" [It does not occur to him that these images might be so vivid and convincing (but also fleeting and intangible) because they are events that have already happened or may still happen to him at another time, in another place (or even in someone else's dream!). This might lead him to the conclusion that different people are all simply manifestations of the same life-force—that the past, present and future are really all one thing called by three different names: was, is, and will be. He is not ready for such a conclusion yet, and such pedagogical gymnastics are beyond his ability and his immediate needs. What he needs right now is a logical and practical explanation for the ridiculous little rod throbbing in his groin.]

It is a dream, however, that plays a key role in his road to adulthood. It occurs to him one night during the closing days of his sex education unit at school, when he has been struggling to understand some of the more subtle associations of such concepts as "impregnation" and "ejaculation."

In the dream, he feels that he is far away in a tropical rain forest, sitting by the edge of a deep, freshwater pool on a large, flat, black rock. His ears are filled with the sweet dissonance of a waterfall at the head of the pool. The air is thick with the perfume of paradise.

He is not alone. A beautiful, young, dark-haired girl is in front of him, smiling. She is totally nude. There is no one else around. Without a hint of self-consciousness she stands before him. Her lovely, brown body is breathtaking. BP cannot bring himself to move or speak, entranced by the vision.

"C'mon, follow me. I know a special place here. It's wonderful," she says softly and turns, walking away from him and diving gracefully into the pool. He watches her swim towards the waterfall, turning back, beckoning him with a wave of her hand.

Without understanding how he does it, he follows her. He does not remember walking, diving or swimming, but he notices that he is also naked, that the water is crystal clear, and that somehow he is propelling himself, underwater, towards the waterfall, where she has disappeared.

He pushes through the foaming, white curtain of bubbles and surfaces behind it, to find her sitting on a shallow ledge, leaning back on her arms, laughing with joy, as the edge of the waterfall rains all over her glorious body in glistening sheets.

The totality of her allure is absolute, and BP surrenders to it—he cannot stop himself. He struggles awkwardly up onto the ledge next to her and they embrace, pressing their wet bodies together and swaying as the water sparkles and beats down on them, a stinging caress that mixes with their own. He feels the heat rising in his loins and abandons himself to it.

He doesn't awaken precipitously from this dream. Instead, he floats along in a blissful, carefree aftermath, filled with sweet feelings of power and confidence all out of proportion to his real achievements. For when he is fully awake, he becomes aware of an exceedingly wet and cold spot on the front of his pajamas, gluing them to his abdomen. He makes the final connections in a sobering, intellectual, rush. He realizes that he has had his first "orgasm" (he was having trouble with that word), and that the wet, sticky stuff is "semen," which has spurted from the end of his amazing little penis. It all falls together shortly—the how, where, why and when of the sperm meeting the egg become simplistically clear, finally. A shocking revelation, but, all in all, a great relief to finally understand.

He takes some comfort from learning in class, later that week, that the sort of episode he has experienced is actually a common and ordinary result of the hormonal changes taking place in his body during puberty. Just what these hormones are and how they work is not entirely clear to him, nor is it to his teacher, as he finds out when he asks about them.

"The hormones are chemical compounds, secreted by various glands, which control bodily functions through enzyme action," explains his teacher. "Microbiologists are still studying the exact mechanism by which these biochemical changes take place, and I'm afraid it is too complicated to understand completely without some very advanced and specialized knowledge."

Therefore, BP believes that he has uncovered all the necessary information in this instance, and that there is no need for him to worry further. There is even a name for it, he finds. It is called "involuntary ejaculation." Later, when he timidly approaches his friend on the subject, Donny tells him that they are also called "wet dreams."

This revelation of what it means to be a sexually reproductive mammal cannot be underestimated. BP feels as if he has made a huge leap towards adulthood. Many things fall into place and become clearer, while at the same time he is struck by his naivete—how many mysterious and strange things there are about life that he doesn't quite understand, how much he has to learn. It is both empowering and humbling, but definitely unforgettable. Of one thing he is certain, though, and that is the fact that women are much more powerful creatures than he knows.

SILENT MEETING

Every Sunday, for as long as he can remember, BP's mother has taken him to church. Although she has told him that he was baptized a Catholic, BP cannot remember any experiences in the Catholic church. His only memories are of the Presbyterian church she has attended since he was about four years old. His mother has devoutly given her time and his father's money to this venerable Protestant institution for years, and has dutifully dragged BP along with her to afford him a proper spiritual upbringing. She sings in the church choir, having a striking soprano voice, and often takes BP to her choir practices as well. His father has never set foot on the church grounds.

It surprises him, then, when one Sunday morning in mid-October, his mother bundles him into the car in a slightly agitated state, saying "We're not going to our usual services this morning, Bobby. We're going to try another place."

"What's wrong, Mom?" It is obvious that something is disturbing her. "Where are we going instead?"

"Something dreadful has happened, and I just want to be around some people who feel more like I do about it." BP notices that her hands are trembling as she gets in the car. Looking at her face, he can see that she is close to tears.

"What's happened, Mom?"

"There was an article in the paper this morning that upset me, Bobby. They arrested Dr. Martin Luther King, Jr. in Georgia. I don't know if you've heard about him before, but he is a great man, a holy man, a Reverend in his church, and they are going to put him in prison."

"But why? What for?" BP is anxious, and curious to know why this means so much to his mother.

"For being a Negro, Bobby. Dr. King is a colored man, and down south, they don't believe that colored folks should have the same rights as white folks. He was arrested with about fifty other people for demanding their civil rights at a demonstration in Atlanta. Now, he has been convicted and they are sending him to the state prison. I feel awful about it!"

She has closed the door of the car now and assumed a driving position, but pauses before starting the engine. Looking over to BP in the passenger seat, she speaks deliberately, choosing her words carefully. "I believe that God created all human beings as equals, Bobby, but there are still many people who don't. A lot of the people in our own church, the one we have gone to for years, are like that, unfortunately. I have been talking to them for quite awhile now about the civil rights movement, about Dr. King, and how we should get involved, support him, show that we believe in Christ's teachings, but they won't listen, or they don't want to face the truth—that they are actually bigots and hypocrites! I'm sick to death of it. I'm tired of beating my head against a wall. I've heard about some people here in town who feel like I do, and we're going to meet them today." She turns the key and starts the engine, backing the car out of the driveway.

BP feels some trepidation about this change in their Sunday routine, but like it or not, he is along for the ride. "Who are these people, Mom?"

"They're Quakers, honey. They belong to a church called the Religious Society of Friends. You'll see."

BP accepts his fate without further questioning and leans back in the seat as they drive north on La Jolla Boulevard. His mother turns into a residential district, makes her way around a couple more corners, and finally parks the car. BP glances around. "Where's the church, Mom? I don't see it."

"Across the street, honey," she says, motioning with her hand. BP looks where she indicates, but sees only a row of single-story houses up and down the block.

"I don't see any church, Mom."

"It's right there, dear—the white house with the green trim. See it?"

BP peers across the street again, and does notice a small, white house with green trim. It is undistinguished from the other houses on the block except for a small sign in the front yard (which he had assumed was a "For Sale" sign) and a man standing by the front door. "That one?" he asks, pointing to it. "I guess I was looking for something bigger...."

His mother senses some disappointment in BP's tone. "Listen, Bobby, this is a different kind of church than what you're used to. They don't have a big building, or a big congregation, or a minister or a choir, for that matter, and the service is not what you may expect—there's no preacher giving a sermon, no hymns sung—it's a silent meeting for worship. I don't know quite what to expect any more than you do, but I hope you'll be patient and give it a chance, sweetie. Won't you do that for me, please?" She smiles at him lovingly, and BP nods his assent, though he is still a bit confused.

They get out of the car and walk across the street together. BP reads the sign as they get closer. In very small letters, it says, simply, "The Religious Society of Friends. Meeting for Worship, Sunday 10:00–11:00 A.M." As they turn down the walkway and approach the door of the house, the man standing there steps forward to greet them, smiling and reaching out to shake their hands, speaking in a low but friendly voice: "Good morning! My name is Lowell. Are you new attenders?"

"Hello," answers BP's mother. "Yes, this is our first time. My name is Betty, and this is my son, Bob. I heard about your Meeting from the Babcocks."

"Ah, yes, the Babcocks, well, let me welcome you, then," says Lowell, nearly whispering. "As you may know, our Meeting for Worship is a silent one, and some Friends are already seated inside, so we ask that you enter as quietly as possible, and not disturb the other worshippers. You may take any seat you like." He looks down at BP and continues: "We don't expect young Friends to sit patiently for the whole hour, so children are seated in the front rows, and they'll be led out after fifteen minutes by the First-day School coordinators for their own activities. The Clerk will signal the rise of the meeting at eleven o'clock by turning and greeting his neighbors. He will then ask any new attenders to introduce themselves, if they wish. You're invited to stay for a pot-luck brunch afterwards, in the rear building, where you can meet and visit with the other members of the meeting, if you're so inclined." He smiles again, warmly.

"Thank you," says Betty, taking BP's hand and leading him into the Meeting house, as Lowell steps back and opens the door for them.

It takes a moment for BP's eyes to adjust from the bright sunlight outside to the lower level of indirect, natural lighting in the interior, but he finds himself in a large, square room, devoid of any inner partitions, filled with rows of chairs in a semi-circular pattern, facing each other, 3 rows to a side, with a narrow aisle down the center. There are some long, comfortable-looking couches in the back rows, against the outer walls, interspersed with wooden chairs and large, upholstered armchairs, while the middle rows are largely metal, folding chairs, with padded seats and backrests. The innermost rows, facing each other across the corridor, are small, wooden, folding chairs, obviously intended for children.

BP's mother motions silently for him to seat himself in one of the smaller chairs, and she takes a seat in the middle row behind him. BP scans the room from side to side, studying his surroundings. The space is plain, without decoration or artifacts, and eerily silent, with muted sunlight filtering in through a row of rectangular, double-hung windows in the north and south walls, shaded by generous roof overhangs. There are already thirty or forty people scattered around the room, with quite a few children sitting in the front rows with him. More arrive through the front and back doors for the next five minutes or so, until exactly 10:00 A.M., walking in quietly, without speaking, and seating themselves. After that time, no one else enters, and the silence becomes deeper. There is only an occasional rustling of fabric or creak from a chair as someone shifts position, with perhaps the odd sniffle, cough, or muted sneeze here and there, for the next fifteen minutes.

BP does not know what to do, exactly, so he just watches things, as usual. He can only comfortably observe the people in the chairs facing him. Those behind him would require turning his head and upper body to see, and he is hesitant to do that, as it seems to him it would be a bit obtrusive or rude, and he doesn't want to draw attention to himself.

The people gathered here are of every age, from very elderly to very young, and are dressed in every fashion, from formal to casual. Many of the adults have their eyes closed, sitting very still, with heads erect and their hands folded in their laps, but the children in front, closest to him, are a bit more fidgety, and most have their eyes open and are looking around, like him. He avoids meeting their gazes.

At 10:15, two women rise and walk to the end of each row of seated children, motion them to follow, and lead them out the back door, with the least amount of commotion possible. BP rises and follows his row of kids out the door and into the bright sunlight. There is a second, smaller building in the back yard, across a small courtyard, and the children troop silently into it.

The spell of silence is broken once the door of the rear building is closed behind them, and some conversations break out, though still in muted tones for a gathering of youngsters. There are light refreshments laid out on a table for them, crackers and fruit punch, and the kids partake. BP helps himself. One of the adults raises her voice and asks the group: "Who would like to go to the playground today?" Some kids raise their hands. "And who would like to go to the beach?" she asks. More kids raise their hand, including BP. "OK, the beach it is," she says, "so finish your snack, and anyone who needs to should go to the bathroom. Then we'll walk down there together."

"How cool is this?" thinks BP. "I'm going to be able to make a surf-check!" And check it he does, after being led several blocks west to the coast at Marine Street in a loose gaggle of children from ages four to about fourteen, with one adult in the front leading the parade and one at the rear, rounding up the stragglers. The surf is not large, maybe 2'–3', and there is nothing rideable at Marine Street itself, just a shorebreak wave, whomping on the sand and closing out on the steep beach, but BP takes off his shoes and socks and runs up and down the beach. He spies some surfers to the north at Horseshoe Reef and some more at the spot towards the south end, Little Point, who are all getting some fun rides on more shapely swells.

After twenty minutes or so, the women gather up the group and march them back to the meeting house, arriving shortly after 11:00, when the meeting for worship has ended. People are gathered in the courtyard and both buildings in small groups, visiting and circulating. By 11:30 or so, a potluck brunch has been laid out in the rear building, and BP eats his fill of a wide variety of dishes brought by each of the families in attendance, sitting out on the rear porch steps alone.

Around 1:00, an announcement is made that a "meeting for business" is about to commence in the front building. BP's mother, who has been mingling with the other adults, finds him and herds him to the car for the drive home. On the way, she asks him how he felt about the Meeting.

"It was OK, I guess. I liked it that we got to go to the beach."

"I'm not sure that you'll get to do that every week, Bobby. When the weather isn't as nice, I think the kids stay inside and learn a little about Quaker history and their faith and practice. But you wouldn't mind that too much, would you, dear?"

"I guess not, Mom," says BP, doubting that it would be as much fun as going to the beach. "I didn't quite understand what was happening in the big room at the beginning, though, when everyone was so quiet. What was going on there?"

"I'm still learning about it myself, honey, but that is the way Quakers worship—in silence. They believe that each person has the Light of God within, and that everyone is equally qualified to speak in God's name. That's why there is no minister preaching a sermon. They all wait in silence for God to move them to speak, and when that happens, anyone may stand up and deliver the message to the others. It is a kind of silent meditation, waiting to be moved by God's word."

"I didn't hear anyone speak, Mom. Did you say anything?"

"No, Bobby, I didn't, but some people did stand up and say things after you left."

"Did you like the service, Mom?"

"Yes, I did, Bobby, I liked it very much. I didn't know it before now, but I think we are Quakers, and we're coming back again, next Sunday. I met some people after the meeting who're working with CORE, the Congress on Racial Equality, here in town, and I'm going to meet them again later this week to see about doing some volunteer work, too. I feel much better now than I did this morning. I feel like I may actually be able to make a difference in this crazy world, somehow."

BP doesn't quite understand how this all works, exactly, but he is happy that his mother feels better. There is one more thing that puzzles him though, and he has to ask: "Does God ever speak to kids, Mom?"

His mother looks over at him with a quizzical expression, and takes a moment to answer. "I'm sure He does, at times, Bobby, but it may be that children are not prepared to hear Him as well, possibly, or understand what He is saying."

BP is quite sure that the Lord never said anything at all to him during his fifteen minutes experiencing silent worship today, at least nothing loud enough for him to hear. Secretly, he wonders if He ever will, or whether whatever character defect that prevented children from hearing God speak would plague him forever. "I guess I will have to grow up to know for sure," BP thinks to himself.

BIRTHDAY

It is often said that there are no seasons (or any real weather to speak of) in Southern California, but as fall turns to winter in San Diego, the change is more than obvious to BP. Cold fronts generated in the Gulf of Alaska sweep down the coast, bringing occasional clouds and rain, turning to snow in the mountains. The days get shorter and colder, the water temperature drops from its summertime highs by 15–20 degrees, and the prevailing, southwest swells are replaced by a more northwesterly, more frequent and powerful variety—large waves, angry waves, storm waves.

With his daily duty of attending school, the dwindling crowds at the beach (which make borrowing a board a near impossibility) and the harsher weather, the overall result is that BP cannot easily satisfy his yearning to learn to surf. His buddy, Donny, is absorbed in other team sports at school and rarely accompanies him to the beach anymore.

Occasionally, on a sunny weekend, there is enough of a crowd for him to wheedle a board from someone, but the ocean is usually cold and inhospitable, and he is back on the beach in less than half an hour, shivering. Often he must content himself with just watching as the small groups of hardcore surfers hurry in and out of the water, gathering around fires on the beach or getting into their heated cars and driving away to warm showers.

This is a very frustrating time for BP. He is familiar enough now with the sport to survey the enormity of the task. He has set lofty, ambitious goals for himself, but he can chart his progress only in tiny increments, painstakingly gained. Most of the time he blames his puny, undeveloped, boyish body for his shortcomings, the rest of the time he blames his lack of the proper equipment. He feels like he has the mind of an eagle trapped inside the body of a duck, high on a rocky, desert peak with no water anywhere in sight.

He rails against this injustice with a passionate fury: "Why does time pass so slowly?" he often asks himself. "When am I going to grow up? It's no joke being a kid. Big people have all the fun. They've got all the power, all the money—they can do what they want and buy what they want and vote and make laws and talk to God, but I can't do anything!"

The truth is that BP's body is beginning to grow very rapidly, though he hasn't begun to notice it yet. Those mysterious hormones are marshalling forces in his pituitary gland that will result in an alarming rate of growth over the next few years, and indeed, he has gained nearly ten pounds, and an inch in height, in just the last three months.

And he is not without resources—he has already begun a carefully conceived program of wheedling manipulation on his parents, designed to elicit the coveted gift by the end of the year. This program consists of casual suggestions and hints (that a surfboard for Christmas would surely make him the happiest of boys), logical arguments and outright propaganda (that surfing is a healthy pastime and that even though a surfboard is expensive, since his birthday falls so close to Christmas, perhaps they could combine the two occasions), and finally outright begging and veiled threats (oh please, I want one so bad....I don't know what I'll do if I can't get one pretty soon). After all, he reasons, how will they know what to get me if I don't let them know?

The fact is that for as long as BP can remember, there is nothing that he has ever desired, within reason, that his parents have failed to provide him (as far as material possessions are concerned, anyway). In this respect, he is extremely fortunate and quite spoiled.

BP turns thirteen on December 21, 1960. He is on Christmas vacation from school and the weather is glorious—a little chilly, but clear and sunny. After breakfast, his father suggests that they all take a drive up to La Jolla to visit BP's grandparents. "They haven't seen you in a few weeks now, and you are growing up so fast, Bobby."

BP is eager to get on to the serious business of the day, namely receiving his presents, but he sees some room for hope in this suggestion. "They got me a board and hid it up at Grandma's—I'll bet that's it!" They get into the station wagon and head up La Jolla Boulevard. "I'll bet they put it in Gramps' garage because it was so big!" He is so excited and preoccupied with his speculation that he doesn't notice when his father stops only a few blocks from home.

"I think we'd better go in here first," says his father, turning to BP in the backseat, who is just beginning to notice that they are not at a stop sign or a traffic light, but have pulled to the curb in front of the La Jolla Surf Shop. "Your mother and I have decided to get you a surfboard for your birthday, son, if that's what you really want, but we don't know anything about them, so we thought it would be best for you to pick one out yourself."

"Oh boy!" shrieks BP. He can hardly believe his ears. "I get to pick it out myself?" Sometimes parents can be so smart.

"Yes, Bobby, but this is quite an extravagant gift, so while you're looking, keep in mind that even if we gave you $25 for your birthday and $25 for Christmas, you only have $50 to spend, OK?"

"That's great, Dad! Thanks a lot, Mom! This is my best birthday and Christmas ever!" He can't get out of the car fast enough. "For $50 I bet I can get a pretty good used board and a wetsuit, too. Is that OK? If I don't get a wetsuit, I won't really be able to use the board much until the summer."

"Whatever suits you best, Bobby, that's why we left it up to you. As long as you keep your $50 limit in mind, you can spend it any way you want."

On the way into the shop, BP is on top of the world. "Now," he assures himself, "everything is going to be different."

Blissful Absorption

Equipped with his new board and wetsuit, BP begins to log many hours in the water through the rest of the winter and into the spring of 1961. With single-minded, fanatical determination he continues to learn to surf.

He is as devoted to his surfboard as if it were a puppy in need of constant care and affection. It is a 9'3" long Velzy/Jacobs, only a few years old, and it had been a steal for $30. It had obviously seen some hard use, but it had been hand-crafted by experts when it was new (as opposed to the mass-produced "pop-outs" that he has already learned to disdain from listening to the chatter of surfers on the beach), and all of its dings have been patched expertly. He grooms it carefully, scraping off the layers of old, dirty paraffin wax that cover the deck and applying a fresh coating. It lives in his room, not in the garage, so he can rest secure in its safety and awaken every morning to its reassuring presence. Besides its obvious utility for riding waves, it is also a deeply significant symbol of his future, of the promise of adulthood, which remains for him so desirable yet seems so remote.

With the other $20 from his gift fund, he purchases a wetsuit from San Diego Diver's Supply. It is a crudely-made jacket of ¼"-thick neoprene rubber, with long sleeves and a beaver-tail flap in the back, designed to loop between the legs and fasten in front. [At this point in time, purpose-built wetsuits for surfing are still several years away, and a diver's suit is the only option available.] It is a cruel solution, as BP finds out, since the stiffness of the rubber chafes his underarms while paddling until they are raw and red, but it shields him from the cold wind and water to some extent, allowing him to conserve enough body heat to stay out for hours during the winter, instead of minutes.

Surfing is simultaneously his daily consolation and a major source of grief. While engaged in the act, he is totally engrossed, absorbed, and unselfconscious. He is able to escape the monotony of his daily life by losing himself in the ocean. It is only afterwards, when he objectively examines his progress, that he becomes discouraged.

The challenge of learning to ride waves is a highly complex task involving physical coordination, strength, balance and agility. But beyond these motor skills, it requires subjective, intuitive, integrative abilities of a totally different sort in order to be elevated beyond a physical drill to an art. This is the matter of *style*, of not only accomplishing the act, but of making it look easy, natural, spontaneous, inspired and beautiful, the quest of all surfers.

Self-consciousness may be slightly helpful in developing the former skills but it is useless in the latter, perhaps even detrimental. Becoming aware of mistakes and shortcomings through retrospection may help to understand which areas of performance are in need of work and improvement, but trying to think about methodology and technique while performing, being too conscious of the activity while actually engaged in it, is extremely counterproductive, even self-defeating, in this sort of complex task.

The part that BP loves the most about surfing is the unconsciousness, the loss of self, the merging with the waves. When he enters the water, he leaves his shore-bound life behind and is in another world. He allows his body, and his unselfconscious learning processes (which are perfectly capable of modifying behavior without conscious awareness) to take control, absorbing information directly from a myriad of inputs, without interference from the more rational part of his mind, integrating him into the environment directly and automatically.

The oceanic playground is dynamic, fluctuating and cyclic, awesome in its complexity and infinite variety, its sometimes epic proportions. It cannot be attacked aggressively and conquered. It is not a problem to be solved. It is a manifestation of cosmic energy which may be approached and enjoyed in harmonious interaction only if a person is able to properly empathize, to tune in, so to speak, with its underlying rhythms, its natural laws, its recognizable patterns of change. To accomplish this one must, to a large extent, leave one's mind behind on the beach. This is more than agreeable to BP.

It is this intuitive power that allows a great surfer to be in the right place at the right time, to avoid falling victim to the ocean's propensity for blind violence, to harness the energy of a breaking wave and create an object of art—a performance, a dance with nature, fraught with real risks and rewards, uncontrived and unrehearsed—an allegory of life, itself.

This object of art is not a tangible one, however. When the surfer's ride is over (unless it has been recorded on film), there is nothing left of it to be packaged and sold, bandied about by eager agents and greedy capitalists (except, perhaps, for the reputation of the surfer who accomplished it, spread by those who witnessed it). It is esoteric performance art, created and lost in a free-form flow of natural events and spontaneous, responsive, creative activity—"that which destroys itself in its own production."

Since BP has not yet achieved such virtuosity (very few surfers do in less than five years of practicing the art), he is more like an acolyte, a lowly devotee, wholeheartedly committing himself to the service of the Church of the Open Water. It means that great personal effort, sustained by faith, alone, must be expended over a long period of ritual practice and initiation in order to penetrate the outer, institutional mysteries of the Church and arrive at the inner, inspirational core—the true, experiential ecstasy. BP believes with all his heart that he will get there, someday. Without understanding why, when or how, he knows it will come.

AT THE BEACH: PHASE TWO

As spring turns to summer in 1961, BP continues his apprenticeship in surfing. He is beginning to grow at an incredible rate now. His parents are shocked by the vast quantities of food and drink he consumes daily. The constant exercise and his internal, metabolic forge are inexorably transforming his boyish body. With every increase in strength and stature and every hour of practice he spends in the water, he is able to win a little more of his uphill battle, to improve and expand his performance with his board and reach new plateaus of ability, with their concomitant sets of new problems. But it is still slow going.

He learns to stand up and ride the soup fairly consistently first, mastering elementary balance and control skills, learning to keep his weight low and centered over the board, knees bent, absorbing the bumps, controlling the board's direction with his feet and ankles by tilting it side-to-side to keep it under him as he rushes shoreward.

He figures out how to more easily push through broken waves by "turning turtle"—paddling hard toward the whitewater and flipping upside down at the last moment, clutching the board by both rails, from underneath, letting the soup pass over, then rotating it quickly upright and scrambling back on top of it, to paddle furiously forward and gain some more ground before the next line hits.

He recognizes that there are critical limits to the size and power of breaking waves that must be respected, even by the most proficient paddler. The energy generated by a very thick lip (the pitching crest) on a very hollow wave can be considerable, even if it is not that large. Its shape and its progression in the process of breaking, he learns, are just as important factors as its relative size in judging how hard a breaker is going to thrash him when he tries to push through it.

The forces right in the "impact zone," where the lip hits the water in front of the breaking wave, can be formidable, snapping boards in half like dried twigs in extreme cases (large and very hollow waves), or routinely ripping them out of the clutches of unwary surfers caught there through some error in positioning or timing. BP learns to paddle around this zone, if possible, or to traverse it quickly during a lull between sets of waves, if it can't be avoided entirely. On the surface, it can be ferocious, but if necessary, after abandoning his board, he can dive deep and get below the maelstrom, hugging the ocean bottom, letting the energy pass above him.

On the bigger swells, over 6' on the face, and pouring in consistently with few lulls, he is frustrated to find that he is not able to paddle outside at his local beachbreak. It requires more strength, endurance, experience and technique than he is yet able to muster. He invariably ends up with his board being wrenched out of his grip and swept into the beach, leaving him with a slow swim back in for it.

Even on the smaller days, when he succeeds in getting outside to the lineup, he finds that catching and riding an unbroken swell is much different than his previous experience with riding the soup.

He has a terrible time trying to "take off"—to catch the wave. This was never a problem when riding the soup, which has enough kinetic energy to easily push him along, whether he wants to catch it or not. He must learn to judge an unbroken wave's development—whether it is steep enough to catch or still too flat to sweep him up and carry him shoreward. It is a fine line that divides the two conditions. He learns that the speed with which he paddles his board while trying to take off must be matched to the wave's relative development, or steepness, thus broadening the line.

At a critical stage in a wave's development, just before it breaks, while it is very steep on the face, a surfer can take off without paddling at all, by simply sitting back and sinking the tail of the board, then laying forward as the wave approaches. This "no-paddle take off" maneuver requires perfect timing and judgment, however, and can result in disaster if it misfires (usually with the nose of his board digging into the trough of the wave, or "pearl-diving," launching him in front of the wave to be steam-rollered as it breaks on him).

On a flatter, less developed swell, a lengthy paddle may be required to catch it, both to increase the board's speed in relation to the wave's and to allow the wave more time to develop and steepen as it heads into shallower water.

Further variables complicate the problem, of course, including the paddler's relative trim on the board (his position fore and aft), whether the wind is onshore or offshore, the tidal currents, etc., all contributing to the overall challenge.

Once he has managed to paddle outside, BP is very cautious about flirting with the impact zone. He tends to sit farther out so that a larger, "clean-up," set wave doesn't pounce on him and pitch him "over-the-falls" with the lip, one of the most calamitous consequences of poor positioning.

However, sitting further outside means that only the largest waves are developed enough to catch. These set waves are less frequent, giving him fewer opportunities to catch a ride, and a wipeout means that he has a much longer swim to the beach to retrieve his board. [It will be more than fifteen years until a functional "surf leash", or "leg rope," to reliably tether a surfer to his board, is invented and becomes an accepted and ubiquitous part of the sport.]

He eventually comes to recognize the indications of a larger set by scanning the horizon and developing a sense of timing for the swell's interval, which is neither perfectly predictable nor totally random. If he attunes himself to the signs and the rhythm successfully, he can drift inside during the lulls to catch the smaller, intermediate waves and still have sufficient warning to scratch back outside and clear the set waves.

Once he has actually caught an unbroken wave, he is happy to find that riding green water is much easier, initially, than riding the soup, as long as the ocean surface is not too choppy. The acceleration is smoother, without the bumpy turbulence of the whitewater, so it is easier to stand up and to retain his balance during the ride.

What to do after that is another matter, for if he rides straight in towards the beach, the wave will soon break right on top of him. He must learn to turn the board and trim it across the face of the wave, at an angle, if he wants to get a longer, faster ride and stay in the unbroken part of the wave.

This is not an easy thing to do. It takes him months to develop a rudimentary turn to the right, his frontside, or forehand, by taking off on a slight angle, leaning back and into the wave as he drops down the face, digging the rail in with weight on his toes. As the board swings around slowly, angling more to the right, he is also slowing it by shifting his weight back, so, as the turn is completed, he must trim forward to keep the wave from passing him by. The board accelerates quickly as he "walks the nose," and this change of speed must be anticipated or it will shoot out from under his feet, leaving him behind.

Turns to his left and cutbacks while riding right (on his backside or backhand) are even more difficult to learn. When he is riding with his back to the wave, it is harder to see what the wave is doing and judge what his proper trim should be. Going left, he must dig the left rail in by rocking back on his heels, which seems less positive and precise than digging in with his toes, and his butt tends to drag in the face of the wave at times. Therefore, with control at such a premium in these early stages, he prefers going right as much as possible, and always seeks out that side of the wave's peak, given a choice.

When he is released from the obligation of school in mid-June, his time in the water quadruples. With this intense practice, and without the restrictions of cold water and gnarly winter swells, he begins to make some visible progress.

The smaller summer swells, usually two to three feet high and more mushy than hollow, are accessible and rewarding, without as much threat of violence, except from the increased crowds the warmer water brings. He begins to collect some modestly competent rides on a regular basis and falls off less often. His flailing, fledgling efforts of the previous summer are remembered only infrequently and with a remote disdain.

His friend Donny is envious of BP's progress in the sport but is unable to match BP's torrid pace, due to a lack of equipment and his time commitment to Pony League baseball (which BP has foregone).

"What do I want to play baseball for?" BP had told him. "You need a whole friggin' team to play with, another team to play against, then you need umpires and coaches and a field and bats and balls and gloves and uniforms.... I can go down to the beach by myself with just my board and have more fun!"

By mid-summer, when Donny's league play is over, he again becomes BP's comrade in the surf. With savings from his paper route, he purchases a used board and the two spend every possible day at the beach. He benefits from BP's prior experience slightly, and is able to avoid a few pitfalls in the learning process by listening to BP's coaching, but it is no cakewalk for him either.

Transporting their boards to the beach is a major nuisance. It is a tiring walk back and forth carrying thirty pounds of foam and fiberglass, so they often pester their parents to drop them off in the morning and pick them up in the afternoon.

BP's father finally grows weary of their demands and builds them each an ingenious surfboard trailer, designed to bolt to the seat post of their bicycles, made out of scrap metal and a pair of small, rubber, wagon wheels. They can tow their boards behind them, now, tied to the trailers, adding immensely to their mobility and independence. The unassisted range of their available ocean playground increases to all of Mission and Pacific Beach, and even the southern La Jolla reefs.

Toward the end of summer, they encounter some of the best conditions for their ability level when a high pressure area squatting over the inland deserts sends dry, hot Santa Ana winds blowing offshore into a small, but perfectly shaped, 2–3', southwest swell. Daytime temperatures hover at 90–100 degrees Fahrenheit, the humidity at 5–15%, making the beach the place to be. They spend all day frolicking in the 72-degree water, riding wave after wave. Such marathon sessions result in radical sunburns, worn out muscles, and marked improvement in their surfing abilities.

BP begins to develop a drop-knee turn to the left and feels more comfortable riding backside. Donny graduates from riding soup and begins to snag a few outside waves, but he is still learning to stand up, turn and trim without falling off.

The vigorous exercise, fresh air, sea and sun pay additional dividends to both boys in the form of excellent health, deep tans, sun-bleached hair, and lean little mounds of hard muscle sprouting on their torsos (the archetypical "California gremmie" look).

Though he has made tremendous strides in ability in one year for a boy his age, BP is aware that he has only begun to scratch the surface of the surfing sphere. When he consciously evaluates his progress by comparing his surfing to that of the older, expert watermen he sees around him, he realizes that he is still a neophyte, and that his progress, objectively, has been petite at best. He is still far from even achieving journeyman status.

Such thoughts are very discouraging and offset the feelings of pride and accomplishment he garners from Donny's admiration and his own fantasies concerning his ability. At these times, when his self-image shrinks to match his reality, he is frustrated and angry beyond tears. He retreats behind a facade of speculation about how things "could" be, "should" be, and "would" be, "if only...."

How things "will" be seems to him to be a matter of chance, decidedly unfair, and somewhat beyond his control.

Junior High Jerk

When school begins again in September of 1961, BP's spirits fade as fast as his tan. He finds the eighth grade to be generally the same boring, useless waste of time as the seventh. He longs to be at the beach and spends many hours in class doodling pictures of perfectly shaped waves in the margins of his notebooks.

His supercilious attitude towards his teachers and his peers is renewed and reconfirmed. There is scarcely ever a subject, idea or lesson introduced that seems new to him—refreshing and inspiring. He has seen it all before in the books, magazines and newspapers that he has consumed voraciously, effortlessly, and willingly for many years now.

Education seems to him to be largely a matter of one's own volition, and he cannot understand why such authoritarian and competitive methods such as drills, tests, assignments and grades are deemed necessary to induce students to learn. It seems to turn them off to learning more often than not.

It appears to him that school is less an institution of education, of intellectual stimulation, than it is a bastion of oppression and submission—to teach children such essential social skills as how to shut up, stay in their seats, and listen to the teacher, regardless of how boring and shitty the class is. He imagines that this is society's meticulous preparation of its loyal subjects for a lifetime of standing in line and waiting, and of working at a boring, unsatisfying job for a regular paycheck (the adult version of the report card).

The arbitrary authority with which the teachers are empowered seems absurd to him. They do not appear to be any more intelligent (though, perhaps, a trifle more knowledgeable) than many of their hapless victims (himself included).

Try as he might, he is unable to discern the reason for, or source of, their power, unless it is true that they deserve and win their favored position by virtue of their greater age and experience alone. Such a "Conspiracy of Age" theory seems to be the only logical explanation.

"They've just been playing this game longer, that's all," he consoles himself. "If only I could grow up faster!"

To patiently become older seems to be the only solution to his problem—the only way of escaping the oppression of youth. Luckily, growing older happens to be inevitable. Patience is harder to come by.

His routine remains nearly unchanged from the previous year. He attends classes, surfs when he can after school and on weekends, goes to Quaker Meeting on Sundays with his mother, continues consuming mass quantities of food, eating four or five meals a day, with hearty bedtime snacks as well, and his phenomenal growth spurt persists. In secret, he masturbates nearly daily, struggling to come to grips with his awakening sexual persona. He is gratified to find the merest peach-fuzz of a beard sprouting from his chin and cheeks, and he begins shaving with an electric razor his mother has given him, although it is not necessary to do it very often.

BP cannot wait to grow up. He tries very hard to figure out just exactly what it is that differentiates childhood from adulthood. There are, he can see, the obvious physical differences, but he realizes he has no control over the rate of development of his body.

Deciding that there are fewer limitations on matters of mind than of body, he tries to determine the essential characteristics of "adult" thinking. It seems obvious to him that one of the major differences is that children are generally told what to think and expected to act accordingly. This rule applies down to the smallest of life's details, on pain of punishment. Adults, on the other hand, are expected to think for themselves, to make their own decisions regarding a wide array of issues and activities, circumscribed only by the rules of law and morality (if any) that they choose to recognize, and their own personal resources and abilities.

He resolves, therefore, to begin to think for himself as much as possible. This is a daunting prospect, however. He realizes that it is impractical to reconsider and rebel against every single restriction imposed on his life by others. A certain amount of unexamined cooperation is necessary to ensure and simplify his survival. "I'd like to ditch school every day and go surfing if it was up to me," he notes, "but my parents would *kill* me!"

Outright civil war is inadvisable, he decides, but limited insurgency against isolated and vulnerable positions seems very plausible, and this becomes his guiding notion, his order of operations, his *raison d'etre*.

One day in the spring of 1962, during the last half of the school year, after carefully preparing some materials and developing the proper rationalizations to bolster his confidence, he enters his homeroom class and sits down purposefully in the first row, right in front of the teachers desk. Usually, he prefers the anonymity of the back rows. When the class rises to salute the flag, as is the morning custom, he refuses to participate. He sits stock-still, under the glaring eye of his teacher, Mr. Foley, as the rest of the class put their hands over their hearts and recite the *Pledge of Allegiance*.

The silence which fills the classroom after the pledge has ended is deafening. It roars in BP's ears as the teacher approaches his seat.

"What is your problem this morning, young man?" asks Mr. Foley, unsure how to deal with such unprecedented behavior by one of his pupils. "Are you deaf or just glued to your seat?"

"No sir," answers BP, "neither."

"Then why didn't you stand up and salute the flag?"

"I didn't want to do it, sir. I'm sorry if that upsets you, but I've been thinking about that pledge, and I don't believe it is absolutely true, so I've decided not to say it anymore."

"Of course that upsets me, Mr. Pilhaus. Saluting the flag is your duty as a citizen and a privilege, besides, I might add; a small price to pay for being able to live in a free country. You are defying school regulations, as formulated by the Board of Education, and I order you to obey instantly! Now *stand up* and recite the pledge!"

BP realizes he is treading on shaky ground. He briefly considers a full retreat but decides instead on a compromise: "OK, I'll stand up and say most of it—I love my country—but I won't say the last line, 'with liberty and justice for all,' because it's just not true and I've always been taught to tell the truth."

"You are being impudent, young man," says Mr. Foley in a rising voice, veins beginning to bulge in his neck. "By what arrogant authority do you claim to amend the pledge? Each and every one of these phrases is part of our nation's sacred history. It is not up to the individual to decide what to say and what to omit. That is like deciding that you will only obey the laws that you agree with and ignore the others—that's anarchy!"

"No sir," says BP calmly, "it's civil disobedience, I believe."

"I don't care what you call it, just answer my question. Whatever gave you the idea that our country does not provide 'liberty and justice for all?'"

"These do, sir," answers BP, playing his trump card. From his desktop he lifts a manila folder containing the material he has prepared, which he offers to his teacher solemnly and humbly, like a lawyer handing an exhibit to a judge to be entered as evidence for his case.

Mr. Foley is taken aback. He had expected BP to capitulate to his intimidating tactics immediately, and is not prepared for this ploy, this counter-thrust. He realizes that time is growing short in the homeroom period, which is only ten minutes long, so he accepts the folder from BP, saying: "I don't know what you're up to, young man, but I can assure you that we are going to get to the bottom of this right now!"

Turning to his pet pupil, a girl sitting next to BP, he hands her the small notebook he is carrying. "Cheryl, will you please take attendance for me this morning?" he asks politely.

Having delegated this responsibility, he turns back to BP. "You stay right where you are, young man, until we get this straightened out. Understand?"

BP nods his head. The girl calls roll as Mr. Foley retreats to his desk to examine the material. Inside the manila folder are copious, carefully clipped photos and articles from various newspapers and magazines. All of them concern events of the struggle for civil rights for minorities, many of them violent, beginning with the 1954 decision of the U.S. Supreme Court in *Brown vs. Board of Education of Topeka, Kansas,* continuing with the passage of the

Civil Rights Act of 1957, then snowballing and raging throughout the nation since Feb. 1, 1960, when four black students sat down at a "whites only" lunch counter in a department store in Greensboro, North Carolina and demanded service. There are articles about lynchings, abuses of voting rights, boycotts, protest demonstrations, sit-ins, and freedom-riders.

Mr. Foley is only able to skim through it briefly before the bell rings, ending the homeroom period. Everyone gets up from their desks and exits the room except for him and BP.

"You know, Bobby," he lectures gently, "you mustn't judge the whole country, the entire political system, on the basis of the actions of a few troublemakers." Mr. Foley feels that there is a young mind at stake, here, that he must formulate a convincing argument that will mend this poor boy's rash stupidity. "Our system is really the best in the world. It might not be perfect, there may always be someone who feels like they're not getting a fair shake, but everyone has the same basic opportunities and rights. It's just a few people, making excuses for their own incompetence, who are creating all this ruckus."

"It doesn't seem to me like there are only a few of them," insists BP. "It seems like there are more and more of them every day, as people become aware of the injustices that exist and find the courage to do something about them."

"You really don't understand, though. The press has a way of blowing these things all out of proportion. The situation is really not all that bad—they are sensationalizing it to sell their product! Worse than that, some of it is just plain, old Communist propaganda, designed to upset people and destroy our democracy." Mr. Foley picks up the folder and brandishes it at BP. "I happen to know that the groups involved in many of these incidents are suspected by the F.B.I. of being Communist-front organizations. Do you know what that means?"

"No, not exactly," admits BP, ashamed that his careful research has not prepared him for this question.

"Well, it means that some organizations, even legitimate ones, can be infiltrated by Communist agents, who worm their way into positions of leadership and use their power to manipulate the organization for their own evil ends."

"You mean that all this stuff is being done by Communist spies?" scoffs BP, totally unconvinced.

"Not exactly. There may be many people in the organizations that are well-intentioned—they are just misguided, that's all. It only takes a few radicals to control a group like that, if they are in the right places."

"Well, what about some of the facts that are quoted in there?" BP gets up from his desk, walks over to Mr. Foley, taking the folder from his hand, leafing through articles until he finds the one he wants. "Look at this—this is a quote from John F. Kennedy, our President." BP jabs the page with his finger for emphasis. "You're not trying to tell me that he is misguided or a Commie, are you?"

Mr. Foley reads the quote: "The Negro baby born in America today, regardless of the section or state in which he is born, has about one-half as much chance of completing high school as a white baby born in the same place, on the same day; one-third as much chance of completing college; one-third as much chance of becoming a professional man; twice as much chance of becoming unemployed; about one-seventh as much chance of earning $10,000 a year; a life expectancy which is seven years shorter, and the prospect of earning only half as much."

"It may be that these are accurate statistics, son," says Mr. Foley condescendingly. "It is the nature of propaganda to take facts and twist them in the interpretation. There may be other reasons for these numbers that are not being considered properly. It doesn't mean that our system has failed. Many of these poor coloreds can't be educated and they have no ambition."

The bell signaling the beginning of first period rings, preventing Mr. Foley from putting his foot any further down his throat, but BP has heard enough.

"I think that maybe the problem isn't with this stuff," says BP, when the bell stops ringing. "I think the problem is that you're a bigot, Mr. Foley—you're so prejudiced you can't recognize injustice when it's right in front of your face!"

Mr. Foley bristles. "I don't have to take that from you, young man, and I haven't got any more time to waste here, either—I have to be in another class right now. You're going up to the principal's office with me and *he* can deal with you!"

He gathers up the materials on his desk and takes BP by the arm, jerks him out of the room and up the hall, depositing him finally on a wooden bench in the outer office of the principal. With a few whispered words to the secretary, he hurries out of the office without looking at BP again—off down the hall, on his way to teach social studies to thirty eager innocents.

Further Adventures in Adulthood

Through some minor errors in deduction, BP has decided that certain "adult" activities, such as drinking alcohol and coffee, smoking cigarettes, and fornicating, among others, must be closely linked to growing up, since children are not allowed to do them. It seems logical to him that experimenting with such prohibited activities will somehow contribute towards accelerating the process, so he is determined to try them all, as soon as possible.

He had been able to satisfy his curiosity about one of these items, coffee, fairly easily. He had overcome his mother's early protests that it would "stunt his growth," since he had now sprouted taller than she, nullifying her argument, and had been allowed one cup of this mysterious brew on Sunday mornings for several weeks. He found it bitter and uninteresting, unless it was liberally laced with cream and sugar, and soon went back to drinking hot chocolate milk.

Smoking is next on his agenda. He cannot figure out why so many people in his parent's generation smoke cigarettes. He imagines it has something to do with World War II, since that seemed to have been the major formative event of their generation. Perhaps the war had made them all very nervous. Many of them had certainly had to grow up in a hurry during this crisis—maybe cigarettes had helped them do it? If it worked for them, maybe it'll work for him, too.

His grandparent's generation seems to prefer smoking pipes and cigars, if they smoke at all, but his father smokes Winston cigarettes, and BP wants to grow up to be like his father. (Sort of.)

After much preparation, requiring a small amount of stealth and cunning, he is ready for his next great experiment, just a few days before Easter vacation.

He has been appointed Audio-Visual Monitor in his fifth-period science class, which means whenever a film or slides are shown, he gets to operate the projector, something he enjoys immensely. It also means that whenever a piece of equipment is needed, he is sent to the A-V storeroom to fetch it.

He is issued a "hall pass" by his teacher, Mrs. Shay, for these errands, since it is a violation of school rules for a student to be out in the halls during class time. He abuses this freedom to the utmost, always loitering as long as possible, enjoying his immunity, visiting his locker.

One of his favorite things about junior high school, a great improvement over elementary school in his mind, is having a hall locker. Since students have five or six classes a day in different rooms, all requiring different books, the school provides banks of metal lockers, lining the hallways, for their convenience. This concession to individual needs is a rarity in such a factory of conformity, and BP takes delight in it.

He visits his locker as often as possible, refreshing himself at this tiny oasis of individuality. He always keeps some kind of food on hand there for quick snacks, since it is illegal to eat in class and his need for caloric input these days is prodigious.

He has customized the interior of his little sheet metal cubicle with all manner of paraphernalia essential to his identity. Surfing photos clipped from magazines are taped up to the sides of the locker and the back of the door, interspersed with decals from some of the major surfboard manufacturers, which he has collected and carefully applied.

The privacy of the hall locker is not exactly inviolable, since they are subject to inspection by school staff (given with one hand and taken with the other), so BP's two most prized possessions are disguised within the general clutter of his locker's contents.

Several months before, he had shoplifted a copy of *Playboy* magazine's gala Christmas, 1961, issue from a local shop (he had been *forced* to steal it, he tells himself, because he couldn't legally buy one at his age). To avoid detection in any locker inspection, he had carefully grafted the cover of one of his mother's old *Sunset* magazines over its illicit contents. He has spent hours since then, five and ten minutes at a time, thumbing through this eye-opening periodical and pretending that he would know exactly what to say and do if he should ever happen to meet one of these naked Playmates.

At the very bottom of his locker he has a box of Parowax, the paraffin bars he uses to wax his surfboards. This particular box contains only three and one-half bars instead of the usual four, however. Though it would appear full if it were opened, the space under the half-bar is occupied by a pack of Winstons he had recently boosted from the carton his father keeps in one of their kitchen cabinets at home. After carefully observing his father's pattern of consumption, he had stolen the pack when the carton was half full and moved the remaining packs forward to cover up the theft, hoping that his father would not be keeping track of exactly how many packs were left. So far, his father has not appeared to notice, or at least has not voiced any suspicions.

He has been screwing up his courage for days and waiting for the right opportunity. Finally it comes. A bulb burns out in a projector during a slide presentation in his fifth period class, and he is sent for a replacement by Mrs. Shay, while she continues with another lesson.

He goes straight to his locker, breathing hard and thinking fast, excited by the unknown prospects laying ahead. "I've got plenty of time, really," he tells himself. "If Mrs. Shay asks me why it took so long, I'll just tell her that they couldn't find the right bulb and had to look around for it."

There is no one in sight as he dials in his three-digit combination on the chromed MasterLock padlock cylinder. He looks up and down the hallway as he opens the door, digs the cigarettes out of the bottom of the Parowax box and transfers them to his pocket, next to the book of paper matches he has brought from home.

Closing the locker door quietly, he strolls nonchalantly down the hallway to the entrance to the boy's restroom, and looks around again before slipping noiselessly inside. He quickly checks the interior of the lavatory for occupants and finds none. Without wasting any more time, he hurries into a stall at the back of the room, under an open window, and fumbles in his pockets to retrieve his precious contraband. His hands are trembling slightly and seem to resist his intentions, not wanting to cooperate in this forbidden act. He nearly drops the whole load into the toilet in his clumsy anxiety.

"Don't blow it now! Get the matches wet and it's all over, dummy!"

There is something strangely familiar about the motions he goes through in lighting the cigarette, something curiously hypnotic, calming him down; cigarette from the package, tipped to his lip, match torn from book, striking the flame, hold it aloft, suck and inhale.

"AAARRRGGGHHH! AAAWWWHHHOOOOEEEYY!" A gagging cough leaps from the depths of his tortured lungs and brings tears to his eyes, twisting his body like a pretzel.

"Holy shit!" he says to himself when the fit finally subsides, leaving him gasping for breath. "I must have taken too big a puff! That wasn't good *at all*. It seemed pretty neat right up until I sucked that smoke in. Maybe I should just take a smaller drag." He steadies himself and takes a couple of shallow, tentative puffs on the cigarette without gagging again.

"There! That's more like it! I guess this is pretty cool." He continues smoking, trying to figure out what the most stylish way to hold the cigarette might be. To do this, it is necessary to leave the stall in order to check his image in the mirror over the washbasin. He is thinking that he does look quite a bit older, and much more sophisticated, when he hears footsteps approaching in the hallway outside.

He rushes back into the stall and closes the door, dowsing the butt in the toilet and climbing up onto it, so that his legs will not show under the privacy partition, which doesn't extend all the way to the floor. He waves his hands over his head in a windmilling motion, vainly attempting to clear the incriminating smoke from the room, hoping with all his fiber that the footsteps will pass him by.

"Why did I go over to that mirror?" he asks himself forlornly. "I should have stayed right here and blown all the smoke out the window, just in case something like this happened. I'm so stupid, sometimes!"

Entering the restroom to relieve his troubled kidneys is Mr. Conroy, a custodian at the school. He is a tall, thin, wiry, middle-aged bachelor, with a gentle (some say effeminate) manner, for which he is often misunderstood.

Mr. Conroy does not smoke (or drink, or fornicate, for that matter, despite rumors to the contrary around the school), so his sensitive nose recognizes the aroma of tobacco smoke in the air as soon as he enters the door.

"All right," he says quietly but authoritatively, "who's in here? Come on out! I know what you're up to..." This is not the first time he has encountered a student smoking in the restrooms.

BP doesn't want to show himself. He wishes he could disappear. He knows there is no way out, but he searches frantically for any idea which might include the possibility of escape, adopting the first strategy that comes to mind.

Flushing the toilet to eliminate the evidence, he puts his hands over his stomach and moans, stumbling out of the stall to face his fate.

"Oh, I'm sick," he groans, "I just threw up!" (He does feel a bit queasy.)

Mr. Conroy discerns that BP's misery is only partly genuine. "Of course you're sick. Smoking cigarettes would make any kid your age sick, I imagine."

"I wasn't smoking," lies BP. "I think it was something I had for lunch that made me puke. I'm feeling a little better now."

"You're not fooling me, young man, I can smell it."

"It smelled like that when I came in here," claims BP. "I just got here! It must have been someone else before me who was smoking. Not me!"

"Then you won't mind showing me everything you've got in your pockets, will you?"

"Why should I do that?" asks BP, beginning to squirm.

"So I can see that you don't have any cigarettes or matches on you. Then I might believe that you weren't smoking."

"Jesus Christ!" BP curses himself silently. "Why didn't I just bring one and leave the others in my locker?" He can see that he has run out of room on this tack, so he tries another. Looking sheepish, he pulls the remaining cigarettes out of his pocket and hands them over, pleading for his life. "Can't we keep this to ourselves, sir? I only tried one and I didn't even like it! I won't ever do it again, honest! Please don't turn me in! I'm in so much trouble already they'll probably suspend me and my parents'll kill me! Please, let's just forget about it, OK?"

Mr. Conroy is not without pity, but righteousness prevails. "I'm sorry, son. There's nothing I can do. It's my duty, you know. You're breaking school rules. I'll have to take you up to the principal's office."

"Don't take *their* side, sir," BP is poignant. "You're not like them. They don't like you any better than they like us kids! They treat us both like dirt! We've got to stick together! We're both on the same side, don't you see?"

"Well," says Mr. Conroy, surprised by BP's acumen, "you might be right about that, young fellow. I don't want you to think I *like* doing this, but a rule's a rule. It's not up to me to judge you—that's up to your parents and the principal. I'm afraid there's no way to keep them out of this. It's their names on my paycheck every month, do you understand? Don't worry, I don't think they'll come down too hard on you for this—at least you weren't smoking that other stuff! Come along, now."

BP is desperate. He makes a break for the door, but Mr. Conroy grabs him by the arm as he rushes past, holding him firmly as they march up the hall towards the familiar wooden bench in the principal's reception area. Mr. Conroy is not a small man and quite strong.

"Lemme go, you fuckin' faggot! Why are you doing this to me!" he screams, losing his temper. In the back of his mind he is wondering what the "other stuff" Mr. Conroy mentioned might be, exactly.

"It's for your own good," says Mr. Conroy.

A Conference

BP's mother and father, Joseph and Betty, are sitting side-by-side on the same wooden bench outside the principal's office at P.B. Junior High School that BP has so frequently occupied. It has become quite a familiar landmark in their existence of late, much to their chagrin and dismay.

"The principal will see you now, Mr. and Mrs. Pilhaus," announces the receptionist politely, standing up and opening the door to the inner office for them. Together they trundle into the office, heads bowed, legs barely moving, carried along on tiny, invisible wheels of shame and embarrassment.

"Good afternoon. Won't you please be seated?" The principal greets them standing, with a cordial but formal air, shaking their hands, indicating two cushioned office chairs arranged in front of his desk.

"As you know," begins the principal, Mr. Rutledge, "the school term is ending in one more week and I promised you that we would try to come to some decision regarding your son by the end of the year. That's why I called this conference with you today. The district psychologist, Dr. Dourmann, and I have formulated a plan to try to deal with young Robert's behavioral problems, but I must admit to you that it is quite radical and progressive—we will need your permission and cooperation to implement it."

"Excuse me," says BP's mother automatically, regretting the decision that was made fifteen years ago for the umpteenth time. "Bobby's given name is Bob, not Robert. His birth certificate reads 'Bob B. Pilhaus,' sir—it's that way on all his records."

"Of course, I'm sorry," apologizes the principal, checking the papers in front of him. "Oh yes, yes, I see.... Hmmm.... What does the 'B' stand for?"

"Nothing, actually," answers Betty miserably. "It's just an initial, a different way to write 'Bobby.' His father thought it was clever." She shoots a glance at Joseph, sitting next to her, which could have informed him just how little she has forgiven him this ancient piece of domination, if he had only noticed it. "We call him Bob or Bobby, but his nickname is 'Beep,' of all things—that's what he began calling himself when he was very young and it stuck." (Despite her resistance to it.)

As the principal pauses, reviewing his file, she remembers Bobby explaining to her how he had derived that name for himself, at age five, while watching Saturday morning cartoons on a neighbor's TV set (another thing for which she is determined never to forgive Television). "You should see it, Mom," he had said, "there's this little, blue roadrunner who's so fast and so smart, he just runs circles around this poor coyote that's trying to catch him! And he never says anything, he just goes 'BEEP, BEEP!' That's almost exactly like my initials, you know, BP, don't you think? That's a pretty neat name, huh?" She cringes at the memory.

"Yes, well, calling him Robert was my mistake, then. I meant Bob, of course. As we discussed last month, Bob's problem is quite extraordinary and seems to have escalated in a fairly short period of time. That's why I had you authorize the special testing we've just completed. It must be remembered that he is going through a period of rapid development at the moment, a difficult but temporary 'phase,' so to speak. Dr. Dourmann assures me, after analyzing the results from a full battery of behavioral and I.Q. tests, that Bob is actually a 'gifted' pupil, and is only manifesting his frustration with the lack of challenge in the school environment through these acts of rebellion. His I.Q. tests out at over 170 points and he already has the reading, writing and comprehension skills of the average senior in high school."

This news comes as a shock to both of BP's parents. Joseph believes that it must be some kind of mistake, an error in the testing. After overcoming her initial surprise, Betty is more inclined to accept this interpretation of her only child's abilities. "He's really not a bad boy at heart, then, is he?" she half-asks, half-states.

"As I said," continues Mr. Rutledge, avoiding a direct answer, "Bob's problem is an exceptional one. Many ordinary behavioral problems stem from learning disabilities, usually caused by perceptual-motor deficiencies, which cause a pupil to perceive school as impossibly difficult. For Bob, just the opposite is true, we believe. He views school as impossibly *easy*. It is failing to present him with suitable and timely challenges to occupy him adequately. So, out of frustration and boredom, he's begun to challenge the authority of the institution he believes is holding him back—the school! You've told me that he's not a behavioral problem at home, correct?"

"Not particularly," answers Joseph, "although all he ever wants to do is go to the beach and go surfing. Sometimes we have to force him to sit down and do his homework, or do his household chores, but he usually knuckles under and does what you tell him, especially if we threaten to take his surfboard away from him for a week or two."

"This supports our theory, I believe," claims Mr. Rutledge. "I think this shows that he perceives school as the problem, not his home or family life. This hypothesis is borne out in several other respects as well. For instance, Bob's academic grades have always been excellent, in the ninety-ninth percentile, but his marks in 'citizenship,' which indicate his level of social integration, have not been as stellar, to say the least. If he is well-integrated at home, then why this failure at school? Also the specific circumstances of many of his offenses, aside from the smoking incident, have shown exceptional ingenuity, resourcefulness, and creativity in some ways.

"I don't believe you're familiar with the details of the last two incidents, which occurred last week. I was waiting for this meeting to inform you about them. It seems that last Tuesday, Bob refused to participate in a standard civil defense drill called during first period. Mr. Foley, his homeroom teacher, was still a bit upset with Bob over the previous incident, with the *Pledge of Allegiance*, so he sent him to my office immediately. As near as I could determine, Bob was trying to protest against the threat of nuclear war, stating that 'there is no defense possible, so it is pointless to prepare for an attack.'" Mr. Rutledge consults some reports on his desk.

"He said, and I quote, 'I'd rather show the Russians that I'm prepared for peace instead of preparing for a war that nobody can win.' To support his argument he had numerous documents concerning the build-up of nuclear arsenals on both sides of the Iron Curtain, articles on the cold war, the nature and effects of nuclear weaponry, and the resulting radiation that would be released into the atmosphere in a major exchange, etc., which would assure global annihilation. It was quite impressive to see the initiative and conviction he displayed, even though his tactics were, as in the case with the pledge, quite disruptive."

"The second incident occurred just yesterday and appears to have been a bit more spontaneous. Mrs Shay, his science teacher, sent him to me for discipline because he had adamantly refused to take part in an experiment in class involving the dissection of a frog. He called it 'gross and disgusting and an invasion of the poor frog's privacy.'"

"Don't you think that shows a sensitivity and respect for life in all forms?" asks Betty meekly. "I've always taught him to appreciate and respect animals."

Joseph's eyeballs roll up in his head in exasperation. "Fer chrissakes, Betty, how do you ever expect the kid to get ahead in this world if he won't keep his mouth shut and follow orders?"

"I agree with both of you," Mr. Rutledge says soothingly. "I believe that we must offer Bob greater intellectual challenges, and at the same time work on his social skills. That's why we are proposing to you that next fall, after some custom-tailored, personal attention in our six-week-long, intensive summer program for gifted students, we enter him into high school on the tenth-grade level, skipping ninth grade entirely. This is a radical solution and a bit of a compromise, but it's absolutely the best suggestion that we could come up with. Dr. Dourmann and I agree that Bob possesses the necessary physical and mental abilities to compete easily on the high school level, and we think it might be just the thing for his emotional development as well. We have consulted with the administration at Mission Bay High School and they will accept him in September. Of course, we would never do this without your permission and his agreement, so we are asking that the three of you talk it over together, and give us your answer soon. The summer session starts in two weeks."

Mr. Rutledge stands up, indicating that the conference is over. "If you have any more questions, just give me a ring. You have my number, yes?" He shakes Joseph's hand, takes Betty's arm and escorts them both to the door.

"Yes, thank you," says Joseph, as they exit the office semi-stunned.

On the drive home, Betty is thinking about the time she had tried to enroll Bobby in kindergarten, when he was four and one-half years old. The district officials had refused to enroll him because his fifth birthday was one week after the cut-off date, and had told her to bring him back the next year. She had protested that he would be almost six by that time. He had already learned to read, she told them, was as large as any five-year-old, and needed to be enrolled in school. She had ended up taking him to a private pre-school for the year. Now she was vindicated. The public school was going to put him forward a grade, where he belonged in the first place.

BP's father is seriously wondering if his son is a sociopath or a genius. It's really not clear to him now. He had gone to the school expecting to be informed of his son's impending suspension or dismissal, and they say they're going to skip him forward a grade for his misbehavior. It doesn't make sense to him. When he was in school, troublemakers were kicked out or held back a year, they were not rewarded with a promotion!

He is sure that this is some sort of bleeding-heart liberal, humanist-type, psychological coddling of the child, and he begins to make some private plans for instilling a little discipline (or at least a proper respect for authority) in the boy.

DEVILPUPS

When his parents introduce the subject of their conference with the principal, BP is apprehensive. By the time they are finished explaining the proposal, he has mixed feelings. He is relieved that he doesn't seem to be in as much trouble as he had thought he would be, but the idea of going to summer school does not thrill him at all.

Skipping ninth grade sounds reasonably pleasant to him. He figures that he will be able to grow up an entire year faster that way—an exciting prospect for advancing to adulthood. He is sure he can handle it academically, even without the extra summer session.

"Couldn't I just go on to tenth grade without going to school this summer?" he wonders aloud. "The water is getting warm again and I really wanted to surf a lot this summer..."

His father interrupts him curtly, irritated by this *laissez-faire* wish, this "something-for-nothing" attitude on the part of his son. "Be quiet and listen! You've had things your own way for far too long now. We've been much too permissive with you. You're *going* to summer school and you're going to work *hard* at it. We've found you out—you're not dumb, you're just *lazy*! Well, there are plenty of kids, as bright as you, who are also willing to *work* hard, and they are going to leave you eating their dust! If you want to go to college and make something of yourself, you're going to have to compete with them. You may be way ahead right now, but if you don't keep working at it, they will all pass you by. Where is this *surfing* going to get you? It'll never put a *dime* in your pocket. Most of those surfers are just *bums*! You've got to learn to apply yourself to the things that will do you some good, that will help you get ahead in this world, whether you like them or not. It's a cold, cruel world out there, and you've got to learn that no one gives a damn if you make it or not!"

"But Joseph, *we* give a damn," points out Betty, trying to calm him down.

"Of course we do, dear, I don't mean to include us. Eventually he is going to be out on his own, though, and the vultures are just waiting to pick his bones. You know who I mean—the mortgage holders, the bill collectors, the loan officers, the bureaucrats! He's never had to work for anything in his life. We've handed it all to him on a silver platter. If he doesn't get a little discipline and a sense of responsibility knocked into him pretty soon, he's going to find himself at the bottom of the heap, and we're not going to be around to help him up again." Joseph's anger is moderating. He looks straight at BP and says: "You just need to understand, son, how important these decisions are! I don't think you have a proper perspective on how crucial this may become, later on in your life. Things change, that's all."

BP is sure that this must be true. It is one of his greatest fears. He is thoroughly intimidated and acquiesces. "I'll do anything you say, Dad, whatever you think is best. I'll go to summer school and I'll work hard," he says sincerely.

"That's a good boy, Bobby," coos his mother, hoping to bring this discussion to an end for the sake of Joseph's blood pressure. "I'm sure we'll be proud of you!"

However, Joseph is not through. "That's fine, son, but there's one more thing. After summer school, I want you to attend another program. It's called the 'Devilpups.' It's run by an old friend of mine, Colonel Borman, for boys just like you. It's only for two weeks, and it'll do you a world of good, I think."

Betty is listening to this in slack-jawed disbelief. "Joseph! We haven't discussed this! How could you!" She is irate. Words fail her.

Joseph ignores her protest and continues. "I'm not going to kid you, Bobby. This camp is not all fun and games. It's tough, just like the real world, and there's no backing out of it once you're there. I think it would be the best thing you could do for yourself."

BP is scared. There is something truly ominous about the name of this operation, and the flabbergasted look on his mother's face increases his sense of impending doom. "I'm not sure I want to go to that. Do I have to?"

"I've already signed you up," says Joseph adamantly. "You're going to *go* and you're going to *like* it, or I'm going to take your surfboard away from you and never give it back! Do you understand?"

"OK," mutters BP, "if you put it that way."

"And I don't want to hear another word about it!" concludes his father, to both of them.

Summer school is both better and worse than BP imagined it would be—better, because it is only four hours long and the classes are smaller, the instruction more personal; worse, because those four hours are in the early morning, when the best waves of the day come rolling in, by and large.

The summer weather pattern consists of night and morning low clouds and fog along the coast, which are slowly burnt off by the sun and swept away by an afternoon sea breeze. This wind builds out of the west almost every day, due to the convection caused by the land heating up much more quickly than the sea. Thus, by the time he gets to the beach on most days, while it is sunny and warm, the onshore wind has made the waves choppy. He often ends up waiting to go surfing until after supper, just before the sun goes down, when the sea breeze dies out and the ocean begins to glass off again.

He tries not to think about what is going to happen after summer school. "How bad could it be?" he rationalizes. "They can't *kill* me!" His confidence in this assumption is shaken somewhat when he feels the tension in the atmosphere of his home throughout the summer. He can sense that his mother is adamantly opposed to this Devilpup business, and he sometimes overhears her arguing about it stridently (behind closed doors) with his father. Apparently, she has not taken his father's statement about "not hearing another word" as seriously as he did, but no change of plans is announced, no reprieve issued.

He has a whole week after summer school to himself, to surf. He is blessed by the sudden appearance of a consistent, well-shaped, 4' southwest swell generated by the sustained, high winds of a cyclone off the coast of New Zealand. The resultant wave train has pushed through seven thousand miles of open ocean, losing some of its original velocity and amplitude, but refining its individual pulses under the calming influence of the north Pacific high pressure dome. After crossing the equator, this southern-hemi swell finally begins to rumble onto southern California shores some ten days after it was propagated.

BP is treated to the best waves of his second year of surfing—a veritable orgy of large, long, fast, smooth walls of water peeling cleanly under sunny, windless skies for days on end. He is much better equipped now to extract the sweet nectar from this well-shaped swell. He has become a competent surfer, if not an artful one, able to catch waves easily and stand and ride both ways, frontside and back, walking the board to trim it, cutting back and kicking out as necessary. He is an order of magnitude stronger than when he had begun, a much more capable swimmer and paddler, and he has absorbed the lore of the waterman like a sponge, learning to "read" the ocean conditions and the way that individual waves break at various spots well enough to avoid the most serious pitfalls, and put himself in position to harvest their energy without much punishment. He gorges himself on ride after ride during this swell, rarely losing his board because the waves are so smooth, so mechanical, so predictable. [Or is it that he has earned a new perception, a new consciousness of them, by his years of effort?]

BP is surfed out, oblivious, and resigned to his fate by late August, when his father drops him off at Camp Pendleton, a sprawling Marine Corps military base in northern San Diego County. He assembles with sixty other boys between the ages of fourteen and sixteen in a large, outdoor amphitheater to hear the opening address by Colonel Borman, his father's friend.

"Good afternoon, gentlemen. Welcome to Camp Pendleton. I am Colonel Borman, your company commander. For the next two weeks, you are going to be living the life of a Marine recruit—sleeping in the same barracks, eating in the same mess hall, wearing the same fatigues, and doing some of the same drills as a real Marine. It is a hard life, in some ways, and it will be difficult for some of you to adjust, especially those of you who have led soft lives on the outside. There will be no one for you to lean on here! Everyone must pull his own weight and then some. But there is a reason for this difficulty. Remember that! You may have heard the phrase—'The Marine Corps Builds Men.' That is not just an empty slogan. You are all here because you chose to be. You want to know what it means to be a *man*. Well, there may be times when you want to quit, to just give up, roll over and play dead, but a Marine *never* gives up! A Marine *never* quits! Just follow every order and stick with it, give it your utmost effort and you will earn the name 'Devilpup,' which is as close as you can get to being a Marine, at your age. If some of you decide to enlist in the Corps later on, this training will prove invaluable.

"Thank you for your attention. When I say 'dismissed,' you are to fall in under the flagpole on the parade ground to the rear of the amphitheater, in rank, according to height, so that the drill instructors can divide you into platoons and squads. There will be no talking unless you are addressed by an officer. Dismissed!"

BP moves silently with the blundering, dazed bunch of boys out onto the parade ground, where they begin to mill about under the stony, motionless glare of two unsmiling sergeants, trying to sort themselves into some semblance of the required stratification. There is some jostling and chattering down the line from him, and the two drill instructors are instantly galvanized—leaping forward and shouting in the loudest, harshest voices he has ever heard.

"SILENCE! No talking! Into line! Find your place! Look to the man on your right! If he is shorter than you, then change places without speaking. Keep at it. You there! You think this is funny? Wipe that smile off your face! Get down and do ten push-ups! The next boot who smiles does twenty. The next one who *talks* does thirty. Do you understand? Listen up! This is the Marine Corps. You don't laugh, you don't talk, you don't even think. We do all that for you. You do what we tell you to do and nothing else, is that clear? Every order is to be obeyed instantly! Do you hear? I want you to tell me you hear! When I ask you again, I want each and every one of you to shout 'Sir, yes sir' as loud as you can! Do you hear me?"

"SIR, YES SIR!" from sixty frightened voices.

They are quickly divided into two equal platoons and ten six-man squads, each with a squad-leader. Each sergeant takes a platoon and begins to teach them the basics of precision, close ordered drills.

In about two hours, they are cohesive enough to be marched as a unit over to the supply house, where they are issued uniforms and ill-fitting, stiff boots. BP's feet, accustomed as they are to going bare, soon learn the true meaning and derivation of the term "boot camp."

They visit the mess hall and are fed bland, tasteless (but filling), steam-table food for lunch, cafeteria style, then they are returned to the parade ground for the remainder of the afternoon to be drilled unmercifully by their instructors. They are taught to stand at attention and at rest in rank, how to face left and right and turn 'about-face' on command, in unison. They learn to march and maneuver in file, as a column, while calling out cadences to keep in step. Any failure in precision is dealt with swiftly and severely by physical punishment, usually push-ups, although the instructors do not hesitate to slap and shove around the less adept or recalcitrant learners.

By the time BP falls asleep that night, after more uninspired chow and a shower, he is one whipped puppy among a kennel full.

They are awakened before sunrise to dress and fall in. They do calisthenics at dawn. The physical training is intense and competitive; one recruit is pitted against another, squad against squad, platoon against platoon, depending on the exercise. Losing is treated with scorn and contempt, as is weakness, and they are encouraged to dehumanize their opponent, to win at all costs.

They are drilled in hand-to-hand combat, they run the obstacle course, they simulate forced marches at double time carrying heavy packs and equipment. And always the endless drilling in formation, until their moves are automatic, carried out precisely and mindlessly in cadence, on command.

The pace is exhausting and there is never a guarantee of an uninterrupted night's slumber. They are rousted out of their beds at all hours of the night for meaningless "inspections," which usually result in more push-ups for somebody.

BP manages to avoid being singled out for any extreme punishment by virtue of his previously cultivated skills of anonymity, which serve him well. He does not resent the rule of silence as he has no interest in conversing with his fellow Devilpups, whom he is convinced must all be crazy, or seriously warped, for volunteering to come to this place. He feels he has been forced into it as some form of penance, which is entirely different. He never bothers to ask anyone else if they were bad boys too.

His physical fitness and coordination are his other saving graces. He is able to hold his own with all of the other boys except for some of the oldest and largest. The clumsiest and weakest of the group seem to incur the wrath of the sergeants most often.

Nevertheless, he is wearing down by the end of the first week. The days begin to blend into each other in a haze of fear and fatigue.

Just when he begins to think that he isn't going to make it, the pace slackens slightly. The midnight inspections disappear and their last days are interspersed with less strenuous lessons in all sorts of armed forces esoterica. There are lectures on military history, strategy and weaponry, and they accompany actual Marine recruits to rifleman's training, practicing marksmanship on the shooting range. BP enjoys this, as his mother has always prohibited him from having any sort of gun, even a toy one.

The last session in weapons training is an event that BP will remember forever. [Even though he may already have forgotten it before.] It is scheduled late in the afternoon of their last day in camp. The next morning they will be released to their families.

It is the grand finale of the Devilpup program, the rite of initiation, staged in conjunction with the entire complement of the base's personnel, with the kind of realism and budget that would satisfy Cecil B. DeMille.

The recruits have no idea or forewarning of the nature or magnitude of this particular event as they assemble in a large, fortified bunker on the edge of the artillery range at 1630 hours. They know only that it is the last activity of the day before a cold shower and chow time.

It is cramped and hot in the bunker after all sixty of them have crowded in. One of the D.I.'s begins his lecture quite routinely.

"Men, this is a tear gas grenade. It is used in wartime primarily to flush the enemy out of a concealed position when there is reason to believe that more deadly force is unnecessary, such as the case might be with an unarmed, wounded or hopelessly outnumbered enemy, who might be persuaded to surrender without a fight, or when there is a desire to take prisoners for purposes of gathering intelligence. It is used in peacetime primarily in police work for crowd control, flushing out barricaded suspects, etc. Every Marine Corps regular and reservist is required to be familiar with the tear gas grenade."

"This grenade is hand delivered, activated by pulling this pin and throwing, which releases this lever, starting an internal timer which will deploy the gas after a five second delay. Other types of grenades can be delivered by a wide bore, projectile gun such as this." He holds up an example of each item automatically for all to see as his voice drones on hypnotically.

"Now, this is a gas mask. I want each squad leader to step forward and take six of these masks out of the boxes in front of me and distribute one to each man in his squad." They do so without speaking.

"Examine your mask!" he commands. "It is worn tightly over the face. Try it on and adjust the straps until it fits firmly."

The boys are busy for a moment, putting on and adjusting the masks until they all look as if they just got off the bus from Venus—dark green, rubbery faces with huge, bulbous, shiny eyes and pendulous, green/black noses. Nobody dares to laugh.

"Now when I release this lever and deploy the gas, you will see that the masks do indeed protect you." He pulls the pin as he speaks and throws the grenade in the corner, spewing dense clouds of white smoke, as the entire troop takes an involuntary step backward in fear and surprise.

"This particular chemical agent is called 'tear gas,' due to the pronounced irritation it causes on the tear ducts and mucus membranes," he continues monotonously, voice muted slightly by his mask. "Although it is very unpleasant, its effect is only temporary and causes no permanent damage, unlike the more dangerous C-2, or 'mustard gas,' named after its pale yellow color, which has been used in modern chemical warfare." BP does not find this comforting, somehow. He has an intuition of impending doom.

"When I say 'begin,'" says the sergeant, speaking very loudly, slowly and distinctly so that his muffled voice is still clear from behind his mask, "I want you all to take off your masks and sing the *Marine Corps Hymn*." He pauses for emphasis. BP cannot believe his ears.

"This is a direct order, and I'm going to repeat it so that there will be no misunderstanding and you will act swiftly, correctly, and in unison, as if your lives depended on it. When I say 'begin,' I want each and every one of you to remove your gas mask and sing the *Marine Corps Hymn*. You all know the words. All I want is the first verse. It's not going to be easy, but I want you to imagine that your best buddy is lying wounded outside. The only way out is through these doors." He indicates the thick, steel double doors behind him. "The only way I'm going to let you out there to help him is if you follow my order, unmask, and sing the hymn. All of you! When I *do* open the door, there will be no panic. You will file out by rank at double time. There are some troughs of water outside for you to wash the gas residue off your face, which will help to relieve your temporary discomfort."

The entire bunker is filled with swirling, white gas. Some of it has leaked out of the gun ports by this time, but it is still quite thick. The sergeant raises his arm. "DEVILPUPS...READY...BEGIN!" he shouts, dropping his arm.

There follows the most pitiful, disjointed rendition of the *Marine Corps Hymn* that has ever been heard, from the halls of Montezuma to the shores of Tripoli, performed by sixty gagging, choking, crying, coughing, slit-eyed young men. The sergeants keep their masks on, and when the verse is finished they fling open the doors.

"LEFT FACE! FORWARD MARCH!" they bellow.

The troop streams out of the bunker into bright sunlight, staggering up to the line of 55-gallon drums filled with water arranged there, frantically gasping for a breath of fresh air, while dunking their heads, splashing and rubbing their faces, trying to get rid of the infernal stinging and burning in their eyes, noses and throats. Some of them simply sprawl on the grass retching, coughing, and moaning.

Several minutes pass before they realize that they are being greeted outside with a full-scale, practice, tactical field maneuver, mobilized especially for their benefit, and timed to commence with their exit from the bunker.

An entire brigade of infantry is staging a mock assault on the hill across the shallow valley below them (though it is a while before any of them can see clearly enough to distinguish any details), supported by armored units, artillery and air strikes. The din is tremendous as rifle, machine gun, mortar and artillery rounds explode. Jet aircraft and helicopters roar overhead strafing and bombing. Armored vehicles and heavy tanks rumble in the valley.

There is nothing at all wrong with BP's ears—"HOLY SHIT! THEY'RE GOING TO SHOOT US ALL NOW!" he screams to himself, as he exits the bunker and is struck by the noise, before the effects of the gas wear off enough for him to see clearly what is going on outside.

The next morning he is safely at home once more. The only concrete reminders of his recent ordeal are a pair of bloodshot eyes, some sore muscles, and a T-shirt, which he had received from Colonel Borman at the closing ceremony, on the last night in camp. It is made of bright red fabric, with a picture of a fierce-looking bulldog and the legend "USMC DEVILPUPS" emblazoned in yellow silkscreening on the front and back.

The psychic scars are burned more deeply into his soul, however, filed away and stored, but not forgotten. Seated on the couch in his own familiar living room, he heaves a deep sigh of relief. Looking at the T-shirt folded in his lap, he makes a solemn pledge to himself, a pledge that his mother has secretly hoped and prayed would be the end result of his experience. In his own words, this is what he vows:

"I must remember, no matter what happens, to never, *ever,* let those crazy bastards get hold of me again!"

Welcome to the Tube

During his first year of high school, BP's feelings of alienation, persecution and fatalism persist and deepen. Despite the good intentions of his captors, his program of rehabilitation is nearly a complete failure. For him, school is jail. In December of 1962, he turns 15, still a prisoner.

The school administrators and teachers (as his judges and guards) are impotent in their effort to achieve what they perceive as his proper social integration. They have assumed that engrossing and enriching BP's rational self nearer to his potential abilities will naturally lead him to wholeness and allow him to take a proper, productive role in society. In this unidimensional misjudgment they are not malicious, only naive. To assume that access to greater knowledge and a more robust challenge to his intellect would be automatically linked to increased socialization and civility is presumptuous on their part.

His parents (as co-wardens) are locked in an uneven power struggle over administrative policy (usually dominated by his father) which renders their leadership inconsistent and ineffective. BP often mistakenly perceives himself as the sole source of their marital discord and blames their arguments on his own inadequacies.

His fellow inmates are a quandary to BP. He desperately wants their approval and acceptance, but the distance separating their individual cells seems insurmountably huge. Many of them don't even seem to realize that they are in prison. (Can't they see the bars?)

The few faces and names of his former peer group, that had so slowly become familiar to him in years past, have disappeared from his classes since he has been advanced so abruptly in grade. They have been replaced with a new group of strangers who must be painstakingly differentiated, identified, contacted and classified. BP finds many of the girls—no, they are young women now—exceedingly attractive, causing flutters in his stomach, light-headedness, and stirring in his lower parts when he studies them, but he does not know how to deal with this.

Such work takes time and BP is in a hurry. Many unforeseen obstacles block his progress, seeming to conspire against him, and he allows himself to be easily discouraged at times. He feels that many of his new peers resent his sudden intrusion onto their level and believe that he doesn't truly deserve such an advancement. Eventually he realizes that some of them *do* believe he has earned this preferential treatment, by virtue of superior "intelligence," and are *afraid* of him for it, intimidated by the dark shadow of reflected, comparative judgment this casts over their own paltry, "normal" achievements.

He finds some of his classmates to be hopelessly immature and fearful, others to be needlessly proud and mindlessly cruel. Many of them he ends up classifying without very much contact at all, due to his own peculiar prejudice, which is a mixture of shyness and selfishness—a preference for separateness which makes him a true "loner." His best friend, Donny, has not advanced to high school with him, so BP does not see him at school, and only occasionally at the beach. In his adolescent struggle for purpose, meaning and identity, no one is much help to him. It is ultimately left to himself, alone, to penetrate these mysteries.

In the pursuit of knowledge and truth, his educators are not much help. While he dutifully collects the various snippets of information and broad concepts his teachers present on a myriad of subjects, both scientific and sociological, their ideas seem to lack an overarching coherence and actually conflict in some ways. [The inarguable 'first principles' of the world, what the ancient Greeks called 'arche,' which would integrate all this data—telling him who he is and how he should lead his life—are unclear, or absent entirely from their teachings.]

While he has continued to attend Quaker Meeting with his mother and has learned a great deal about their beliefs, been very impressed with their religiosity, their egalitarianism, and their determination to apply these principles in daily life, God has still not spoken to him, even though he has ceased to leave meeting with the children for the last two years, steadfastly sitting through the entire hour of silent worship, waiting to be moved. Blind faith, as an ultimate answer, fails to prove itself to him, and when he thinks about it, he has no hard evidence that God even exists.

Surfing is his only solace, and by any common definition of the word, his true religion, giving his life meaning and purpose. Through his intense involvement with the waves, he feels connected and whole, an integral part of the wondrously complex natural environment, instead of a hopelessly lost and confused solitary organism. It is excellent therapy for him precisely because it is almost exclusively a right-brain activity, allowing his intuitive, spatial organization skills to assert themselves, to the exclusion of his left-brain chatter, which has been cultivated to excess.

For him, surfing is meditation, it is freedom, it is his only sphere of clear success—the only matter in which he has total control, the only endeavor he can enter without restraint, without inhibition, focusing his energy and expending it explosively, to reap his own sweet, private rewards. When all is said and done, the only identity that fits, which seems correct and true for him, is as a surfer.

As BP has initiated himself into the surfing realm, struggling through flailing kookdom to achieve a rudimentary competence after nearly three years of effort, there are few signposts to mark the way to virtuosity, though there are countless milestones to be reached.

The unstructured nature of the sport and its relative newness, its lack of historical tradition, contribute to its mystification. Surfing's essential qualities are extremely subjective and resist analysis, investigation, quantification and even communication. The direction in which he must move in order to progress becomes less clear and explicit as he advances. The route from mere proficiency to true artistry is the most well-concealed.

Surfing's evolution has been meteoric in Southern California in the early sixties, even though the sport is still in its infancy. It was conceived (in its modern incarnation) from seeds of the ancient Polynesian monarchies deposited by the legendary Duke Kahanamoku during his trips to California in the early 1900's. After a long gestation period, nurtured by a few hundred intrepid, colorful, pioneering watermen, riding wooden boards in solitary conditions, it was birthed into full glory during the early fifties, from the fertile womb of the post-war plastics industry, by the invention of the lightweight, polyurethane foam and fiberglass surfboard.

This innocent, newborn babe was given a massive overdose of megavitamins, protein powder and steroids in 1959, when some sharp operators in the communications industry in Hollywood released the first "Gidget" movie. The resulting explosive, mutant growth has been phenomenal, but uncontrolled and chaotic, approaching malignancy at times.

Stumbling along in the midst of this overgrown, cancerous-infant-surfworld in 1963, there are few references to guide BP to the core, the heart of the matter. The few books he can find in the library concerning surfing are largely historical and simplistic, offering him little help. Other than the direct experience he obtains in his daily *mano a mano* with the waves, the only outside input that gives him any clues about the true nature of the beast are his observations of, and interactions with, the other surfers at his local beaches, the stories and photographs which are published in the specialty surfing magazines, and the cult movies about surfing which he attends.

Surf movies are his favorite and most appreciated source of "stoke," the expression that surfers use to characterize their unique brand of motivation and enthusiasm. Not the made-in-Hollywood, big budget, saccharine extravaganzas which play at his neighborhood theatres, featuring the latest teen idols in starring roles and containing precious little actual surfing footage—these he rejects as contrived, exploitative buffoonery for a mass market. The films that he enjoys are the low-to-no budget productions that proliferate underground, and are shown in school auditoriums and small halls at widely scattered dates. These films are made *by* surfers, *for* surfers. They are usually shot in cheap black and white film, sans soundtrack, accompanied only by taped music and live narration by the producer (acting also as director, photographer, editor, booking agent, projectionist and ticket-taker), who is traveling up and down the coast with his one technically crude print, trying to squeak out a living and a stake for his next film. They invariably contain nothing but hard-core documentation of the best rides, on the best waves, of the best surfers that the producer can find and film, by hook or by crook. Occasionally a moment or two of comic relief is inserted to break up the rapid-fire surfing sequences, but usually there is not the slightest attempt at a coherent plot.

BP is not looking for a story from these films, so this shortcoming is easily forgiven. He wants information from them, not diversion, and their dense, starkly realistic, documentary format provides him with a wealth of input in a very short time. He attends every one that comes to his neighborhood as many times as possible, beginning in 1960—losing himself in the flickering images on the screen, empathizing totally with the surfers displayed there on ride after ride. He longs to be like them, to become fluent in their language, to sing his own song on a wave. It seems to him that these great surfers know something that other people do not, though he cannot quite clarify this to himself, and he longs to actually meet them in real life and talk to them. He is sure that they must lead the most perfect of lives, very different from his own.

He pores over each detail of every scene, soaking up subtle nuances of performance, absorbing every maneuver on every wave and trying to interpret its sense, its appropriateness, its elegance, its utility, its difficulty, and its meaning, in order to develop and refine his own standards, his own concepts of "style" and "position," the two issues which seem to be at the heart of good surfing.

In the winter and spring of '62–63, the fourth or fifth generation of these cult surfing films arrives in San Diego and the evolution of the genre is amazing. Instead of black and white, many producers can afford color film and processing by now, and because they can also afford to travel more widely, much of the footage is international in scope. BP witnesses surfing in many exotic locations he has never heard or imagined had waves, making him feel very limited and provincial. Beside California, Mexico and Hawaii, there are waves in Africa, South America, Europe, Indonesia, the South Pacific, Japan, and Australia to be explored, he finds, and people are taking up the challenge all over the world. Already there are thousands of avid surfers in Australia, he discovers, as the renowned Duke had visited "Down Under" and strewn more of his prolific (some might say "profligate") seeds in that receptive, aquatic nation as well.

Hawaii is still the capitol of surfing, however, the undisputed pinnacle, the proving ground for the young sport's elite, and every movie pays its respects to this modern Mecca. The north shore of Oahu Island lays claim to the highest density of quality surf spots and accomplished surfers each winter, and every photographer of repute is on hand to record the action. This season, it seems, the big news is the "conquest" of a difficult break called the "Banzai Pipeline" at Ehukai Beach Park in Pupukea, and every movie he sees has sequences of absolutely riveting action filmed at this spot which effect BP in a strange way. When he had first seen this wave the year before, introduced in Bruce Brown's 1961 film, *Surfing Hollowdays*, the riding had looked tentative and exploratory. Now, with more time to become familiar with the break and more comfortable with its risks, surfers are beginning to explore its potential more fully.

The Pipeline is such a majestic and photogenic wave, which breaks so close to the beach, with such epic proportions—a very square, wide-open tube is formed by the towering lip, jacking-up to twice the wave's original height and pitching forward several yards in front of the wall when the wave hits the shallow reef as it travels in from deep water—that BP's skin tingles when he sees it. It feels like he has an itch everywhere. One that can't be scratched. It grabs him in the gut and tweaks him, nudging his outlook in new directions, with profound and far-reaching consequences in his surfing and his life.

Up to this time, BP has considered a "tube ride" to be just another minor trick in a surfer's arsenal of "hot dog" maneuvers, on a par with "shooting the pier" or pulling off a "head-dip Quasimodo." Most of the tubes that BP has been inside have occurred on closed-out sections of relatively small waves when he has failed to kick out in time and found himself "locked in." Ordinarily, he never *looks* for the opportunity to get in the tube, it is taken only as a last resort, when there is no other way out of a fast, peeling, walled-off section. In this situation he usually trims up, crouches down, grabs the rail, sucks in a last breath, closes his eyes, and waits to get bounced off when the tube collapses around him.

Now he realizes that tube riding has another dimension, a deeper challenge. He sees that with the right conditions (namely, offshore winds and large, hollow waves with stand-up barrels of "Hall of Fame" proportions) combined with consummate skill and daring, it is possible to surf in a portion of the wave that is even *steeper* than the face under and in front of the curl. It is possible to ride *behind* the curl, inside the tube, on the edge of disaster, out of sight from the beach, and make it back out. He witnesses such displays of brinksmanship on ride after ride at the Pipeline, some less successful than others. The price to be paid for admission is simply total commitment. The cost of failure ranges from indignity to death.

It is obvious to BP that this is a very different type of surfing than that which he has done so far, based on totally different premises. It seems to him that he has mistaken "fashion" for "style," a common, modern mistake. The tricks and posing of small-wave, hot-dog surfing are not what real surfing is about. True style springs from the attitude of the surfer, the way he uses his position on the wave to make a statement, much in the way that a matador uses the horns of the bull.

After this realization, BP takes immediate steps to delete non-functional maneuvers from his surfing, making tricks subordinate to position. He begins to shun nose-riding (for any reason other than forward trim speed), and looks for opportunities to get into tubes and make it back out. Instead of just closing his eyes in the barrel and waiting to be knocked off, he trains himself to keep his eyes wide open, concentrating on staying on his board and riding it out to the bitter end.

The visual perspectives he receives from these changes in technique and attitude prove to be tantalizing, requiring further inspection. The short duration of his first tube rides does not detract from their intensity, and the fact that he wipes-out on every one of them does not discourage him. Before the axe comes down, he catches his first views of the "green room"—the inner sanctuary of the wave, so animated and so brief—an elongated cylindrical space behind the closed curtain of the falling lip, a whirling vortex of green water, casting cobalt shadows, giving the enclosed volume a kinetic, otherworldly aura. It is mesmerizing and tantalizing in a way he cannot understand or fully explain.

He begins to collect tiny increments of this sublime time in the tube at every opportunity. Unfortunately, the quality and quantity of hollow waves in California does not match that of the Hawaiian islands. His experimentation proceeds painfully slowly. He will purposefully pull into unmakeable sections (which he would have previously avoided) and tuck under the lip, even though he knows he can't possibly win the race to the shoulder. He crouches tightly to fit into the smaller, less spacious tubes available in average surf. It is enough to snatch the view and get the sensation of being in that special space, no matter how short the time and how violent the end. He truly doesn't mind these wipeouts, when the tube collapses around him, jerking him about, even if it means a swim for his board. The few, rich moments gained inside the tube are enough to last him all day. Indeed, while they are happening they seem to last impossibly long—much longer than they objectively should, or could—with the passage of time inside the tube stretching out, or slowing down, somehow.

Eventually, instead of looking for a place to jump off when he gets locked into the green room, he begins to look for a door, a way out. If the wave is not a total close-out, the whole wall dumping over at once, it is usually there, even though he can't reach it, due to lack of speed from his board. It appears as a shining orb of light at the end of the tunnel, retreating rapidly into the distance until it shrinks to nothing, winks out, and comes rushing back towards him closed—a shadowy grey-white disk of solid, whirling whitewater, slamming in his face.

The first time he makes it out of a tube from deep inside he is ecstatic. He is watching the bright, elliptical door twisting, spinning and closing in front of him, as usual, and he is straining to squeeze more speed out of his slide, when he realizes that he is finally going fast enough—the door is not receding anymore! It is growing larger and brighter, rushing towards him, until he bursts out of the eye of the tube into the glaring sunlight, flying high across the face of the wave, faster than he has ever gone before.

It is a very cathartic experience. He feels reborn, cleansed and powerful, as if his chosen path has intersected with the wave's process in a way that is timeless and eternal. He feels certain that he is on the trail of something big, some awesome revelation which will transform his life and allow him to make it whatever he wishes it to be.

A Shocker

The most noteworthy events of BP's second year of high school revolve around the latest Beatles releases—until November 22, 1963. The rumors fly fast and furious around the cafeteria at lunchtime: "The President has been assassinated!"

Many people refuse to believe the rumor at first, but somehow, BP knows immediately that it is true, even before he sees the stark reality of the TV news coverage, of Walter Cronkite crying in front of the nation.

BP is shocked and profoundly disturbed for days, without really understanding all the reasons why. [Even if he could remember that he had already experienced this before, it would not have helped.] It is like being kicked in the gut.

He listens to everyone express their feelings and ideas about this horrific event—his parents, his teachers, his fellow students, the newscasters and columnists—but no one seems to know exactly what this terrible thing means, and what it portends. In all of the analyses, explanations, commentaries and emotional outpourings, BP is never able to fully correlate or express his own feelings of abject fear, helplessness, and paranoia. It seems to him that everyone is missing some crucial point, some hidden meaning of tremendous significance, but he can't quite put his finger on what it is.

Weeks later he is still wondering, still dwelling on it. He reviews the known facts endlessly, but the answer he is seeking is not contained in them.

Here was a man, John F. Kennedy, who had played the game to perfection. He had been born into good fortune and had never looked back. He was rich, good-looking, charismatic and had become the most powerful person in the world, and yet all his luck, cleverness and charm had brought him to a premature and violent death. Does this mean that there is no reward in this life for living well? Is Jack reaping his reward in another place? Was he simply the victim of insane, random violence? Or was his murder a manifestation of some greater conspiracy, some overwhelmingly evil new trend?

Perhaps he had not played the game as perfectly as it appeared. He was, after all, the youngest man ever to be elected President. Certainly there are older, more experienced people in other seats of power. Perhaps he had not reckoned with them properly. Perhaps being President isn't really as powerful as it sounds.

No rational explanation he can muster accounts for the depth of his anxiety, however. He humbly assumes that he does not know enough about life to conclude anything [just as he has been conditioned to do] and blames this on his tender age again, even though it is now obvious that his "Conspiracy of

Age" theory has some gaping flaws in it.

The real problem is that it frightens him to death to think that growing older might not bring him any greater understanding of this phenomena called life than the fuzzy notions he already possesses. This is his last great hope—that as he grows older, everything becomes clearer.

It seems definite to him that adulthood is not the panacea he had imagined it to be. If it was, then the wisest and most powerful person on earth would be the oldest living human being who had not yet lost his or her wits.

Unless, of course, it is true that the great secrets are revealed to each person only upon their death—that it is impossible to discover ultimate truth in this life.

BP prays that this is not the case, for it means that the quickest solution to his quest for understanding would be to take his own life. Malcontented as he may be, the alternative of suicide has no appeal to him.

Mobility and Socialization

On Dec. 21, 1963, BP receives that passport to freedom, that ticket to adulthood, which is so coveted by his generation—his first California Driver's License.

Six months earlier, to the day, he had applied for his Learner's Permit, which entitled him to operate a motor vehicle while accompanied by a licensed driver over the age of eighteen, but now he can legally drive solo, unencumbered by a nervous parent, after passing the DMV driving test on his birthday with flying colors.

His vital statistics and picture are recorded on the document—Name: Bob B. Pilhaus; Address: 443 Obsidian St., Pacific Beach, CA.; Date of Birth: 12/21/1947; Height: 6'2"; Weight:170 lbs.; Hair: Brown; Eyes: Brown; NO VISIBLE SCARS.

Holding it in his hand for the first time and carefully stowing it in his wallet, he is elated. "I'm almost a real person now!" he thinks.

By borrowing his mother's car, a brown, '57 Ford, four-door, Country Squire station wagon that his father had bought for her two years earlier, he is able to begin exploring for rideable waves throughout San Diego County. He surfs as far north as the Oceanside Pier, and as far south as the Tijuana Sloughs off Imperial Beach, almost to the Mexican border, usually accompanied by his friend, Donny Miller. They save their longest trips for the weekends and holidays, often camping out in the wagon overnight, folding the rear seats down and sleeping in the back.

Donny does not yet have his driver's license (he is seven months younger than BP) or such easy access to a car (his is not a two-car family), so he feels privileged and liberated on these adventures with BP. He has not kept pace with BP's development as a surfer, in favor of a more well-rounded social and athletic life, but he can hold his own in the waves and surfs competently, if somewhat erratically and without any coherent style. Donny envies BP's more advanced ability in the surf, and BP wishes he possessed Donny's social skills, his ability to get along with people.

While BP is aware of the cultural norms to which he is expected to conform, namely going to school, getting a job, marrying, having a family, career, etc., he does not see his way clearly down this path. To begin with, marriage requires picking a suitable mate, and BP is still deathly afraid of approaching women. On one of their surf trips, BP finally screws up the courage to ask his friend for advice. This is difficult for him to do. Donny is his closest friend, but like most young American males, they do not usually talk about things that actually *matter*. They are far more comfortable with "small talk" chatter, jokes, and nonsense. "Hey, Donny, can I ask you something? You go out on a lot of dates, don't you?"

"Sure, Beep," answers his friend, "I've been going out on dates for a couple years, now, I guess. What's up?"

"I'm just wondering, you know, um, how do you ask a girl out? I mean, how do you get to know her good enough? What do you say to her? Now that I can drive, I've sorta been thinking about trying to meet a girl, maybe, and go on a date...."

"You don't need to be able to drive to go on a date, Beep—shit, I used to walk over to Cherie's house and take her to the movies when I was 14. You remember that, don't you? But it'd be cool, yeah, to be able to pick a girl up and take her somewhere—I'm definitely going to do that as soon as I get a car."

"But how do you know which girl to ask, and whether she'd even want to go out with you?"

"Well, you just kinda talk to them and figure it out. You've gotta know if they already have a boyfriend, I guess, or if they're going steady with someone, or whatever, and then if they're available, ya gotta just flirt with them a little, and see if they flirt back. You can tell if they like you. They'll let you know. They have their ways."

It is just this quality of easygoing sociability in his friend that BP covets. Donny makes it sound so simple, and indeed, BP has seen how easily he engages people, makes friends, meets girls. He is very popular at school, and has more friends than anyone BP knows. He feels fortunate that Donny even spends any time hanging out with him—he's sure he must have more important and fun things to do. He's still puzzled, though: "But whaddya say to them, exactly? You're so good at that—you've got the gift of gab. I get around a bitchin' babe and I just choke up!"

"You could do it, Beep. You're a smart guy, and you're not too bad lookin'—there're plenty of girls who would go out with you. I don't know why you don't even try."

"I've thought about it plenty," admits BP, "but I've never been able to really do it. I always figure out some way to chicken-out, I guess...."

"I could fix you up, Beep," says Donny, blithely. "You know Jodie, that girl that lives on the corner by me? She's a junior like you, I think. You've seen her at school. She was asking me about you the other day. I think she's got the hots for you, and she's pretty cute."

"No way! She doesn't know I exist." BP is intrigued, though, by this piece of news. "What'd she say about me?"

"You know...she was asking me why you're so quiet, whether you were going with anybody, that kinda stuff. She was sorta casual about it, but I think she wants your bod."

"No way! She's too hot. She's a friggin' cheerleader—she only goes out with your jock friends, doesn't she? Wasn't she going with Crayton, the quarter-back—Mr. Varsity-Letterman-Guy?"

"Nah, they broke up awhile ago. That's old news. I'm tellin' ya—you should hit this, you could score! Chicks do not ask guys questions about their buddies for no reason. She is interested."

"What should I do?" BP is excited, but embarrassed by his own ineptitude at the same time.

"Listen, you should come over on Saturday and hang out at my house. We'll throw a ball around in the street or something. She'll be around, probably—heck, I'll let her know you're going to be there and she'll show up for sure, and I'll introduce you. Then it's up to you, pal."

"Oh man, Donny, I'll be there. Thanks a lot, buddy!" BP is hopeful, but has a sneaking suspicion that things will not be as easy as they seem, as usual.

At 11:00 on that Saturday morning in early February, 1964, after a quick morning surf, BP heads over to Donny's house. He has carefully made arrangements with his mom to borrow her car for the day, offering to wash it first, figuring that would make a good impression on her, and perhaps on Jodie as well. He parks in front of Donny's house, and they grab a football and toss it around, playing catch in the street. Sure enough, within fifteen minutes or so, Jodie walks by.

"Hey, Jodie," Donny calls out to her as she approaches. "How are ya? C'mon over here, I want you to meet my friend, Bob." They stop their game of catch as the young woman walks toward them. She is a tall, thin, pretty, and very shapely blond, wearing a pair of floral-print pedal pushers and a tight white blouse, her face perfectly made up (which seems strange to BP for this time of day), with a big, bouffant hairdo, sprayed stiff, not a hair out of place. Her smooth, measured, swaying gait as she walks up to them reminds BP of a young lioness, somehow. His eyes widen and his breathing seems to stop, involuntarily. With a struggle, he manages to suck in some air, and resists the urge to bolt away.

Donny makes the introductions as she joins them: "Bobby, this is Jodie Noll, my neighbor, she lives right over there," he says, pointing towards the corner. "Jodie, this is my friend, Bob Pilhaus, but I just call him BP, or Beep."

"Hi, Bob," says Jodie in a husky voice, full of self-assurance, smiling at him and offering her hand. BP forces himself to smile back and shakes her soft hand limply, afraid of squeezing too hard. He tries to speak, but there seems to be a frog in his throat.

"Hello," he finally croaks, "glad to meetcha."

"What are you up to today, Jodie?" asks Donny, breaking the awkward silence that follows.

"I'm just heading home for lunch. I was down at the salon on Garnet Avenue getting my hair done."

"Oh yeah? You're looking good, for sure," says Donny smoothly. "Hey, I'm getting hungry, too, maybe you and me and Beep can go grab a burger or something, whaddya say? Bob's got his car right here—we could cruise down to the Jack-in-the-Box and then head out to the beach for a little bit, maybe, whaddya think?"

Jodie looks over at BP and he manages to nod his head. "Y-yeah, that would be fun," he stammers out.

She smiles again at BP, her eyes seeming to sparkle a bit at him, somehow. "OK, sure, let me go home and tell my folks I'm going out for lunch instead, and I'll be right back." BP watches as she turns and walks down the street towards her house. He can breathe again.

Donny pokes him in the ribs with his elbow as she disappears into her house, and laughs. "You're in there, man, she likes you!"

"What do I do now?" asks BP, nervously. "I don't even know what to say to her."

"Oh c'mon, Beep, it's easy. I'll help you out. Just act natural and be interested in her—ask her what she likes to do and compliment her whenever you can. Listen, when we get back, drop me off here and drive her down to her house, then maybe ask her for a date before she gets out."

Jodie comes out of her house and waves at them, walking back up the street to the two boys. "My mom says I can go for a couple hours, but I have to be back for my dance lessons at 2:00."

"Cool," says Donny, "lets go!" They all climb into the station wagon, with Jodie sitting between them on the front bench seat, and drive off. Since he has to drive, paying attention to traffic, BP is relieved from having to carry much of a burden in the conversation that ensues. Donny turns the radio on to a rock station, and he and Jodie chatter away about things, mostly gossip relating to people at school, some of whom BP is familiar with, but mostly not. At one point, as the car leans around a corner, Jodie slides slightly over towards him and braces herself on his arm. He can smell her perfume, feels the heat of her thigh against his. He wishes he had not gotten so sweaty playing catch before they went on this ride.

They drive through the newly constructed Jack-in-the Box on Grand Avenue, order burgers, fries and milkshakes, and drive back to the coast, parking on the bluffs by Crystal Pier to eat their food and watch the surf. Jodie and Donny continue their conversation. They talk about the football and basketball teams, both of which Donny plays on, and for which Jodie leads cheers. They talk about the different cliques at the school—the Jocks, the Surfers, the Soshes, the Greasers, and the Nerds. Eventually, BP becomes more relaxed in this familiar setting by the ocean. Watching the surf soothes him, just as it has many times in the past, and he is finally comfortable enough to join in their chatter.

"You know, you can't classify people strictly into those groups," he says at one point. "There are always some crossovers—people who fit into more than one category. Look at Donny—he's a jock, but he's also a surfer. The greasers are into their cars and bikes and stuff, but some of them surf, too."

"And what are you, Bob?" asks Jodie, looking straight into his eyes.

"I'm a surfer, for sure...but I guess I'm also kind of a nerd," he says honestly. She smiles at his answer.

The three of them continue their conversation all the way back to Donny's house, and BP actually surprises himself by being somewhat witty and glib at times. They drop Donny off at his house, as planned, saying "goodbye," and BP continues down the block with Jodie, parking the car in front of her house. Just then, the Beatles song "I Want to Hold Your Hand" comes on the radio.

"I just love those guys," says Jodie. "Their music is all *so* good. It just makes me want to dance every time I hear it."

"Yeah, they *are* good, I really like them, too. So you are into dancing? You have a dance lesson now, or something? It's almost 2:00."

"Yes, I started out with ballet, but now I am learning modern and jazz dancing. So you really like the Beatles? Did you know they are going to be on Ed Sullivan tomorrow night?"

"No, I didn't," BP is ashamed to admit. "We don't have a TV at my house, actually."

"You're kidding!" Jodie laughs. "I thought everyone had a TV these days. Would you like to come over to my house tomorrow and watch it, then?"

BP can't believe his good fortune. The pressure is off. "Sure I would. What time?"

"It's on at 8:00. I'll tell my parents you're coming over. It'll be fun!" She smiles at him and slides across the seat to the door, opening it herself and hopping out. Turning once more to look at him as she walks up the driveway, she smiles again, waves, and calls out, "Bye-Bye, Beep. Don't forget—8:00!"

BP is over the moon. "I'm going to be normal, now," he says to himself as he watches her leave.

PUPPY LOVE

BP is excited but a bit confused. He tells his mom of his plans to go out the next evening, and obtains a promise of the use of her car again, so that detail is solved easily. The next morning, he seeks out Donny for a little more advice, though. "What do I do now? *She* asked *me* out, and I'm going over there tonight."

"Oh man, you've got it made!" says Donny. "That's the best possible sign. All you've gotta do is put a smooth move on her and she'll be yours."

"How do I do that?" BP asks. He's not quite sure what this "move" is and how one makes it.

"You'll know how. It'll just happen. When you're close some time, say something nice to her. Show her you like her. Smile at her. Hold her hand, or put your arm around her. It's easy!"

That evening, BP showers and shaves after dinner, puts on his best Madras shirt, clean Levis and his newest pair of Converse tennies, sneaks a splash of his father's Brut cologne, and drives over to Jodie's house. She meets him at the door and invites him inside to meet her parents. They are nice folks, and BP exchanges pleasantries with them politely. "We're going to watch the Beatles on the TV in the den," Jodie announces, taking BP by the hand and dragging him towards the next room.

"OK, whatever you like," says her mother, "I don't understand what you see in that music, though."

"You kids have fun," says her father. "Just leave the door open."

BP follows Jodie into the den and they sit on the couch in front of the TV to watch the show. The group's performance is certainly impressive, but BP can remember little of it, later. At one point, when the band has just about finished their set, Jodie seems to sigh slightly and snuggle a bit closer to him on the couch. He remembers Donny's advice and raises his arm, draping it across the top of the couch and loosely around her shoulder. She snuggles even closer into the crook of his arm. He tightens his hand on her shoulder, she looks up at him, he looks back, and soon they are kissing each other on the lips, madly. He is a little surprised when her tongue insistently parts his lips and explores the inside of his mouth. It is his first encounter with "French" kissing, but he finds it exciting and provocative, soon countering her lingual thrusts with some small probes of his own. In a few moments, they come up for air.

"Wow, you're a good kisser," BP whispers.

"So are you," Jodie lies. They go at it some more, and BP is astounded when she takes his hand and guides it to her breast. "Don't be afraid, I want you to touch me," she says. He is more than happy to oblige, caressing her breasts, feeling the stiffness of the bra underneath her blouse, the soft swelling behind it. They begin to breathe a little heavier as their mouths, lips and tongues continue to interact and their hands grasp and grope about. Except for the situation (with her parents in the next room) the two would probably have been naked and writhing on the ground in passion within the next few minutes. When Jodie's hand finally finds its way into BP's lap, there is no denying the stiff swelling there. "You want me too, don't you?" she asks.

"Oh, God, yes," gasps BP.

"We need to be alone, sometime—sometime soon! Will you take me to the dance on Friday at school?"

"I don't know how to dance."

"Don't worry, I'll show you."

The girl is not kidding. BP takes her to the dance that next weekend, and she teaches him how to move with the music, both fast and slow. She is patient with him, and she is confident, athletic and graceful on the floor. He learns from her quickly how to feel the rhythm, tune in to it, and lose his inhibitions. BP can hardly stop looking at her when they are together, she is so magnetically attractive.

They fast become an "item," seeing each other constantly, attending more dances, games, parties, concerts and a host of social activities with which BP is unfamiliar, a world which he didn't even know existed. When they attend athletic events at the high school (something BP had largely shunned to this point in his life), Jodie performs in the cheerleading squad, and BP loves to watch her move in synchrony with the others, leading the crowd in cheers for the home team. He thinks she is the most lovely and stylish creature in all of creation, and his head swells with pride and wonderment that she has somehow chosen him to be her boyfriend.

They double-date with Donny and his latest flame, Megan, going out to eat and to the drive-in movies, laughing and playing together, fogging up the windows with their make-out sessions. He even takes Jodie to the beach one weekend while he surfs, but she does not seem that happy to be left on the sand alone for two hours while he goes in the water.

Eventually, she initiates him into the mystery dance of love as well, guiding him progressively through the preliminary steps and foreplay until they end up "going all the way" after a couple of months together—he loses his virginity in the front seat of the car, parked high up on Mt. Soledad one dark night. They profess their love for each other and talk it through. It is not the first time for her [and truly, if BP could only remember, it is not his first, either] and though they feel very much in love, they agree that they are not yet ready to be married, either one of them, or to be making any babies. Up to this time, they have explored each other's bodies and pleasured themselves in every way possible, short of full intercourse, and the next step is inevitable. "We should use protection," BP says, recalling some of the basics from his sex education studies, "you *can't* get pregnant right now."

"Don't worry about that," says Jodie, "I'm on the pill."

Through the end of the school year and into the summer, they are nearly inseparable, stealing any time or opportunity they can find alone to have wild, orgasmic sex. By necessity, this is often in BP's mother's car, which they are agile and flexible enough to accomplish in the front seat, as they have proven, but by storing his sleeping bag in the back of the station wagon (which does not seem too odd to his mother, since he sometimes uses it to camp on surf trips) and lowering the rear seat when necessary, they have their own semi-private, traveling boudoir. BP scouts out and becomes familiar with the most deserted and least traveled roads in town, searching for places to park at night with Jodie after their dates. If these locations also happen to have a panoramic view to enjoy during their trysts, all the better. Occasionally, they are able to steal a few sessions together in their own beds, at their own homes, when their parents are absent, though such opportunities are scant, forbidden and fraught with the risk of discovery.

Though he is ecstatic with their relationship, extremely grateful for her companionship and the social integration it has helped him achieve, and absolutely, overwhelmingly lustful for her body and the sexual relationship they enjoy together, in the back of his mind, there is a nagging realization that it is illicit and not condonable. But it is so enjoyable, so powerful, so commanding and compelling, it is a simple matter for him to push any doubt and guilt over their actions into the far reaches of his psyche, elbowing his way up to the trough of instant gratification without remorse and drinking deeply.

BAD DAY AT BIG ROCK

His relationship with Jodie is not all-consuming, however. Though he devotes much time to her, especially in the evenings, which costs him many an early morning session while sleeping late, BP's thirst for surf has not abated. He has become semi-maniacal in his quest to advance his skills and especially to accumulate time in the tube. Nothing else (except sex) seems as immediate and important to him. Most events of his ordinary, day-to-day life seem dull and meaningless compared to the few vivid seconds he has experienced behind the shimmering curtain, in the barrel. These stolen moments are not easily wrenched from the bosom of our mother ocean, however, and BP must pay his dues.

The fact that waves of sufficient size and quality to offer makeable tubes are a rare commodity along his local beaches presents a new challenge to him. On most days, the waves are either too small or too junky to get tubed, but he goes out anyway, surfing for hours whenever he can, perfecting his technique, conditioning his body, and recording the day's conditions in a personal journal he begins to keep, cataloguing the size and direction of the swell, how well it is showing up at different breaks, the effect of winds and tide on the waves, as well as his impressions of any noteworthy rides he obtains.

As his surfing ability has expanded and his body has matured, his opportunities for encountering sufficiently challenging waves has shrunk in an inversely-proportional relationship. When he had first begun surfing, any crappy, small wave was enough to test his limits—now he needs quality waves of good size, shape and power to further his pursuit. This necessitates traveling more extensively, and it is also the reason for keeping his diary. He hopes that by building up a base of data cataloguing past conditions and analyzing it, he might gain an advantage in predicting where the best waves will be on a given day in the future, according to whatever conditions exist at that time.

Time is once again his most frustrating adversary. The days with conditions that produce the kind of waves he is looking for are few and far between, he loathingly discovers. In the entire year of 1964, up until the middle of August, they number less than twenty.

It is his journal that steers his search north to La Jolla, especially on days of larger-than-average swells. When his local beachbreaks are starting to wall-off and close-out as a new swell builds, the rocky reefs surrounded by deeper water off the bluffs of La Jolla are just starting to come on strong. By the time the swell surpasses a consistent 6' it is a struggle, if not impossible, to paddle out at his local spots, and the waves are often breaking too fast to be makeable anyway.

The reefbreaks to the north have very short, steep beaches at the water's edge (or sometimes no sand beach at all at high tide, simply rocks or a steep sandstone bluff) leading out quickly to deep water channels; so though the shorebreak may be ferocious, it is very localized, and if a surfer can time his entrance into the water correctly, once he is ten yards off the beach he can have a clear paddle out to the break.

The relative shallowness of the reef, surrounded by deep water, causes the ocean's swells to break more abruptly and with a more predictable and desirable shape. Unlike sand bars, rocky reefs do not shift and erode with the current, so they are less fickle and changeable, although sand transport may still play a role in changing the complexion of a reef by alternately filling and excavating space between the rocks, according to a seasonal cycle.

For these reasons, anytime the surf shows signs of creeping above 4' these days, BP heads north for La Jolla. Unfortunately, even though his journal may be a well-kept secret, the quality of the waves in this area is well known. Large crowds at the best surf spots have become a reality in Southern California surfing, an inevitable result of its explosive growth.

The surfing population has grown in a few short years by several orders of magnitude. BP is far from alone. On a "primo" swell, hundreds of other surfers, on their own personal quests for their own idiosyncratic reasons, descend on this area from all over San Diego County and beyond. The competition for the best waves is fierce, sometimes even violent. This is an appalling reality for BP, another unexpected obstacle to face along his chosen course.

One of the best reefbreaks in La Jolla lies at the foot of Bonair Street and is named Windansea. It has been surfed regularly for many years, since the '20s or '30s at least, and is very popular. The first tentative forays BP has made there have been disappointing, however, to say the least. He has a difficult time adjusting to the speed and power of juicy, overhead waves, which are fearsome enough for him *without* a crowd. With 30–50 energized, wave-thirsty maniacs scrambling around the lineup intent on getting their share of the action, a definite "conflict of interest" situation is created.

In the best-of-all-possible worlds, this situation might be resolved by a shared spirit of cooperation and brotherly love, which would allow everyone to reap nature's benefits equally and magnanimously. However, the surf world at Windansea in 1964 is less than an ideal, utopian situation, and BP discovers there is a distinct hierarchy, a pecking order, which has been culturally established at the spot to deal with the overcrowding problem. He finds himself, once again, an outsider, looking in on a strange scene.

The crucial elements in establishing one's place in this hierarchy, he finds, are complex and not perfectly defined. They may consist of how well one can surf (excellent surfers are allowed some privileges), how close to the break one lives (proximity establishes some "ownership" interests, somehow), who one knows (friends and/or relatives of established locals may be granted some entrée), and how big and tough one appears to be (a propensity for violence and/or an actual criminal record for assault, or simply a reputation as a totally unpredictable nut case, combined with a professional wrestler's physique, is enough to draw some slack from most of the local crew).

The most accomplished and skillful surfers generally catch the best waves by virtue of their superior experience and wave judgment, and they are rarely molested by "shoulder-hoppers" out of respect for their ability. However, this is not always the case. The exception to this rule might be when a surfer who is definitely hot, but not a local, and not very big or tough looking, vies for the same wave as a local surfer who is very large and loves to fight. The locals have no qualms about dropping-in on anyone they don't recognize as being particularly deserving or menacing, since they feel they have some sort of proprietary privileges in the matter. The craziest, alpha-dog locals don't even care about the "deserving or menacing" part, they just take what they want and enforce order in the lineup ruthlessly, to their own advantage, of course.

If you don't surf particularly well and you happen to live twenty miles inland, you must be over 6'6" tall and a solid 240 lbs., preferably a black belt in some martial art (or just well-armed and certifiably psychotic), to possibly get a wave to yourself. If you are a smallish, unconnected, powder-puff of a kook, you might as well forget it; everyone will cut you off unmercifully at the first sign of weakness or faltering (unless, of course, you are flying under the protection of an alpha-dog's wing—say, his little brother, or good friend).

BP is a larger, well-developed youngster (if a bit skinny, still) and a proficient surfer (not "hot," though), but he doesn't really know anyone and he is not particularly rough-looking. No one recognizes him as a local, or even a "regular," so although he is not harassed, at first he must content himself with snagging whatever overlooked waves he can find on the inside break—the "tweeners" (smaller waves that come in between the larger sets). This is the bottom of the totem pole, the first rung on the ladder.

It means he must sit inside many of the riders, in order to be able to catch the smaller waves, which break in shallower water, and thus expose himself to being "cleaned up" by the larger sets. He must pay strict attention to the horizon, try to spot the larger on their approach, and paddle swiftly towards the safety of the channel as they are forming. He must get far enough out of the way, to the side and out, in order to avoid having the waves break in front of him, possibly ripping his board from his hands, or, more importantly, to avoid getting in the way of anyone who might catch and ride the set waves. This is one of the biggest *faux pas* in the surfing world—to spoil someone's ride by poor positioning. This includes not only taking off on someone when they are in a better position, closer to the peak (or already up and riding the wave, heaven forbid!) but also applies to paddling out. If you are faced with a breaking outside wave with a rider already standing on it, you may not take the easy way and paddle for the unbroken shoulder if it would impede their path. You must turn towards the whitewater or the breaking lip and try to push your way through the turbulence. If you can't hang onto your board when pushing the soup, that is your problem, and you have to swim for it. It is far worse to cause a collision or make the rider change course, especially if it causes them to wipeout, or not "make" the wave.

BP enters this arena and surfs quietly and hard, but must be very patient to reap few rewards. He is uniformly polite and well-mannered to everyone, trying to act especially respectful towards the older, more experienced, hard-drinking, rowdy, "A-team" crew, which costs him many waves and a lot of paddling and swimming, but keeps him out of any fights.

The saving grace of surfing the inside break at Windansea is that there is a very hollow closing section on the right side, which allows BP to further his plodding exploration of the tube there. According to his journal, of the nine days during the summer of '64 that he surfs Windansea when it is breaking well, he is able to manage only six, short tube rides on this inside hooker, which all result in horrible, grinding wipeouts and a swim to the beach (the journal does not lie).

It is past mid-summer, on August 15, as a matter of record, that he reaches the momentous milestone of making it out of his first tube there, on a pumping south swell, saving him from his spiraling discouragement and frustration, renewing his hope and determination to press onward. This event is duly logged into his journal with a large star scribbled next to it, along with the words "SO BITCHIN!" in great, big capital letters.

During the last day of this swell, on a grey, overcast afternoon, he and Donny pull into the parking lot at the foot of Bonair Street on a surf-check. The waves are still fairly large, but not as straight or consistent as at the beginning of the swell. Even with the poor weather, there is quite a pack of riders at Windansea. The wind is not very stiff, so the heavy kelp beds beyond the outside peak are able to smooth the short wind-chop on the surface. Though it is fairly clean, the tide is high and the waves are mushy, not very hollow.

"Shit," says BP from the driver's seat of the Ford, after watching a few waves break on the reef, "look at all those guys. It's not even that good out there!" They wait fifteen minutes to see another set. There is quite a bit more west in the swell, so the lefts are not as makeable, further concentrating the crowd on the rights. The lips of the waves are crumbling forward instead of pitching out, even on the inside section, and all of the surfing they see is being done on the face of the wave, not under the lip.

BP's eyes scan the beach to the south. "We're not going to get tubed out there today, man, even if we could get a wave to ourselves. Let's go check out Big Rock," he suggests.

Riding shotgun, Donny is dubious. "You aren't going to go out there, are you Beep?" he asks, a note of incredulity in his voice. Even though it is within sight of the parking lot where they sit, barely 400 yards south of Windansea, Big Rock (or Lobster Lounge, as it is sometimes called) is never very crowded, and for good reason. It is an extremely shallow, rock ledge (barely awash at low tide), that produces a vicious, boiling, sucking-out, spitting, lefthand tube that is only regularly challenged at higher tides by a few intrepid kneeboard riders and the infrequent expert, goofy-foot, standup surfer on a longboard. Neither BP or Donny have ever surfed the spot. Bulging out of the water, right in front of the take-off zone, is the Rock, standing tall, proud and dry, except on the highest spring tides. If you lose it on the take-off, the Rock is almost sure to eat your board, if not your body.

"The tide is right, at least," says BP noncommittally, "and I can see right into the barrel down there—it's working, for sure. The crowd out here is crazy. Let's go check it out."

He starts up the Ford and they cruise slowly south on Neptune Place to Palomar Street, parking the car and walking down to the bluff, watching the set of waves that is coming through. There are a pair of kneeboarders and one lone standup surfer out riding tricky, wrapping barrels. The west in the swell is making the waves even more treacherous, the end section closing-out and collapsing, sometimes trapping a pocket of air inside which is expelled explosively, in a haze of spray, out the mouth of the tube—a cosmic burp.

"It doesn't look too makeable to me, Beep," says Donny, as he watches one of the kneeriders bite it in the end section, getting "clam-shelled" by the lip. He has no desire to go out there.

"Aw shit, he *almost* made it," lies BP. "At least he was locked-in for a second! I'll bet it's an awesome view in there...."

He has wanted to try this break for a long time—ever since he heard that it is *the* California spot that most resembles the Banzai Pipeline in Hawaii—but he is not sure if he is ready for it. It is a difficult ride for goofyfoots and he has a normal stance, left foot forward, so it is on his backside. The wave jacks-up swiftly as it sucks water off the ledge and deposits it in the thick lip (which registers on the Richter Scale when it crashes down). The takeoff is always late, the drop is ultra-steep, and the first turn is *very* critical, with the Rock right in your face. He waffles, wondering if he can handle it.

Just then, the longboarder catches the best wave of the set, driving straight down the face of the wave in a compact crouch and extending his body in a perfectly timed, soul-arch, bottom turn as the lip arcs over his head. He trims up and casually matches his speed to the wave's peel for an inspiring, three-second tube ride, pumping BP to the maximum. He is sure it is a sign that he should be out there.

"AAAWWHHOOOO!" he hoots. "I'm stoked! Let's go out! Did you see that!" He scrambles back to the car to get his board and wetsuit.

"You're nuts," says Donny, unconvinced. "It's *gnarly* out there! That guy is really hot! I would've 'toaded' on that wave." ("Toad" is their verbal shorthand for "Take Off And Die," a syndrome familiar to surfers everywhere.)

BP refuses to be intimidated. Despite his friend's protestations and some nagging doubts about his own ability, he is determined to go for it. He puts on his wetsuit and waxes his board thoroughly. Carrying it down the short bluff to the beach, he watches the shorebreak pound on the sand.

As the last wave of a set rushes up the beach, he runs out with the backwash and launches himself into the water atop his board, paddling furiously on his stomach to clear the shorebreak during the short lull between sets. The surge of the backwash gives him an extra boost and he makes it over this hurdle easily.

As he paddles out to the line-up, his perspective of the wave changes constantly. As he comes closer, he can see that the waves are a little larger than they appeared from shore and even more hollow. When he draws abreast of the impact zone, he stares directly into the gaping mouth of one of the smaller tubes coming through. It is easily large enough to drive a V.W. Bug through (if it were amphibious and one had lost all concern for living).

He waits out several sets, sizing up the break and trying to deal with his fear. He watches the other riders, studying their strategies, and scrutinizes the waves, timing the interval and counting the number in a set, checking how far over and out the largest ones break. There is a deep water channel just to the north of the reef, where he can sit and watch from the side, without danger of being picked off by a cleanup set.

The kneeboarders definitely have the advantage at this spot, as they do not have to get all the way to their feet after they catch the wave, making them quicker on the "get-up" and keeping their center of gravity lower on the drop-in. Also, their short boards are easier to turn and trim, and they can use the swim fins on their feet, as well as paddling with their arms, to catch the waves and get over the ledging lip early. BP edges into the line-up from the channel slowly, carefully, after a set has taken all the other riders inside.

While the others are paddling (and kicking) their way back out, he goes for the first wave of the next set. It seems to him that he is lined up perfectly but the wave passes him by, rolling under him even though he is stroking powerfully.

He sits back on his board after missing the wave, looks behind him, and sees the second wave of the set bearing down on him. It appears to be much larger and overdeveloped, already standing very steep and looking like it is going to break right on his head.

He wheels his board around and paddles in a panic for the channel, the safety of deeper water. Surprisingly, he makes it over the second wave and into the clear with room to spare, and he scolds himself for being so frightened.

"I'm never going to get tubed by avoiding the juice like that! I've got to get right in there and go for it," he tells himself. "Those other guys can do it, so I should be able to do it, too, right?"

He musters up his courage with such rationalizations, as he paddles to the left again and lines up on the third wave of the set. He chokes back his fear as the house-high wall looms over him, blotting out the horizon, dominating his attention in a way that only the deadly can.

The face of the wave is nearly vertical as he feels the tail of his board lift and break loose in a plane. He leaps to his feet in a single smooth movement, knees bent, taking the drop. He can see the ocean floor clearly in front of him, even though the surface of the water is roiled and pockmarked as it is sucked off the ledge and boils up the face. It seems so shallow that he is sure his fin will drag on something.

He starts his turn early, before he reaches the bottom, swinging his nose around conservatively and carefully to the left with a drop-knee technique. Glancing quickly over his shoulder, he can see that the wall is vertical and jacking for a considerable distance down the line. He knows immediately that he has no time to waste if he is going to make this wave.

He trims up quickly, walking forward two steps while his board is still coming out of the turn. The lip is already pitching out over his head, and as its shadow crosses his face he instinctively ducks and crouches, grabbing the outside rail of his board and leaning into the face of the wave to draw a tighter line. He is totally committed and magically absorbed, no longer afraid.

The tube is deep and square and bumpy. Its dimensions are unlike anything BP has experienced before. The lip is landing so far in front of the wall that there is a large, flat floor to the tube, and he has enough room around him to stand up and wave his arms, though he is content to stay in his crouch, with his eyes wide open and his hand gripping the rail, steadying himself against the boils coming up the face.

In less time than it takes to think about it, he realizes that he is not going to make it out—the wave is quickly leaving him behind. He feels the tail of his board slowly creeping up the face of the wave. He shuffles forward another foot until he is right on the tip of the nose, hanging five, eliciting every ounce of thrust out of his board, trying to drive it down and out of this cavern.

He speeds along at maximum amperage for several more circuit-breaking seconds, while the tail of his board lifts inexorably behind him. He sneaks a look backward just as the fin breaks loose, releasing it's grip on the face, allowing the tail to sideslip down, spoiling his forward motion. Instead of sliding ahead, he is suddenly a hopeless chunk of flotsam stuck on the face of the wave.

He is promptly sucked up the face and pitched over the falls, still clinging to his board. For an instant he is riding upside down on the ceiling, insanely glued to the roof; then he goes weightless and everything turns white.

He and his board and the lip land only milliseconds apart in the trough of the wave, and BP finds himself eating a surfboard sandwich. The rail of the board catches him squarely in the mouth, snapping his head back with the impact. He is knocked temporarily senseless by the blow. He sees silver shooting stars. He sees lobsters laughing at him as they lounge on the ledge below.

He goes limp, though not unconscious, as the whitewater churns and thrashes around him, then struggles dazedly to the surface as it releases him. He puts his hand to his mouth and is surprised to find that his front teeth are still there, though they feel quite loose. He can wiggle them around easily with his tongue. He is not yet in pain, but his hand comes away bloody and he realizes he is hurt.

He swims slowly in to the beach, letting the broken waves push him towards shore, where Donny is waiting for him with his board, collected from the shorebreak.

"Boy, did you eat it *royal* on that one, Beep," he is shouting, as BP comes out of the water holding his hand to his mouth, where the tender flesh has begun to throb rather smartly. "Your board missed the rocks OK, but it's still got a little ding over here...." Just then, Donny notices the blood trailing down BP's arm and puts two and two together. "Oh Jesus, it hit you, didn't it...."

BP nods and rushes past him without speaking. He runs all the way up to the parked car and twists the side mirror around so he can see his face. It is not a pretty sight. His upper lip and gums are torn and bleeding, as is his nose, which is weirdly twisted. His front teeth are definitely mobile, and one of them is heavily chipped.

He heaves a sigh of despair as Donny comes running up behind him, carrying his board. "Leth get out of heah," he lisps, keeping his tongue over the jagged edge of his tooth, which has become quite sensitive. "I juth ruint my fathe, man!" He is beginning to feel nauseous.

BP drives home silently in his wetsuit, sitting on a towel, holding his t-shirt to his nose and mouth to try to keep the blood off the upholstery.

"Just go straight to your house, Beep," Donny suggests. "I can leave my board in your garage and walk home." He is feeling quite sorry and worried for his friend.

BP's mother takes one look at his swollen, bloody face and shudders, hustling him directly to the emergency room at the local hospital. His nose is set and taped, and many stitches are taken to close the split in his upper lip, which extends clear up beside one nostril.

The doctor tells him that if everything goes well, there will be no permanent scar, and his wound will virtually disappear in eighteen months or so.

"Eighteen months!" laments BP to himself. "Christ! I'll be done with high school by then!"

The next day he goes to a dentist, who gives him novocain and fits a temporary cap over his chipped front tooth, blessedly soothing the exposed nerve there. Finally, he can take his tongue off it. He explains that BP's teeth will probably firm up again in their sockets as the gums heal, and it will be at least two weeks until he can come back and have the permanent cap fitted, when the swelling subsides.

Other nerve endings, strangely stimulated by this accident, deep within his memory banks, are not so easily assuaged.

Equipment Problems

BP must stay out of the water for seven days, until he has the stitches removed from his lip, so he has plenty of time to think, in the aftermath of his injury, which is not to say that he gets much of anything figured out. He spends most of his time in bitter recriminations and futile self-pity.

"Why did this happen to me?" he laments. "Is God punishing me for something I've done?" Since his relationship with God is still in doubt in his mind (they certainly are not on a "first-name" basis, by any means), he discards this idea. He wants desperately to understand the reason for his misfortune, though, the meaning behind it. He knows that this event is irretrievable, and wishes he could have had the foresight to avoid this incident entirely. He wonders if there was some portent that he had missed, some forewarning—a sign that he ignored or failed to notice.

After some agonizing sessions of self-examination, he decides that this is not likely, that everything had seemed to point him in the direction he had taken, and that he would most certainly do it again, faced with the same circumstances. He *had* to try to ride that wave. And it had been *worth* it, up to a point. The cost was fairly steep, though—the outcome pretty damaging.

He believes that if there is any way he is to benefit from this disaster, it will be by searching out the root causes and facts surrounding his failure, so that his errors can be eliminated and future success insured. In this belief, this dedication to rational methodology and man's domination of nature, he is acting according to some of the most cherished ideals of western civilization, a tradition in which he is thoroughly indoctrinated. If someone were to tell him that he should have known he was going to be hurt before it happened, he would think that they were crazy.

In the end, the damage to his physical appearance is the most upsetting to him, the most devastating consequence of his mistake. "I'm a mess!" he must admit. "I can hardly stand to see myself in the mirror. What must other people be thinking of me? I look like I was in a terrible fight and lost heavy! Nobody likes a loser. What will Jodie say when she sees me?" He avoids any contact with her at first, finally telling her in a brief phone call that he was hurt and had to stay home for a few days.

Indeed, the tape over his swollen nose, his two puffy, black eyes, the gash in his lip (closed with tiny, criss-crossing tracks of bloodstained, black thread), and the sickening damage to his teeth and gums, all contribute to the disheartening image of himself as a beaten, broken-down prizefighter, past his prime at the tender age of sixteen.

All sorts of wild doubts and fears besiege him. "I wonder if my nose will ever look the same again? Will this cut ever really heal up and disappear? Will the DMV have to recall my driver's license and change the 'NO VISIBLE SCARS' to 'HUGE SCAR ON FACE'?"

He patches the ding in his surfboard. This portion of the accident is easily reconstructed, at least. He trims away the shattered fiberglass, noting the distinct impressions left by his teeth, shuddering to find some dried, tattered shreds of his flesh still embedded there. He fills the ding with some polyester resin and fiberglass shavings, and shapes it smooth with a rasp. After a brushed-on coat of pigmented glossing resin, the board is repaired, though the color of the patch is not a perfect match. He wishes his confidence was as easy to restore, but the worst is yet to come.

After three days of separation (perhaps their longest in six months), Jodie calls him to say that she is going on a vacation with her family to visit relatives in northern California for the next several weeks. She will be gone nearly until the start of the school year next month. She misses him and desperately wants to see him before she leaves. He screws up his courage and goes over to her house.

When she meets him at the door and sees his battered face, she shrinks back reflexively in shock, shrieking "OMIGOD, what happened to you?" and starts crying uncontrollably, "OMIGOD, OMIGOD!" BP is not prepared for this, and cannot console her. He hugs her and tries to tell her that it's OK, that it doesn't hurt much anymore, and that he is healing fine, but every time she looks at him, she breaks out crying again, and all she can say is "Oh Bobby, Bobby, Bobby...." through her tears. "I'm so sorry," she sobs. BP just holds her, and after a few minutes her body stops heaving and shaking so heavily.

"I wanted to be with you so bad before I go," she says, finally, her voice cracking and breaking, still. "I just can't take this, though, it's too much for me right now. I'm sorry. I'm such a mess. Maybe you should just go home now and we'll talk when I get back, OK?" She looks at him through bleary, pleading eyes, and he can tell that she is about to break down again. He feels terrible, and figures the best thing to do is to leave her alone right now.

"Sure, babe," he says, leaning over to kiss her on the cheek. "I'm sorry, too. It'll be OK. I'll see you when you get back." He turns and walks away, and she shuts the door quickly behind him, without another look.

He has an additional subject to add to his bag of recriminations now. He wonders about her reaction to him and what he might have done to make their last meeting less traumatic. Maybe he should have told her more about the specifics of his injuries beforehand, so that she would not have been so shocked? Living inside his body, he had gotten used to it quickly, but he doesn't have to look at himself unless he's in front of a mirror. When he does study his reflection, he must admit that it doesn't look very good. Some might certainly find him ugly and repulsive, perhaps. But it's just temporary, no?

The grotesque swelling has already receded, and the black around his eyes has turned from purple to green and is starting to fade away. The stitches in his lip make him look like a young Frankenstein, admittedly, but in two weeks, he should heal up even more, and his appearance should return to normal.

It is his fervent hope that he will see her then and everything will be like it was before. It is his greatest fear, one that he refuses to contemplate fully, that she seems to be judging him solely on his appearance. Isn't he more than just the way he looks? He doesn't want to think about this any further, as it makes his heart ache.

By chance, while checking the surf with Donny a few days later, he happens to recognize the other surfer who had been out with him that fateful day, sitting in the parking lot at Windansea.

"Hey, who is that guy?" asks BP. "He's the one I was out at Big Rock with, remember?"

"Oh yeah," says Donny, "That's Dale Keeling. Don't you know him? He's really a hot surfer, man, probably one of the best around. But everybody says he's not quite playing with a full deck, you know, he's pretty crazy, I guess. I thought you knew who he was."

"No, I mean, I know the guy rips, I saw him get *so* tubed that day—that's why I went out there! But I've never met him...."

It occurs to him that Dale may be a valuable source of information and knowledge that he has overlooked. He has always preferred to struggle through his problems alone (like a man), and is hesitant to ask anyone for advice. The fact that Dale is several years older, and one of the more well-known (or at least notorious) surfers in the city, doesn't help. He is pretty sure Dale wouldn't recognize him, couldn't care less about his problems, and would probably laugh in his face.

"I've got to talk to him," he decides, an indication of his desperation.

"What for?" asks Donny.

"I need to find out how he does it. Maybe he can tell me where I screwed up. He was there. He came through and I got eaten alive. I need to know where I went wrong. It's important to me."

"Why? It's over and done, Beep. Let it go! It doesn't matter that much, does it? It was an accident, that's all. You were just unlucky."

"I don't know, I've just got this feeling that it's something way worse than that."

He swallows his pride, reasoning that Dale might be flattered by his attention, stifles his fear, and walks up to him.

"Hey, man, how's it going?" he begins, as casually as possible, sitting down next to Dale.

"What's happening?" answers Dale, looking over at him with a blank face.

"Uh, my name's Bob, my friends call me Beep," he stumbles ahead. "Could I talk to you for a minute?"

"Sure, man. My name's Dale. My enemies call me 'The Goon,' so don't you call me that, OK? Jeez, what happened to you? Someone rearrange your face?" he chuckles.

He seems jovial enough, so BP plunges ahead. "Nah, I did it to myself—that's kinda what I wanted to talk to you about. I was the guy out with you at Big Rock last week, on Tuesday, with the orange board. I went over-the-falls on my first wave and mashed myself with my stick."

"Oh yeah, I remember you. I wondered why you went in so quick. I saw that ride you got while I was paddling out—man, you were deep! That was some outrageous gas you took. I didn't know your board hit you, though, that's too bad. You should try to get away from it when you're going to eat it like that. 'Course, it would be better to never fall off at all, huh?"

"Yeah, I think that's what I shudda done—I shudda bailed out sooner. I was still trying to ride it out when I got sucked over."

"Oh man, that musta been radical. You were really going for it. You disappeared as you went by me, but then I looked back and all I saw was the fin of your board poking through the top as it went over. But you gotta remember, if you're going for it at the Rock, you're gonna get nailed, sooner or later. It's a nasty wave. Why do you think we were the only two stand-up guys out? There were thirty goons up at Windansea that day!"

"I know, I checked it out, that's one of the reasons I came down there with you. There were plenty of waves and they were so hollow. I wanted to get tubed."

"Yeah," purrs Dale, "that's pure, unfiltered juice out there...."

"How do you handle it so well, Dale? I've gotta know—what did I do wrong? I watched you rip that place and then I went out and almost killed myself."

"Shit, man, I don't know," Dale shrugs. "I only saw that one ride of yours, but it didn't look like you were blowing it, it just seemed like your board wasn't that fast. Maybe you're having some equipment problems. What are you riding?"

"It's a 9'3" V-J. It's the only board I've ever had."

"A 9'3" Velzy? The only board you've ever had? Christ, that thing's an antique! How long have you had it?" Dale sounds truly shocked by this revelation.

"About four years, I guess. I learned on it. I've never really thought about getting another one. I guess I'm just used to it."

"You should get yourself another stick, man, that thing's holding you back. It's an old pig-board design—way too wide in the tail for those waves—not nearly fast enough. You need something gunnier. Shapes are changing all the time. You've gotta stay on top of the latest designs and try them all out for yourself if you want to stay ahead of the pack, and even have different boards for different conditions. I bet I've had thirty or forty boards in the last eight years."

It is BP's turn to be shocked. "Thirty or forty boards? How can you afford all those?" He has never considered giving up his old board.

"You've got to have a sponsor. I ride for Challenger Surfboards and they'll give me a new board every month, if I want. You should get into some contests and get a sponsor—it's the only way to go."

"What else should I do?"

Dale considers his question. "Just surf your brains out, every chance you get. And think about learning how to switch stance. That's what I do, so that I can face the wall in either direction. You fit into the pocket better when you face the wave, and you have better vision, so you can see what's coming up down the line. Other than that...just remember when you have to bail out at the Rock, your board isn't the only thing to worry about. You've got to stay flat, don't *dive* off—the bottom is right there! Just lay off the back and kick your board out in front of you when you know you've had it. But you've gotta stay with it long enough to get past the Rock or you can kiss your board goodbye."

"I think I had that part under control, I was past the Rock, OK. I just sort of got hypnotized in the tube and forgot to bail out in time, I guess. There's really a lot to be afraid of out there, huh?"

"That's right, there's a lot to be afraid of, buddy, but really nothing to fear, if you know what I mean. Hey, I gotta split, man. Nice talking to you. I'll see you out there again some time."

"I hope so," says BP.

Baby Beep

Two weeks later, in the first part of September, only a few days before the start of his senior year in high school, BP sees Jodie again, but things do not go as he'd hoped, by a long shot. While his appearance has almost returned to normal, and she doesn't recoil in horror upon seeing him again, she seems a bit distracted and distant when he picks her up at her house. She hugs him, kissing him briefly on the lips, and brushes past him, grabbing his hand and pulling him towards the car. "Let's go for a ride," she says, "we need to talk."

BP follows her down the walkway, scooting ahead to open the car door for her (he has become more of a gentleman under her tutelage), and they drive off towards the beach. He can sense that something is wrong, and has a feeling of foreboding and dread. There is no carefree banter between them, catching each other up on what has happened since they were last together, sharing their recent experiences and feelings freely, as they would have done in the past. She seems preoccupied and nervous, and BP cannot think of the right thing to say to break the ice. They drive the few blocks to the pier and park the car. Jodie finally shatters the awkward silence that has built up between them with a piercing announcement: "Bobby, I'm pregnant," she says, finally.

BP is stunned. "B-but, that's not possible, you're on the pill," he stammers. "How could that happen? Are you sure?" This is not what he was expecting. His pulse starts pounding and his mind is racing around this new set of variables, searching for suitable responses.

"I don't know how it happened, but I am sure, now. I missed my period almost three months ago and it hasn't come back. I didn't want to believe it, but I finally went to the doctor last month and the tests were positive—I'm going to have a baby. Your baby! The doctor said the pill isn't always 100% reliable, and I don't know, maybe I missed taking it one day or something.... Oh, Bobby, I'm so sorry! I didn't want this to happen, and I know you didn't either....What are we going to do?" Her voice trails off in a strangled little gasp. BP looks at her and sees tears welling up in her eyes. He desperately wants to comfort her.

"We'll get married, then," he blurts, putting his arm around her and pulling her closer. "I love you, Jodie—everything will be OK, don't worry." He tries to project a confidence with his words that simply does not exist within him at the moment, and his voice rings hollow in his ears.

"Oh, Bobby, we can't do that. We aren't ready to be married, and our parents will never allow it," she sobs softly, burying her head in BP's shoulder, wiping the tears from her eyes on his shirt.

"We'll run away then—we'll go to Las Vegas or something...." BP is grasping at straws in his confusion. Even in Nevada, 16-year-olds are not allowed to marry without parental consent.

"That won't work, Bobby, how would we get there? How would we live? We don't have enough money. We can't take care of a baby. We need to finish school, still."

"I'll quit school and get a job."

"You *can't* do that, I don't want you to. I won't let you," insists Jodie. "You could ruin your life. What kind of job could you get without even a high school education?"

BP realizes she is right, in a practical manner of speaking, and his mind searches frantically for other alternatives. "What about an abortion?"

"I couldn't, Bobby. I thought about it right away, and I was going to do it—I even went to the family planning clinic and talked to them, but when it was time to go through with it, I felt horrible—I couldn't let them cut this helpless little baby out of me and kill it! I just can't let that happen. It's not right." She begins to cry again.

BP is close to tears himself. He is frightened and dismayed by this development, but somehow he knows it is a natural consequence of their actions, of the choices they have made, and they must bear the responsibility somehow. "Have you told your parents about this yet?"

"No, I'm too afraid. I wanted to talk to you first, but they are going to find out—I've already gained a little weight, and I'll be showing soon. My mother will know. We can't hide it for long."

BP does not see any easy way out of this quandary. His own meager teenage knowledge and resources are not sufficient to deal with such a serious situation. He feels he must respect Jodie's choices and feelings in this matter, for he realizes that it impacts her far more profoundly than it does him. He recognizes his own responsibility for what has happened and does not want to shirk it. He wants to support her, to comfort her, and he wishes he could solve this problem himself, quickly and cleanly, but no solution comes readily to mind.

He realizes that they need help, that they cannot deal with this alone. Although it brings a sinking feeling in his gut, an alarming sensation that events are spiraling out of his control once again, and a devastating intuition of where this is all leading, he comes to the only conclusion which he is capable of finding: "We have to tell them." Deep down, he knows that they are about to pay a heavy price for the lustful fun they have had with each other.

That evening, he sits down with his parents and breaks the news, at the same time that Jodie is doing so with her parents, as they had agreed. His mother and father are shocked and dumbfounded, just as he expected, but less angry than he had anticipated. They are sad and deeply disappointed in his irresponsible behavior, it is obvious, but there is no ranting and raving, no punitive measures handed down in haste. They seem to sense BP's despair, and deal with him calmly and assertively. This supportiveness in the face of his transgressions is a relief to BP. He could have fully understood his father beating him to a pulp over this news.

What he is totally unprepared for, however, is how completely powerless he becomes in the situation. Once he has spilled his guts and laid the problem on the table, his parents take control, and things start happening quickly, with no further input from him.

A meeting is arranged for the next day, with all the players. Jodie and her parents arrive at BP's home and assemble in the living room, sitting opposite BP and his parents. The adults do all the talking, while BP and Jodie just look at each other wistfully, across the room.

BP's father begins, with his usual business-like manner: "I'm so sorry we have to meet under these circumstances, Mr. and Mrs. Noll, but I thought it would be best that we work out a mutually agreeable solution to this situation, in the best interests of our children. Bob has admitted his wrongdoing to us and is ready to assume full responsibility in this matter, but we need to hear from you what your wishes are for your daughter, as she is the one who is most severely effected by his mistakes."

"Thank you," says Jodie's father, "we appreciate your concern. We have no desire to place blame, here. After discussing it with our daughter, we realize that this was a mutual breakdown in self-control by both of them. We, as parents, can probably share in the blame ourselves, for not having been more vigilant and less permissive with them in many ways, but there is no use in crying over spilt milk at this point.

"As far as what to do now," Mr. Noll continues, "after looking at all the alternatives, we have ruled out the possibility of marriage, I think—even the kids agree with this, I believe—they are much too young and immature. So there are very few options left. An abortion is out of the question, for us. Therefore, we have come to the decision that Jodie will have the baby and put it up for adoption.

"We have decided to send her to her Aunt's home in Sacramento next week to attend school, until she gives birth, and this will avoid further embarrassment or temptation for all concerned. As it happens, I have just found out that my company has plans to relocate me there in the next few months, so we will be selling our home and moving north anyway, shortly. Bob and Jodie's relationship would have ended then in any case. But for now, we think it is best that they do not see each other in the meantime, for obvious reasons, so we will send her there ahead of our move, and she can at least begin the school year in her new environs."

"That sounds very reasonable," says BP's father, "and we fully respect your decision. Rest assured that our son will comply with your wishes, and we will see that he bears full responsibility for the financial burden of her care as well. Please let us know what the costs are for the delivery and adoption services, and I will make sure that he repays you, sir."

"Thank you very much for your understanding and cooperation," says Mr. Noll. "I think this is about the best we can make of a bad situation. I guess we are done here, then."

Just like that, it is over. Their fate as a couple and that of the child they have created is sealed, without BP or Jodie ever uttering a word. BP sits in disbelief, stunned, as Jodie and her parents leave. Once again, he has been blind-sided by developments which are totally beyond his control, taking him in directions he never would have wished. One of the most important aspects of his life has been ripped from his grasp and he is powerless to do anything about it at all. It seems so unfair to him, so unjust. "How could they do this?" he agonizes to himself.

After escorting Jodie's parents to the door, BP's father approaches him, as he sits in an aporetic stupor. "As for you, young man," he says in a commanding tone, "I'm afraid it is time for you to grow up and face the music. You've had your own way for far too long and things are going to change, starting right now! You've done some adult things, and now you must act like an adult. You're going to begin looking for a job tomorrow—a part-time job that will not interfere with your schoolwork, and you're going to earn the money to pay the bill for this little escapade, no matter how long it takes. Do you hear me? And you are not to see or speak to that girl again under any circumstances, do you understand?"

"Yes sir," BP replies meekly, unable to object, or defend himself. Later, though, alone with his thoughts, he rails against the injustice of it all. He cannot believe that he has been cut off from the one he loves so abruptly and so finally. He tries to devise some plan where he can see her again and find out how she feels about this disastrous turn of events. He thinks about sneaking over to her house and spiriting her away somehow, but ultimately cannot figure out how to do this without making matters even worse. "If only we were eighteen, they would not be able to do this to us," he thinks. "We would be able to make our own decisions and they couldn't control us this way." (Another piece of evidence to further support his Conspiracy of Age theory that he files away.)

He considers perhaps waiting until he comes of age (it is only another fifteen months, after all), then running away to Sacramento and finding her, renewing their relationship and living happily ever after. But he finally realizes that this is just a fantasy. "Fifteen months is a long time, and a lot will have happened by then. She may have even found another boyfriend by that time," he thinks. "How will she feel about me by then? What if she doesn't love me any more? And what about the baby?"

As he ponders the complexities of his situation over the next several days, doubt begins to enter his mind and dominate his thoughts. "Does she really even love me?" he wonders. "Do I even know what true love is? Isn't it forever—'until death do us part?'" He knows how powerful his attraction to her was, how much he enjoyed her company and how much he learned from her. The deliciousness of their physical passion was undeniable and heady—absolutely intoxicating—but is that all there was to it? They had never really shared much with each other about their ultimate hopes and dreams, or made any plans for sharing their lives together. They had been too busy having fun. And now, it didn't seem that she was making any real effort to escape this cruel repression and come to him, somehow (although he recognizes that this is impractical, if not impossible at the moment).

He remembers her revulsion when she had seen him with his disfigured face, and wonders if this was a sign that theirs was merely a physical infatuation, based only on appearances and lust. Or was it that she had already known at that time about her pregnancy and was already upset over that, and his mutilated appearance had just been the final straw that had pushed her over the edge, into hysteria? He doesn't know, for sure, and realizes he probably never will.

He remembers the tiny seeds of guilt that had sprouted in the fields of ecstasy they had created together, and how he had so quickly stamped them out. Even as he had given in to his libidinous urges, drawn by the shining glory and the overwhelming newness of her naked body, overcome by his fascination with the wondrous pleasures she could bring him, he knew somehow, deep in his heart, he was doing something wrong. But how could he have done anything else? It was so sweet—it seemed so right at the time.

In the end, all his mental contortions do him no good at all—he only becomes more confused, paralyzed by doubt, guilt and fear, and ultimately does nothing to try to change his fate. He never sees or speaks to Jodie again, and never even knows what happens to their child, or whether it is born a boy or a girl.

TROUBLE AHEAD, TROUBLE BEHIND

BP has landed in a world of hurt. On September 14, 1964, he begins his senior year in high school and Jodie is not there. It is a lonely place again. His physical wounds have healed nearly completely, relieving him of this badge of disgrace. His nose retains a telltale bump where the cartilage was shattered, but largely resumes its normal configuration. The permanent cap on his chipped tooth is an adequate match and blends well with his natural teeth. The split in his lip closes cleanly, leaving only a thin, white line, which will fade further in time. The scars on his psyche are deeper.

The very day before school starts, he finds a job washing dishes in a local restaurant for minimum wage ($1.15 per hour). He spends five hours a day each afternoon and into the evening in a hot sweaty kitchen, running dirty dishes, pots, pans and utensils through a commercial dishwashing machine, for the grand total of $5.75 per day. This was the first job he was offered, at the first place he inquired, but time was of the essence, he felt, to comply with his father's orders.

It is not a great job, but the people he works with are friendly, and there is one excellent perk to it—all restaurant employees are allowed to eat one meal before or after their shift. This proves to be a huge bonus for BP, who manages to eat enough of the restaurant's food to nearly double his meager salary (if, somehow, he could be paid the resultant savings to his parent's weekly food bill.)

This obligation, combined with his school work, cuts heavily into his surf time. When he does begin to surf again, it is with more caution and less abandon. His accident, and his talk with Dale Keeling, has destroyed his confidence in his beloved surfboard. He can never look at it again in quite the same way. Its flawed obsolescence seems so obvious to him now. Though it had served him so well in the past, he cannot trust it fully anymore.

This change in perspective about his board is almost as hard for him to accept as the developments in his relationship with Jodie, which parallel it uncannily, feeding his despondency. In both cases, it is extremely depressing for him to think that something which brought him such joy and contentment in the past could be so easily transformed, in such a short period of time, by a few calamitous events and a slight change in his perception, into a source of frustration and anxiety. The evidence cannot be denied, however. The reality is that Jodie is lost and gone, and his board is a piece of shit.

He sees no easy way out of his predicament, but it is obvious to him that the most immediate need is to earn some money, so he puts his head down and works hard, without complaining, grinding out the hours, days and weeks.

School, work, eat, sleep, and surf a little when he can—if it is not prison, it at least seems like indentured servitude.

After two months, he learns from his father that he will owe approximately $600 to Mr. Noll, so at least he has an idea of the magnitude of his problem. During that time, he has managed to save only a little over $200 from his job. At this rate, he calculates (adding the $125 he needs for a new custom board), it will take him 6 more months to get his head above water. This is a disheartening prospect, but he gives the $200 he has earned to his father, who, thankfully, offers to loan BP the $400 balance so that Mr. Noll can be reimbursed fully, on the condition that Bobby continues to make monthly payments on the debt.

BP agrees to this, and looks for a way to increase his monthly earnings. As a solution, he decides to start a neighborhood gardening service. For several years, since he was 14 or so, he has earned a $5 per week allowance from his father for doing chores around the house, which include mowing the lawn. He asks his father if he can use their lawnmower, a small, gas-powered rotary rig, to mow some of the neighbors' lawns. His father is delighted to see him display this entrepreneurial initiative and quickly assents.

By soliciting work door-to-door in his immediate neighborhood, he finds enough gardening work to bring in about $50 more per month, without taking up too much of his already scarce time. His father secretly encourages this activity by taking upon himself all the expenses of maintaining the lawnmower, just as he always has, increasing BP's profit margin. He fills it with gas and oil, sharpens the blades regularly, tunes the motor (always when his son is not around), and BP never questions why the mower always works so well and doesn't ever seem to run out of fuel.

His parents are pleased at his apparent rehabilitation. He has become a model of good behavior at school, and has even taken a more active interest in some of his classes (especially math and science, which fascinate him). His high school record has been spotless, to this point, mostly because he has realized that above and beyond "thinking for oneself," it is a much more adult attitude to keep quiet about what one knows, until one sees a clear opportunity to use such knowledge to one's own advantage, at the most propitious time. (This is sometimes known as "discretion.") He has taken his private war against authority deeply underground, since his overt "guerilla" tactics have previously won him only tiny, idealistic victories, at huge, practical costs.

He takes all the "Advanced College Placement" classes at school and does well. His education in mathematics has progressed through arithmetic and geometry to algebra, now, and he has sensed some of the grander aspects of this discipline, which have beguiled others before him. The magic of logical transformations carried out unerringly, within a rigidly defined, closed system, in a universal symbology, to produce undeniable truths, is immensely appealing to him. He wishes that truths were so easy to seize from the real world of everyday life, which seems so much messier to him, with so many shades of grey instead of black and white, true or false.

He marvels at a system which can express concepts like "infinity" and "nothing" with simple symbols (a drunken, sideways 8 and a circle) that everyone seems to understand and manipulate perfectly easily, even though he suspects that no one has ever truly experienced these qualities in the real world. He knows *he* hasn't, but he naively believes that when he finally understands everything there is to know about mathematics, the correspondence of these symbols to his reality will become clear. [It will still be several years until he encounters the chilling quotation by Albert Einstein in which the great physicist admits that "to the extent that mathematics is certain, it does not relate to reality, and to the extent that it relates to reality, mathematics is not certain."]

His indoctrination in modern scientific theory and method progresses as well, to the point that he accepts it unquestionably as the cornerstone of all wisdom and civilization. He admires the expertise and accomplishments of the many great scientists he learns about, but he wishes that some of them had been surfers, so that they might have applied their erudition to designing the perfect surfboard for him. He toys with the idea of becoming a Great Scientist himself, so that he can solve this pressing problem, but he realizes this will take a great deal of time and effort.

He imagines himself as Dr. Pilhaus, heading up an intensive, national research effort in hydrodynamics to reveal the secrets of surfboard design. He is certain that if the methods and brainpower of the Manhattan Project, which had brought us nuclear fission, could be applied to his equipment problems, they would be solved in short order, and the world would be a better place for it. Unfortunately, there is no Ph.D. offered at any accredited university in surfboard design.

When he does investigate what science exists in this area, he can only find theories and descriptions regarding the nature of displacement and planing hull forms that apply to warships and commercial vessels in the open ocean—there is no widespread interest in determining how a surfboard works on a wave. He figures this must be because no one wants to spend any money on research that doesn't either save people's lives, or find better and faster ways to snuff them out. There doesn't seem to be any middle ground in this area.

BP wants to familiarize himself with the current concepts of surfboard design, so that if and when he does become a Great Scientist, he will know how to proceed with inventing the perfect board. At the very least, he hopes to learn enough that when the time comes that he is able to order the new custom board he wants, he will know what works best and why.

Unfortunately, unlike the technical aspects of surfboard construction, which have become fairly standardized throughout the industry, ideas about their design are neither well defined nor widely agreed upon. There is no written body of documentation on this subject for him to consult. The complex parameters of a surfboard's shape—its length, width, outline, thickness, rocker, and foiling—are ultimately resolved on the floor of the shaping room in less than two hours, he finds, by a single person, bringing an artful eye to bear on an oversized blank of polyurethane foam. Wielding a pencil, some templates, a handsaw, an assortment of hand and power planes and some sandpaper, the final shape is rendered in a flurry of white foam dust. It is not academic or scientific, but a "folk knowledge," not unlike that of many crafts, and to obtain an understanding of it he must go to the source—the shaper himself. In the few spare hours he has, when the surf is flat, he seeks these people out at some of the surfboard factories in the area, to pick their brains and see how it is done.

They are an eclectic group, these shapers, some of them quite eccentric and secretive, others open to talk to him and share their ideas. He is surprised to find that many of them cannot articulate exactly what they are doing or why. They speak in generalities about a board's performance, how it will work differently according to various design characteristics, but they often contradict each other, and admit that there is no formula for the perfect board.

BP had always assumed that much more objective and specific criteria were involved, and he is disappointed to find that every design is a compromise, optimizing some performance features at the expense of others. There seems to be a great deal of subjective "luck" involved in satisfying a customer's requirements, and the shapers are the first to admit that no single board will work well in all conditions (relieving themselves of any further responsibility for a customer's dissatisfaction).

He has no intention of spending his hard-earned money on an unknown quantity, so he postpones his decision. He examines all the new boards he sees in the shops and on the beach with new interest and increasing discrimination, recognizing design subtleties that had previously escaped him. He attempts to relate these nuances to the board's performance, boldly going so far as to ask total strangers in the water if they might trade boards for a few rides. They are sometimes difficult to persuade when they take note of his ancient, orange hulk.

During this period, he slackens his all-out pursuit of tube rides in favor of a more conservative approach to his surfing, which he hopes will avert further injuries. In addition to his investigation of the role his board plays in his surfing (which he begins to realize is much larger than he thought), he practices switching stance, as Dale Keeling had suggested.

Learning to ride with his right foot forward turns out to be an alien and challenging task for him. Unlike Dale, he is not naturally ambidextrous, and he must constantly fight to control his instinctual preference, which is to ride with his left foot forward. It is like trying to throw a ball with his left hand—awkward and uncoordinated.

It is difficult to enforce this new order in his surfing. He must relearn the most basic relationships and responses that have become unconscious habits in his regular stance. It is necessary to accept a precipitous plunge in his performance level (clear back to kookdom) in order to reap future dividends, but he rationalizes it by reminding himself that his old board is no good anyway, and works just fine for falling off (which is all he can seem to do as a goofy-foot). He contents himself with practice/maintenance sessions at the softer, less crowded breaks whenever he can steal the time, and misses many of the better swells and more ideal conditions because of his busy schedule.

He shuns the social events and activities at school once more, due to time constraints and the lack of a suitable partner. He is totally gun-shy and heartbroken over his affair with Jodie, and he has no desire to repeat his mistakes with someone else. Just before the Christmas break, he takes the SAT (Scholastic Aptitude Tests) for college entrance and aces them, finding them easier than he had anticipated. When the results are returned early in 1965, his school counselor informs him that he can probably win entrance to any California state college or university to which he applies, with his excellent grades and test scores.

While he has little use for news or current events, it has not escaped his attention that a war (although it is originally called a "U.N. police action") has been raging in Southeast Asia for some time, and that his country's involvement in it is ramping up. The *Gulf of Tonkin* resolution was passed by Congress on August 7, 1964, giving President Johnson broad powers to conduct military operations without an actual declaration of war, and on March 2, 1965, *Operation Rolling Thunder* begins, with American B-52 bombers raining death and destruction on North Vietnam in a program of "strategic persuasion."

In the Quaker Meeting (which he still attends on Sundays), there is much consternation and outrage over this aggression, as it is at odds with their testimony of peace, and BP learns that he may be swept up in this growing conflict by means of the Selective Service Act, or "draft." At the age of 18, which is less than a year away for him now, he will be required to register with his local draft board and could be "selected" for military service. This possibility does not appeal to him whatsoever. Although he learns of the provisions for conscientious objectors under the law from the Quakers (indeed, his mother becomes heavily involved in counseling young men regarding their choices), he also finds out that there is a deferment status for full-time students which allows them to complete their studies and delay their conscription. This seems by far the easiest route to take, and BP decides that he must indeed go to college, and right away, immediately after high school.

He researches his choices and sends in his application to the University of California. There are nine undergraduate campuses in the UC system, all around the state, but only three of them are located in close proximity to the ocean, which will provide him with adequate opportunities to continue surfing: San Diego, Santa Barbara, and Santa Cruz. He lists them in exactly that priority order on his application, as required, and sends it off. As a backup, just in case he is denied admission to UC, he sends in an application to San Diego State College, which both his parents had attended.

By the end of March, he has saved enough money to retire his debt to his father completely, and also order a new custom surfboard from Carl Ekstrom's shop in La Jolla. Carl seems to him to be one of the most thoughtful, experienced and articulate shapers with whom he has come in contact, with the added bonus that he is a meticulous craftsman—his boards are always extremely well-constructed and beautifully finished, absolute works of art, in BP's eyes. In addition, Carl is a longtime La Jolla local, and knows the reef-break waves there intimately, designing boards which are well-suited for those conditions. He has also recently come up with an asymmetrical tail design, which is intended to make backside turns as easy as frontside, without switching stance, and BP wants to try this feature out, as he is still struggling with riding goofyfoot, and doesn't think he will ever master it.

He has enough money left over, by virtue of working two jobs, to buy himself his first car as well—an older, beat-up, 1953 Chevrolet panel truck that had once been used for deliveries by a local bakery. It is in poor cosmetic condition so it costs him only $200, but it runs well, with a rebuilt six-cylinder engine, and his surfboard fits inside perfectly, along with his gardening equipment. Relieved from the pressure of his debt, he quits his dishwashing job and concentrates on expanding his freelance gardening business, searching out more distant customers than before. This allows him a more flexible schedule, of his own choosing, and is still sufficient to bring in enough money for his immediate needs.

In mid-April, he takes delivery of his new, 9'10" Ekstrom surfboard, just days before he receives admittance offers in letters from all three UC campuses, as well as San Diego State. He is in the fortunate position of being able to choose between them all. His parents are very proud of this achievement, and encourage his path towards higher education. UC is a slightly more expensive institution than San Diego State, and BP is not eligible for any scholarships (their family income is too high), but his parents offer to pay his tuition and expenses for any school he chooses. "If you go to a San Diego school," they point out to him, "you can live at home and commute there at first, so our other costs will not be much more than they are now, except for the fees, books and the gas money to drive there each day."

The deal is sealed when he thinks about the fact that the UCSD campus is located in La Jolla, right on the coast, and just a few miles north, while San Diego State is located some twelve miles east of the beach and several miles south. There is no contest. He sends off his acceptance letter to UCSD, and soon begins to receive orientation materials from them. His new surfboard and the forward-thinking anticipation of college help to rid him of depressing thoughts of the past, and he begins to climb out of his year-long funk. Nevertheless, when he graduates from high school in June of 1965, he attends neither the graduation ceremony nor the senior prom. He is ready to move on.

Coming of Age

During the summer of 1965, BP begins to feel better about his situation, that he is finally achieving more control over his life, moving along the road to adulthood and independence and leaving recent traumatic events behind. He has earned his high school diploma. He has started a small, home business which allows him a flexible work schedule, and as he recruits more customers, he is earning more money all the time, enough to eventually provide for him to live by his own resources, if he should become so inclined, or obliged. In just three months he will be entering college. In six months he will be eighteen years old, the age of majority.

He has more freedom and surfs more during this summer than ever before, usually two sessions a day if there are rideable waves, both morning and evening, fashioning his work schedule around the best conditions. His new board is a joy to him, easy to ride, easy to paddle, loose and maneuverable, yet predictable, and a great noserider. He has achieved true journeyman status as a surfer, now, after nearly five years of apprenticeship. While still undistinguished, perhaps, in his wave riding, he is experienced enough to handle any conditions he encounters at his local breaks, competent enough to position himself well, catch any wave he wants, draw his own line on them at will, and aware enough to fit into any lineup without conflict.

His physical fitness and strength levels reach all-time highs from the many hours of paddling he puts in, as well as the manual labor he performs daily, cutting people's lawns, raking their leaves, trimming their hedges and trees. His titanic growth spurt has finally tapered off, and he has reached his full adult height of almost 6'4", surpassing that of his father by an inch, and has added another ten pounds of lean, knotted muscle to his frame by summer's end. His mental development, however, has been much less robust, and is far from peaking.

He begins to think about how he wants to shape his life as an adult, what he wants to become, in the long term—what he wants to achieve, where he wants to go. When he contemplates his future, it is not a comforting endeavor. From what he has been able to gather from his youthful perspective, the world is a stunningly contradictory place, at once both astonishingly vast, complex, wondrous and beautiful, yet full of cruelty, suffering, and violence. He does not know what to make of it, exactly, or how he is supposed to fit into it.

He is fairly certain that his further education is essential in penetrating this mystery, and he is excited about the prospect of attending college. He knows that he is fortunate to have such an opportunity, and hopes that his immersion in higher education will help him fill in the missing pieces of the puzzle, illuminating the darker, shadowy corners of his meager understanding of life. (At the same time, he furtively hopes against hope that he will also be able to meet some fabulously intelligent, stunningly attractive woman, who will find him irresistible.)

He does not yet know exactly what he would like to study most, but he is aware of his parents' preferences for him. His father, he is sure, would like him to become a physicist or an engineer, obtaining advanced technical knowledge with an eye towards commerce. He goes so far as to mention at one point that a person with a scientific background, combined with a law degree, specializing in contracts, would be highly sought after by major corporations in the defense industry (who are mainstays of the San Diego economy and have employed him ever since he graduated from college on the GI Bill, after World War II). His mother reminds him (separately) that it would be a worthy goal to become a physician, helping to alleviate disease and injury among his fellow human beings. He is relieved to learn at a freshman orientation session that it will not be necessary for him to declare a "major" area of study until his third year, as the program at UCSD for lower division students is largely the same for everyone, with few elective courses.

BP decides to treat himself with some of the extra money he has saved by buying a motorcycle, something he has desired for quite some time. He approaches his parents about the idea one evening, rationalizing the purchase as an economical means for commuting to school when the weather is nice. As he expects, his mother objects to the idea. "Those things are too dangerous, Bobby, you'll get hurt!" she argues.

His father, however, is supportive, as he had hoped. "Now, Betty, you know it's not the bike that is dangerous, it's the other drivers. I rode my old Indian to school and then my Norton to work for years, remember?" (Some of BP's fondest early memories were of short rides around the neighborhood as a very young boy, tucked between his father's legs, clutching the gas tank of that shiny, snarling, twin-cylinder Norton, cradled by his father's arms stretching to the handlebars—experiences that are undoubtedly feeding his yearning.)

"Yes, I do, and I'm sure you remember that I never once got on that thing with you," his mother retorts. "And I remember very well when you crashed it!"

"I didn't crash it, dear, I had to lay it down when that idiot turned his car right in front of me, without ever looking. I wasn't even hurt, just a little road rash."

"Well the bike was wrecked, that's for sure, and it could've been much worse," Betty counters.

"If he's careful and alert, and gives other drivers a wide berth, nothing bad will happen. Let the boy have some fun. You'll be careful on it, won't you, Bob?"

"Yes, sir. Except for riding it to school, I mostly want to use it off-road, anyway, where there aren't any cars."

Realizing she is not going to prevail against the two of them, and unwilling to lay down any ultimatum, his mother settles for having the last word: "If you're going to buy one of those things, you're going to get a helmet, then, and you're going to wear it! I don't want your brains splattered all over the street somewhere."

BP shops around and finds a good deal on a used, 250cc Honda Scrambler, a reliable hybrid model suitable for use both on the road and in the dirt, and buys a cheap helmet to go with it. While a bit heavy and underpowered, it is fun to ride and very economical. With a few pointers from his father on shifting, braking, and handling the bike, he is quickly up to speed and comfortable on it, enjoying the open-air feeling of freedom on a two-wheeled vehicle.

For the rest of the summer, whenever the surf is flat, he enjoys exploring the local backcountry inland from his home, riding on the dirt roads, trails and graded firebreaks. [In this less densely-developed era in San Diego, before the ticky-tack housing tracts have filled in the landscape, and the new, burgeoning, interstate highway system has totally dissected the community, open space is not such a scarce commodity. It is possible for him to ride his motorcycle off-road, clear from the Miramar mesa to Santee or Lakeside, while crossing only a single, paved road at Murphy Canyon.] He finds the challenge of hill-climbing and trail riding on the bike exhilarating and satisfying, somewhat like surfing in the dirt, demanding his complete attention and coordination to pick the correct line through surface ruts and obstacles, while maintaining his balance and forward momentum.

On a couple of occasions, he manages to exceed his capabilities, falling over and dropping the bike at low speed (causing no physical injuries to himself, luckily, and only minor damage to the bike—breaking a rear-view mirror, and bending the brake and clutch levers, which are easily repaired). He realizes that the consequences of "wiping out" in the dirt could be far greater than in the ocean, and overall, he takes a more cautious, less "gonzo" approach, in the interest of safety, after these incidents.

Despite the failures he had suffered earlier in experimenting with adult pastimes, he deviates from his conservative routine to venture into another forbidden area: drinking alcohol. He must be 21 years of age to purchase or imbibe such beverages in California, and he chafes at this limitation. He is extremely curious about this phenomenon, and thinks that it is certainly a stupid and arbitrary regulation. If he is nearly old enough to go to war and die for his country in the armed forces, shouldn't he also be old enough to drink booze? He manages to overlook the fact that his previous escapades in the forbidden have not turned out well. With sufficient time and distance between himself and his earlier troubles to render the more painful memories a bit hazy, he hatches a plan.

His father enjoys a daily cocktail after work, usually a martini. BP knows where the liquor is kept, and he begins to stealthily take an ounce or so at a time (so that it won't be noticed) from the bottle of gin his father keeps in the kitchen cabinet, stashing it in an old quart canteen he uses for camping. Over several weeks time, he accumulates a little over a pint of the distilled spirits, thus avoiding having to try to make an underage purchase from a store, or some other, more risky, tactic.

He recruits Donny into his little conspiracy, figuring that there is safety in numbers, and together they decide to execute their experiment at the drive-in movies one Friday night. "This'll be fun," insists BP, "and really cool, I think." Donny has no reason to disagree, so he goes along for the ride.

They take BP's panel truck and arrive at the drive-in just as it gets dark and the first movie is about to begin. "I tried it straight, Donny—took a little sip of it one day," BP had explained earlier, "and the stuff tastes like crap by itself, really. We're gonna need to mix it with something." Wasting no time once they are parked, they head up to the concession stand and each buy a large cup of 7-Up. Returning to the car, they drink half of the soda down quickly, then break out the canteen and fill the cups back up with the gin, splitting it evenly between them.

While BP still finds the taste of the mixture a bit vile, he is able to choke it down, gulping it rather hastily, so that it spends the least amount of time on his taste buds, suppressing a gag instinct several times. He finishes the drink in less than fifteen minutes, and begins to feel the effects quickly. At first, it is pleasant enough. He feels happy, even euphoric. He and Donny chatter about the movie, and everything that is happening on the screen seems humorous, even the serious parts.

At one point, though, he finds it hard to make sense of what is playing on the screen. This confusion turns his mood a bit towards the dark and angry side, as he is sure he could have written a better story than whatever this dumb-ass screenwriter had come up with. He begins to have trouble understanding what Donny is saying, as his speech seems to be slurring. His stomach is feeling a little upset, and he decides he needs to stand up and walk around a little. "I've gotta get a little fresh air," he says to Donny.

"Me too," Donny answers. They both get out of the car, and BP finds it is a difficult matter to muster the coordination to walk. Donny is in the same general condition, and they meet at the front of the truck, bracing themselves from falling down by grasping each other's arms. They lurch forward together, stumbling ahead towards the screen, until they find themselves in a sandy area, which BP fails to recognize as the little kiddie playground, a sandbox with a jungle gym and slide in it, that is at the front of the theater, directly under the huge flickering image being projected on the screen.

"Thish looks like...the beach," he says haltingly. "We betta shiddown." They collapse in the sand and lay prone, instead of sitting, as that seems to be the most stable position at this point. Looking up at the giant, distorted images flashing brightly above him makes him dizzy and instantly nauseous. His mouth begins to water and he can feel the bile rising in his stomach. "I think I'm going to puke..." he says, rolling over. Donny isn't even listening, as he is already hurling violently himself. The last thing BP remembers, laying in his own vomit, staring skyward, is a twirling sensation and everything going black, as if he is being flushed down a huge toilet, floating on his back, in some giant monster's deep, dark dungeon. It is the first case of the "black whirlos" that he has ever experienced. [And, unfortunately, won't be his last.]

When he regains consciousness, several hours later, the worst is over Though he feels bleary-eyed and achy, and is still having some problems with making his body do what he asks of it, he is able to sit up and take stock of the situation. Donny is laying to his right, so he crawls over and shakes him awake. "Hey bud, are you OK?"

"I dunno," answers Donny slowly, shrugging off his stupor, "I don't really feel very good. What time is it, anyway?"

BP looks down at his watch and tries to read it, but has some trouble focusing his eyes. "Around midnight, I think." They sit in silence for a moment, looking around, trying to recall how they got where they are. "I think we maybe overdid it a bit with that gin. It was kinda fun for awhile, but then it made me sick."

"We better get back to your truck, Beep."

They navigate their way back to the car unsteadily, and sit for an hour or so inside it, sobering up a little more all the time, rarely talking. Eventually, they realize that they are very dirty and their clothes are smelly. "Cripes, we're a mess, Beep!" Donny finally states the obvious. "We better get cleaned up and get home pretty soon, man, or we'll get in trouble." They stumble up to the restroom and clean up as best they can, using the water out of the faucet in the sink and paper towels out of the dispenser on the wall.

BP is still fairly impaired, but he manages to make the short drive home without hitting anything or being stopped by the police, suffering from a bit of tunnel vision, which requires immense concentration and constant scanning from side to side to control the car properly. He drops Donny off at his house and then sneaks into his own bed without waking his parents, relieved that he doesn't have to deal with any confrontation.

The next day, he showers early and washes his own clothes, so that his mother does not catch a clue from them about what he had been up to the night before. While he suffers no immediate penalty for his actions this time, he senses how wrong the night might have gone, and he is not eager to ever repeat it.

As the summer draws to an end, he takes a week off from work and packs his board along with some camping supplies into the panel truck for a surfari up the coast. He explores the southern stretch of the Pacific Coast Highway, all the way up to Santa Barbara, stopping to check out all the well-known surf spots along the way, from the Wedge in Newport Beach, to the Huntington Beach Pier, to the magnificent point breaks at Malibu and Rincon. While he finds only mediocre surf at many spots this time of year, he is able to see the setups and experience the environments of all the southern California breaks he has heard and read about, and seen in the movies, for so many years. This solo adventure makes him feel very grown-up and capable, more experienced, and ready to face the unknowns in his future.

In the last days before he begins his college career, BP's mother takes him shopping and buys him two suit coats, with matching slacks, shirts and ties, and a pair of wing-tip shoes, so that he can make a good impression in more formal situations. When she has him dressed "to the nines" in the store, she hugs him and tells him how handsome he looks, how proud of him she is. BP wishes his usual summer attire of shorts, T-shirts and sandals would be adequate, but apparently, this is not the case.

His father sits him down one day and unexpectedly presents him with a rare gift—his own, prized, Keuffel and Esser, 10" long, ivory slide rule (or "slipstick"), a finely-crafted and engraved instrument, kept in a well-worn, protective leather carrying case. It is the same instrument he had used for math and engineering calculations since his post-war student days and into his aerospace career. The significance of this gift is not lost on BP, even though it is accompanied by the sort of stern, pithy, lecture his father is capable of giving.

"Son, I want you to have this. We're using the new electronic calculators at work now, so I don't use it anymore, but I believe you will need it for school. From what I've heard, the new electronic gadgets are still too expensive for the average student, so the University does not allow them in class, and a slide rule is still required. You remember how to use it, don't you?"

"Sure, I do, Pop," answers BP, feeling a bit like a young samurai in training, being handed his first, hand-forged, laminated steel blade. "I still have the little short one you gave me way back, when you first showed me how."

"Well, this one is full size and duplex, engraved front and back, with more scales for trig functions, logarithms, square roots and such. It's more accurate, but, of course, you must still keep in mind the order of magnitude of your calculation—it's easy to be off by a factor of 10, or even 100, if you don't estimate the result properly in your head, remember?"

"Thanks, Dad, I do remember that."

Pausing and clearing his throat, Joseph continues, getting to the lecture portion of his presentation, finally: "Bob, I want you to understand how much harder you're going to have to work at college than in high school. Think about this—while you may have been in the 95th percentile of your graduating high school class, only the top ten percent of that class will be moving on to college with you. Your peers, now, will be only those who were in the 90th to 100th percentile, which will raise the bar considerably. If you were in the 95th percentile in high school, you will now be in the 50th percentile in college. If you want to compete, earn good grades and get into graduate school, you're going to have to work much, much harder, because everyone there will be as smart as you are. The class average will not comfort you, anymore. Do you understand what I'm trying to say?"

"Yes, I do."

"Are you going to knuckle down and do what it takes?"

"Yes, I will, Dad."

"And one more thing, Bob," continues his father, quite incongruously. "I know you haven't been dating anyone lately, but you're probably going to be meeting more women, now—more *mature* women, and it may happen that you will once again...umm...err...have sexual relations with one of them. I want you to remember, if this happens, that you *must* use a condom, no exceptions allowed. Ever! Do you hear me?"

"Yes, sir, I hear you," says BP, blushing mightily at this change to a subject which has always seemed like a taboo with his father.

"I should have talked to you about this a long time ago, I'm sure," admits his father, uncomfortably, "but it's not just a matter of birth control, and avoiding another unwanted pregnancy, it's a matter of your health. There are too many venereal diseases floating around out there, and you could pick one up easily, without using some protection. Before you even think about doing it again, I want you to buy some condoms and use them, OK? Promise me!"

"OK, Dad, I will, I promise," says BP, meekly.

"Thank you, son. Using a rubber may not be quite as pleasurable, it's sort of like trying to wash your feet with your socks on, but anything else is just too risky."

College Boy

When he begins attending UCSD on September 25, 1965, BP finds himself one of slightly more than a thousand students at the university. The campus is just newly born, although a portion of it, the Scripps Institution, had been established in La Jolla in 1907, and been accepted as a field station for graduate-level biological research by UC in 1912. The first undergraduate class of less than 200 students had only been admitted the year before, in 1964, with an additional 600 accepted in 1965, augmenting an existing population of some 260 graduate students.

The new campus in San Diego had been established largely through the effort and vision of Roger Revelle, the eminent scientist whose research first called attention to the "greenhouse effect" and "global warming." As director of Scripps Institution of Oceanography (renamed in 1925, due to its emphasis on marine biology) from 1950 until 1964, he initially sought only a cluster of graduate-level science and technology institutes, to expand SIO and gain more autonomy for it, as the Ph.D. programs there were still administered and approved by UCLA at the time. He got much more than he wanted in the bargain.

Beginning back in 1955, Revelle's lobbying and fundraising efforts for the addition of these independent, organized research units at SIO touched off a complex and titanic struggle between the regents of UC, officials from the other UC campuses, the governor and legislature of California, the federal government, as well as the local politicians, business leaders, media powers, and philanthropists in San Diego, culminating in the chartering of a full-fledged UC branch, the granting of some 1,200 acres of city and federal property on the ocean bluffs, just east of the existing SIO campus, and the appropriation of funding for the construction of the first permanent campus buildings.

By the time the fledgling university reached the point of having its first chancellor appointed, in 1961, the tumultuous political infighting and machinations involved in its creation had resulted in Roger Revelle alienating some very powerful people in the conservative, San Diego community (who already suspected him of Communist sympathies, due to his defense of academic freedom and his anti-loyalty oath stance during the McCarthy era). He had also made enemies in the generally anti-Semitic town of La Jolla by hiring Jewish professors at SIO, and helping to provide housing for them in a village which tried to deny the sale of property, or even residency, to anyone other than white Christians. He lost other supporters in a bitter struggle for city land with Jonas Salk, the inventor of the first polio vaccine, who wanted to locate his new institute for biological studies at the same site along Torrey

Pines Road that Revelle coveted for UCSD, and was ultimately forced to share it with the folk-hero physician.

Although Revelle certainly deserved the job, for his magnificent efforts in championing the university, and while the first college established at UCSD was eventually named for him, the UC president, Clark Kerr, for purely political reasons, appointed Herbert York, a young Berkeley physicist and "ex-whiz-kid" of the Manhattan Project, as the first chancellor instead.

York landed in a hornet's nest, however, and presided over the development of the new campus for only three years, recruiting faculty and graduate students, finalizing the land grants from the city and federal authorities, and reshaping Revelle's plan for a cluster of scientific institutes into a broader one of a great, world-class university, based on the Oxford model, with twelve small colleges emerging in a stepped development, over the next 24 years, each with their own Provost and particular specialization, loosely integrated into the larger university structure.

By the time applications for the first undergraduate students were to be solicited in 1963, the politics involved—the lack of executive power, of true authority and autonomy in his position as chancellor—had grown tiresome to York, and he asked to be relieved. Once again, Kerr passed over Roger Revelle in considering York's replacement, appointing John Galbraith, a former history professor from UCLA, to be UCSD's second chancellor in 1964. This was the last straw, the final slap in the face, for Roger Revelle, who promptly resigned and accepted a position at Harvard.

BP is largely unaware of this history, having selected UCSD almost solely for its proximity to his home and good surf. As a freshman at Revelle College, he is totally ignorant of its namesake, assuming, like many colleges, it must have been named for some famous dead guy. The newness of the campus, however, is readily apparent to him, as it is a veritable construction zone when he arrives. Many of the major, high-rise buildings that will comprise the Revelle campus are still not completed, and most administrative activities, as well as some classes, take place in temporary quarters to the east—in the Quonset huts and old, single-story, wood-framed buildings of Camp Matthews, the decommissioned Marine Corps base that was part of the federal land grant to the university. The bookstore, he finds, is located in the old Marine Corps mess hall. The art gallery is in the old bowling alley.

In just one year of existence, the campus had not yet formed any social cohesiveness, or the kind of spirit of identity, or traditions, found at older universities. There were no national fraternities or sororities on the campus, no intercollegiate sports teams, no marching band. What it did have, however, was one of the highest faculty/student ratios in the country, and a very demanding science and math curriculum. The original graduate institute, the School of Science and Engineering, which had attracted 260 post-grad students since

1960, had been merged into the new undergraduate college, along with all of its eighty faculty members, mostly science professors (including two Nobel Laureates and thirteen members of the National Academy of Sciences), so the focus at Revelle was determined by default. While additional faculty had been hired to provide undergraduate instruction in the liberal arts and humanities, of course, there was no denying that the core purpose of the university was still scientific research.

Without any history to constrain it, the school had adopted the new "quarter" system for its calendar, dividing the year into four, ten-week terms, with a break between each one, instead of the traditional semester system. This was intended to allow someone on an accelerated schedule to graduate in only three years, by going to classes year-round. There were not sufficient staff and funding available to maintain the full, year-round schedule, however, so no classes were offered yet during the summer session in 1965.

The Fall quarter begins at a breakneck pace for BP, and ratchets up from there. All the lower-division students are required to take the same rigorous program of math and science classes, plus a specially designed series in the humanities, as well as obtaining proficiency in a foreign language. He begins his college career with enthusiasm and discipline, riding his motorcycle to campus to attend classes on most days, when the weather is nice, wearing a sport coat and slacks under a grubby Army-surplus flight suit, which he peels off on arrival to present a more cosmopolitan, professional and dapper appearance, as his mother wished. Freed from the constraints of his high-school's dress code, which prohibited any facial hair whatsoever, he grows a mustache in an attempt to look more mature and worldly, as well as to hide the trace of a scar which still lingers on his upper lip.

His classmates are composed of mostly nerdy, upwardly-mobile white males, he discovers, with a smattering of women and a very few kids from ethnic minorities. Everyone who has chosen this school purposefully (unlike himself) is generally committed to a serious pursuit of academic excellence and little else. Studying is their major pastime, and they are all very intelligent, as BP's father had predicted. Classes are intense and fast-paced, homework is mountainous, and aside from his part-time gardening work, he can find little time for anything but reading, studying, eating and sleeping. His surfing time suffers horribly under this academic onslaught, but he is determined to succeed in this new arena, and reap the harvest of truth and knowledge which he is sure awaits him.

The curriculum leaps straight into a rigorous exposition of physical science along with the analytic geometry, calculus and differential equations which accompany it. The pace of the math courses is dizzying for BP, even though he had taken advanced algebra in high school, and the humanities course requires reading a major work of some great thinker or another each week. His inexplicable, fairly random choice to learn the German language for his proficiency requirement complicates matters further, as he finds it exceedingly difficult, and spends many hours in the language lab trying to master its strange words and inflections by mimicking recordings of native speakers. There is little time for distractions, and he often gazes longingly at the surf as he rides past the beach at Scripps on his way up the hill to the university. He is only able to grab a few short sessions in the water during the entire ten weeks, usually in sub-optimal conditions on the weekends, when it is most crowded.

He keeps his head down, survives midterms, and then final exams, and is released from his studious slog for Christmas break, just before he turns 18 years old. He manages a grade point average of 2.75 for his first quarter, earning mostly "B" grades, with one "C" in German, a performance which his father seems to find mildly disappointing. "I told you that you would have to work much harder to excel at this level," his father reminds him. BP cannot think of anything more he could have done, other than to give up his gardening work, which he had already cut down to less than ten hours a week by shedding a few customers, and he is reluctant to eliminate this source of income completely.

He is able to surf a bit more over the break, and it feels good to get back into the waves, but the holiday season seems to be a bit strained at home, compared to usual. He senses some tension in his family life that he doesn't understand completely. The joy of the Christmas season seems to be missing, somehow, and he can't quite put his finger on the reason why, but he suspects that it might be his fault.

On his eighteenth birthday, he is required to register with the Selective Service System for possible conscription into the armed forces. It is an event that he has anticipated with some foreboding for quite awhile. Some of the young men he had known in high school, who had not gone on to college, have already been drafted. Many were sent to Vietnam. Some came back whole, some returned missing parts of their bodies or minds, and some came back in bags to be buried, or were never heard from again. He had no desire to serve in the military at this point in his life. When he registers, he applies for status as a conscientious objector, as he had learned from the Quakers that one may do. It is many months before he hears anything from the draft board, but when his card comes in the mail, it shows that he has been assigned the "2-S" status of a student, and not the "1-O" status of an objector.

The most important discovery he makes during this time off is that there is a surf club at UCSD. While surfing at Scripps Pier one morning, he strikes up a conversation with a couple of surfers he recognizes from classes at UCSD. When they get out of the water, they show BP the way to an outdoor shower behind the graduate student lounge at SIO, where they can rinse off the saltwater. Then they open the door to an adjacent storage shed, where they place their surfboards on horizontal racks, beside many others, each with their own lock and chain looped around the tail to secure them. He learns that by joining the surf club, he will be eligible to use the storage locker, and it occurs to him that if he kept a board there, it would make it possible to surf on some days between classes, since he could ride his motorcycle down the hill, go out, ride some waves, shower off, and get back to school in only a few hours time, without having to go home and get his board.

Within a few days, he has been to the Recreation Department, signed up as a member, and is pleased to find that it is free—the cost is included in a small Recreation Fee that is collected as part of his registration at school. Before the beginning of the Winter quarter, he slips his board into its newly assigned slot in the shed.

As 1966 begins, he is back to the grind. The next quarter is a repeat of the first, but with even more intensity. Subjects seem to get more dense and challenging, the workload heavier. BP notices that there are fewer of his classmates around—there is some major attrition as people drop out or transfer to other colleges. An immense amount of information is crammed into his cranium again, in a short period of time, and he is required to regurgitate it on demand, during the testing periods.

The only portion that he finds even halfway enjoyable is a short stint that his math class spends in the computer center. Each student is required to learn the Fortran programming language, and write, debug and execute a simple program on the CDC 6400 mainframe computer housed in Urey Hall. This impressive device is one of only two such computers in existence, sitting in a glass-walled, climate-controlled room on the first floor. This giant, electro-mechanical installation can perform calculations faster than a million medieval monks scratching on their parchment sheets. It fascinates BP, and he relishes typing in commands on its terminals, creating punchcards which will execute his rudimentary program when fed into the machine, and print out his results in moments on a noisy line-printer. Mounted over the front door of the computer room, BP notices, when entering for the first time, is a large, glass-fronted display case containing an oversized replica of a slide rule. A sign hung under it says: "In case of power failure—BREAK GLASS!"

Despite his best efforts (and largely resisting the temptation to bail from campus, run down the hill, grab his board and go surfing), the results of his second quarter in college are slightly worse than the first. His grade point average drops to 2.5, with two "B" grades and two "C's." During the short Spring break, he is sure he perceives a certain discontent in his parents' demeanor, and attributes it to his failure to achieve better grades, which must surely be a disappointment to them.

The first cracks in his ivory tower dreams start to appear in the final quarter of his freshman year. Having progressed through Newtonian mechanics, learning to manipulate the equations for mass, velocity, force, acceleration and momentum that describe mechanical motion, then into classical field theory, learning how forces like gravitation and electromagnetism interact with matter at a distance, they proceed to wave theory, which begins pleasantly enough, but ends in a nightmare.

During ripple tank experiments in a physics lab section, his interest is aroused. It seems to him that this introduction to the scientific formalism of wave theory, explaining the propagation and transmission of waves, including the definitions and relationships of such concepts as the amplitude, frequency and wavelength of oscillations, as well as their reflection, diffraction, refraction and interference, might actually have some relevance to his surfing endeavors in the ocean.

The ripple tank is a simple apparatus—a glass box approximately 36 inches on a side and a foot deep, filled a little less than halfway with water. It allows the students to observe the propagation and progress of waves, generated from different sources, as they interact with the walls of the tank, as well as various barriers placed inside it. He lingers after class one day, setting up his own experiment with an inclined pane of glass at one end of the tank, simulating a beach, and sending tiny, perfect, peeling tubes towards it, generated with a flat paddle that he plunges into the water from the other end of the tank at regular intervals. He changes the angle of the waves to the beach, and even drops a small piece of cork into his imaginary lineup to simulate a surfer, watching its motion as the waves pass underneath it.

What he finds curious is how slowly the cork moves across the tank, until it is finally caught up by one of the miniature breakers and tumbled up onto the simulated shore rapidly at the very end. He plucks up the cork and deposits it offshore again, then begins generating more waves, observing the dynamics of its transport towards the beach once more. When viewed from the side of the tank, the cork bobs up and down on the waves he sends surging towards it, describing concentric circles, almost, displaced only a slight amount towards the shoreline by each cycle. In fact, the drift of the cork seems maddeningly slow to BP, as he waits for it to finally be carried into the miniature impact zone, next to the beach, where the waves are breaking.

Just then, Dr. Lee, the post-doctoral teaching assistant who leads the physics lab, walks by on his way out of the room, so BP accosts him, asking about this phenomenon. Dr. Lee stops and listens, looks at the cork in the tank, and answers quickly, once he understands what it is that BP is questioning. "You must remember, Bob," he says, "It's the wave—the disturbance, the oscillation—that is moving on the horizontal axis, not the water. The water is only the medium. The wave, or pulse of energy, is moving through the water, but the water itself is moving in a little circle, an orbital motion, as the wave passes, with only a very small horizontal displacement. What you see the cork doing is exactly what the individual 'pieces' of water around it are doing. It is drifting slowly along with them, not moving swiftly through the water side-ways, like the pulse of energy that you generated with the paddle is. When the pulse reaches your little beach, there, where the medium becomes shallow, it 'feels' the shore rising underneath it, and it's transformed, or translated, back into energy, as the wave rises, shortens, tumbles and breaks on the shore. There is a different set of equations to describe shallow water waves. When they break, the wave functions collapse—you'd need a bit of chaos theory to describe the situation at that point," he laughs.

"I guess I've always thought of waves as breakers, then, or breakers as waves," admits BP. "I like to surf, you know, and the waves close to shore are the only part that you can ride. I've never even paid much attention to them out in the deeper water. When they rise up and break, it really does feel like it is a wall of water moving forward, and I guess I've always thought of them that way. You can't really *see* the energy moving, you know, it seems like the water moves...."

"Well, in shallow depths, the water is displaced horizontally to a greater degree by the wave," explains Dr. Lee. "When the depth is less than half the wavelength, the circular motion of the water becomes more elliptical, a phe-nomenon that is called 'Stokes drift.' When you're surfing, you are dealing with breaking waves, though, where the amplitude has increased and the wave length decreased—the base can no longer support the top of the wave because it is too steep, it becomes unstable, and collapses. At that point, the simple physical models we've been discussing break down, and are no longer valid."

"Things are always more complicated than they seem, I guess," says BP.

"It's natural for us, as humans, to wish that things were simpler than they really are. It's just more comfortable, easier, but that doesn't change the fact that all phenomena are quite complex, when you try to get to the bottom of them. Just wait until we start looking at electromagnetic radiation—self-prop-agating waves that don't need a medium to exist, which can travel through the vacuum of free space. That's when things *really* get complicated."

Dr. Lee's promise comes true for BP when the class is introduced to the wave-particle duality of light, by means of the "double-slit" experiment, in the next week. All the "sensibleness" of Newtonian mechanics comes crashing down when he finds that light can act as both a particle and a wave at the same time. How a single photon can enter one of two slits and still interfere with itself completely baffles him. The fact that the interference pattern disappears if a detector is added to determine which of the two slits a photon passes through defies all reason, and the rules and expectations of his normal experi-ence. The explanation that the photon is actually a "probability wave," about which nothing can be known between the time it leaves the emitter and the time it is detected, comforts him little. The suggestion that the emitted particle might take every possible path through time and space to arrive at the detector, including passing through both slits at once, seems entirely impossible to him. It rattles him thoroughly that Nature could give two different answers about a phenomenon, depending on how one poses the question.

The unavoidable fact that all matter displays both wave-like and particle-like properties becomes clearer to him, but no less shocking, as they progress through an explanation of the photo-electric effect and begin studying quantum mechanics. His previous notion, inculcated in his lower education—of atoms as the primary building blocks of nature—is exploded with the introduction of sub-atomic theory. His understanding of the nature of science, with its various methods of observation, measurement and experimentation, is forced to evolve in a very uncomfortable way.

He is accustomed to thinking of observations as they happen in the macroscopic world, of noting phenomena according to what he sees, through his eyes, and what he hears, through his ears. He understands now that his eyes can only perceive visible light, which it turns out is only a very small spectrum of the energy that is present in the world, and his ears only hear waves of an audible frequency. The energy that exists at higher and lower levels is basically imperceptible and invisible, which is not to say that it cannot be observed and measured, at least indirectly.

At the level of the very small, such as sub-atomic particles (or probability wave-forms, as he is led to think of them), direct observation is impossible, even with the most powerful microscope. By inducing collisions between these particles in an accelerator, however, physicists have been able to discover and quantify many of their properties, leading to the Standard Model of fundamental particles, which he is taught next, explaining the electromagnetic, weak nuclear, and strong nuclear interactions between them. This model has only recently been developed, and is still undergoing rapid advancement and refinement, as more and more particles are discovered and classified according to their interactions.

The "fly in the ointment," he finds, is the Heisenberg Uncertainty Principle, which states that both the position and the momentum of a particle cannot be determined with certainty. If a particle is determined to exist in a certain region of space, it makes knowing the momentum of the particle uncertain, and conversely, measuring the momentum of a particle precisely makes its position uncertain. The existence of any fundamental particle can only be described as a probability distribution, a wave function that has a statistical "potential" to exist in any particular place, at any given time, with any specific momentum.

When we actually try to observe the position of a particle, usually by bombarding the region with other particles until a collision takes place, so that we can detect the effects of the collision and work backwards to determine where the original particle was, we alter the state of the original particle's momentum in the collision, rendering it uncertain to a degree which is inversely proportional to the accuracy of our position measurement.

This leads to perplexing questions of "superposition," where the subatomic particle can exist in a combination of all possible states until it is observed (to which Schrödinger objects with his famous thought experiment involving a cat in a box). Issues of instantaneous action at a distance, which would exceed the speed of light are raised, as well as questions regarding the observer's effect on the experiment, of his "entanglement" in the very system he is trying to objectively study. He learns that the controversies surrounding these paradoxes of wave-particle duality still continue, and that despite the confirmation of Einstein's theory of gravitation (with the confirmation of the curvature of space-time by Sir Arthur Stanley Eddington's eclipse experiments), no one has been able to reconcile gravity completely with the forces of quantum mechanics yet—though both theories have proven to be so effective that they have led to the construction of the hydrogen bomb and the successful launching of satellites into space, followed by the commitment by NASA to put a man on the moon! The "Grand Unification Theory," to explain all fundamental interactions of nature in a single "Theory of Everything," is an unrealized dream of physicists, he learns, and he wonders if it will ever be achieved.

When BP adds it all up in his head, the overall result is extreme disappointment, along with utter bewilderment. He had always envisioned his college career as the culmination of his education; that is, he had always anticipated that it would bring him complete and certain knowledge of how the world works—that the smartest people in the world would teach him the ultimate truths, the kind of information that would provide him with the sort of perfect wisdom which would enable him to make correct choices in every aspect of his life.

Now, as he bumps up against the current frontiers of scientific knowledge for the first time, and sees the depth and breadth of what is known and what is not, he realizes that even a lifetime of study and contemplation might not bring him to such a point. He suspects that *no one really knows what is absolutely true*—that indeed, there may not be a single "right" answer to every question. Quantum physics suggests that the descriptions that different observers give of the same events are not universal. The actions of bodies at the sub-atomic level contradict many classical concepts which seem incontrovertible in the normal, "macro" world, and he struggles mightily with the implication that our normal waking reality may not be what it appears to be—that objects which appear "solid" may not actually be so, for instance, or that something may be here, and then there, without any interval of time passing, or that the arrow of time might not always fly linearly forward, moment by moment, into the future (a notion that he finds particularly disturbing, for some reason).

His most pressing concern is to figure out where and how the "ultimate" truth might be learned, or if he might just be wasting his time in college. If reductionism won't reveal it, deconstructing matter into its ever-smaller, constituent bits, perhaps he should study cosmology, or astronomy, to learn about the greater universe as a whole? Or maybe the questions he needs answered are basically philosophical, or even religious in nature, and no science will resolve them? What should he study? How much is it possible to actually learn in a lifetime? The possibilities seem both endless and pointless, at the same time, a very discouraging proposition.

For lack of a better idea of how to resolve these questions, he decides to approach Dr. Lee. Of all his teachers, Dr. Lee has always seemed to be the most accessible, and one of the smartest. The already established, very distinguished, full professors who populate the faculty are mostly involved in their organized research units, as well as graduate-level seminars and classes, and rarely offer any direct help to undergraduates. It is the junior faculty, the assistant professors and their TA's, mostly graduate students, who carry the majority of the undergraduate teaching load, and have the most contact with students like himself.

Catching Dr. Lee after class one day towards the end of the year, he tries to glean some direction, asking him directly: "Why did you choose to study physics?"

Dr. Lee seems slightly taken aback by the question and pauses a moment before answering. "Actually, Bob, I never really thought about doing anything else. My father was a physicist, you see, and I was always interested in what he did. I wanted to be like him, I suppose...."

"My father's an engineer," offers BP. "but I'm not sure that I want to follow in his footsteps. There's so much to learn about, and so little time. I can't decide what subject I should choose for a major. I want to know about the big questions, you know—who we are, the nature of the universe, the meaning of life, our purpose in being here. Should I be studying philosophy or psychology instead of science, maybe?"

"I don't know if I can answer that question for you. Different people want different things from their education. My feeling is that everyone should study those things that grab their interest, that instill some passion for knowledge in them. It's easier to do the hard work, I think, when there's a fire and a thirst driving you on. For me, that's physics, but for you, it might be something else, I don't know. I think that when one delves into any subject matter deeply, some insights into those larger metaphysical questions can be gained, but I'm not sure that they can ever be answered completely. People have been asking them since the beginning of recorded history with no perfect consensus. Most physicists believe that they're not really proper scientific questions at all, and ignore them, since they don't lend themselves to empirical and experimental investigation, which are the tools of science. They leave those questions for the philosophers to answer, if they can."

"Isn't that limiting their knowledge, then?" asks BP.

"Not if you define knowledge as that which can be known with certainty," answers Dr. Lee. "Most metaphysical questions deal with ideas which aren't verifiable or testable, though they may seem reasonable, so scientists regard them as moot and pointless, and concentrate on asking the questions that can be proven, one way or another, by evidence."

"But it seems to me that the questions which have already been asked and answered have always revealed another layer of questions underneath each discovery. As we dig deeper and deeper into what constitutes our reality, we can never seem to get to the bottom of it—there's always another layer of complexity to be investigated, requiring ever more elaborate equipment and greater and greater time and expense. We have specialists branching out into each new area and revealing a myriad of other questions to be answered. Will we ever get to the bottom of things this way? Do we need to take a step back and look at the bigger picture somehow, instead? Are we getting lost in ever-increasing dimensions of details?"

"No one ever said it was going to be easy or quick, Bob, but there is no denying the advances that have been made with this method of inquiry over the last several centuries, with practical applications in every aspect of our lives. I don't see an end to it in the foreseeable future, and certainly not in our lifetimes. Advances occur in leaps and bounds, sometimes, and then science plods on for awhile, digesting the new information and expanding upon it, until another breakthrough in understanding occurs. It may be that we're in one of the ebb cycles in this flow right now, historically speaking, but I still find it exciting and promising. There's no telling what new discoveries might be just around the corner."

"OK, I understand, I guess. From what I've learned in my humanities sequence so far, philosophers do tend to disagree about more things than scientists. I just feel like I need to learn more about other areas. It seems like it's all been math and physics this year." BP does not mention that he has found these subjects more baffling than interesting.

"You're just a freshman, Bob," counsels Dr. Lee. "Be patient. You have another whole year of lower division study before you have to choose a major. Next year you'll learn about biology and chemistry, too, and I think you'll find that the math this year prepared you well for that. In your upper division work, you'll be able to take elective courses and learn about other things, and for sure, I encourage you to broaden your horizons. It seems that many of the most important discoveries have been made by people who were fluent in at least two disciplines, and applied insights from one to the other, in ways not previously recognized. Diverse knowledge can lead to a great synthesis, sometimes, but I think you have to be careful of losing your focus. You don't want to become a 'dabbler.' Remember what an old professor of mine once told me, and I have never forgotten: 'The specialist knows more and more, about less and less, until he knows everything about nothing. The generalist knows less and less, about more and more, until he knows nothing about everything. Find a middle path!'"

BLACK'S

It is with the greatest relief that BP completes his final exams and is released from the travails of his first year of college in June of 1966. He has barely mustered the discipline to survive the grind—the regimentation of being in class on time, of completing assignments by the deadlines. When it is over, he rejoices in the three months of freedom the summer break brings.

More than anything, he has missed surfing on a regular basis, and the joy of being back in the water every day is intense and undeniable. Though summer conditions are uninspiring, for the most part, with mainly small, short-period waves generated by local winds, the water is warm, the weather is idyllic, and most importantly, he has the time to surf every day. Unfortunately, the explosion in popularity of the sport, due to its continued cooptation and assimilation into popular culture, has resulted in ever-increasing crowds at the more well-known surfbreaks, along with an ever-dwindling ability on the part of the average surfer, as more and more clueless beginners take up the sport and clog the lineups.

BP avoids this depressing congestion by careful planning, often surfing the "dawn patrols," paddling out just as the sun is rising in the morning, then getting out of the water when the crowds show up later, and by taking advantage of his local knowledge of the more obscure breaks, which escape the attention of the "kooks" and "newbies."

It is impossible to avoid this competition for waves entirely, though, and when a less skilled surfer, with poorer position, tries to drop in on what BP considers to be *his* wave, he begins to be more aggressive in his reactions, as his physical size, strength and surfing abilities have advanced. When attempting to establish wave possession, a surfer involved in a paddle battle for the same wave with someone else will often try to call the other surfer off it audibly—usually yelling out "Got it!" or "Coming down!" or issuing a loud whistle to call off the encroacher, so that the lame excuse of "I didn't see you" won't be applicable. BP develops his own unique warning system. Mimicing the voice of his cartoon namesake, the Roadrunner, he simply bellows out "Beep! Beep!" towards any trespassers, then takes off and barrels down on them like a Mack truck, if they persist.

He hooks up with his friend Donny again, who has graduated from high school, and together they explore the surfbreaks in upper Baja California, which are within an easy day's trip from San Diego, often crossing the border at Tijuana and driving the coastal road down towards Rosarito and Ensenada until they find rideable, uncrowded waves. They plan and execute several more extended surfaris together as well, camping and surfing for days at a time at K-38, K-42, and San Miguel, enjoying the differences they discover in the Mexican culture, the local food (and drinks, since it is legal for them to buy beer in Mexico), and the relative emptiness of the lineups, often sharing good waves with only a few other surfers out in the water.

The real saving grace for him, though, and the site of his most important revelations during this summer, is Black's beach. Due to its relative isolation, surrounded by high cliffs, with no direct access by road other than a single, private driveway winding down a steep canyon from the La Jolla Farms housing development to the beach (which is always secured by a locked gate), Black's is an oasis within the teeming cityscape. To surf at Black's requires a concerted effort—either a long walk, or a long paddle, or a little of both—which discourages the less dedicated and hardy, suiting BP just fine.

An added bonus is that the peculiar bathymetry offshore—several underwater canyons dropping abruptly into very deep water—provides bigger and better waves on most days. When conditions are mired in the usual summer 1'-2' range, Black's will often be 2'-3', due to the deep water offshore stealing less energy from the swell. With the final, abrupt rise of the bottom, the waves jump up and pitch out further when they hit the sandbars, making hollow, tubular conditions more common than at most spots in San Diego.

Whenever possible, BP makes the trek to Black's and reaps the rewards. He usually just rides his motorcycle up to SIO and parks it, grabs his board out of the storage shed, jumps into the water at Scripps Pier and paddles the mile or so north to the break. While it is possible to scramble around the rocky point just north of the pier at low tide and walk the rest of the way on the beach, he enjoys paddling there more, stroking rhythmically on his board, alternating between kneeling and prone positions, breathing fully and evenly, working on his strength and fitness, releasing endorphins in a hormonal process that floods him with a sense of well-being.

When he arrives at the break, there are usually only a few other surfers scattered among the various peaks. In general, having made the extra effort to access this spot, they are all a bit more serious about the sport and more advanced in their waveriding skills than the average surfer, interfering with each other minimally and extracting maximum enjoyment in sharing the waves, even though there are no "locals" enforcing order in the lineup.

He will sometimes pack a few sandwiches in plastic bags, along with some water, put them inside an old rucksack, and strap it to his back for the paddle. This way, he can spend all day surfing there (when he doesn't have to work), taking breaks on the beach to refuel and hydrate at intervals, then paddle back in time for dinner that evening. Although sometimes on sunny, hot days he will wear a long-sleeved T-shirt both in and out of the water, he does little to protect himself from the ravages of the sun's rays, suffering many a sunburn so severe that it blisters and peels his skin in areas, but tans him deeply in the process, bleaching his hair to a lighter, blond shade.

The hours he spends knee-paddling exacerbate the case of surf knots, or "housemaid's knee," he has been developing for years, building up calcium deposits in knobby bumps below his kneecaps and on the top of his feet, which eventually become scraped and abraded from sand stuck in the wax on his board until they bleed and ulcerate. It's a small price to pay, he feels.

The offshore canyons, cliffs and relative insularity of Black's beach provide more than an unimpeded path for waves to break on an uncrowded shoreline. They also offer a haven for wild creatures of the sea and air. BP spends many magical sessions surfing with pods of porpoises that patrol the waters there, enjoying the waves as much as he does. They will charge towards shore in groups of three or four at a time, matching their speed to a swell, swimming within the wave in synchrony, with their blunt bills just inches behind the face as it builds, banking sideways as it develops, and racing the wall down the line until it breaks, when they turn out the back abruptly and leap from the water in spectacular fashion, seeming to celebrate the end of the ride with a flying "kickout." BP hoots and applauds these magnificent aquatic acrobatics and aerial arcs. He also witnesses harbor seals frolicking in the waves as well, and wonders if his surfing might be some sort of a primordial instinct, etched in his soul from some amphibious anscestor.

On some occasions, when huge balls of bait fish are boiling in the lineup, large flocks of pelicans, cormorants and seagulls will be feeding all around him as well, squawking, wheeling and banking in the sky, diving into the water to catch the anchovies in their beaks. At such times, paddling through the sparkling water with all this activity transpiring around him, he can be filled with a sense of peace and joy—of *belonging*, feeling completely within and part of the moment, like an integral piece of the oceanic wilderness. This is his church, now. He has never felt any closer to heaven.

As a result of many summer hours of practice and experience, his surfing takes another leap forward, lifting him from a plateau of development induced by his previous injuries. With its fairly friendly sand bottom, and hollow, but thin-lipped and not fearsomely powerful waves, Black's allows him to overcome his trepidation and continue with his exploration of the tube. He is scrupulously careful about the way he ditches his board while bailing out on a wave at the end of a ride, when it closes out and there is nowhere else to go but down, so he has no further problems with injuries.

Being enveloped in the heart of the breaking wave, with shimmering water surrounding him on all sides, hurtling through a liquid vortex, strikes him as such a peak experience [which he will soon learn to call a "rush"] that it is massively seductive. His senses are always so heightened when locked in the tube, his mind so clear, so purged of mundane details and alert to the sense of *now*, that these few moments seem to last forever, slowing and expanding the passage of time. He wonders idly if there might even be some "quantum relativity effect" of tube-riding, which makes it seem this way.

One day towards the end of summer, he is having an especially good session during a small but consistent 3'–4' south swell, which sends long lines of waves marching through in sets, connecting three peaks in one long wall stretching up and down the beach at Black's. He catches a very fast left from the south peak and rides it in a long way, kicking out as it meets the curl of the middle peak, breaking to the right. Caught inside by the next few waves, he has to grab the nose of his board tightly and dive under each one, pushing through the turbulent soup, before there is enough of a lull to roll back onto his board and paddle back outside.

In between the lines of soup, while he is floating next to his board and catching his breath, with his arm still draped around the nose, he watches a surfer take off from the middle peak on the biggest wave of the set and ride to the right, directly towards him. At first, BP thinks it is a kneeboarder, because his board seems very short, and he is carving up and down on the wave in some very tight arcs, generating a lot of speed down the line, but as he gets closer, it is apparent that the surfer is standing up, although in a tight crouch.

He is flying along faster than anyone BP has ever seen when he pulls into the tube as the wave begins to close out, racing along impossibly fast behind the curtain, matching the speed of the lip as it curls and snakes swiftly sideways, down the line, riding deep in the barrel for an improbably long time, before popping out at the last moment. Then, instead of straightening out towards the beach as the wave dumps over, he turns his board sharply, straight up into the pitching lip, as if to kick out over the back. BP is sure he is too late to pull off such an exit, and is bound to get pitched into the pit, but unexpectedly, he banks off the lip as it throws out, arcing his board to finish a tight, sweeping S-turn, pointing him back towards the beach. The lip, the rider and his board all hurtle down into the trough together, yet he emerges erect in front of the explosion of spray caused by the wave's collapse.

BP loses sight of the surfer as the next wall of soup bears down on him. He must take a deep breath, tighten his grip on the nose of his board and duck under it, but he is dumbstruck by this display of talent. It is like nothing he has ever witnessed, so instead of paddling back out, he decides to take a break on the beach and just watch this guy surf. For the next hour or so, he sits on the beach and takes in a performance that is utterly flabbergasting, and seminal for him in ways he does not even realize.

This surfer rarely rides standing totally upright, never walks the nose and poses, as is the common style—he is almost constantly crouching and in perpetual motion, turning one way or another, up and down, pumping the board for speed and then changing direction, carving tracks on the wave face that baffle BP, and send rooster tails of spray into the air on the tighter arcs. He gets many deep tube rides, making it out of almost all of them, and repeats the "re-entry" maneuver off the lip when the wave sections or closes out several times, landing every one of them in the trough with the lip, bouncing in the turbulence of the soup a bit, but never falling off.

If the wave is only sectioning and not completely closing out, he sometimes even ends up perfectly balanced over his board on the re-entry, with lots of speed to spare, shooting out in front of the soup and leaning over into a powerful bottom turn, to sweep around the section and skirt it, attaining the shoulder again, the unbroken part of the wave that is ten or twenty feet down the line from him, to continue his duel with the lip.

It is a most unusual and powerful exhibition, somewhat manic, and bordering on arrogance in its confidence and power. Rather than trying to blend and flow with the wave, he seems to challenge it at times, asserting his dominance and control in places that BP never would have gone. It is an utterly different way of surfing, clashing with the classical approach in a way that some traditionalists might call ugly, but BP somehow knows that he is seeing the future.

Eventually, the surfer rides a wave to the beach and leaves the water, toweling off just a short distance up the beach from where BP is sitting. "I've gotta check out his board," he says to himself, getting up and walking over to him.

"Man, you were surfing really good out there," he calls out as he approaches. "What's that board you're riding?"

"It's my Zen Flyer," says the young man, flashing a friendly smile as he wipes the last of the saltwater off his face with the towel. "I made it myself."

BP is even more impressed by this piece of information, as he looks at the board lying next to them in the sand, placed carefully upside down to keep the sun from melting the wax, with it's nose propped up on a clump of kelp to keep the sand off the sticky film on its deck. "Can I check it out?" he asks. "My name's Bob, by the way, but my friends call me Beep."

"Sure, man, knock yourself out!" the surfer says, in a very amiable way, sticking out his hand to shake BP's. "I saw you catch a few out there when I first went out—it looked like you knew what you were doing on that longboard of yours. My real name's Adolph, and that's no lie, but my friends just call me Bumper."

When he had first seen him in the water, BP had thought that he might be a very young and precocious kid, but now he can see that Bumper is a mature adult, probably a few years older than himself, but not nearly as tall, with a thin, gangly, but wiry and knotted physique. His skin is deeply tanned, with the same sun-bleached brown hair as BP, though it is lighter, longer, straighter, and bushier than his own, cut in a sort of "page boy" style that covers his ears, framing a handsome face. From a distance, any onlooker might mistake him for BP's younger brother, they are so similar in appearance, except for their relative size.

The board is the most bizarre thing he has ever seen, and during his lengthy examination, it seems to tug at his psyche somehow. It is extremely short, compared to his own board, or any other one on the beach that day, only about 7' in length and very light in weight, he finds, when he picks it up and hefts it, turning it on its side to examine its rocker and the foiling of the rails. "I thought at first you were riding a kneeboard out there," he says, "your board was so short, and you were drawing such tight lines, but then I saw that you didn't have any flippers on, and you were standing up on it."

"Yeah, sometimes I kneeboard," says Bumper. "I've made a few of those too, and still keep a couple of them around for the right conditions, but on a day like this, the Zen Flyer gets the call."

The outline (or plan shape) of the board looks like two ellipses joined together; a stubby, wider one for the nose, joining a longer, more drawn-out one for the tail, which ends in a rounded pin shape. It sports a long but shallow keel fin on its flat, red-tinted bottom. The top is clear, but there is a circle of red pigment towards the nose, with a graceful squiggle bisecting it, which looks familiar. "Is that your logo?" asks BP, indicating the circular symbol.

"Ah-yup, but it's not my design. It's an ancient sign of the Tao, the symbol of Yin and Yang, you know, from Zen teachings. That's why I call it the Zen Flyer."

"Well, you were really flying on it out there, that's for sure. What made you shape it so short?"

"I wanted to be able to surf stand-up like you can on a kneeboard—only different, of course, since you're standing up and not kneeling down. It really isn't that short, at least for my weight, if you compare it to what some of the guys in Australia are riding these days."

"You've been to Australia to surf?"

"Sure, a couple of times. That's one fuckin' surf-crazy nation down there. Did you know that over three-quarters of their population lives on the coast? And a *lot* of them surf—it can be more crowded than here sometimes."

"And they're all really riding boards this short?"

"Well, not *all* of 'em, but a few of 'em are. There're still the old wankers who ride the same old logs as here, but a lot of the hot, younger guys are trying some crazy new stuff. Didya ever hear of a guy named George Greenough?"

"I think so—he's a kneeboarder from Santa Barbara, isn't he?" guesses BP, having read the name in some surf magazine or other, sometime in the past.

"Yeah, that's the guy. He's the one who told me I ought to go down there and check it out. He's been there several times himself, and when the Aussies saw him ride his 5' spoon in rockin' point break waves, they went berserk for it, and started shaping smaller and lighter stand-up boards. I brought home a McTavish V-bottom last year and I've been experimenting with different things. This is probably the eighth board I've built since then. I tried to get some of the shops here to build my designs, but they wouldn't, so I had to do it myself."

"How much does it weigh?"

"About fourteen pounds, I think. It's glassed really light—you don't need the two layers of ten-ounce glass that most people use these days. They just do that for durability, but the extra weight really hinders performance. If you don't care how long the board lasts, one layer of six or eight-ounce is enough, and that's all I use. I just think of the board as more disposable—if I break it, I'll build another one. I'm telling ya, 'Light is Right,' man. You can go so much faster and change direction quicker when there isn't all that extra weight to move around."

"But isn't it a lot harder to paddle fast and catch waves?" wonders BP.

"Yeah, a little bit. You have to take off later and make steeper drops, and you might not catch as many waves as you are used to, but it's totally worth it when you feel the speed and the maneuverability. You can't let it bog down, though, you gotta keep the water moving under it, keep it up on a plane. It takes a different style of surfing, that's all. You wanna try it?"

"I'm not sure I could even stand up on that little thing," BP allows. "It's just a little potato chip! My Ekstrom is 9'10" long."

"Well, it is a little small for your size. You could probably use something a little bigger that'd float you a little better, but you should take it out for awhile anyway, just to get a taste of the speed. I'm going to soak a few rays here for the next hour before I split, so have a go on it!"

BP is a little hesitant, but something in the back of his mind is telling him he shouldn't miss this opportunity. "That's really cool of you, Bumper, but I don't want to hurt it. It seems kinda fragile...."

"No worries, mate! If you break it, I'll build another one. Like I said, they're disposable! Not quite 'use once and throw it away,' like a Kleenex, but by the time it's all dinged up, I'm usually ready to make some design changes anyway. It's only about $30 for me to make another one."

"No shit? That's really cheap! My board cost me $125 last year. OK, in that case, I'll give it a try, if you're not too worried about it."

"Go for it," says Bumper, spreading his towel out on the sand and lying down to sunbathe. "I'll be right here."

BP picks up the board and heads down to the water. Pulling a chunk of paraffin out of the wax pocket of his trunks, he freshens the coating on the deck and then paddles out. He is immediately aware that it is a whole new ball game on this tiny stick. Knee-paddling it is out of the question, of course, and even when paddling on his belly, he can feel how much less stable it is, due to its narrower width. The lack of flotation from the smaller volume of foam is most apparent, as with his weight on it, the entire board is underwater as he paddles, except for the very tip of the nose. It takes him much longer, and many more strokes, to reach the outside lineup, as there is less glide and more drag than with his long board.

When he finally catches a wave, after missing several because he can't seem to paddle fast enough, the board becomes a different animal, though. He remembers what Bumper said about late takeoffs, so he sits a little more inside, and waits for a wave with more steepness to the face before even trying for it. As he finally paddles into one, feeling the tail lift, he leaps to his feet and the board takes off like a rocket as it drops down the face, surprising him totally. He falls right off the back as the board skitters out in front of him so quickly he is unable to anticipate it and adjust his balance.

It takes several tries before he is able to synch his body with the acceleration of the board as it leaps up to speed on the drop, planing on its flat bottom, losing the sluggish, unstable feeling it exhibits while immersed during paddling entirely. With a lot of water rushing under the bottom, lifting it up on a plane, the feeling of the board immediately firms up and becomes more stable. He notices that it is still very sensitive to weight shifts, though, so it is difficult to find the ideal trim position. He widens his stance, spreading his feet further than normal and bending his knees, as he had seen Bumper do, giving up the noble and erect, relaxed stance of the ancient Polynesian wave riders (which he has always held as an ideal), for a more stable, crouching position (which he had previously disdained as a "stink bug" stance only fit for beginners). He finds this compromise is necessary, though, and very effective in keeping his weight centered over the board, so as not to fall off as it squirts rapidly one way or another with the slightest lean of his body. It is obvious that "walking the board" to trim it is unnecessary, as simply leaning forward, or shuffling his feet only slightly, is enough of a weight shift to trim the board for various positions on the wave's face.

In an hour, he has not come close to mastering the board's dynamics, but he has made enough adjustments to see some of its potential, and understand how Bumper was able to make it do the amazing things he had seen earlier. He prones-out on his last wave and rides the soup in to the beach on his stomach. Carrying the board back to where Bumper is laying in the sand, he is convinced that this is a direction he needs to explore.

"I've gotta have one of these things," he blurts out bluntly. "It's really hard to get used to it, but I can see the potential—the speed is fuckin' amazing, and it turns on a dime. Will you build me one?"

"I don't really make 'em to sell, although I've given a few away to my friends when I'm done with 'em, I'm glad you like it, and I'll tell you what—I'll show you how it's done if you want to build one for yourself. You know what they say: 'Give a man a fish, and you feed him for a day, but teach him how to catch a fish, and you feed him for a lifetime,' or something like that," Bumper says, smiling. "I've got a shaping room behind my house up in Del Mar, and all the tools you need, if you want to give it a try."

"That sounds bitchin'," says BP, "I'm up for that! How do we get it together?"

"Well, you can go up to Laguna and buy a blank from Grubby Clark for twenty bucks, but you could also just buy a beat-up, used, long board and cut it down. That might save you a little money, if you can find some crappy old board with a lot of dings for sale for ten bucks or so. It's a little more work to strip off the old glass, and you don't want one with big, wide, redwood stringers in it—that'll add too much weight—but otherwise, it'll work OK. Then, just go to one of the marine suppliers and buy six yards of woven fiberglass cloth—don't let them sell you any chopped-strand mat, you want the woven cloth, in six or eight-ounce weight at most. Pick up a couple quarts of polyester laminating resin and one of finishing resin, too, along with the catalyst. When you get the materials together, just give me a call. You can come on up to my place and I'll show you what to do."

BP cannot believe his good fortune. "Wow, that is really cool of you, Bumper, I really appreciate it! I'll start looking for that stuff tomorrow. What's your phone number?"

"Oh shit! I forgot about that. It's unlisted and I don't have a pen or a piece of paper down here—do you?"

"No, I don't have anything to write with in my pack," says BP, thinking fast to overcome this obstacle. "Just tell me what it is and I'll memorize it. Or just scratch it into the wax on my board, maybe, and I'll write it down when I get home...?"

"Heck, I'm splitting now anyway," suggests Bumper, "so if you just follow me back to my car, I'm sure I've got something to write with in there."

"I didn't drive here today, though—I paddled down from Scripps."

"That's OK, I drove down the road. My car's right up there in the lot," Bumper says, gesturing over his shoulder. "It's right on your way back."

"You drove down the road? Don't they always keep that gate locked?"

"Oh yeah, it's always locked, but I have a key," explains Bumper.

"How'd you get that?"

"A friend of mine lives up in the Farms and he gave me one of his. All the Farms residents get two. C'mon, get your stuff and we'll head up."

BP gathers his board and rucksack and follows his new-found friend up the short path to the small, dirt parking lot at the end of the private Black's beach access road, which is located just above the beach on a low bluff, a little bit south of where they are standing. He is dutifully impressed that Bumper is so well-connected that he has a key to the gate, but when they arrive at the lot, his jaw drops even further when he sees Bumper's car, the only one parked there that afternoon. It is a brand new, candy-apple red, 1966 Chevy El Camino

SS model, with a 396 cubic-inch, V-8 motor, making about 375 horsepower, and a 4-speed Muncie transmission—a lip-smacking, tire-burning, bona fide hotrod dream car. BP had drooled over such a model on the showroom floor when it first came out, and would give his left nut to own one.

Bumper unsnaps the black tonneau cover fastened over the rear bed and slips his board under it, then unlocks the door and reaches into the glovebox, coming out with a small note pad and a pen, scribbling his phone number on a sheet and handing it to BP, who is still staring at the car.

"Man-oh-man, what a cool car! It must be really fast."

"Yeah, it goes pretty good," says Bumper. "I ran a 12.9 with it in the quarter up at Carlsbad last month, and that was with a couple sacks of cement in the back to get a little traction for the rear wheels. Anyway, here's my number, just give me a call when you're ready to roll. I'm going to be around for another month or two before I leave for the Islands, so as long as you get hold of me before then, we can get this done, easy."

"You're going to Hawaii?"

"For sure! I've gone over for the winter season every year since I was 16. Wouldn't miss it—the best waves in the world! You ever been there?"

"Not yet," says BP. "I'm still in school."

"Well, school's good—not for me, but for most people, I guess. But the North Shore...mmmmm...that's surf paradise. You gotta go sometime."

Bumper climbs into the driver's seat, starts the engine, and backs the car around BP in a tight half-circle, facing it up the hill. He waves out the window and shouts over the rumbling engine noise, "See ya soon, brahdda!" He drops the clutch and peels out up the driveway, leaving BP standing in a cloud of dust.

"There seems to be a lot I don't know about this guy," says BP to himself, "but I really like his style."

CRAFTSMANSHIP

Within three days, BP has found an old, yellowed, 10'6" Hobie beater with a single, ½"-thick, balsa wood stringer at a local garage sale for $15, rounded up the necessary resin, catalyst, and fiberglass cloth from Kettenberg Marine, down on Shelter Island, and calls Bumper to make an appointment to shape his new board. He is quite excited about the whole idea of building a new surfboard for himself. It seems right on so many levels—he wants a second board because picking up and dropping off his Ekstrom at SIO is inconvenient at times, and he especially likes the idea of saving about $100 on buying a new one. He has watched shapers making boards in the past, and has always wanted to try it himself but didn't know where to start, so this is a great opportunity. Most importantly, he wants to explore the possibilities revealed by his brief taste of riding a shorter board, and learn to do it proficiently.

True to his word, Bumper invites him to come up the next day, after his morning surf session, and gives him directions to his house in Del Mar. BP loads all the stuff he has collected into his panel truck and drives up the coast about 10:00 A.M. to meet him, following an early surf at Crystal Pier.

He finds Bumper's house fairly easily, located on the mesa just south of Del Mar and inland from the Coast Highway, winding through the last stretch on a dirt road that begins at a large gate. He pulls up in front of an old farmhouse on the edge of the bluffs, overlooking Carmel Valley, with several outbuildings surrounding it, situated on a large, fenced parcel of land, with no other homes in sight.

Bumper is standing out front when he drives up. "Ya found it OK, huh?" he says, as BP parks his truck and gets out.

"Yeah, it was easy. Wow, this is a nice place! I didn't even know it was out here."

"I like it just fine. It's old, but it's comfy, we've got a lot of room out here, and it's private. Lemme show you the shop." He leads BP towards one of the outbuildings, pointing out some other features on the way—the view out Carmel Valley to the ocean, with La Jolla in the distance; an old cactus garden, surrounded by a low fence made of smooth, rounded, river rock; the remains of a small citrus orchard that died long ago.

"This was the old chicken coop," he says, pointing BP towards a low, board-and-batten, flat-roofed shed on the north side of the house, "but I made it into two rooms, one for shaping and one for glassing. No one's worked this farm in 20 years, I don't think. They're just holding onto the property, waiting for housing developments to fill in around here, and then they'll sub-divide it, I bet, but I got it on a long-term lease awhile ago at a really good price."

As they enter the shed, Bumper flips on a couple of wall switches and eight large, double-bulb, 4' fluorescent fixtures hung on the ceiling (and also on the walls, at about waist height) illuminate the small, stark space brightly. Everything is painted white, reflecting the abundant light coming from the fixtures, as well as a row of narrow windows set high on the south wall. BP sees a set of racks with several boards laying in them at one end, a bench and cabinets along the north wall, with a pegboard full of hand tools hanging next to it, and a shaping stand anchored to the floor in the center. Built into one wall is a large, industrial exhaust fan.

"This is the shaping and sanding room," Bumper says, leading him through a door in one corner, down a short hallway, and opening a door into the other end of the building, "and this is the glassing room." It is also brightly lit, but smaller and completely bare, except for another stand in the center of the room, surrounded by a 10' by 12' patch of asphalt roofing felt nailed to the floor. BP notices mounded drippings of multi-colored, hardened resin on top of the tarpaper, in an elliptical shape around the stand. There is another large ventilation fan built into the far wall. "We try to keep the dust from the shaping room out of here with the double doors."

"This is really cool—you're totally set up here!"

"Thanks. Some of my buddies helped me put it together, and I let them use it to build their boards, too. But nobody's working in here now, so let's get you started on your stick."

They return to BP's truck and retrieve the old Hobie and the glassing materials he has bought, carrying them back to the shed. Bumper lays the board flat on the shaping stand, which is essentially a specialized pair of cushioned sawhorses, about 5' apart, with a U-shaped pocket made out of carpet strips in the middle of each one, forming a padded yoke to set a blank down into and hold it on its edge, while working the rails.

"First thing to do is strip this old pig." Bumper goes over to the cabinets and pulls out an electric saber saw, grabs an extension cord off the pegboard, and plugs it in, handing it to BP. "What you wanna do is cut about an inch off the rails, all the way around the board, then use some of those chisels on the pegboard over there to lift the edge of the glass off the foam, and peel it back. Try not to damage the foam too much in the process. Be careful of the edges of the fiberglass—they can be sharp! Use these gloves," he adds, going over to the bench and pulling a pair out of a drawer, "and wear a mask, so you don't breathe any dust that gets in the air. There's a box of them over there. Got it?"

"I think so," answers BP.

"Go for it, then, and I'll be back at the house when you're ready for the next step."

BP puts on one of the particle masks, lines the long saber saw blade up on the board, and starts cutting down one rail from the nose. Bumper watches him get started, sees that he seems to have the right idea, then interrupts him briefly before leaving: "Oh yeah, I forgot to tell you—just cut off the tail in front of the fin. You don't need to wrestle that thing off, it's got a lot of glass holding it on, and you'll have plenty of foam to work with in front of it."

"Got it," says BP, waving a short, two-fingered salute towards him as Bumper steps out the door.

It takes him a little over an hour to strip the yellowed, old fiberglass skin off the foam core, breaking it into pieces as he peels it up, trying not to gouge the soft foam underneath. When he finishes, he gathers the biggest pieces up from the floor by hand and throws them in a garbage can sitting in the corner, then sweeps up the rest of the smaller bits.

Ready for some more direction, he takes off the gloves and mask and heads over to the house to find Bumper. As he knocks on the door of the main house, he can hear loud, bluesy, rock music blaring inside. When the door opens, he is met not by Bumper, but by a gorgeous, young, brown-haired woman. "C'mon in," she says to him. "I'm Eva. Bumper's in the kitchen. We were just making some lunch. Are you hungry?"

"M-mostly just thirsty, I guess," mumbles BP. Beautiful girls still make him nervous.

"We can fix that," Eva says, brightly. "C'mon in! Would you like a beer or a Coke?"

"A Coke would be great." He follows her into the kitchen where Bumper is slicing up a big loaf of french bread. "I've got a clean blank out there now," he announces.

"That's bitchin'!" says Bumper. "We'll attack it after lunch. How about a tuna sandwich?"

"Ummm, sure, I guess so. Thanks!" He goes over to the sink and washes his hands.

Eva brings him a glass with ice and a bottle of Coke, and he sits at the kitchen table. "Hey Griff," Bumper yells out. "Lunch is on!" Ambling into the kitchen from the living room comes a young man dressed only in shorts, with long, black hair growing straight down to his angular and bony shoulders. He is so extraordinarily thin, without an ounce of fat anywhere, that he reminds BP of pictures he has seen of Mahatma Ghandi during his periods of fasting—just skin and bones.

"Griff, this is Beep," says Bumper, nodding in his direction. "Beep, meet Griff. He's one of my roomies. He doesn't surf, but he's a helluva musician, so I let him hang around."

"Hiya, Beep," says Griff, smiling his way, "how's it hanging?" They all sit down and devour their sandwiches, with only a little small talk over the music, which still emanates from the living room.

"Who's that on the stereo?" asks BP in passing, at one point.

"It's John Mayall and the Bluesbreakers," answers Griff, between bites. "They're an English group. I just picked up this album."

"Oh, I haven't heard of them."

"You will," Griff assures him. "They've got a new lead guitarist, a young guy named Eric Clapton. He's an incredible player—a fuckin' genius! They're goin' places, for sure."

"Are you in a band?"

"Yeah, but we're kinda in between gigs right now. It's hard to find work in this town."

They finish their lunch, and Eva offers to clean up. "You boys can just get out of here and go back to your little projects," she says magnanimously. Bumper and BP head back out to the shaping room.

"Griff seems like a cool guy," BP says, on the way. "He's *really* skinny, though!"

"Yeah, he is. What he didn't tell you is that his last gig was almost the U.S. Army! He got drafted a few months ago, and didn't want to go in the service, so he starved himself until he was under the minimum weight for his height. He just went for his physical last week and failed it, so he's started eating again now. He lost about forty pounds, I think, and he wasn't fat when he started! He hasn't always looked like that."

"What about you, Bumper? You said you aren't in school, so don't they want to draft you, too?"

"Oh sure, they already did! I'm '4-F' too—unfit for military service. They think I'm a physical wreck, and that's fine with me," he laughs. "It's a long story, though, maybe I'll tell you some time, but let's get to work on your board for now."

Back in the shaping booth, Bumper pulls out two pieces of thin masonite sheeting, each with smooth, parabolic curves along one edge. He makes some reference measurements on the blank, marking them with a pencil and arranges the templates on one side of the stringer, explaining his methodology to BP as he works. When they are placed just the way he wants them, he traces their outline down one side of the board, then flips them over to the other side, aligning them to his reference marks until they form a mirror image, then traces that outline as well. "Here's your plan shape, now. This is the template I used for my last board, only we've stretched it to 8' to give you some more float. Now, just cut it out with this handsaw—try to stay just outside the pencil line and keep the blade as vertical as you can."

BP dutifully follows his direction, cutting carefully along the lines, all the way around the board. When he is done, Bumper flips the blank over on the rack, bottom side up, and pulls another, longer, less curvaceous piece of masonite out of the rack. "OK, now, this is your rocker template. See how there's more curve for the nose rocker, and then it flattens out towards the tail?" He stands the template up vertically on edge, aligned to the stringer, and points to the spaces between the edge of the template and the surface of the blank. "Your next job is to make the bottom conform to this curve everywhere, front to back." He walks over to the cabinets and pulls out a power plane. "This'll make short work of it!"

Bumper explains the controls of the power plane, plugs it in, and makes a couple of demonstration passes on the blank with it for BP to see. "Use this straightedge across the blank to make sure you aren't getting any humps or hollows anywhere," he says, handing him a yardstick, "and eyeball the bottom often as you go. You just need to take off the high spots until the template lays flat on the board everywhere. Once you get close with the power plane, we'll use this Surform rasp for final smoothing, with this little hand plane for the stringer, and finish up with a flat sandpaper block," he says, pointing out the various other hand tools on the work bench. "Think you got it?"

BP nods and goes to work with the planer. Bumper watches him, stopping him once to show him how to adjust the depth of the blade. "You can always make another pass and take off more material," he warns BP, "but you can't put it back on if you take off too much!"

After about thirty minutes of flying foam bits, interrupted by careful eye-balling and checks with the template and straightedge, the bottom is roughed-in with the plane, and BP moves to the Surform rasp to smooth out the small furrows left by the planer blade, finishing up with a sanding block. The balsa stringer, being denser than the foam, stands a little proud from the surface in several places, and Bumper shows him how to carefully shave it down with the small hand plane.

"Now you're ready to put the Vee in the tail and a little belly in the nose," he explains, "which will help it turn and paddle better." Together, they work the rear 18 inches of the bottom into a shallow, inverted V-shape, with the highest point at the center stringer, where the fin will be attached, sloping outwards towards the rail at a very slight angle, increasing constantly to the very tip of the tail. Turning to the nose of the board, they remove the flatness from the first two feet of the surface, shaping it into a very gentle, rounded arc, like the bottom of a canoe.

When Bumper is satisfied with the contours of the bottom, he flips the board over on the rack. "This is the toughest part. Now you have to taper the deck to meet the bottom, foiling the rails. You can start with the planer again, and dome the deck a little, taper the nose and tail thickness out, keeping the thickest part of the board about where your chest will lay on it when you're paddling, and then just bevel the square edges off the rails, like this." He makes several long passes along the edge of the blank, with the planer held at an angle, walking completely up one side and down the other, altering the angle of the planer slightly with each pass.

"Once you have the volume distributed like you want, then you cut multiple chines or bevels in each rail like that, then smooth the ridges with the Surform, and do the final blending of the deck to the bottom with the sandpaper. Up near the nose, the foil can start kinda egg-shaped, like your longboard, but this is gonna be a 'down-railer,' so as you move towards the tail, the 'apex' of the egg drops down and gets sharper as you work your way back. You want it foiled like an aircraft wing, with a profile like this," he says, drawing an example in the foam with the pencil. "Just try to make the transition smoothly from nose to tail, and be sure you keep both sides symmetrical. Lift the tail of the blank up to your eye level every once in awhile, tilt it back and forth, and use the shadows cast by the lights to show you any lumps or bumps. You can shut off the overhead lights and just use the side lighting sometimes—that might help you spot them."

"I think I got it," says BP.

"OK, I'm gonna head back over to the house again, but gimme a shout if you need me."

For the next several hours, BP struggles through these final steps of shaping the board. Though he understands the concepts, except for the "down-railer" part, which is new to him, and he has watched shapers make the same moves with the same tools before, he begins to appreciate the artful element of sculpture involved in blending all these curves together nicely, to please the eye. He whittles away at the blank fitfully, with a flurry of action on one side and then the other, pausing to study the results at arms length, always discovering a bump or two that must be carved down, or a flaw in the symmetry from side to side that must be corrected. Each time he thinks he is done, he sees something else, and the board gets a bit thinner or a bit shorter each time he corrects it.

Though he doesn't ask for help, he is grateful when Bumper shows back up in the late afternoon and asks how it's going. "Fuckin'-a, you were right, Bumper, this is really hard." says BP, a little exasperated and discouraged. "I thought I had it right a couple of times already, but there's always something else I notice...."

"No worries, mate, it doesn't have to be perfect—this ain't brain surgery. Let's see what you've got." Bumper examines the board carefully, with a more practiced eye, and pronounces it satisfactory. "It's almost there, it just needs a few little finishing touches." Setting the board on its rail into the yoke of the stand, he takes a piece of sandpaper and holds it at each end, wiping it up and down and along the rail like a shoeshine boy working on buffing a boot, sighting carefully in between flurries of strokes, flipping the board over and repeating the process on the other side. "That's plenty good enough, Beep—the water isn't going to know that it's not perfect. Let's clean it off and it'll be ready to glass."

Using a fine-bristled bench brush, Bumper sweeps all the loose foam bits off the surface of the blank and himself, examines it one last time, and then carries it carefully into the glassing room. "Just stay here," he warns BP, "you've got too much foam dust on you, and we try to keep the glassing room clean, ya know."

BP brushes the dust off his clothes and body, then busies himself with sweeping up the thick layer of foam debris on the floor all around the shaping stand.

"I wanted to install a compressor out here," remarks Bumper, when he returns, "so you could use an air gun to blow off the blank and get the dust out of your hair and stuff, but we used up all the electrical capacity on the lights and the fans. I'd have to run another circuit from the house to power it, so we just shined it. Anyway, ya done good on that board, Beep! We can start glassing it tomorrow, if ya want."

"Thanks a lot, Bumper, I never could have done it by myself. It really means a lot to me—I'm very grateful. I'll have this place cleaned up 'Spic and Span' right away, and I'll definitely be back tomorrow to glass it."

"Shit, man, no problem! Let's just get the big stuff into the can and take it out to the dumpster by the barn. This place is just going to get dirty again real soon, anyway. I've got a slogan that I live by: 'You can't beat dirt!' All you can do is just try to stay ahead of it a little, or work your way around the biggest piles of it, if you have to, and not get caught in any landslides, if you can avoid it."

"That's pretty funny, man," laughs BP, "and so true!" Together, they quickly pick up the bigger chunks of foam and sweep up most of the dust on the floor, depositing it all in the trash can, along with the old fiberglass shards. "Where do we dump this?" he asks, as they finish up.

"Follow me," says Bumper. BP picks up the can and trails him out of the shed, over to the big barn sitting to the east. They hoist and empty it together into a tall, green, roll-away dumpster that sits alongside. "The trash service is only out at the paved road, and I don't wanna haul everything out there all the time, so I just rent this from a construction company and have a truck come out every month or so to pick it up and drop off an empty one. It's a lot easier that way...."

As they set the trash can down, through some holes and cracks in the weathered wood siding of the barn, BP catches a flash of bright color out of the corner of his eye. Trying to focus and peer inside through the cracks, a gleaming reflection of the sun's light, as it lowers in the western sky, nearly blinds him for a moment. "What's in the barn, Bumper?" he asks, blinking.

"Oh, just a few of my cars. You wanna check 'em out?"

"Sure! How many cars do you have?"

"I dunno," replies Bumper, shrugging. "10 or 12, I think. I haven't counted them up lately, and not all of them are here...."

They walk over to the big, double doors at the front of the barn and Bumper opens one side. Sunlight floods the interior enough for BP to see that there are at least a half-dozen cars parked inside, all painted in different, bright colors. It had surely been the glint of chrome or glass that had flashed in his eyes. As Bumper flips on the overhead lighting, he discovers that there are exactly six—two parked sideways on each side of the large doors, and two parked parallel down the middle, just inside them. "Holy shit...." BP's eyes widen, as he takes them all in. "Whaddya do with all these?"

"Well, I drive 'em, of course," answers Bumper, laughing. "Not all at once, needless to say, but I use each one on different occasions, for different purposes, you know...like, the Kombi van is good for little overnight beach trips, and the '40 Ford Woodie is cool to drive to surf contests, and the Dodge Powerwagon is great on trips to the desert, or Baja. The Porsche and the Lotus are bitchin' for spirited mountain drives, or carving the canyons, and the '32 Ford roadster is perfect for car shows and races...."

While they are all obviously in excellent condition, the cars are not spit-shined like those of a collector. They all sport a patina of use—some small rock chips in the paint, some dirt on the tires, BP notices. "B-but, how can you afford all this stuff, Bumper? Are you rich or something?"

"I guess so, by some people's standards," allows Bumper, blushing slightly. "I've got enough money not to have to worry about it for the rest of my life, anyway. I was born lucky, I suppose. My parents were pretty well off, and they divorced when I was still young. Some trust funds got set up for me and invested in stuff—stocks, bonds and whatnot. I don't really even know how much money I've got, but it's enough. A financial guy up in Beverly Hills takes care of it for me, and if I need more, I just call him up and he deposits it in my account. I don't go too crazy with it, but I do like cars, and I like to travel around to surf and stuff...."

BP is fairly stunned at the realization that his new friend is independently wealthy, and (unlike himself) will never have to work a day in his life. Having a job and thinking about a career has always been central to his existence, for many years now, severely inculcated by his parents. It is hard for him to imagine being in Bumper's position. What would he do if money was no concern, if he didn't have to earn a living? The idea stymies him, so he immediately discards it, trying to regain his previous train of thought. "Where's the El Camino, though?" he wonders aloud, coming back to his senses.

"Oh, it's over in the garage by the house, with my motorcycles. It's my daily driver right now."

"You sure are full of surprises, Bumper. Motorcycles too?"

"Just a 250cc Bultaco dirt bike and a Harley Davidson chopper—that's all I've got down here right now."

After staring at the quiver of cars for several long moments, speechlessly, BP finally finds his voice again: "Look, I gotta get home for dinner pretty quick—I'd love to check these cars out better sometime, but I'm gonna hit the road right now. I'll see ya tomorrow, OK? Around the same time?" BP is suffering from a bit of sensory overload, and feeling the effects of a long day in the shaping room. The dust from the foam and fiberglass stuck to his skin is making him feel a little uncomfortable and itchy. More than anything, he wants to take a shower and get cleaned up.

"How about after lunch tomorrow? I'm going to surf again in the morning, and then I've got some errands to run, but after 1:00 would work OK," suggests Bumper. "We can't get much more done on the board tomorrow besides glassing one side. It's gotta set up over night before you glass the other side, anyway, then ya hafta wait again to hot-coat and sand it, but we'll have it done in a few days."

"Allright!" says BP. "See ya then." He gets into his panel truck and drives home in a semi-daze, tired and day-dreaming all the way, thinking about having unlimited money and leisure time, imagining what it would be like to be Bumper.

The next day he is back at the farm, though, raring to go. Bumper shows him how to glass the board, starting with the deck. They clean the surface off carefully again, using a shop vacuum, then tape off the lap line on the bottom first, using a double layer of masking tape, trying to lay it exactly 2" in from the rails, all the way around. Flipping it over on the rack, they unfold and drape the glass cloth over the deck, centering it, then trimming the fabric roughly with a pair of stout scissors, so that the edge will fold under the rail and land on the tape, cutting a few darts for relief at the nose and tail.

Mixing the resin and catalyst carefully in a cardboard tub, they let it sit for a moment, putting on some rubber gloves to protect their skin. When they can feel some heat building in the mixture, they pour it down the center of the board in a long puddle and stroke it smoothly out towards the rails with rubber squeegees. The resin soaks through and saturates the cloth, turning it clear from its original opaque, white color, and adhering it to the foam. The resin drips and runs down onto the floor in places when they sweep the excess over the edges with the squeegees, adding to the mounds on the floor, but they try to catch these drips and spread them sideways as they occur, saturating the short margin, or valance, of cloth hanging downward.

When all the excess resin is skimmed off of the top, they use a small, disposable paint brush to dab the remaining resin left in the bottom of the tub over any dry spots around the valance (which are easily spotted, since they have remained white), until all of the cloth is saturated and sticky. Then, working quickly, as they have only about twenty minutes of pot-life to complete this operation before the resin begins to harden, they use the squeegees to wrap the cloth around the rail and up onto the tape on the bottom, forming the lap, cutting the cloth with the scissors and a single-edged razor blade wherever necessary to relieve it and keep it from wrinkling or trapping air pockets as it stretches around the curves of the rail. They finish up just as the resin starts to gel, then clean up their tools with acetone, before retiring to the house for a cold drink.

BP meets Bumper's other two roommates, Skip and Rocky, who had been surfing up at Trestles the day before. This surfbreak is on the far north coast of San Diego county (actually located inside the Camp Pendleton Marine Corps base), just south of the Orange county line, and they hadn't gotten back home until after he'd left. BP has never surfed there before, and listens to their description of the break. It is off-limits to civilians, so dodging the Marines who often patrol the beach and kick the surfers out is part of the drill to surf there. It sounds like it's a combination of surfing with a game of high stakes, hide-and-seek thrown in the mix. If the Marines catch you on the beach, they will confiscate your surfboard, apparently. Skip and Rocky seem like nice guys, and they make him laugh with the story of their trip.

After an hour's break, they return to the glassing room to check the status of the chemical reaction that turns the resin into a hard plastic. It is going off nicely, and they wait until the coating is leather-hard and no longer very sticky, then turn the board over carefully and cut the glass at the lap line on the bottom with a single-edged razor blade, tracing the outer edge of the masking tape carefully, peeling the tape and the excess glass back together, as they work all the way around the rails of the board.

Nothing more can be done that day, so BP heads home and returns the next afternoon, when they repeat the process on the bottom of the board, lapping the glass up over the top in the same manner and trimming it, so that there are two full layers of cloth laminated all around the rails, and a single layer everywhere else. Once again, they leave the board to cure overnight.

The next day, Bumper shows him how to do a "hot-coat" to prepare the board for sanding. The laminating resin, though it is fairly hard now, approaching its final, cured strength, never quite cures completely on its outside surface, where it is exposed to the air, remaining slightly tacky to the touch, and the texture of the cloth weave still shows through the thin coat of resin bonding it to the foam. A coating of finishing resin, with a wax additive that rises to the top and seals the outer surface off from the air, solves this problem and serves to fill the pores of the cloth weave at the same time, rendering a smooth, sandable surface.

"You put more catalyst in the finishing resin to make a hotter batch, and you have to get it all on the board in a hurry, 'cause it'll go off quick," explains Bumper. They prepare the board for this operation by smoothing any drips, ridges or wrinkles left in the lapped glass cloth on the rails, nose and tail with the Surform rasp, and vacuuming the loose bits off the surface. Then they form a short skirt all around the rails, using 2" masking tape, to allow the excess resin to run off the deck and onto the floor, without forming any unwanted runs or drips on the underside.

Before they mix the half-quart batch to fully coat the deck, Bumper mixes a tiny batch of resin in the bottom of a small paper cup and adds some red pigment to it. "First we do the logo. You're on the 'Zen Flyer' team now, after all!" He takes one of the big, empty cardboard resin tubs and places it in the center of the board's deck, towards the nose, and using it for a pattern, applies the pigmented resin with a small brush in a circle, freehand. Lifting the tub off the deck when he completes the circle, he carefully draws the S-squiggle thru its middle, forming the Yin-Yang symbol, filling in one side with the colored resin, leaving a small circle within it clear, and painting a complementary red dot in the corresponding spot on the clear side. "There ya go," he says, as he steps back to admire his work. "We'll wait about fifteen or twenty minutes now, until that batch of pigmented resin goes off, then we'll coat over it all with the clear and the logo will be protected when we sand."

"How'd you pick that symbol out?" asks BP. "I don't really know anything about Zen."

"I saw it when I was surfing in Japan a few years ago, and I really liked it. It's just so symmetrical—unifying complementary shapes in a circle, you know, which is so much like life. I don't know that much about it either, except what my friends over there told me. It comes from ancient Chinese Buddhism and is thousands of years old. It represents the opposites in everything—the male and the female, the earth and the heavens, winter and summer, the good and the bad—there's always a little of each in the other, and nothing's ever all black or all white, ya know what I mean?"

"You've surfed in Japan, too?"

"Oh yeah, they have some big waves during typhoon season. It can get gnarly over there, but most of the time it's pretty small. All in all, I didn't really like it as much as other places. It's really crowded in the cities and everything is so strange, you know—the food, the language—and I always felt so different, like I stuck out and couldn't just blend in anywhere. I'm a lot more comfortable in Hawaii or Australia, where they speak English, at least, and the waves are generally better there too, so I haven't been back to Japan."

"Geez, I've never been anywhere but California and northern Baja, yet. Where else have you gone?"

"Lemme see. You mean to surf, right? Well, I went to South Africa, Morroco, and France a couple years ago on one trip, and got really good waves. And I went to Peru once—that place can get insane! There's a left there called Chicama that just goes on *forever*. Then I've been to mainland Mexico a few times. It can get really good down there on a summer south swell, better than northern Baja, and way warmer. I went to Florida once, too, but I didn't see any good surf. They told me I should head down to Puerto Rico, but I didn't have the time on that trip. I'm gonna go back and explore that place some day, and maybe the rest of the Caribbean...and Indonesia, I definitely want to go there some day. The Aussies told me there's great surf in Bali, and there're thousands of islands all around it with more good spots, waiting to be discovered. I just like to travel, you know—it's a big world out there, and I want to see it all, especially the places with good waves."

By now, the red logo has begun to gel, and they mix a big batch of clear resin for the hot-coat. They pour it on the board when the exothermic reaction begins to build up heat in the mixture, brushing it sparingly and swiftly, just enough to spread it out, covering the whole deck thickly and evenly, and then stand back, letting it flow and level itself. The brush strokes disappear quickly, and the excess resin runs off the deck, down the tape skirt, and drips on the floor for a few minutes, until the resin thickens and gels, freezing some of the drips on the tape in long strands, as they solidify while falling.

In twenty minutes, they pull the tape, and in another ten, the coating is hard enough to flip the board over on the rack and repeat the process on the bottom, overlapping the coatings on the rail by a quarter-inch or so. In another thirty minutes, the bottom has set up, and when they pull the tape, BP is excited by how finished the board is beginning to look. As he lifts it off the stand, he is impressed by how light it is as well. "This is going to work so bitchin', I just know it! I can't wait to try it out."

"You'll be riding it pretty soon, but we need to make the fin next. Have you thought about what kind of fin you want?"

"Uh, nope...not yet..."

"Follow me," says Bumper, walking back over to the shaping room. Pulling a cardboard box out from under the bench, he lifts out some flat pieces of solid fiberglass laminate. "I've got some extra material left over here that I laid up awhile ago. And there are some templates around here somewhere..." He rummages through the cabinets and finally comes up with some pieces of thin cardboard, cut into different shapes.

"I've been messing with these keel fins lately, and they work pretty good in small waves," offers Bumper, displaying one of the templates, "but the tail slides around pretty easily on a steep face. If you're going to ride this board in bigger, hollower waves, I think you should stick with a higher aspect-ratio, deeper fin, maybe like this one." He picks out a longer, skinnier shape and holds it up.

"Looks good to me," says BP, "kinda like a shark's tail. Let's do it."

Bumper traces the outline of the template on one of the sheets of flat fiberglass, clamps it to the bench, and cuts it to shape with the saber saw. "Now you just need to foil the leading and trailing edges, and thin out the tip in a nice taper," he says, pulling an electric angle grinder out of the cabinet with a flat, abrasive disk attached to its rubber wheel. "Put on your mask again, clamp it to the bench and use this for the rough shaping, and then you can finish up with a sanding block. I'm going to take the board outside and wash it off with the hose. That'll take the wax coat off the surfacing resin and make it easier to sand."

"Aye, Aye, Captain!" says BP, giving him another mock salute, but smiling and not resenting his orders in the least. He tackles this next task happily, and finds it is fairly simple. As he tapers the edges of the fin, the various layers of fiberglass show telltale white lines, as their bare glass fibers are exposed from the surrounding resin when material is ground off. This makes it easy for him to see how thin it is getting everywhere, and keep the foiling even on both sides. The grinder cuts through the material quickly, and he must keep a light touch to make sure he doesn't gouge it. The only nuisance is the itchy feeling he gets again on his arms from the ground-up glass fibers that cling to his skin, but it is no worse than when he had stripped the glass off the old longboard, and doesn't bother him that much.

When he has finished shaping the fin, he brushes the dust off himself and takes it back to the glassing room, where Bumper has been preparing the board by sanding the middle of the tail section and wiping it down with acetone. He takes the fin from BP and sets it on the board with the tip of the fin touching the furthest edge of the tail, aligns it with the stringer, and then rocks it up into position. "These seem to work best when they are set forward on the bottom the same distance from the tail as they are tall."

Making two small pencil marks on the stringer at the fore and aft points of the fin's base, where it sits on the board, he removes it, mixes another small batch of laminating resin in a paper cup, paints some of it on the bottom of the fin and the bottom of the board with a small brush, and then plants the fin down firmly, upright, between the marks, sliding it back and forth slightly until it is perfectly aligned with the stringer. "Get the masking tape and run a couple of pieces from the top of the fin to the sides of the board, will ya? I don't want to hold this here until the resin goes off."

BP complies and fashions a little tape tent to brace the fin while Bumper holds it in place. Once it is supported, Bumper takes a small carpenter's square and checks the vertical alignment of the fin, adjusting the tape strapping without moving the base, until he is satisfied with the placement. "OK, that's it for now. Tomorrow, when it's dry, we'll add some fiberglass to the base of the fin to strengthen it, but we don't want to touch it anymore today."

The next morning, they proceed with the final steps to complete the board. Removing the tape on the fin, taking care not to disturb its thin, fragile bond at the bottom, Bumper shows BP how to place short pieces of fiberglass rope around its base and saturate them with more resin, then lay several rectangular pieces of woven cloth on top of that on each side, like little angle brackets, lapping each piece progressively further up the fin and out onto the bottom of the board at the same time, creating a strong fillet joint to reinforce the fin.

Once the resin sets up, they shape the fillet to a pleasing radius with sandpaper, blending the fin into the bottom of the board seamlessly. Then they attack all the other surface imperfections of the board with 80-grit sandpaper, knocking down any high spots and smoothing the surface. They finish up with progressively finer grits, wet-sanding with 220 and 400 at the end, until the entire surface of the board is as smooth as a baby's bottom.

"Most production shops would put a pin strip on it now, to hide the lap lines, and then a gloss coat on top of that, to get rid of the cloudy look of the sanding scratches," explains Bumper. "Then they'd buff and polish it up like a car, with rubbing compound, but I think all that stuff just adds weight to make it look a little prettier. Here's what I use instead." He retrieves a metal can from the corner and shows it to BP. "Plain old 'Mop & Glo' wood floor finish works just fine, and weighs a lot less."

They wash the dust off the board and dry it off, then apply a coat of the acrylic varnish to the bottom of the board and the rails. BP has to admit that it looks pretty good. Although the varnish is thin, and doesn't quite fill the sanding scratches completely, it makes the glass job look more shiny and less cloudy. "You're going to put wax all over the deck anyway, so most of the time I don't even coat the top," says Bumper. "As far as I'm concerned, as soon as this stuff dries, the board is done. 'Light is Right' and 'Functional is Fine,' I always say—we aren't out to win any beauty contests with it."

"Sounds good to me! I can't wait to try it out."

"Well, come on up early tomorrow, and we'll go down to Black's and give it a go," suggests Bumper.

"Dynamite!" says BP.

FLYING HIGH

The next morning they pile into Bumper's VW Kombi van, which he has pulled out of the barn for some exercise. "More room for boards, people, food and drink than the El Camino, anyway," he says. Skip and Rocky accompany them for the session and they strap all four of their boards to the racks on the van's roof, setting out for the drive down the coast highway to Black's.

BP is as excited as a little kid before Christmas about the prospect of trying his new board. It is something that he has crafted with his own hands (and Bumper's help) out of raw materials, into an organic, functional implement, which is more than just the sum of its parts. He is both proud and nervous about what he has created. How will it actually work when he puts it in the water, he wonders?

They have a rollicking good ride down to the beach, with the stereo blasting tunes out of the custom four-speaker sound system Bumper has installed in the van. The fun-loving duo of Skip and Rocky sing along at the top of their lungs from the back seat, even though they don't really know all the words to the various songs. Their random, spontaneous substitutions for the actual lyrics are fairly comical.

They zip along at a fast pace, as the VW van has a Porsche six-cylinder motor and five-speed transaxle transplanted into it, another customization Bumper has applied, overcoming the rather anemic power level of the stock, four-cylinder engine. When they arrive at Black's, unlocking the gate and driving right down to the beach (a definite luxury for BP), it is obvious that conditions are not quite as "primo" as the last time BP had surfed there with Bumper. But there are rideable, if not perfectly shaped waves to be had, so the four young men wax up and hit the water, with BP lingering a little longer on the beach, having to apply the first wax job to his virgin board, which takes quite a bit longer than a freshening.

He watches the first rides taken by Skip and Rocky, and can immediately see that they are fairly skilled riders, like Bumper, already well adapted to the new style of surfing required by the shorter, lighter boards. As he paddles out, he is aware again of the differences in flotation and trim required by the new board, and is thinking about what he must do differently.

These constant internal reminders cause him to struggle a bit when he catches his first few waves. Eventually, as thinking about what to do is replaced by instinctual reactions, through repetition, he begins to get the hang of his new vehicle and snags some fair rides, linking more than one maneuver together before falling off or bogging down and losing the wave. After several hours of practice, he is starting to get the idea, or rather the feeling, mastered a bit, and swoops through two longish rides in a row, climbing and dropping, generating considerable speed down the line, and begins to feel elated. While it has its quirks, the board does actually work! He is able to go faster, turn sharper, and ride different parts of the wave than has ever been possible for him with his longboard, even if it is much harder to paddle and catch waves.

After about three hours, they get out of the water and gather at the van, refueling with the sandwiches and sodas Bumper had stashed in its icebox that morning. They joke with each other, making fun of their biggest wipeouts and worst waves ridden, mercilessly critiquing the surfing of the few other people out with them as well, all of whom were riding much longer boards. BP is the butt of several of their jokes, and takes their good-natured ribbing in stride, without resentment, as he knows that he is on the steep side of a new learning curve, and cannot yet match their proficiency.

Since the usual, afternoon, onshore winds have not started blowing and the surf is still fairly glassy, after a brief rest, they go out for another session. BP continues to adapt to his new equipment, and although the waves are nothing special, he has an excellent time of it—the most enjoyable and inspiring he has had in many years. Despite the difficulties involved in learning new techniques, and suffering from a lower total wave count, he is convinced now that his premonition regarding taking this new direction was correct, and that with further work and practice, his surfing is bound to leap forward into new, unexplored territory. Given suitably juicy, hollow, well-shaped waves, he is positive his new board will facilitate another level of tube-riding that he is anxious (even driven) to experience fully.

When he finally gets out of the water, after another three hours or so, he is totally exhausted and drained. His shoulders ache from the paddling effort, and his arms do not want to do any more than just hang limply at his side. It is all he can do to carry his board up the short path to the parking lot and hoist it up on the van's racks, setting it down carefully, bottom side up, fin forward. He is very glad that he doesn't still have to walk all the way up the hill, or paddle down to Scripps, to get home. He sits down on the low bluff to rest, and is soon joined by Bumper. "So what's the verdict?" he asks, as he sits down next to BP. "How do you like it?"

"It's totally bitchin', Bumper, I am super-stoked!" answers BP, grinning widely. "I still have a long way to go to get used to it, but I don't think I'll even be riding my long board any more, except when it's really small and I need the extra glide. I really had fun on it!"

"Yeah, there are only a few times when a longboard will work better. The shorter board doesn't have the volume and weight to carry speed out on the flats. You need to stay in the steeper part of the wave to keep it going, and cut back more often when it mushes down the line. As much as it will bog in the flats, though, it will squirt in the steeper stuff. Stay closer to the curl and use the soup, even—with less volume, you'll find the soup won't effect the board as much, it won't knock you off as easy. You can bounce off of it, use it like a springboard to get more speed, at least on days like this, when it's not too hollow and thumping. When you have enough speed, you can drop down in front of it and get around sections. You were catching on out there, though. I watched you, I can tell."

"Thanks," says BP. "I watched you too, that day we met down here. I could see how you were riding it. I understand what you mean, totally. I just have to adjust to it—it can be so sensitive on the turns and so fast on acceleration. It's hard to stay on top of it. And it is definitely a lot harder to paddle! I'm beat. But I feel good. I can't wait to try it in some good waves."

Skip and Rocky have also left the surf now, arriving at the parking lot as sunburned and surfed-out as BP and Bumper. "Hey, guys," Bumper announces, as they walk up, "I brought a celebration doobie down for the christening of Beep's new board—ya wanna get high?"

"Oh hell yeah!" Skip and Rocky shout out simultaneously. "Break it out!"

"It's in the pack of Marlboros in the glove box. Bring it on over when you towel off."

BP is a little confused. "A doobie?"

"Sure, man," answers Bumper matter-of-factly, "a joint, you know, a reefer—a big fat one I rolled up this morning, just for you."

"Y-you mean m-m-marijuana?" BP is a little shocked at this development. "I've never done that."

"You what?" Bumper is incredulous. "You've never smoked dope?"

"Nope," admits BP, quietly, not wanting to advertise the fact that he is so inexperienced and unworldly, but not wanting to lie about it either.

"Well, I'm turning you on right now, then. You'll dig it!"

"B-but Bumper, I've got to drive home still, once we get back...."

"No worries, mate, this won't fuck you up like, say, six beers would right now. You'll still be able to drive home."

"I don't think I've ever had more than two beers at once, Bumper. I'm kind of a lightweight, I guess. I tried getting drunk once when I was younger, back in high school, and I didn't really like it. I just spun out and puked."

"This isn't anything like that, Beep! It'll just give you a mild buzz. Ya gotta try it! Trust me. Have I ever steered you wrong, yet?"

"Ah...nope."

"If you feel like you can't drive when we get back to my place, you can just crash on the couch for the night, no problem. But you won't have to—you'll be back to normal in a couple hours. You'll see!"

Skip and Rocky return from the van with the pack of Marlboros and a book of matches. Sitting down next to Bumper and BP on the bluff top, they take out the joint and light it up, inhaling deeply and passing it around. BP watches, thinking rapidly about what he should do, and when it gets to him, he decides—what the hell, how much could it hurt?

He takes the joint and inhales deeply, holding the smoke in his lungs, like he had seen the others do. Handing it back to Bumper, he can feel it expanding in his chest, until he bursts out coughing, suddenly.

"Don't take such a big hit next time, Beep," says Skip, laughing, "there's enough to go around."

"I'm OK," chokes out BP, his eyes watering. By the time the joint gets back to him in the rotation, he has recovered somewhat. Taking a smaller puff this time, he doesn't hold it in as long, resulting in a less furious internal reaction. They continue to pass it around until the joint becomes too small to handle easily, at which time Rocky tears off the cover of the matchbook and rolls it up into a tube, wrapping it around the butt of the joint like a cigarette holder, then puffs on it again and hands it off. "This makes a good roach clip in a pinch."

BP isn't sure exactly what that means, but he does his part and takes another hit off the smoldering little stub, through the end of the cardboard tube rolled around it, and passes it on. They smoke it down to the final scrap, wasting nothing, and sit in silence for awhile, watching the afternoon sun lowering into the sea.

Other than the little bit of irritation left from his coughing fit, BP does not feel any different, at first. Try as he might, he cannot detect the intoxicating effect he had anticipated. Everything seems quite normal to him. He experiences no dizziness, and doesn't feel the kind of nausea rising in his stomach that he had when he experimented with alcohol. He straightens his posture and sits up, breathing fresh air deeply and waiting for the worst, watching the few surfers remaining in the water chase and ride the waves below. Nothing untoward seems to be happening to him at all. After a few minutes, he voices a question that occurs to him: "So, you guys, when does this stuff take effect?"

For some reason, this utterance sends all three of his companions into a rollicking fit of laughter, nearly rolling on the ground. He fails to see the humor, since he had simply asked the question out of curiosity, not cleverness.

"Well, this is just some Mexican dirt-weed," chortles Bumper, when he recovers from his mirth sufficiently to reply. "It's nothing exotic, but I'm already getting buzzed myself, Beep, so I know you're high, too. You probably just haven't noticed it yet. It's really kind of a subtle effect, especially for a first-timer, who doesn't know what to expect."

"This is your first time smoking weed?" asks Rocky, who had not overheard BP's earlier admission. "I thought you were making a joke, being sarcastic!"

"Yeah," says Skip, "I think I said the same thing the first time I smoked dope. Everybody does! That shit was plenty strong, though, and if you aren't buzzed yet, you will be pretty quick. Is your mouth getting a little dry?"

BP is a trifle embarrassed that his secret is out now, but it doesn't seem to matter much at this point. He thinks about Skip's question and examines how he feels once again. "Yeah, my mouth is a little dry, come to think of it."

"Ah-huh, a little 'cottonmouth' is a sure sign. Next, you'll have the full-on munchies."

"That reminds me," interrupts Bumper, "there's a Hershey bar in the 'frig in the van. Let's split it!"

Rocky jumps up, retrieves the chocolate bar and returns quickly, splitting it up equally. They all munch away in unison, enjoying the taste treat. BP realizes that his taste buds do seem to be delighting in the sensations far beyond normal, and that he seems to have recovered rather miraculously from the aches and fatigue he was feeling previously. Or is it that he just isn't worried about them anymore, since he is feeling quite euphoric, warm and fuzzy on the inside, freed from cares? "I think I'm getting it, now—I feel pretty good!"

He also feels like he owes some sort of explanation to his friends, somehow, and launches into a lengthy monologue at this point about how happy he is—how fortunate to have made friends with them all, especially Bumper, who showed him how to make his new board, which works so bitchin', and on and on, in a spontaneous, wandering, stream-of-consciousness discourse.

The other three pass the pack of Marlboros around, and each light a cigarette as he drones on. Eventually, after much tangentiation, when BP finally meanders onto the subject of Bumper's logo on his new board, elaborating how it reminds him of the wave/particle duality of modern physics, with the S-shaped squiggle through the middle being the wave and the two dots on each side representing particles, he is finally interrupted.

"Just listen to yourself, Beep," says Bumper. "This is proof positive that you are higher than a kite right now—you're babbling on like Albert-Fucking-Einstein with this shit!"

BP stops talking in midstream, realizing Bumper is right, that he is making a fool of himself with his rambling speech. All he can say is "Oops!" This makes everyone laugh.

"C'mon, it's getting late, we need to load up and get on back to the hacienda," says Bumper, stubbing out his cigarette and standing up.

As promised, by the time they return to the farm, BP is still feeling a bit high, but not the least bit physically impaired, and he drives back home easily, without incident. On the way, he reflects on what seem to him to be the numerous and quite momentous developments of the day, ones he surely will not forget, ever. Before he drops off to sleep that evening, he repeats the mantra that has occurred to him in the past: "Things are really going to be different, now!" [Truthfully, they have always remained the same as they ever were.]

On His Own

His second year at UCSD does not begin until the first week in October, so BP has several more weeks of vacation to enjoy, even after the official end of summer, before he must start the college grind again. Whenever he isn't working, he spends his free moments surfing and hanging out at the farm with Bumper and his crew. He can't think of any more enjoyable or worthwhile way to pass his time. They surf like madmen, every chance they have, and get high every day.

He bonds with these new friends like no one he has known before. He feels accepted and welcomed into their midst, and is fascinated by the many new things he learns and experiences with them on a daily basis. After "turning him on," his new pals feel somewhat responsible for him, initiating him further into the ways and means of smoking dope, including the politics of stoners and survival in a hostile world.

He learns how to clean the seeds and stems from the weed and roll his own joints, and how to build a makeshift pipe in a pinch, if no cigarette papers are on hand, out of a toilet paper roll or a hollowed-out potato, with a pinholed piece of tin foil for a bowl. They are always willing to share a toke with anyone they trust, but they remind him that possession of even a single joint is a felony offense, and urge him to be very cautious. "Let the wrong people know who you are, and they'll eat you!" Bumper tells BP. (This is one of the corollaries to his 'You Can't Beat Dirt' philosophy.) "If you smoke dope, you are an outlaw to many people, especially the cops. If you're going to be an outlaw, it's best to only break one law at a time, so be careful! Try not to be caught holding any more dope than you can eat. Don't take your whole stash out in public, just roll up a joint and take that. If you get in a hassle, you can eat one joint, but you can't eat a whole bag of weed. If you're going to make a buy or something, and you are holding a quantity, don't jaywalk, or if you're driving, don't run any stop signs or have a tail light out in your car, or anything trivial like that. That'll just give the cops an excuse to pull you over. If you do get stopped by the cops, never agree to let them search your car."

Surfing is one of the most unifying forces for BP's new crew of friends, and even more so due to their early adoption of shortboards. There are very few surfers who have accepted this new paradigm yet, and there is a certain undercurrent of discontent whenever they show up in the lineup. The cruising era of slow turns, stalling, noseriding and posing on longboards has not yet passed away for most surfers, although an Australian, Nat "the Animal" Young, is about to put the lid on its coffin at the end of this month. Riding a shorter, lighter board and carving the waves mercilessly (opening many eyes in the process), Nat defeats the king of noseriding, David Nuuhiwa, along with all the other highly competitive members of the mighty Windansea Surf Club, at the 1966 World Surfing Championships held at the Ocean Beach jetty. BP and Bumper drive the fifteen miles south to attend the contest and watch the slaughter. They agree that it would have been even worse if Nat had lopped another foot off his board and really cut loose.

The differences in style and technique between the shortboard and longboard surfers is enough to cause consternation and friction between the 'old guard' and 'new-wave' riders when they occupy the same peak and compete for the same waves. The longboarders can catch the wave sooner, when it is less steep, and feel that they have established priority, or wave possession, in the act of standing up. The shortboarders have a slightly divergent concept of priority, based more on positioning—that being deeper in the peak, closer to the curl, in the steeper part of the breaking wave, has more to do with wave possession than merely being first to your feet.

This difference in opinion gives rise to a new surfing concept, that of being "rat-holed," where a longboarder takes off early on the shoulder of a peak, while a shortboarder takes off deeper, but later, and quickly catches up to the other rider from behind—like a rat coming out of his hole, according to the longboarder. The shortboarder, however, having performed a more difficult take-off, in a more critical position on the wave, feels "snaked" if the longboarder does not yield to his deeper positioning, pull out and give him the rest of the wave.

Along with the radically different lines and speed produced by the two different types of boards, this new notion of wave priority is a source of conflict between the two groups, and BP and his friends are still very much in the minority. Surfing at uncrowded breaks is their first preference, but surfing together, as a group, reduces the chance of any angry confrontations in the surf at the more popular spots, as there is safety in numbers. Both Skip and Rocky are quite large and robust fellows, a bit older, rougher, and more streetwise than BP, with a fondness for brawling that he doesn't share, but he is happy that they have his back, if push comes to shove. Bumper, though the smallest in stature of the four of them, is a long-time student of the martial arts, and could easily surprise a larger foe in any hand-to-hand combat. And God help anyone who might want to escalate any violence beyond fisticuffs, as BP learns one day, when Bumper shows him his collection of weapons stored in a large, locked, metal cabinet at the farm—everything from samurai swords to firearms of every description!

When the surf is bad or non-existent, BP spends some time riding his motorcycle with Bumper in the back country, hill-climbing and scrambling on the trails, but the favorite, non-surfing summer pastime for all the boys, by far, is "trolling for tuna" together. "Tuna" is their private, cryptic synonym for members of the opposite sex, and they apply it without malice or fore-thought, to both individual specimens or to groups ("schools of tuna") that they encounter in their travels. [The sexist connotation of naming women after a game fish that is routinely caught and consumed along the coast largely escapes them, naive as they are, at this point in their lives, as to how women might actually wish to be considered, or treated.]

The most populous beaches, during the midday heat, are the most productive spots for observing wild tuna in its most delicious state, stripped down to a bikini and seared by the sun. They spend hours cruising La Jolla Shores and the boardwalks at Pacific and Mission beaches, which are a veritable cornucopia of skin and suntan oil. They observe and catalog every feature of every specimen extant, with Rocky and Skip often approaching the most appealing with a lame line or two, hoping to snag one, perhaps score a phone number or a date. Bumper and BP prefer to troll without actually baiting the hook or even casting a line into the water, since Bumper is in a relationship with Eva, at the moment, and BP is deathly afraid of what might happen if he actually caught something.

Bumper is full of all sorts of interesting information and stories, which BP finds fascinating, and he seems to have more friends than could be humanly possible, given his young age. There is an incredibly diverse bunch of people showing up at the farm to visit all the time—not just surfers, but artists, musicians, intellectuals, tradesmen, and students, including a dazzling array of young, healthy, attractive women. Every weekend at the farm seems like a party to BP, whether declared or informal, with Bumper enjoying the company immensely, displaying a generous and easy hospitality, seemingly truly interested in everyone with whom he interacts.

BP admires this natural sociability, and wishes he was not so shy and reserved himself. Bumper is the sort of person who sets off sparks when he walks in a room. BP asks him where he got his nickname and Bumper answers: "One of my friends said to me once: 'No matter what the situation, man, you just seem to bump it up a notch. You're just a mad "Bumper."' Pretty soon, all my friends were calling me that, and it stuck."

Eventually, with a few joints to loosen him up, BP begins to feel a little more comfortable at these larger gatherings on the weekend, but it is when he is hanging out with just Bumper and his roomies that he really begins to open up and share details of his life, his thoughts and dreams, his fears and aspirations, in an honest and trusting way, as their friendship deepens.

They have many discussions on a wide range of subjects, sometimes sober but most of the time fueled by a pleasant marijuana intoxication. BP learns much about their lives, and sincerely shares the reality of his own as fully, truthfully, and humbly, as possible.

He finds out that Skipper, whose real name is Warren (which he detests), came from a military family, had served in the Coast Guard for four years after graduating from high school in Oceanside, and is working as a waiter in a ritzy restaurant at night, while attending a few classes at a community college by day.

Rocky had grown up in Los Angeles as an orphan, and been shuffled between several foster homes, landing finally in Santa Monica, where he learned to surf. He had joined the National Guard after high school to avoid being drafted and sent to Vietnam, and was still serving about a month in military training every year, while also working as a bartender and bouncer at a local nightclub.

Griff is a talented guitarist and vocalist, a slightly taciturn type with a decidedly spiritual bent—a listener and a seeker, who tries to write a song out of every experience. He is the most inscrutable of the group, and seems to enjoy shocking people with his appearance and loud, raucous music, as well as interjecting an occasional *bonmot* like "Bizarre is beautiful!" into conversations. At one point, BP asks him why he wears his hair so long, and Griff answers: "Our creator gave us hair, but didn't give us scissors—we invented those."

Bumper, the de facto ringleader and benefactor of the group, had been born to the dissolute heir of an old-money, San Francisco fortune, whom his mother had divorced, marrying a famous Hollywood movie star when he was five years old. Privately schooled, he had grown up in the fast lane in Los Angeles, and tested out of high school through the GED to become an emancipated minor when he was sixteen. They all four become his close friends in an amazingly short period of time, and BP begins to care for them enough to overlook any of their perceived shortcomings.

It is the last weekend in September when Bumper takes him aside and asks him if he would like to move in with them at the farm. "Griff is moving up to L.A. next week to play with his new band, and there's going to be a free bedroom that you could have. You would fit right in here. I know you're still living at home to save money, but it would be cheap enough. Skip and Rocky just pay me $30 a month to cover the rent and utilities, and we all chip in together for food, so you could do the same. It's almost as close to your school from here as it is from P.B., so it wouldn't cost you any more in gas. Whaddya say?"

Since he is already living there, for all intents and purposes, except for sleeping, such an arrangement would suit him perfectly, BP decides, and quickly agrees. "I'd love that Bumper. I've been thinking about it a lot, and I really need to get out on my own, anyway. That would be perfect, to live here with you guys."

"Cool! You can move in next Saturday, then. And Beep, you know, in November I'll be heading to the Islands for two months, and while I'm gone, it would be great if you could sorta act as the landlord here for me. Skip and Rocky are great guys and all, but you've probably noticed that responsibility isn't exactly their strong suit. I need someone I can count on to get the rent money to the real estate office each month while I'm gone, and pay the utility bills on time. It's not that much trouble, you just have to be organized and disciplined enough to remember to do it. I feel like you're more that kind of person, you know, running your own gardening business and going to school and whatnot. You're really smart and you're used to dealing with deadlines. I know you could handle it fine. I'll show you what needs to be done on the first of the month, and while I'm gone, you don't need to pay anything to live here, I'll forgive your portion of the rent. Does that sound OK to you?"

"It sure does, Bumper!" BP is excited over this sweet icing being added to the cake. "Thanks for trusting me so much. I won't let you down, don't worry. I can handle it."

His biggest immediate concern becomes how to introduce his parents to the idea that he is leaving home. He worries that they will resist or forbid it, but when he finally musters up the courage to break the news to them at dinner a few days later, they seem to be resigned to the concept of him moving out, or even expecting it, and give him their blessing. "You're 18 and an adult now, Bobby, and it's probably time that you learned to live on your own."

It is a simple matter for him to pack all his worldly possessions into his panel truck (leaving the tools for his gardening work in the garage, since most of his customers are in his parent's neighborhood or nearby) and move his whole act up to the farm. The next day, after surfing together at Law Street in the morning, Bumper drops him off at his parent's house to pick up his motorcycle, which he rides north to complete his relocation.

Before leaving P.B., though, he stops by Donny's house to let him know he is moving, give him his new address and phone number in Del Mar, and invite him up to see the place sometime soon. Though he hasn't seen him much in the last month or so, Donny is the only person he will really miss from his old neighborhood, besides his parents, and he wants to keep in touch and maintain their friendship. He is excited to be entering a new, independent phase of his life, and feels very grown up, but it also scares him a little to be casting off so many of his roots to the past.

He falls into his new routine at the farm easily, adding new life skills as necessary. He learns to shop for food and cook a bit, things his mother has always done for him, and to do his own laundry. He makes an effort to help out with housekeeping and maintenance chores around the place, sharing the load of mundane responsibilities and pulling his own weight. At one point, a week or so later, when they are rolling up yet another doobie from their seemingly endless supply of weed, it occurs to him that he has never contributed anything to the group on this front. "Hey, you guys," he exclaims, "I really ought to buy some of this stuff sometime, instead of you always breaking out your stashes to turn me on!"

"You wanna buy some dope for us, Beep?" asks Rocky, grinning.

"Well, sure," answers BP, "or rather, I wanna buy some for myself, so I can share it with you guys, instead of you just sharing yours with me all the time. It's only fair...."

"That's right sportin' of ya, man. I can probably help ya out with that. Let me call my man down in Mission Beach and see what we can do."

The next day, BP huddles briefly with Rocky, who has arranged the deal for him. "My man, Jerry, wanted me to come myself, but I told him you were cool, and way too young to be a cop, so he's OK with it now. He's not a real talkative guy, but he'll help you out."

BP heads down that afternoon to the address on San Jose Court that Rocky gives him, with the $40 in his pocket that he was told would be required. He knocks on the back door of the house, in the alley, at the appointed time, as instructed. A burly, dark-haired man, badly in need of a shave, his barrel chest showing through the front of a tattered, unbuttoned, Levi jacket, with the sleeves cut off, answers the door, checking BP out slowly, from head to toe. "I'm Bob," he says to the man, a bit nervously. "Rocky sent me."

The man sticks his head out the doorway briefly, looking up and down the alley, then steps back into the house, motioning with his head, opening the door wider. "C'mon in, then," he says. "I'm Jerry."

BP steps inside to find himself in a narrow kitchen area, barely wide enough for two people to stand side-by-side. There is a counter, with a sink and cupboards to the left, and a stove and refrigerator to the right, separated by more countertop. As Jerry retreats a few steps to let him in, he notices a big, horseshoe-shaped, white patch on the back of his denim vest, with "HELL'S ANGELS—SAN DIEGO" embroidered on it in large, red letters.

"You got the dough?" asks Jerry, curtly.

"Sure," answers Beep, pulling two $20 bills out of his pocket. "Right here."

Jerry takes the money from BP's outstretched hand, and wasting no time, opens the refrigerator door, takes out a brown, paper grocery bag, and hands it to him. "Here ya go, then. Have a blast, and say 'Hi' to Rocky for me."

BP takes the bag, can't think of anything else to say, so tosses out a "Thanks a lot, man!" as he heads back out the door quickly. He walks back to his truck and climbs in, shoving the bag under the seat, and drives back to Del Mar carefully, obeying all the traffic laws and watching his mirrors closely.

It isn't until he arrives safely back at the farm that he even opens the bag to see what is there. Parking his truck, he pulls the grocery bag out from under the seat. Inside is a large, rectangular brick, wrapped tightly in several layers of blue cellophane. Folding the top of the bag back up, he carries it inside the house, where Skip and Rocky greet him. "Allright! You're back. Did you score OK?" Rocky asks.

"Yeah, I think so," answers BP. "I haven't even looked at it close yet, though, it's all wrapped up."

"Well, let's dig into it, then, and see what you got," says Rocky, heading into the kitchen for a few implements, returning in a few moments with some newspaper and a box of plastic bags. "Jerry's usually got some good shit!"

"He seemed like a nice enough guy," says BP. "He told me to say 'Hi' to you, Rocky. Hey, what does the "Hell's Angels" mean that he had on his vest?"

"Oh, that's just the motorcycle club he belongs to," explains Rocky, spreading several sheets of the newspaper out on the floor. "Those guys all ride Harleys and like to raise a little hell here and there." Taking the brick from BP, he unwraps the cellophane to reveal some butcher paper underneath, which he strips off as well, uncovering a greenish-brown core of tightly packed vegetable matter, which he begins to break apart over the newspaper. "Wow, this is really dense. They really pressed this kilo hard, but that makes it good on the weight, I can tell—there must be close to three pounds here."

As Rocky breaks the brick up bit by bit, it seems to grow bigger in volume all the time, reminding BP of a batch of popcorn expanding in the pan as the kernels explode. He takes a pinch or two of the loose stuff and puts it into a cardboard shoebox top, handing it to Skip, who cleans it and rolls a huge bomber of a joint. "The proof is in the toking," Skip says, lighting it up and passing it around.

As they smoke the joint, they continue to crumble and fluff up the brick together until they have a huge pile of weed sitting in front of them, and a nice buzz in their heads. "This is some good shit," Rocky intones finally, "and you definitely did not get shorted on the quantity. Jerry came through again."

"I thought $40 was kind of a lot of money," says BP, "but I didn't realize it was going to be so much weed!"

"Well, Jerry only sells by the kilo or more, and a kilo is supposed to be 2.2 pounds, but when they're pressing the bricks, I don't think anyone is really weighing them up every time. Better to be heavy than light, anyway, it makes for happier customers."

"But what am I going to do with all this?" asks BP in dismay.

"Well, smoke it, of course!" laughs Skip. "And if you can't smoke it all, then you can always sell some of it. I'll buy a $10 lid of it from you right now, Beep, if you want, I could use some more for my stash."

That sounds like a good idea, so BP picks up one of the quart-sized Ziplock bags that Rocky had brought out from the kitchen and stuffs it almost full, handing it to Skip. "Here ya go, then!"

"Wow, Beep, that's about a quarter of a pound, man. A lid is usually only an ounce or so!"

"Hey, what are friends for?" says BP, stuffing up another bag full. "How about you, Rocky?"

"Sure, man, that's the most righteous $10 bag I've ever seen. I'm down for that! And I can help you sell a few more lids to some of my friends if you want."

"So can I," chimes in Skip.

They pack up the rest of the pile of weed, stuffing another four ounces or so into a big bag for Bumper (who is out with Eva at the moment, but will definitely want to buy it when he gets home, Skip and Rocky assure him). They divide the balance up into smaller, but still generous, increments of well over an ounce per bag. Within a few days, Rocky and Skip have each sold several of them for him, and BP has doubled his $40 investment, while still having nearly two pounds of weed left in twenty more bags. Without even straining his brain, it is obvious to him that there is some considerable profit to be made in this commodity.

In the second week of October, BP begins his sophomore year at UCSD, and classes are just as difficult and fast-paced as before, while the campus has become more crowded and busy. Though only half of his original classmates remain, over a thousand more new admits and transfer students take their place. He tries hard to apply himself to his schoolwork, but finds it increasingly difficult to muster the discipline to study hard, for a number of reasons that seem to accumulate and compound as time goes on.

He manages to arrange his class schedule so that he only needs to be on campus on Monday, Wednesday and Friday, leaving Tuesday and Thursday free to work, surf, or party, though he should really spend them all studying, if he truly wants to earn good grades.

One Tuesday morning towards the end of the month, he drives down to Pacific Beach to take care of some of his gardening work. Pulling up to the garage at his parent's house, he is loading the mower and tools into his panel truck when his mother comes out, looking a little pale and nervous. "Bobby," she says, "I want to talk to you for a moment. Will you come inside, please?" Without looking at him directly, or waiting for a reply, she turns around and walks back into the house. BP is puzzled and taken aback, but he obeys her request, following her through the door and finding her sitting on the sofa in the living room, looking quite sad, eyes downcast.

"Is something wrong, Mom?" he asks, moving across the room to sit beside her on the couch.

"Son," his mother begins, looking up into his face, finally, "I've been struggling with the way to tell you this, but I didn't want to just phone you about it. You're here now, so I want to tell you in person. Your father and I have separated. He's taken an apartment downtown, and he isn't living here with me any more."

BP is aghast. After sitting in shock for a moment at this news, he blurts out the first thing that comes to his mind. "Is it because of me, Mom? Is it something I did? Does he think I'm a failure or something?"

"Bobby, this isn't about you at all," his mother tries to assure him. "It's only about us, just your father and me. We haven't been getting along for quite awhile now. For many years. More than you know. You've seen that we haven't always agreed on a lot of things, but we hid a lot of our deeper disagreements from you. This has been building up for a long time, but nothing about it is your fault. We both still love you very much! If anything, you kept us together. I think we tried harder to remain a family than we should have, possibly, so that we could give you a good home, and a head start in life. I think now that you've grown up and are out on your own, your father has decided that it's time to let it go—to give up trying to be something we're not. We just can't be together any more, for our own sakes."

BP does not know what to say. This is an entirely unforeseen development that he can't quite get his arms around completely. He just sits in stunned silence for quite awhile, mouth agape.

"Let me give you your Dad's new address and phone number," his mother continues, getting up from the couch stiffly and awkwardly. "You might need it. He said he wanted to talk to you after I did, so you should probably give him a call."

"Does this mean you're getting divorced?" he asks, as his mother hands him a slip of paper she has retrieved from her purse.

"Not just yet, Bobby, we've just separated for now. I don't know what exactly will happen in the future, though."

BP takes the slip of paper from his mom and gives her a big hug, fighting back tears from his eyes. "Everything's going to be OK, Bobby," she tells him. "Things are just going to be a little different, now, that's all."

He leaves without saying anything more, and attends to his gardening, finishing his chores in a fog, mowing and edging two lawns and trimming some hedges automatically, with a dazed sense of dread hanging about him. Another blazing stunner of a surprise has swooped in from left field and smacked him on the head, without him ever seeing it coming. "What's next?" he wonders.

Getting back into his truck when he's finished the last job, he heads for the beach, intending to park at some overlook and smoke the joint he had rolled up as a reward for after work. He decides instead to make a run past Donny's house to see if he's home, feeling the need to talk to someone. It's been quite awhile since he's seen or talked to his friend.

Donny is out in his driveway alone, shooting a basketball at the hoop mounted on the garage roof, when BP drives up. He parks in the street and waves him over to the car. "Ya wanna go for a surf check?" he asks, as Donny runs up to the passenger-side window.

"Sure, man, let's go." Donny answers, throwing his ball in the back of the truck and hopping in. They drive west towards P.B. Point.

"I just found out my parents are getting divorced," he tells Donny, without wasting any words.

"Oh jeez, that's tough, Beep," says Donny, sympathetically. "It happens to a lot of folks, though, from what I've seen." They continue driving in silence to the foot of Archer Street, pulling up into an empty dirt lot on the bluff overlooking the ocean and parking. From here, they can check out four different surf breaks, from South Bird Rock to the Point, without leaving the car.

"Well, there's nothing I can do about it," sighs BP, leaning back in his seat, "that's for sure. What have you been up to lately?"

"I signed up for some classes at the junior college, Beep, but I don't really like it all that much. We started five or six weeks ago, and I'm pretty bored. It seems just like high school, only with cigarettes allowed."

This mention of smoking reminds BP of the joint he has stuffed in his windbreaker. He wonders briefly how to broach the subject with his friend, but decides the direct approach might be the best tack. "Hey Donny, have you ever smoked any marijuana?"

"Ummm, why do you ask, Beep?" Donny fidgets a bit.

"Well, I've got this joint here," says BP, pulling it out of his pocket, "and I was going to smoke it, and I wondered if maybe you wanted some, too?"

Donny relaxes and grins broadly. "For sure, man, light it up!"

"So you've done it before, I guess? I was hoping maybe I was going to be the one to turn you on to it."

"Yeah, I've smoked it quite a few times already at parties and stuff, but I didn't know how you would take it if I told you. I didn't want you to think I was a fool, or something, for doing it. The Barzo brothers turned me on to it a few months ago. You know those guys—what a wild couple of muthas they are! I kinda dig the shit, how 'bout you?"

"I think it's bitchin'," says BP, smiling and firing up the joint. "The guys I'm living with now are totally into it. I've been getting high every day."

They smoke the whole joint together and check the surf, jabbering away all the while, catching up with each other's lives, dredging up old memories, feeling close again over their many shared experiences, no longer separated by concealing the secret of their drug use from each other. BP is relieved from his recently depressed mood. The pall of doom that had encircled him since the morning lifts.

An hour later, when Beep is dropping him off back at his house, Donny thanks him. "That was some good smoke, man."

BP has a mild inspiration. "Would you like some more of it for yourself? I've got a bunch at home."

"Well, hell yeah, Beep! I know plenty of people who would like to get their hands on some good shit like that."

"What the fuck, then," says BP, "I think I can help you out! Are you going to be home Thursday? I'll bring you some in the morning if you want."

"I'll be around, for sure!"

When he gets back home, he screws up his courage and phones his dad to tell him that he has heard the news from mom about their split. They have kind of a stilted conversation, talking around the issue, as men tend to do, and BP is a little shaken by his father's pronouncements about his financial situation. "We're maintaining two households now, Bob, and I have to pay rent on this apartment besides the mortgage on the house," his father tells him. "Don't worry, I'm still going to pay your college fees, like I promised. I'll send you $75 every quarter to take care of your tuition. If you can make the rest of the money you need to pay for your books, rent and food costs, that would really help out at this point."

"No problem, Dad," says BP. "I can handle that."

On Thursday, as promised, BP brings five bags of weed down to Donny, and tells him he can keep two if he can sell the other three for $10 each. By the end of the next weekend, Donny is calling him asking for more. He delivers five more to him the next Tuesday, picks up the $30, and in another week, they are doing it again. In no time, he is running out of weed, turning it into $200 along the way, so he sets up another buy with Rocky, and spends $80 on two more kilos from Jerry.

By the time Bumper leaves for Hawaii in mid-November, BP is feeling pretty flush. He has about $500 in dope money stashed away already, as well as his savings from his gardening work, enough for him to live for the rest of the school year, especially since he is not going to have to pay rent for a couple months while acting as Bumper's surrogate landlord on the farm. He is also still sitting on a bunch more of the herb to smoke and sell off in lids over the next month or two.

With his newfound cash flow, he makes the decision to give up his gardening work, as it is unnecessary and time consuming. He tells his customers that he is quitting the business to devote more time to college, and that they will have to find someone else to take care of their yards. This is a bit of a fib, because he doesn't actually use much of the time he saves by quitting his job on his schoolwork.

After receiving some last-minute coaching and written instructions from Bumper about his new duties in maintaining the homestead, he gives him a ride to the airport to catch a plane for Hawaii about a week before the Thanksgiving holiday. Bumper is traveling alone, and on the way, BP wonders aloud why Eva isn't going with him. "Well, you might have noticed she hasn't been around much for the past week or so," explains Bumper. "We had a little disagreement about exactly where our relationship was heading, you might say."

"I wish I was going with you, Bumper," says BP, with a tinge of longing.

"It would be awesome to be paddling into some warm water waves in a tropical paradise tomorrow. If I were you, I don't think I would ever even come back!"

"Well, you don't know the whole story about the place, Beep," says Bumper, "but I'm sure you'll figure it out for yourself eventually, when you get a chance to go over there. Sure it's warm and tropical, the waves and weather are outasight, but I'll definitely be back here by the end of January. It's a great place to visit, but I really couldn't live there for too long. After awhile, you realize you're just on a tiny rock out there in the middle of the ocean, and you can drive all the way around it in a day. And being a *haole* boy can make for some tense situations. There's a lot of racial problems and hatred going on under the surface, all the time, that people don't really talk about very much."

"Whaddya mean, Bumper? I didn't know that."

"Well, how would you feel if you were a native Hawaiian, and these white, European guys sailed up and snaked your whole kingdom out from under you over a couple hundred years, and they ended up owning everything and you were left with next to nothing?"

"I guess I'd be pretty pissed off," allows BP.

"That's exactly the situation," declares Bumper. "There are some pretty pissed-off natives over there these days. The last things they feel like they still own are the beaches and the waves, and they don't want to give them up without a fight. Let's just say that if a big Hawaiian guy gets in your face and asks 'You like beef, brah?'—he's not inviting you over for dinner to share a nice pot roast with his family."

Seeds of Radicalization

The next two months at the farm are a bit more sedate, without Bumper's presence to instigate weekly parties and attract the usual influx of visitors. BP tries to concentrate on his college classes, but the lure of surfing is strong. He very much wants to master the intricacies of riding his new shortboard, and that requires more time in the water, especially when there is a significant swell running that can offer challenging conditions. Small, gutless waves, which are the prevailing circumstances 80% of the time in southern California, are a waste for him, other than providing exercise opportunities and a few meditational moments away from the brain-racing thrash of academia.

The problem for him, as it is for all dedicated surfers, is that the ocean does not offer up its gems on a regular schedule. The 20% of the time that sizeable, exciting waves are available comes in spurts, at infrequent intervals, and must be grabbed when available, or missed. The swells do not conform to anyone's timetable or commitments, such as class schedules, or a steady job. This is why both Rocky and Skip work at night, to have their days free to chase the waves when they come, and BP envies them this freedom.

Even though he must spend only three days a week on campus now, he sometimes finds himself cutting classes if there is a swell running, with good waves begging to be ridden. His obsession with tube-riding continues unabated—heightened, even, by the possibilities his new equipment offers to seize more of those scarce, sublime moments spent enveloped in a barreling wave. He is driven to pursue them, to make them happen more often.

These rare and brief peak experiences of being tubed seem more enticing, more intense, and more satisfying to him than anything else—better than food, drink, sex, money or power, the common motivators of humanity. Although these fleeting, exciting instants seem to stretch and elongate in duration while being experienced, they remain somewhat dreamlike in his mind after they happen—foggy and unavailable for total recall, partially incomplete, mysterious and incongruous, somehow. However vague these memories are, they seem to offer some veiled answer that he seeks, to a question he cannot even fully articulate, held just beyond his grasp—a carrot on a stick, dangling in front of his face, beckoning him urgently onward towards further exploration and discovery.

Though he knows he must dedicate himself to his studies in order to succeed in college, his disillusionment with the ability of his science and mathematics education to offer him the kind of overarching wisdom for which he longs continues to grow, rendering his efforts in that direction increasingly irrelevant.

His introduction to molecular biology reinforces the same doubts he had experienced with physics. UCSD is on the cutting edge of this subject as well, including on its faculty Dr. Francis Crick, one of the Nobel Prize winners who had delineated the double-helical structure of the DNA molecule in 1953. But as he learns about this monumental scientific breakthrough, and the subsequent revolution in biological research, it only reveals to him the immense complexity of natural organisms, and of genetics, when pursued to the molecular level. Though it has undoubtedly opened many paths for scientists to investigate and confirm theories of evolution, heredity, disease mechanisms and prevention, which are already leading to practical applications in the fields of medicine and agriculture that will benefit humanity, the cracking of the genetic code reminds BP of the same, gigantic, bottomless Pandora's box that had been opened by sub-atomic physicists.

The moral and ethical dilemmas posed by genetic engineering are as critical and serious as those engendered in the development of nuclear weapons in his eyes. Even disregarding those, however, the main question raised in his mind when exposed to the scale and depth of the processes involved (including tens of thousands of genes and a possible three billion base pair combinations in the 46 chromosomes of the human genome) is how will anyone ever sort this all out? And even if they do succeed in solving the molecular genetic code, without uncovering another baffling layer of underlying complexity in their reduction (as had happened so often in physics), what exactly will any of it tell us, ultimately, about where we come from, who we are, why we are here, and how we are supposed to live? Very little, he suspects.

The rapid growth of the campus has made it a more interesting place to be in many ways, though, and some of his discouragement is tempered by the increasing social and political aspects of his education. The Revelle campus buildings are largely completed now, grouped around a central plaza, and the construction crews have moved on to the north and east, where the second campus, Muir College, and the School of Medicine are being built. The student body has grown to the point where there is a virtual flood of humanity pouring into Revelle Plaza at fifty minutes past each hour, as students end one class and start another at the top of the hour. Groups of people congregate in the plaza between classes and lounge around on the benches, grass, and low rock walls that bound the landscaping. There is a sense of community in the student body that was not there the year before for him.

On the days he is on campus, he begins to hang out in the plaza as well. People gather there and talk. Sometimes a student activist or two will make a speech on the steps, gathering a small crowd to listen to sometimes brilliant, sometimes banal, oratory—usually protesting U.S. involvement in the war in Vietnam, or the injustice in civil rights in America, or rehashing the issues of the Free Speech Movement which had begun at Berkeley the year before, generally condemning the University's involvement in the war machine, or its failure to serve the underrepresented poor and minority populations. Often there will be at least one person who has brought a guitar and is playing music, while more than a few folks assemble in small groups on the fringes and smoke dope unabashedly, but semi-furtively, he discovers. The unmistakable smell of burning herb, which he couldn't even have identified earlier, often wafts through the air and attracts his attention. This serves as an entrée for him into peer group interactions with which he would not have been comfortable previously.

He makes a habit of rolling a big joint every morning before heading to campus, and on his breaks from class, usually seeks out someone with whom to share it. He makes many new acquaintances this way, and has some stimulating conversations in the aftermath, meeting many very bright, very articulate, very curious, and very fun-loving people.

The members of this fast-growing subculture of the university community, into which he slowly integrates himself, consist of those who are becoming widely known as the "hippie" movement [which will culminate and, some say, die during the upcoming "Summer of Love" in San Francisco]. They are a free-thinking and highly individualistic bunch of people, beginning to establish their own unique style on campus. It is a loosely affiliated, diverse, open and welcoming group, with an insatiable appetite for marijuana, it seems. He happens to be in an advantageous position to satisfy this need, and gains an instant status of credibility by supplying small quantities of weed to many new, appreciative customers.

By the time the end of the first quarter arrives, just before the Christmas break in 1966, BP finds himself ill-prepared for his final exams. His extracurricular activities have limited his class and study time in such a way that he is hopelessly behind the curve, on the verge of failing some courses. A last minute, stop-gap reprieve comes to him from an unexpected source—his old buddy Donny.

While surfing together on one of his infrequent trips to P.B., the week before finals begin, he mentions his dilemma to Donny, admitting how much he has slacked in his studies lately, and his fear of the upcoming tests. "No problem, Beep," Donny assures him, "all you need is some speed!"

"Some what?"

"Some speed, some amphetamines, you know—some 'uppers,' like bennies or dexies. They'll fix you right up! You can stay up all day and all night and study, read all the books you need to in a few days, or whatever."

"Do they really work? How do they make you feel? They won't fuck me up too bad, will they?"

"Oh yeah, they work bitchin'," claims Donny. "If you don't take too many of them, they don't screw you up too much. They just make you really alert and help you concentrate when you wanna fall asleep. As long as you don't keep taking 'em for too long, they're pretty safe—hell, they sell them over the counter down in TJ, and truckers all over the country take them to stay awake on long hauls and stuff. I heard they even gave them to pilots in the Air Force in WWII, when they had to make long flights. I've got a bottle of them at home that I traded some weed for, if you want some."

Thus begins BP's next experiment in drug use. By taking some of the small, pinkish-orange pills containing 20 milligrams of pure methedrine that Donny supplies him (in exchange for another small bag of weed), he is able to cram a month's worth of studying into the next week. While he loses quite a bit of sleep, does not eat well, and ends up feeling like a pile of hammered dog shit by the end of the binge, he succeeds in passing all his tests by the skin of his teeth. His retention of the information crammed into his brain while under the influence is poor, though. Deciding that this is an emergency tactic only, he vows to stay ahead of the academic game during the next quarter. He finds the initial rush of the meth, the surge of energy it seems to send through his body, quite enjoyable, however, and doesn't discount its occasional recreational use in the future.

This is the first Christmas holiday that he has not spent at home, and although he visits his mother on Christmas Eve, it is too sad of an experience for him to linger. She is obviously feeling alone and abandoned in a way that hurts him deeply, though she tries to show a stiff upper lip, talking about her plans to stay busy by possibly returning to school and completing her teaching credential—perhaps looking for a job in the public school system, afterwards.

He cannot help but feel some resentment towards his father over this situation, which is only reinforced when he visits his apartment for the first time, a little after the New Year holiday, to pick up his tuition check, and discovers his father is not living alone there, as he had imagined. He has taken up housekeeping with a young woman only slightly more than half his age, whom BP recognizes, from prior visits to his father's office, as his secretary! This dreadful revelation makes him extremely uncomfortable, and leads to a growing alienation from his father that will last for many years. He instantly realizes that his mother's hopes for any reconciliation of their marriage are likely futile, and that their relationship is almost certainly headed for divorce in the near future. He does not know if she is aware of his father's new companion yet, but he is certain that he will not be the one to mention it to her if she isn't.

The only upside for him of this shocking discovery is the realization that his fears over being the cause of his parent's breakup are probably unfounded. In all likelihood, he reasons, there must indeed have been other longstanding issues at work between them, as his mother had claimed, possibly partly sexual in nature (which he finds difficult to contemplate or visualize), as his father's rapid flight into another intimate relationship would seem to indicate. He realizes that nothing he can do now will have much, if any, effect on their marriage, but that he must forge ahead and make his own place in the world, whatever that may be, using the attributes, resources and tools they have given him. It is a watershed moment for him in the march towards independence and adulthood.

He plunges back into his schoolwork during the first part of January, but his determination and focus fade again rather quickly. Bumper returns from Hawaii towards the end of the month, with stories of huge, hollow waves breaking in warm, blue water, and the partying at the farm begins again with a vengeance. He also brings back some new ideas on surfboard design, which initiates another flurry of activity in the shaping shed. Nothing draws BP's attention quite as much as the few chunks of dark brown, Afghani hashish Bumper brings home, though.

BP has never seen hashish before. He is curious about it, and asks Bumper what it is, exactly, and how it is made. Bumper explains that it is just processed and concentrated marijuana, with a higher THC, or cannabinol, content than the leafy weed. There are many different types of hash that he has smoked, from light tan, soft and crumbly stuff from Morocco, to this darker and harder type from Afghanistan. He has never seen it done, but has heard that it is made by rubbing the oily, flowering buds of the plant in your hands, then scraping the gummy deposits of resin and pollen off your skin and pressing it into blocks or plates. He has also heard of other methods that involve sifting or sieving the buds, or even running through the fields of mature plants wearing leather aprons, to collect it.

They sprinkle a small amount of the hash onto a pinch of marijuana, rolling it up and smoking it. The hash turns the milder weed into the strongest dope that BP has ever tasted to this point. Only a few hits on this tiny "pinner" of a joint are enough to send him flying, higher than he has ever been.

Motivated to learn a little more about this practice into which he has fallen, BP researches cannabis at the university library. He finds that evidence of it and its derivatives date back to pre-history, and that there are known traditions of its cultivation and use as an entheogenic drug as long ago as 1500 B.C. in Hindu culture. References to its use in spiritual and religious contexts appear in the histories of pagan, Christian, Jewish, Muslim, Sufi and Sikh rituals as well, and continue to this day in the Rastafari movement which emerged in Jamaica in the 1930s, he finds.

Considering this, he wonders what has brought about the prohibition and condemnation of this herb in the twentieth century, so he investigates this question as well. Hemp had been legal in the U.S. until the early 1900s, he finds, when it appeared that a wave of immigrants from Mexico, induced by the revolution there in 1910, brought its recreational use into the public eye. Somehow, marijuana was lumped together with narcotic drugs and prohibited entirely in the mid-1930s, even though the prohibition against alcohol instituted in 1920 was repealed in 1933. As near as he can determine, propaganda by the newly created Federal Bureau of Narcotics, as well as lobbying by the paper, chemical and cotton producing interests, including industrial titans like DuPont, Mellon and Hearst, who saw hemp as a competing interest, were more responsible for its prohibition than any actual societal damage or harm it had caused, which had never been documented. Despite the LaGuardia Commission report of 1944, which carefully refuted prior governmental claims that marijuana led to addiction, criminality, overt sexual behavior and insanity, mandatory sentencing and increased punishment for what were largely victimless crimes were enacted in the early '50s.

The irrationality of the nation's drug policies ultimately produces only doubt and distrust of authority in his mind. If an innocuous and non-debilitating drug like marijuana can be banned, and its recreational use severely punished for dubious reasons, while a more harmful substance like alcohol is freely used and openly manufactured, sold and promoted by commercial interests, what other governmental policies might be equally misguided?

His research leads BP to begin to doubt governmental integrity, question its authority, and not accept the major media pronouncements and propaganda as gospel in a number of different areas as well. Thus, a floodgate of possible disinformation, mistaken policies, hidden agendas and outright corruption is opened. BP is determined to think for himself, and independently investigate the other pressing social and political issues of the day, examining them more thoroughly, through his own research and reasoning, without jumping to conclusions or accepting the commonly held beliefs and opinions, which seem to be tacitly accepted by an easily manipulated majority. This work is time consuming, but eventually begins to seem to him to be more relevant to his life than his formal classroom studies.

The most polarizing issue in American society at this time, beside the civil rights movement, is the U.S. involvement in the Vietnam War, which has been escalating at a frightening rate over the last few years. Voices of protest are being raised all across the country, and the college campuses have become a focal point for youth activism against the war. Though BP knows quite a bit about the struggle for civil rights, through his earlier involvement with the Quakers, whose "Peace Testimony" had also aligned them against the Vietnam War, his knowledge of the history and justification of this conflict is less well developed, though he knows in a visceral way that he wants no part of it.

When he looks carefully into the underpinnings of the military actions taken by his country against the small nation of North Vietnam, on the other side of the world, it is difficult to find any reasons that make sense to him. It is not actually a declared war, in fact, but is called a "police action" by officials instead—a politically-motivated military intervention in the civil war of another country, which does not itself represent any direct threat to America. The justification for this, he finds, is based in the cold war with the USSR which had built up after WWII—the struggle between Communism and democracy that has resulted in the nuclear arms race, with ICBM missiles pointed from east to west and vice versa, assuring mutual annihilation if an all-out, "hot" war ever broke out.

The prevailing "Domino Theory" of U.S. foreign policy contends that it is in our national interest to resist Communist expansion in Southeast Asia in order to contain it and avoid its spread throughout the region and beyond—to prevent the "Red Hordes" from ultimately engulfing Hawaii and invading the western United States. The official reasoning seems to be that since the North Vietnamese have turned to the Chinese Communists (and by extension, the Russians) for support in their struggle with the South Vietnamese government, it is vital for America to oppose them, and fight a proxy war against the Communists, in order to avoid having to fight it on American soil down the line.

American military involvement began under President Kennedy, who was essentially continuing the foreign policy of President Eisenhower, and faced increasing pressure in his term due to the partitioning of Berlin, with its infamous Wall, and the Cuban revolution, which represented a Communist incursion into the western hemisphere, only 90 miles from the Florida coast. After the failure of the Bay of Pigs invasion to topple the Castro regime, Kennedy felt that U.S. power and prestige were at stake, and committed military aid and "advisers" to the fight, as much to help the South Vietnamese government as to maintain U.S. credibility in the eyes of our allies.

The problem, however, was that the South Vietnamese government was ineffective and corrupt, lacking in popular support, and no amount of aid and "advice" seemed to help them in their struggle with the North. Chaos, corruption and coups were the overriding characteristics of their government, with regime changes the only constant. Kennedy may have finally seen that there was no military solution to what was a political power struggle between the insurgency and the puppet government propped up by the U.S., but he was assassinated before he could find a way out.

Vietnam was not a large priority for Lyndon Johnson when he took over as President. It represented a distraction from his dream of a "Great Society" and he wanted it wrapped up. Since the South Vietnamese seemed incapable of defeating the guerillas on their own, he seized on two reported attacks on U.S. warships in the Gulf of Tonkin by North Vietnamese torpedo boats, in August of 1964, as provocation to launch retaliatory air strikes against their bases.

These two incidents were played up in the press far beyond their importance, it seems to BP, and there were lingering questions about the nature of the attacks (even whether or not the second one had ever actually happened). Nevertheless, Congress reacted quickly, in patriotic fashion, and passed a joint resolution in a matter of days, giving President Johnson the power to conduct military operations in the area without a formal declaration of war.

Consulting with his military commanders and the National Security Agency, Johnson's administration devised a plan for the Communists, as expressed by Chief of the Air Force, Curtis LeMay, "to bomb them back into the Stone Age." A massive bombing campaign was undertaken to destroy the infrastructure and defenses of North Vietnam in March of 1965. Ground troops were committed to protect U.S. air bases there also, which the South Vietnamese army had proved incapable of doing, quickly reaching a level of 200,000 soldiers, as well as many other civilian specialists and contractors, by the end of 1965. General Westmoreland had promised victory then in a year, or 18 months at the most.

Here we are, nearly two years later, still stuck in a quagmire over there, BP observes, with no end in sight. The resistance by the insurgency, despite the application of all our country's military might, has not abated. If anything, it has intensified. American and South Vietnamese soldiers are under attack and dying in all parts of the country, and an astounding amount of our country's resources are being expended daily to support this undeclared war. Either our leaders have been incredibly arrogant, unforgivably stupid, or downright deceptive, he concludes.

The Johnson administration had initially enjoyed public support for their mission, by playing on the fears of citizens regarding the "Communist hordes," but BP cannot imagine any scenario where a foreign invader could successfully occupy American soil. If the tables were turned, and America was the invaded rather than the invader, wouldn't the resulting insurgency by American citizens be even more fierce and effective than that of the Vietnamese people? We are, after all, just as proud and independent a people, probably more belligerent by nature than most, and considerably more well-armed and better equipped!

As far as "protecting our interests" goes, he wonders exactly what these interests might be? Who is profiting from this massive military effort, other than the corporate suppliers of the war machine? How is our stature in the world community increased by being the aggressor against a tiny nation, propping up a failed democracy, which has devolved into a corrupt military dictatorship?

Worst of all, what are the moral implications of our actions? We have abandoned the high ground implicit in our reputed Christian ideals of love and compassion for others with our unmitigated aggression. Rather than "turn the other cheek," we have struck the first blow! What worthy end result do we have in mind to justify the terrible means we have employed?

Try as he might, he can see no credible justification for the war, and he is certain there will be no successful outcome from it. In discussing the issue with his friends, acquaintances and teachers, in many conversations and dialogues, he learns nothing else that changes his mind.

What he should do about his conclusions is a different story, though. Taking part in anti-war protests is a possibility, he decides, but he is not sure how effective this will be. His will just be one more of a rising chorus of voices being ignored by the government, but it is worth a try, he supposes. On a personal level, he determines that he will never allow himself to contribute to the military-industrial complex that is waging this war in any way—certainly not as a soldier, to be sent into combat, or even, if he can help it, through any vocation or career that would contribute to this destruction in any way.

He makes the decision to stop cutting his hair and shaving his beard, as a token display of his separation from the mainstream of society, which allows this travesty to continue. His hippie friends call it "letting your freak flag fly." His conservative style of dress has long since been abandoned, as dry-cleaning sportcoats and slacks (without his mother to take care of that chore) is an expensive hassle for someone living on a budget, who can barely manage getting a load of laundry done once a week. He is more comfortable in Levis or shorts and a T-shirt, anyway, and tennis shoes or sandals suit him better than wingtips.

On the home front, he finds Bumper's evolution of the Zen Flyer design after his trip to Hawaii intriguing. The finished product is shorter, narrower, thinner, and more streamlined than before, with an even sharper edge to the down-turned rails in the tail. He decides he must follow suit to see where it might take him, so he builds a similar new board for himself in his scant spare time. He spends the money to buy a new blank for this iteration though, saving him the time and effort of cutting down and stripping the glass off an old longboard. When it is finished, he is pleased with the result—it is 7'6" long, 21" wide, and seems to be faster than his other board and even more maneuverable, although another bit more difficult to paddle, due to its decreased volume. The most positive offset to this decrease in floatation is that "duckdiving" becomes more feasible—doing a "push-up" from the prone position and sinking the board underwater with all your weight as a wave breaks in front of you, pushing it as deep as possible before the impact, then ducking your body under the turbulence and letting it pass overhead, floating back up to the surface with the board after the soup has passed, in perfect position to continue paddling. He works hard at perfecting the mechanics and timing of this technique to aid in getting through the breakers, losing less ground to each incoming wave the deeper he can duck.

When he is satisfied that the new design suits him, he follows Bumper's lead and gives his old board away. His friend, Donny, is still into the old school of longboarding, and BP wants to urge him ahead, into the future. When he presents him with his old board, Donny is skeptical. "I don't think I can even stand up on one of these little chips, Beep!" he says, but promises to try it out anyway and thanks him profusely for the gift.

It is when Griff returns to the farm for a visit one day in March, just before the Spring break, that his life takes another unexpected turn. Everyone is happy to see Griff again, and they all take time out to get high together and listen to stories of his recent life, playing in a blues-rock band at a popular Hollywood club. But Griff is not just on a visit, he is on a mission. At dinner that evening, he makes a strange and provocative announcement: "I am going to take you guys on a trip tomorrow like you have never been on before. I've brought you something very fresh to sample, and it is not just another cool buzz. It is a mind-blowing experience, guaranteed!" Reaching into his pocket, he pulls out a brown, plastic vial containing a multitude of small, white pills to show them.

"What is it?" asks BP, very curious. "What'd you bring?"

"Some LSD, my young friend," answers Griff. "Lysergic acid diethylamide—a psychedelic pipeline straight to God."

LSD is not completely unknown to BP. He has heard it mentioned casually by some of his hippie acquaintances, and had learned something about it from his research into drug prohibition. He knows that it has only recently been outlawed, and that previously it had been freely available to medical researchers as an experimental drug from the Sandoz Laboratories in Switzerland, where it was discovered. He is aware of the very vocal Timothy Leary and his research associate at Harvard, Richard Alpert, who had advocated for the beneficial use of psychedelics through their research projects, and were fired from their jobs at the university. Just recently, he had seen reports in the news media about the "Human Be-In" that had taken place in January at Golden Gate Park in San Francisco, where 30,000 hippies gathered to protest the prohibition of LSD, with Leary telling them to "Turn on, tune in, and drop out." Needless to say, BP's curiosity is piqued by Griff's pronouncement. "Where'd you get that stuff, Griff?"

"Why, from the boys in the band, of course. Each tab in this-here, little brown bottle contains 250 micrograms of Owsley's pure White Lightning, straight from San Francisco. But listen up, you guys—this stuff is no joke. It is some seriously strong shit. It ain't like tossing down a couple of beers and having a nice doobie in the afternoon. I want to turn you on to it, but you're going to have to be in a positive frame of mind, in a peaceful and secure setting, where you feel safe and comfortable, and ready to be *really* high for 6 or 8 hours at least. It can be really intense, even scary, for some people, sometimes.

I don't want any of you freaking out on me. No bum trips!"

"Well, let's go to the beach, then," pipes up Bumper. "I don't feel as good anywhere else than when I'm at the beach!"

"That sounds good to me," chimes in Rocky.

"How 'bout Black's in the morning?" suggests Skip.

"That'll work," says Griff. "I just dropped some two days ago, so I'm not going to get high with you this time. It's better to give it a week or so between hits—kinda let the experience sink in a little. I'll just be your guide for this trip, your guardian, stone sober, OK? If you need someone to lean on, I'll be there for you."

They all look over at BP. "I'm in," he says. "Tomorrow is Tuesday. I don't have any classes."

Tripping

The next morning, all five of them pile in the Kombi van and head down to Black's beach after a nice breakfast. It is a rather overcast, grey, spring day, with an onshore wind chopping up the small surf early, making it look fairly uninviting. "Well, at least we aren't missing anything in the water today," remarks Bumper.

They park the van at the bottom of the hill. There is no one else around. They each swallow a little white pill, doled out by Griff (who abstains, as promised), then grab some towels and an old blanket out of the van and walk down to the beach. Sitting on the blanket in the sand, they make small talk and wait for the drug to come on.

BP does not notice anything different for the first thirty minutes or so. It is just another day at the beach. Eventually, he begins to feel a tingling of excitement rising in him from nowhere, which slowly builds into a rush of euphoria. He looks around at his friends and can tell by their wide-eyed looks that they are feeling it too. No one has spoken in several minutes. He has been idly lifting up handfuls of sand and letting them sift back to the beach through the bottom of his clenched fist in a single stream, making a small pyramid grow where they fall, sort of like the sand falling into the bottom chamber of an hourglass. He is just beginning to think that this reminds him of something when he notices the stream of sand seems to be glowing as it falls. He looks up to see if the sun has suddenly come out—whether this is just a reflection glinting on the sand, but it hasn't, and it isn't.

Indeed, when he looks back at the sand, it is not only glowing, but small sparks seem to be flying off the pyramid as the individual grains land on its top and slide down its sides. His excitement is intensifying rapidly. He wants to tell his friends about this discovery, but he can't quite find the words. "Oh... man...you guys...this sand...it's golden!" he finally manages to say. "It's on fire...."

"It's the same old sand that's always here," Griff says to him calmly. "You're just seeing it differently right now, Beep. Is it beautiful?"

"Oh...god...yes!" gasps BP. "It's awesome...."

"That's cool," says Griff. "Everything *is* beautiful—all of nature. But we just don't always notice it."

"Look at the ocean," says Bumper, suddenly. "It's alive!"

Glancing over at the flushed face of his friend, staring out at the water transfixed, like a deer caught in some kind of cosmic headlights, BP knows that he is feeling this rush too, and that they are all in for quite a ride. An idea comes to him urgently: "Let's walk around a little bit," he suggests. "I wanna see it all...." His voice sounds somehow distant now, as if someone else had uttered the words rather than he, although he knows they came from his own mouth.

"That's a good idea," says Griff, "but let's stick together, OK? I don't want any of you wandering off on your own. We're hanging together here." They all get up, moving down the beach and back towards the cliff slowly, taking everything in, turning around in circles to see it all, in utter astonishment, speechless.

When they arrive at the base of the cliff, about a hundred yards down the beach, after fifteen minutes of meandering and pausing, with Griff riding herd on the group, they are totally peaking. BP looks at the cliff and swears that it is breathing. The bank of earth and rock seems to be moving and pulsating very slightly, but rhythmically—not at all its usual stable, solid state. Looking at the striations of sediment exposed on the face of the cliff, the pattern of horizontal lines seems to vibrate in fantastic colors, moving constantly and merging into each other on the surface. He reaches out to touch them and sees his hand move, though it doesn't seem to be connected to his body anymore. He notices that his hand, too, is surrounded by these pulsating lines of various colors, outlining each of his fingers perfectly, in minute detail. Even before his fingertips actually touch the cliff, he sees the aura surrounding his hand meet the aura projecting from the cliff and merge—roiling and engaging together, flowing into and out of each other, exchanging energy, and information, in a way he has never experienced before.

He looks away, back towards his friends and the ocean, trying to express to them the profound way that he is understanding and knowing, actually *being*, the cliff at this moment, but he cannot find the words. He sees now that each one of his friends have the same energetic, glowing halo, a colorful aura, surrounding them as well. It pulses and emanates from their bodies with every movement, more dense at the surface, and diffusing as it travels outward, but clearly connecting them all together at its periphery, in wispy tendrils. It roots them to the ground as well, while reaching into the sky, and out to the ocean. Everything in view is connected to everything else in the milieu, clearly, by these energetic auras. Nothing is separate, everything is alive and dancing together, intertwined by what appear to be vibrant fields of energy.

Feeling the earth with his fingers, he knows that the cliff is alive as well. He sees it suddenly from the perspective of eons, from its birth in a wave of tectonic movement, of uplifting from the ocean floor, through its long life of slow erosion by wind and water, as its edge crumbles and transforms itself into the sandy beach. As he looks upwards, at its towering expanse looming above him, he momentarily imagines it as a huge terrestrial wave, its top about to pitch out and break like an ocean wave, covering and burying them all in a giant, earthen tube as it collapses. He becomes instantly terrified. "Watch out!"

he screams, turning and trying to bolt away from the base of the cliff.

Before he can run two steps, though, Griff moves in front of him, grabbing him by the shoulders, restraining and shaking him mildly. "It's OK, Beep," he says calmly, confronting him directly, trying to make eye contact and get him to pay attention,. "Nothing's wrong…don't worry…we're all OK, here… it's just the drug…it'll wear off…."

BP slowly calms down as he realizes his imagination has run a bit wild on him, and that the cliff is not actually falling on their heads after all, though it does seem to be moving slightly, still. "Whoa, Griff…thanks, man," he manages to say, finally, with great effort, but finds he is unable to fully express or articulate what had just happened any further. "I've gotta get away from here, though…let's go down by the water…please…"

After Griff rounds up the group and herds them down towards the water's edge, BP is soothed somewhat, and not as scared anymore. The ocean appears to him to be less threatening, though it is also throbbing and pulsing like a vast organism, lapping at the land and sky, reaching out and encircling his feet as he walks its edge, making the sand glisten, sparkle and shine.

An ecstatic peace returns to him, as he slowly walks in wonder at the interface between sea and land, feeling a part of both, noticing every detail—the frothy foam, with rainbow-colored bubbles swirling and bursting as it surges and surrounds the clumps of seaweed, filling the holes where the sand crabs burrow. The sandpipers wade in the shallows with him, rooting after the crabs with their long beaks, while the pelicans, cormorants, ospreys and gulls soar and dive for anchovies just offshore. The dull roar of the surf along with the squawking of the birds sounds like a symphony to his ears.

He notices the bleached skeleton of a sand dollar lying on the beach at his feet. Picking it up, he examines it closely and is thrilled by its texture and symmetry. Everything is so incredibly beautiful, so seamlessly integrated and important, and he is in perfect harmony with it all, it seems, woven tightly into the same fabric. Even the kelp flies, which he usually finds annoying, seem an absolutely necessary part of the whole, as they rise in small clouds and flee upon his approach.

They wander the shore for hours, and it is well after noon when the effects of the acid begin to wane. The rush of excitement and the colorful apparitions begin to fade, and the gauzy fog of his normal, waking reality begins to seep back into his consciousness, replacing the breathtaking, but dreamlike, clarity of his previous visions. Objects resume their normal, discrete shapes (lacking the miraculous, ethereal connections to everything else he had been perceiving) and seem somewhat humdrum and mundane to him now.

While disappointed, he is not exactly depressed about it, though, because he had begun to wonder if he would ever come back from this trip—if his normal perception would ever return. As he begins to sober up, the hallucinations retreat, and he is relieved that these effects are not permanent, that he is not going completely crazy. He is still quite awash in a milder, less frenzied, feeling of well-being, which is pleasant and more relaxing than the earlier electric, orgasmic euphoria. He is also a bit exhausted from the emotional rollercoaster ride of the past few hours, without having any real sense of how long it has been, but knowing that such intensity could not be sustained without ultimately draining his strength and sanity.

Gathering back at the blanket with his friends, where they had started out that morning, he can see that they are just as shell-shocked from the experience, and still pretty high as well, except for Griff, their sober shepherd. Hollow-eyed, they sit and stare out at the surf without speaking much, trying to assimilate the whole affair into something intelligible and communicable, but that is a tall order. Curt exclamations such as "Wow," "Awesome," and "Gnarly" seem to be as close as they can come to expressing themselves at this point.

Eventually they wander back up to the van and smoke a big joint together as the sun drops in the western sky, further softening the edginess of their experience. It is not until they have driven home, showered and eaten dinner that they are straight enough to try to talk cohesively about their trip. As they sit around the living room at the farm that evening, listening to soft, soothing, acoustic blues records on the stereo, they make some halting attempts at understanding and explaining what went down. "I know I have never been that high before, *ever*, that's for sure," offers BP. "Those are some powerful little pills, Griff! Thanks for turning us on to them. And thanks for being there to keep me from freaking out!"

"For sure, my brother," answers Griff. "What happened to you up by the cliff, anyway?"

"I'm not sure," says BP, truthfully. "I thought there was going to be an avalanche or something. The cliff turned into a giant wave and I thought it was going to break on us for a minute!"

"Wow! Whaddya think that meant?"

BP has to think hard before answering, trying to dredge up his fragmented memories of the incident. After a long pause to organize his earlier perceptions into an understandable response, he answers: "Just before it happened, I had this weird vision of the cliff, like I was seeing its whole life throughout time, sort of like a stop-action movie taken frame by frame through millions of years. You know, like those shots you see in science movies of clouds developing and sailing by, or a plant budding and flowering over a period of days, only this was over a much longer span of geologic time. I saw, or felt, the cliff rising out of the primordial ocean and forming the beach! It was sort of like a wave jacking up before it breaks, and I thought it was going to close out on us. Maybe I just got confused or something...."

"Dude, you were *really* high!" laughs Bumper. "But who am I to talk? At one point, I thought I saw a mermaid in the surf!"

"Was she a hot babe?" asks Rocky, laughing with him.

"I thought she was for a minute," answers Bumper. "I was thinking about ripping off my clothes and jumping in to swim out to her, and then I realized it was just a kelp ball in the waves!"

"It was heavy for me for awhile, there," Skip says, very seriously. "I thought something monumental, something earth-shattering, was going to happen at any minute—that the skies were going to open up, you know, and Gabriel and all the angels were going to come marching down from the clouds, or something, blowing horns and playing harps and stuff, ushering God right down to Earth—full-on Judgment Day kind of shit. It was scary for me! I kept wondering what the hell am I going to be able to say to God about my life? I felt pretty pitiful for awhile...I was quaking...and then I finally got blissed-out on it all....I figured if that is what was going to go down, even if I was just a good-for-nothing surf bum, at least I was going to get to meet God! Nothing ever happened though, I just felt like it was going to, at any minute..."

"That *is* heavy," agrees Bumper, and everyone falls silent for awhile.

"One thing I know for sure," says BP, finally. "I gotta try it again. It seemed like I was really close to figuring something important out for myself, but I couldn't quite get there. I was seeing things so clearly, at times, how everything fits together, and I felt like if I could just look sideways fast enough, I might see around a corner, behind the scene—get a glimpse of the true reality of things—how it all really works...who or what exactly is pulling the strings as we dance around..."

"You'll get your chance, my friend," Griff assures him. "I'm splitting tomorrow to head back north, but I'm going to leave that little bottle with you guys. It's in the freezer right now, staying fresh, and it's all yours. There're still almost a hundred more hits in it. Do what you want with it. Give some away, turn some people on, take some more trips yourselves, whatever. There's plenty more where that came from, and its dirt cheap. But be careful with it, and take care with anyone you give it to. It'll go lame on you after awhile, so keep it cold and tightly sealed, out of the sunlight. You'll know when it's losing potency, as it'll take two of them to get you as high as you were today."

"Wow, thanks Griff!" says BP. "Can we pay you for them?"

"Nah, man, my treat," insists Griff. "They only cost me twenty cents apiece. The Bear, the guy who makes them, is not in it for the money. He just wants to turn people on. He's gotta make enough on them to cook the next batch, but that's it. I'll score some more as soon as I go back to L.A. No problem. Our bass player is a good friend of his."

"All right!" says Bumper. "That's really cool, Griff. So, you guys, when are we going to take another trip? This weekend, maybe? I wonder what it's like to drop acid and surf?"

"I wonder what it's like to get tubed on that shit?" asks BP, to no one in particular. "I felt like I was continuously tubed for about four or five hours today. What's going to happen when you're feeling like that, and *then* you get barreled on a wave?"

"It's gotta be pure ecstasy," says Bumper. No one argues with that conclusion.

Summer of Love

BP's experience with LSD has a profound impact on his life and his world view which cannot be underestimated. In this he is not alone. All across the country, hundreds of thousands of young (and some not so young) people are experimenting with psychedelic drugs—each for their own reasons, and with wildly differing results. For him, it becomes a quest, a mission of discovery. Instead of the outward exploration and analysis of the physical world upon which he had been embarked in his education, he is thrust headlong into an inner exploration of his mind, his consciousness and his perception, setting out on a voyage of discovery into a new "spiritual" world.

It is precisely because this tiny quantity of synthetic chemical had so radically altered his perception of the world, temporary as it might have been, that he makes this radical turn in his path. All of the science he had learned to this point was inevitably based on observation—supposedly objective, unalterable, repeatable, experimental observation. Yet the activity and participation of the observer in any experiment cannot be ignored—this was proven in the double-slit experiment, and others in modern cyclotrons. Observations are obviously dependent on our perception. But perception can be easily and radically altered, as he has found out. How can true "objectivity" be determined and maintained, under these circumstances, then? Perhaps "subjectivity" has something more, or different, to offer, in some instances?

Objectivity yields facts, there is no doubt—more of them than a single person can glean, digest and store in a lifetime of study, he is sure, but is it really the route to the ultimate truth, to answering the Really Big Questions? Of this, he is no longer sure. He has begun to suspect that the secrets of life, of the universe, and all that exists, might be entirely subjective, accessed through an individual's mind and perception, in a moment of revelation, enlightenment, and transcendency.

At one point in his acid trip, when he had overcome his fears and his mind was not racing, but he was still perceiving the mysterious, magical, colorful, visual connections between himself and everything in his view, he had given himself up to simply absorbing the awesome beauty and majesty of the scene, marveling at the interconnection of everything and thankful for his opportunity to witness it. It was in that moment he had been struck by a feeling, or an intuition, that it was this awareness, the ability to perceive the natural world and reflect on his place in it, which was the essence of life. Moreover, this was the fundamental connection he shared with everything else—his consciousness of it!

It occurred to him that his awareness might actually be supporting, even helping to *create*, everything that existed, simply by his participation in the world. By the same token, he was momentarily convinced that everything else he saw, animate or inanimate objects alike, were also alive, participating in some sort of consciousness or awareness of these events, of this moment, as well. Perhaps not in the exact same way, certainly not all with the same sort of awareness he possessed, but he felt positive that everything around him *knew* he was there, and knew where everything else was as well, in some way—the sand, the rocks, the cliffs, the ocean, the birds, his friends—everything! In that moment, the division between himself and the world had dissolved. It was a singular and passionate experience of unity and oneness he had never known before, and he was determined to understand and embrace it.

Unfortunately, in the cold, hard, light of day, stone sober and rational, such feelings and intuitions seem foolish and delusional. It is difficult, if not impossible, for him to duplicate them. When he is in a normal, unintoxicated state, he cannot look at a rock and perceive that it is conscious or aware, in any significant way. The ocean does not look like an organism to him, just a large body of water. It is easier to imagine that other animals, ones with a brain, at least, might have some sort of consciousness, but certainly not like his. And the idea that his consciousness might actually participate in *creating* the universe seems egomaniacal, at best. Certainly if he were to die, and his awareness ceased to exist, the universe would not collapse! Plenty of people die every day, and the world persists.

He can see a myriad of logical and rational problems with such feelings, but there is no doubt that he has had them, and that they were both compelling and intriguing. The fact that they were induced by ingesting a chemical does not deter him. "Better living through modern chemistry" was a slogan ingrained in him (and the culture at large) by the promotional efforts of Dow Chemical company many years before, after all. He had not invented the idea.

It becomes even more difficult for him, now, to complete his sophomore year in college successfully. He has lost his enthusiasm for strict rationalism, and dedicates himself instead to a new sensory regime—the search for the miraculous. This is not compatible with the rigorous, scientific curriculum of his lower-division studies at UCSD.

Beside the fact that he begins to drop acid weekly, wasting many days in the process which might have been spent in the classroom and studying, there is a string of early-season south swells leading into the summer of '67 which distract him mightily. Between surfing and getting high (often at the same time), his schoolwork suffers. Even at the odd times he applies himself to it, he can't escape from an undercurrent of sneaking feelings about the possible irrelevance or incompleteness of the whole scientific method.

In the final segment of his physics class, the latest theories regarding the origin of the universe are being taught. The one in greatest favor, the "Big Bang" theory, is supported by a preponderance of evidence, most recently confirmed by the accidental discovery, in 1964, of the cosmic microwave background radiation, or echo, which remains behind from the initial explosion or expansion of the universe. This theory is now almost universally accepted. It is built upon the work of many philosophers and scientists, over thousands of years of accumulated knowledge—from the ancient Greeks, to Aristotle, to Copernicus, to Kepler, to Galileo, to Newton, to Friedman and Lemaître, to Einstein, and to Hubble, who finally proved that the universe consists of billions of galaxies, billions of light years apart, and that it is still expanding at a colossal rate, in every direction, at every moment.

If this is the case, it is logical that in the very distant past, many billions of years ago, before the rapid expansion began, the universe was much smaller. Taken to its reasonable conclusion, at one time, in the very beginning, everything was packed into a single, infinitely small point, a singularity—the *Primeval Atom* or *Cosmic Egg*, which had to exist at infinite temperature and infinite density. When it exploded, everything we know of was brought into existence.

The earliest event that scientists can describe, however, is a tiny fraction of a second later, at about 10^{-43} seconds into the expansion. When BP wonders what was there before that—what exactly this primordial atom was like, where it came from in the first place, and what set it into such radical motion, there are no answers to be found.

The mathematical model is impeccable—gorgeous and logical, but even it reaches its limits at zero, infinity, and the speed of light. Focusing backward in time, towards the singularity, the theory can render an explanation for everything that happened once the initial cosmic inflation slowed down to the speed of light, but before that, the laws of general relativity break down. What existed in the beginning, how and why it originally came into being, and what caused it to change, are only subjects of speculation, not of science.

This seems unacceptable to BP. Once again, it appears to him, the Really Big Questions get short shrift from science. While ignoring these core issues, the best scientific minds in the country are simply scurrying about refining the theory, trying to measure the size, age and density of the universe more accurately, unable to explain what happened in the Planck epoch (that first tiniest increment of time) or before. It seems like a dead end to him, and loses its appeal.

He finds it hard to focus on his assignments, and to do the work necessary to keep up to speed. Despite another amphetamine-laced binge at the end of the quarter to prepare for his final exams, he nearly flunks several of his classes, obtaining only a grade of D in both math and physics, and fails his proficiency test in German. This doesn't bode well for his career as a scientist, but he has already abandoned that notion, deciding instead to declare his major in Philosophy for his upper-division work, and investigate some different ways of obtaining knowledge.

One of these ways, he rationalizes, is direct experience. Isn't that what "empiricism" originally meant, after all—knowledge derived from sensory experience? At this, over the next summer, he certainly excels, indulging in an orgy of sensory experience, in more ways than one.

Foremost, of course, is surfing. Once school is out for the summer, he is back in the water almost every day. He continues the evolution of the Zen Flyer model with Bumper, carving a new prototype every 3 or 4 weeks, tweaking the design based on the performance of the last one, adding or deleting features, trying concave and channeled bottoms, winged outlines and swallow-tails, then testing to see what difference they make. The common, recurring element is that the boards get shorter, narrower, thinner and faster at each evolution.

Second in line is his LSD experimentation. With his friends, BP trips-out constantly. They drop acid while trying everything—going to movies and rock concerts, making the trek up the coast for the Monterey International Pop Music Festival in June, which is a massive, psychedelic affair, but also surfing, hiking in the wilds of the mountains, in the desert, or just staying at home and listening to music while loaded to the gills. At one time, they try spacing-out in a virtual isolation chamber, ensconcing themselves in a small, empty, windowless, basement study room at the Humanities Library at UCSD, which is nearly deserted during the summer session. Turning off the lights, lying on the concrete floor in total darkness, they come on to the drug in silence. While BP has always preferred the more isolated, natural environments for their acid trips, with few other people around with whom they have to deal, he finds being under the influence in the darkness of that basement room is too much for him, as it is for his friends. After an hour or so, they break their silence and mutually agree to move outside, spending the rest of the day wandering around the eucalyptus groves and canyons on campus in the bright sunlight.

Around the Fourth of July weekend, he turns Donny on to the White Lightning and guides him through his first trip, choosing a weekend surf trip to Northern Baja as the venue. Donny is quite enamored of the experience, and wants to know where he can get some more of the stuff.

Having shunned the massive migration to the Haight-Ashbury district in San Francisco by the youth culture that summer, in favor of the warmer waters of the southern California bight, they miss out on a remarkable happening, but also avoid the uglier aspects of that overcrowded, overstressed, hippie scene. Luckily, one of Bumper's acquaintances, an energetic young promoter named Ron, otherwise known as "Anchovy," organizes a series of local "love-ins" and free concerts at Scripps Park in La Jolla. While the level of talent in the bands might not be quite the same as in the Haight, these events prove incredibly popular with the rapidly growing hippie population in San Diego—the young people seeking the same freedom of community, free music, free sex and free drugs as up north. They come in outrageous garb, or nearly naked, with flowers in their hair and sometimes painted bodies, to dance and sway together with the music, meet others of like mind, get high and just roll in the grass together.

It is at these summer gatherings that BP finally loses his reticence and inhibitions regarding the opposite sex. Without any commitment, sometimes nearly wordlessly, he meets, interacts with, and eventually beds in succession several attractive, unrestrained, young women he meets, all in various stages of intoxication, and none requiring or expecting anything more from him than his mutual enjoyment of their sexual activity. This suits him just fine, and it is a great boost to his self-esteem and social confidence that such lovely specimens would find him attractive and seek him out for these mating rituals. It also beats the hell out of autoeroticism, which had been his only means of sexual gratification for far too long now.

It is towards the end of July when they run out of LSD. After a few phone calls, he makes a run up to L.A. to see Griff, who helps him buy a large quantity of Purple Haze, Owsley's latest production run, named in honor of Jimi Hendrix's debut at the Monterey festival. He comes home with over 1,000 doses of it for about 25 cents apiece. With the relatively short shelf life of the drug, he busies himself with distributing it. Adding it to his illicit commodity repertoire, he sells many hits for $2–3 apiece, which enables him to give away many more to his friends for free, and even to strangers, who strike him as worthy, at love-ins, parties or concerts he attends. He becomes a very popular guy in a growing social network.

At the same time, he has not abandoned his intellectual pursuit, just changed its focus. He still reads constantly and visits the local libraries at least once a week, looking into the various mystical traditions and paths of enlightenment, both in the eastern and western worlds. These are the things that interest him now, and seem most important. The possibility of a blinding revelation, of an instant illumination, of some transcendent vision of the order and meaning of the universe, is a terribly attractive idea to him, at the moment. The things he sees and feels on acid make him believe it could happen to anyone, with the right kind of insight, inspiration, or religiosity, the right spiritual mentor, meditation or practice, possibly with the right entheogen added to the mix. Who knows? He feels deep in his soul that there is some obvious clue or secret, floating right in front of his face, that he is somehow missing, and when bumped into, noticed, encountered or finally found, it will lead him immediately to all the answers he seeks.

His embedded enculturation, his stubborn socialization and cynical realism are driven into the background. He doesn't allow himself to think that such spiritual aspirations may be simply his seeking an easy way out, an effortless path to wisdom, which doesn't really exist. He also completely ignores the fact that he is dancing on a fine line between genius and insanity, between enlightenment and imprisonment. He is having far too much fun for such mundane considerations.

MAC MEDA

The city of San Diego, California, BP's birthplace, is a very conservative community, at its core. It is basically a military enclave, built and fed by the Navy and Marine Corps installations that dot its well-protected bay and the surrounding countryside, along with the government contractors who had sprung up during WWII to supply and equip the war effort. A huge number of the citizenry are either active duty or retired military personnel, or receive their paychecks from the booming defense industry, including BP's own father. The majority of the population, as well as the entire power structure in the town—the "movers and shakers," political and business leaders, media moguls, etc., support the war in Vietnam vehemently and are eternally suspicious of the "University of Communism" that has invaded its northern border in La Jolla.

It is no wonder, then, that Anchovy's "love-ins" at the park are not well-received by the community at large. As reports filter in concerning the problems that the city of San Francisco is having with the influx of hundreds of thousands of hippies from all over the country, and they see thousands of their own children being subverted by this youth movement, gathering in wild-eyed and long-haired scruffiness to celebrate freedom and love, the city council moves to squash any escalation of this problem before it gets out of hand.

There have been reports of drug use and underage drinking, even public nudity, during the events at Scripps Park, as well as complaints from concerned residents neighboring La Jolla Cove, who have found it difficult to park their cars anywhere close to their homes when the hordes of hippies descend. By September, the city government reacts by finding "irregularities" in the permits for these gatherings and shuts them down. Anchovy is forced to give up his public venue, taking his entrepreneurial effort private, leasing an abandoned roller rink downtown, remodeling it into an all-ages nightclub called "The Hippodrome," and continuing to promote rock concerts there, eventually bringing many of the bands who play the Fillmore Auditorium and the Avalon Ballroom in San Francisco down to San Diego over the next year.

Kids will be kids, though, and fun cannot be legislated out of existence for this generation. A shadowy, loosely organized, underground social club named the Mac Meda Destruction Company, based in the Windansea surf culture, decides to throw an end-of-summer bash at the beach on Labor Day. BP and his friends hear about it through the "coconut grapevine," the surf-culture rumor mill, as the event is unsanctioned and not widely publicized, the sole notices being some hand-drawn and mimeographed flyers posted near La Jolla surf spots. They decide it is not something to be missed.

On the morning of the event, they load their boards onto the top of Bumper's van, fill their pockets with joints and little purple pills, and head south towards Windansea. Stopping for a quick surf check at Blacks, they see a small, but clean swell rolling in and decide to jump on it. "Never drive away from good waves," Bumper reminds them. "It looks like there's a lot of west in this swell—it might not be that good at Windan'. The wind is liable to come up, too, and it will definitely be more crowded over there. Let's hit it!" They surf for a couple of hours and then continue their trek southward, grabbing some burritos at a Mexican take-out restaurant to fill their rumbling stomachs on the way.

Not knowing quite what to expect, they are blown away by the crowd of kids already gathered when they finally arrive at Windansea in the late morning. The beach is packed, the crowd overflowing onto the bluffs and sidewalks, and cars are jamming the streets, with young people hanging out the windows waving and yelling at their friends as they parade slowly down Neptune Place, caught in the jam.

There are no public facilities to speak of at the beach here, and only a tiny parking lot, so they must search around the residential neighborhood before finding a place to park, finally, several blocks away. Having seen that the surf is not that good on their initial drive by (and quite crowded for the conditions), they take their boards off the roof and lock them in the van, then walk the short distance back down to the beach.

The party is in full swing, with much merriment and general confusion. There is a generator set up on the beach, providing power for the electric instruments of a rock band playing loudly, but messily, from under the thatched surf shack. Kegs of beer are tapped and nestled in tubs of ice under the shade of the bushes growing at the base of the bluffs. Young people of all descriptions—surfers, hippies, greasers, hodads, bikers, students and jocks, are mingling and dancing in the sand, or sitting and standing in groups on the rocky bluffs, most with paper Dixie cups of beer in their hands, some sharing puffs of marijuana. There are schools of hot tuna in skimpy bikinis soaking up the sun everywhere, and hormone-ridden young men trolling desperately for a hookup. "Yowser!" is all Rocky can say as they come upon the scene from the south end of the beach.

Sifting through the crowd, making their way slowly up the beach towards the shack, they recognize some friends and acquaintances, stopping to chat and have a toke or two with them. BP bumps into Donny, who is hanging with a bunch of their old friends from P.B., in the crowd around the sewer pump station at the foot of Kolmar Street. He gives him half of the Purple Haze tabs from his pocket when Donny asks if he has any acid. "Just give them away to anyone looking for a good time," he suggests, moving on through the mass of humanity towards the shack, looking to score a cup of beer to slake his thirst.

The party is still growing by leaps and bounds as the morning sun climbs to its zenith at noon. BP ponders whether or not to drop one of the tabs of acid, but decides against it, feeling a bit uncomfortable with so many people around. He continues to just give them away to friends he meets, and eventually to anyone who asks, as word of mouth spreads from his acquaintances to total strangers, who approach him timidly, each with the same sort of pitch: "My friend, [So-and-so], said you might have some LSD...."

He sits with his buddies on the rocks above the shack, their shirts off, working on their tans and a mild beer-and-pot buzz, listening to the music, scoping the performances offshore in the mediocre surf, and watching the girls go by. BP is trying to decide which one of these beauties he might try to approach when he notices a commotion down by the pumphouse. The crowd surges in a circle around some disturbance. He sees some paper cups flying through the air. "Hey, what's that—a fight or something?" he asks, pointing it out to the others. They stand up to get a better view.

"I dunno," says Rocky, "but aren't there a couple of uniforms in the middle, there?"

"I hope it's not the cops," says Bumper. "That would be a bummer!"

"Let's go check it out," says BP. Sidling through the crowd to the water's edge, they are able to make some fairly swift progress down the beach, dodging the shorebreak as it washes up the sand. As they get closer to the pumphouse, the crowd gets thicker, though, and the mood angrier. When they can penetrate it no further, BP asks someone on the edge of the knot of people what's going on. "They're trying to bust some kids for underage drinking," is the answer. Shouts of "No! Get out of here! Leave them alone!" fill the air. More cups fly, half-filled with beer still, spraying the crowd.

Circling around to the south, they climb halfway up the bluff to gain a vantage point, and see two San Diego police officers struggling through the angry crowd towards the stairs alongside the pumphouse, with two, young, mop-headed, surf groms in their grasp. People are blocking their way and berating them. Suddenly, another police car speeds by on the street above, siren blaring, signal lights blinking, and screeches to a halt at the top of the stairs. Two more officers jump out, one with a bullhorn, who begins blaring through it at the crowd while the other rushes down to aid the two who are surrounded below, billy club drawn, hand on his gun: "CEASE AND DESIST! WE ARE DECLARING THIS AN ILLEGAL ASSEMBLY! PLEASE DISPERSE IMMEDIATELY OR RISK ARREST!"

"Oh-oh," says BP, "this could get ugly." As they stand there watching, three more police cars arrive in unison. They can hear more sirens in the distance. Realizing that he is still holding at least ten hits of acid in his pocket, that his buddies probably have several joints on them, not to mention that he is still several months shy of his own twentieth birthday, making him guilty of illegal alcohol consumption by a minor as well, he makes a calm but urgent suggestion to the others: "I think maybe we should just clear out of here, guys, right now!"

They walk as quickly as they can down to Big Rock, at the south end of the beach, and climb the stairs to the street there, hurrying back to the van. As they pull their boards out and tie them back onto the roof rack, BP takes a quick inventory. He has twelve purple tablets, packed by pairs into small, glassine envelopes. "What are you guys still holding?" he asks, in a low voice.

"I've still got a couple of pinners in my pocket," says Skip.

"I've got one joint left," answers Rocky.

"I'm out of dope already," says Bumper.

"OK," decides BP, throwing two of the packets down the storm drain at the curb, next to the car, "I've got 8 hits of acid left now, so if we get pulled over, we only have to eat two apiece. This stuff is going a little bit lame anyway, so I think we can handle a double dose. We'll have a really good time if we get thrown in the tank, anyway," he jokes, nervously. "Let's go! Skipper, give one of your joints to Bumper to eat if we have to."

They drive south a bit and then circle around on the boulevard back to Little Point, at the north end of Windansea. They cruise slowly back down to the beach, where they can see south again onto Neptune Place, and it is solid cop cars and paddy wagons, with lights flashing, blocking the street for as far as they can see. They hang a U-turn and head back up to the boulevard and north to Del Mar on the coast highway.

"Shit," mutters Rocky. "And they call this 'the land of the free.'"

The Year of the Monkey

In the aftermath of the Windansea "riots," as they are portrayed in the reactionary local press, the city administration expresses a strong commitment to maintaining the peace and tranquility of their constituents, determining to crack down on the "rowdy elements" at the beach who engage in unlawful behavior. In searching for the parties responsible for this corruption of youth, by dispensing alcoholic beverages to minors, the leadership of the Mac Meda Destruction Company cannot be found or properly punished. The purported president of the organization, one Albert Mac Meda, is never identified, even though his picture adorns the back side of the T-shirts worn by club adherents. Though the police are baffled, the truth is that Albert is already behind bars. In reality, he is the oldest, largest, silverback gorilla living at the San Diego Zoo.

Frustrated by being unable to detain any major "perps," the police clamp down in a "shotgun" approach, increasing patrols at all the beaches and hassling anyone they can find who might be flouting the law. Trivial busts are made for sometimes fabricated reasons. Anyone showing any sign of being engaged in an "alternative lifestyle" is under suspicion. A practice of "field interrogations" is instituted where simply having long hair or being dressed weirdly is enough of a reason for the cops to stop someone, especially young people, and ask for identification or question their activities. Invasions of privacy become more common—police searches of a person's body or vehicle without valid cause, resulting in an uptick in minor "possession and use" charges, some of which do not stand up in court, but some resulting in severe criminal penalties for decidedly victimless crimes, ruining innocent lives and crowding the jails.

This abuse of authority is indicative of the severe schisms that are developing in the society at large and continue to widen over the next year. The polarization of American culture reaches a zenith during 1968. It is a year of upheaval and deadly conflict on a number of levels. The young are pitted against the old, the establishment *vs.* the progressives, the liberals *vs.* the reactionaries, the rich *vs.* the poor, the stoners *vs.* the straights, antiwar *vs.* hawks, black *vs.* white. It is a tragic time.

BP hooks up with Donny for one last surfari to northern Baja before the start of the school year. They camp on the bluff at K-42 and enjoy some clean, shoulder-high waves. Donny is making progress in transitioning to shortboarding, though he is still a little shaky with the twitchiness and speed of the smaller vehicle. They have a fun session together and afterwards eat a massive *enchilada* dinner at Raul's restaurant on the cliff (the only building around for several kilometers).

Sitting next to their small campfire that evening, Donny drops a bomb-shell in BP's lap: "I've been avoiding talking to you about something, Beep—I know I should have told you sooner, but didn't know how you would take it. I'm joining the Army next week, and I'm going to be gone for the next four years."

BP is stunned. "Oh, man, why would you do that, Donny? That's crazy! They'll just send you to Vietnam to get shot at! Did you get drafted? I thought you had a student deferment."

"Nah, that ran out in June. I'm not going back to junior college. My grades weren't very good, so I probably wouldn't be able to transfer into a four-year school next year unless I did a lot better, and I probably couldn't afford it, anyway. I thought I might get a baseball scholarship out of it, but that didn't work out. I don't really like college anyhow, except for playing ball. I dunno, I'm just not cut out for studying, I don't think. They haven't sent me a draft notice yet, but I went down and signed up. They're going to get me one way or the other."

"But if they draft you, you'll only have to do two years, Donny. If you enlist, they've got you for four!"

"I know that, Beep, but there are some bonuses for signing up, and there are other benefits—the recruiter told me I would be able to pick my own train-ing program better if I enlist. If you get drafted, they pretty much just tell you where to go, and it's mostly to Vietnam as an infantry grunt. Maybe I can learn a trade and get assigned to a base somewhere else. I wouldn't mind learning how to be a mechanic or something and getting assigned to Hawaii—that would be pretty cool. Anyway, it's a done deal, already. My dad thinks it is the best thing for me to do, and I already signed the papers to join up. I'm leaving for Fort Ord next week for basic training."

BP feels like he has been kicked in the gonads. He has a deep sense of foreboding regarding his friend's future, but he stifles it. Despite his feelings of loss and dread, he realizes that Donny's mind is made up—he is commit-ted to this course of action, and arguing or pleading with him will probably not change anything. Rather than alienate him, BP feels he must support his friend as best he can now, even though he disagrees violently with the idea. "Well, bud, if you gotta go, you gotta go. I'm going to miss having you around, though. Be sure to keep your head down and stay in touch, OK?"

"I will, Beep," is the last thing Donny says to him before they turn in for the night. Rising the next morning from their sleeping bags, they surf another session together, have a big breakfast of *huevos rancheros* at Raul's, and then drive back north across the border, making only small talk the whole time, never mentioning the elephant in the room standing between them.

When he begins his third year at UCSD in October of 1967, the tensions on campus are rising as quickly as the population. John Muir College, the second of the twelve colleges planned for the UCSD campus, admits its first students for the start of the 1967–68 academic year. Their new buildings are not yet completed, so they are housed in the old Camp Matthews buildings, as the first class at Revelle had been, and integrated into the life of the university. This wave of new Muir students, along with another, larger, freshman class at Revelle, plus transfers from other colleges and new graduate students, require the ranks of the faculty to be expanded as well to accommodate them all.

Newly elected Governor Ronald Reagan, the former Hollywood actor, is pressing to impose his conservative political will on the UC system in the name of "law and order," attacking UC President, Clark Kerr, over the unrest at Berkeley. Kerr fights to preserve the neutrality of public higher education, but is ultimately driven from his post. UCSD Chancellor John Galbraith has submitted his resignation as well (though it has not yet been accepted by the regents), preferring to accept a visiting professorship at Cambridge rather than face the "abrasive environment" in San Diego, insisting that "free inquiry and free expression" should be at the core of the university, and that it should "not endorse nor repudiate political viewpoints."

As the war in Vietnam continues to rage, campus protests increase. Military recruiters are prevented from setting up shop on campus by angry students. A Viet Minh flag is hoisted up the flagpole at the old Camp Matthews. The community responds with vitriolic editorials and cartoons in the press, along with the formation of a group named "Citizens to End Campus Anarchy." The schism between "town and gown" is growing rapidly.

BP enjoys his upper division philosophy classes more than anything else he has experienced so far at college. He actually looks forward to the lectures and reads all the assigned books eagerly. Several of his professors have extremely engaging and interesting styles of lecturing, and are very accessible. They treat their students as intelligent, mature, human beings, almost as peers in the quest for knowledge, encouraging them to think critically and reach their own conclusions rather than indoctrinating them with the "correct" answers. Although many of the logical transformations of philosophical arguments follow the same rules as mathematics, there is, in the end, no single, correct approach to many of the questions involved.

His favorite teacher by far is an elderly, white-haired gentleman from Germany, who had fled his homeland during the rise of the Third Reich in 1933, after earning his doctorate at the University of Freiburg in 1922, becoming a naturalized United States citizen in 1940, and working with the OSS, the predecessor to the CIA, during WWII. After the war, he was employed by the U.S. Department of State until 1951, when he was hired as a professor at Columbia, Harvard and Brandeis universities before coming to UCSD in 1965, the same year BP had arrived. His name is Herbert Marcuse, and although BP finds his thick German accent a bit difficult to understand at times, his lectures are stimulating and often humorous. Though he is a noted expert on Kant, his interests and experience are wide-ranging, and BP finds his knowledge of the full scope of western thought prodigious during the first introductory class he attends, covering the history of philosophy. Though it is not assigned for this class, BP looks for his latest book, *One-Dimensional Man*, in the library, checks it out and reads it. He finds it very interesting, speaking to the stifling of individual expression in modern culture, the need for societal tolerance, and making a very thoughtful and innovative critique of the repression that exists in both capitalist and communist societies.

The graduate student leading the course section for Marcuse's class is Angela Davis. She is unlike anyone BP has ever met. A strong and striking young black woman, four or five years older than himself, with a huge halo of afro hair surrounding regal features, she is an imposing figure, with a sharp mind and an even sharper tongue. While he had seen her before at political rallies in Revelle plaza, standing with the leaders of the Students of the Independent Left (which has now become affiliated with the national organization, Students for a Democratic Society), or with other members of the Black Student Council, he had never spoken to or interacted closely with her, finding her both attractive and intimidating at the same time. It is rumored that she is a Communist party member, in addition to being an associate of the Black Panther party, and that one of her brothers has just been drafted into the NFL by the Cleveland Browns. As Marcuse's TA, he finds her very articulate and helpful in explaining some parts of the course material, but it is obvious, from a few of her offhand, withering comments and biting remarks, just what she thinks of the legacy of Jim Crow in America, and the capitalist system's shortcomings in oppressing the poor.

BP has watched the evolution of student political activism over the last two years mostly as a casual observer, not an actual participant, though he has attended some anti-war rallies. He can't help but notice the difference the Black Power movement has made in it, paralleling the same evolution of black pride and black nationalism within the civil rights movement nationally. While previously, white liberals had predominated in leadership roles, black people are now insisting on taking responsibility and speaking for themselves. The same thing is happening with the Latino community and their pride in *La Raza*. The Chicano students have formed their own organization as well, called MAYA—the Mexican American Youth Association. The SDS, consisting of white progressives, forms the third arm of an uneasy triumvirate, with BSC and MAYA, replacing what had previously been a more unified, though white-dominated, activist effort. BP can't help but think that the conservative establishment is applauding this development, as it seems to contain an element of "divide and conquer" strategy, which is always helpful in fragmenting opposition.

Time flies when you're having fun, and the first quarter of school passes quickly for BP. He is so involved in his new philosophical bent that he even surfs less, spending more time on campus, reading and studying, attending every class. There is beginning to be an exciting atmosphere there, as if change might really be in the air. "Participatory democracy" are the words on everyone's lips, and protests, teach-ins, demonstrations, guerilla theatre and performance art occur regularly in the plaza, along with proliferating clouds of dope smoke, rising from multiple, diverse groups, at any given time. He saves any LSD trips and partying for the occasional recreational weekend. Without even cramming for finals, he is amazed to earn straight A's in all his classes.

During the Christmas break, he is able to surf more, while having to attend to a few chores involved in caretaking the farm, as Bumper makes his annual pilgrimage to the north shore of Oahu. BP continues to read on his own, investigating a new interest in eastern philosophy and religion. He studies the *I Ching*, or *Book of Changes*, the ancient Chinese divinatory text, finding it most baffling, and reads the *Autobiography of a Yogi* by Paramahansa Yogananda, whom he only then comes to discover was the founder of the Self-Realization Fellowship, whose golden domes grace the cliffs over the surfspot he knows as "Swami's" in Encinitas.

Just after the New Year holiday, he receives a scribbled post card from Donny, saying that he has completed basic and advanced training, and that he is shipping out for Southeast Asia, without being specific about the destination. It is sent from San Francisco and contains no return address. BP's heart sinks as he assumes that Donny's plan to avoid the war has not turned out the way he had hoped. This is the only communication he has had with his friend since September, and the last he will hear from him for awhile.

The second quarter of his junior year passes as quickly as the first for him. On January 22, 1968, word begins to filter into the popular media of the battle for Khe San, in Vietnam. Things do not appear as rosy on the war front as the administration has been representing. At the end of the month, the news is filled with reports of a "Tet offensive," which stretches into February. There are widespread attacks by the Viet Cong throughout South Vietnam, reaching right into the heart of Saigon, including an attack on the American embassy there. Clearly, the insurgents are not beaten into submission and retreating, as the government has claimed. BP's fears for Donny's welfare heighten with this escalation in violence. On March 16, the My Lai massacre occurs, and in its aftermath, in the eyes of the rest of the world, the U.S.A. loses anything left of the moral high ground it had purported to occupy in the conflict.

On March 31, President Lyndon Johnson announces that he will not seek another term in office, which is widely seen as an admission of failure, reflecting his widespread unpopularity and the growing opposition to the war. Many are encouraged that the door has been opened for Robert F. Kennedy, who is running on a platform of social justice and non-intervention abroad, to assume the leadership of the nation. His popularity with, and engagement of, the younger generation is an undeniable asset.

On April 4, in Memphis, Tennessee, Dr. Martin Luther King, Jr., is assassinated, and everything changes. More than a hundred American cities go up in flames over the next week, as civil disorder erupts in the nation from coast to coast. The murder of this popular prophet of non-violent change, who had won the Nobel Peace Prize four years earlier, and become so effective in tying together the threads of injustice represented by the Vietnam War, the struggle for civil rights, and the needless tragedy of poverty in America, sets off a wave of pent-up frustration and anger in many people, over centuries of abuse and neglect, which results in chaos, looting and destruction.

As the riots rage, the government calls out the National Guard to restore order, assisting local police departments who are unable to cope with the level of chaos. The deployment of massive military force into American cities, at a level which had not been seen since the Civil War, largely contains these disturbances within the ghettos where they arise, scarring them deeply, while the important centers of government, commerce and investment are protected and preserved. The suburbs are saved, while the businesses and residents who are able to do so simply flee the blighted inner cities, leaving them to decay, sprouting poverty and crime in the ashes.

For BP, the murder of Dr. King evokes the same feelings of horror and angst in him as were raised by the assassination of JFK. How could this have happened? Who could have done it, and why? Visions of conspiracies dance through his head. There are no reports regarding the perpetrators of this terrible act, but there is plenty of speculation. He is fairly certain that no final, unassailable explanation for the crime will ever be found, just as with JFK's assassination, and regardless of the intent of those responsible, he is positive it will not have the effect they desired, whatever it might have been. Events like this have a way of spiraling out of anyone's control, in unforeseen ways, he is sure.

He decides that the only thing he can control in these circumstances is his own reaction to the incident. He joins a coalition of activists on campus who are planning a collective response from the UCSD student body. It is decided that another campus demonstration is not enough, in this instance—that some sort of "direct action" within the community is necessary, to carry their concerns outside the confines of the "ivory tower" to the city at large. A protest march through downtown La Jolla is planned for the following Tuesday, April 9, and they are determined that it be a peaceful demonstration, with fervent hope that the local police do not overreact.

The Tuesday the Ninth Committee, as they dub the loose coalition, creates flyers and posts them around campus to publicize the march, as well as holding noon-time rallies in Revelle plaza to inform students and staff of the action and enlist their support. They hastily arrange carpools for transportation of those students who are without vehicles, and in less than four days, despite the impending crunch of final exams for the quarter, nearly a thousand students assemble and march down Girard Avenue, through the heart of La Jolla, waving signs and chanting slogans, blocking traffic, under the watchful, glaring eyes of the local police. Though many fear it, and some are quite prepared to respond, no violence ensues, and no arrests are made. BP's impression is that the residents and business people in La Jolla, as well as the cops, look at them with one of two different attitudes: either an air of tolerant pity—"Oh those poor, misguided kids, when will they ever learn…"; or a more prevalent, and thinly masked, quite malevolent disposition composed of ignorance, fear and mistrust—"There's something happening here, what it is ain't exactly clear…."

The mood on campus is volatile, and moving towards more militant measures. During their Tuesday the Ninth preparations, on April 7, an unarmed Black Panther, Bobby Hutton, is killed in a hail of bullets from Oakland police, and his companion, Eldridge Cleaver, is wounded and arrested. For the BNC members and other campus activists, it is easy to believe that their own lives might be in jeopardy. Some arm themselves.

Death threats are received by Dr. Herbert Marcuse, whom the John Birch Society (and others in the community) hold unjustly responsible for instigating campus unrest. Bodyguards are arranged for his protection by SDS members. When BP is asked if he will take a shift in providing this protection, he declines. At dinner that evening, he mentions to Bumper that one of his professors is under 24-hour armed guard. "Hey bro', if you need to borrow my 9mm Beretta, just let me know," is Bumper's response.

In May of 1968, a student strike in Paris precipitates police confrontations that degenerate into weeks of widespread violence. French workers join the student strike by the millions, and the country is paralyzed. The De Gaulle government is nearly toppled before various misdeeds and deceptions by the leftist union federation, as well as the French Communist party, defuse the situation. "Revolution is in the air…."

On June 4, as the school term is winding to a close, Robert Kennedy wins the California primary election. Late that night, leaving a victory celebration at the Ambassador Hotel in Los Angeles, he is shot by another "lone gunman." This is a wrenching shock for BP and many others, who had held out hope that Bobby would be able to effect a change in the direction of the country. Little is understood, again, regarding the motive for his murder, but it may have its roots in the Middle East conflict, as the man who pulled the trigger is a young Palestinian named Sirhan Sirhan. "Paranoia strikes deep…."

After the school year ends, while some campus activists make plans to head for Chicago and the Democratic National Convention in August, BP retreats into his surfing life for the summer. With his trusty panel truck, his latest surfboard, a sleeping bag and camping implements, a small bag of pot and what's left of the Purple Haze, along with a satchel full of books he wants to read, he makes a three-month sojourn down the Baja California coast. After giving $90 to Bumper for his summer rent, he takes $300 in cash out of his stash and heads south, stopping at the border for a visa, Mexican car insurance, and to exchange some dollars for pesos, then drives further down the peninsula than he has ever gone before.

Once past the border towns and south of Ensenada, the complexion of Baja California changes completely. It is a desert wilderness, mostly, yielding a very hard but seemingly satisfying life for those few who would challenge it. Exploring the coast in search of waves is a daunting task for BP. Outside of the main towns, most roads are unpaved, unmapped, and can become impassable at times, due to either landslides, very deep ruts, or a layer of sandy silt deposited in flash floods, deep enough for a vehicle to sink itself into and become immobile. He proceeds carefully, carrying extra gasoline and water in jugs, in case he becomes stranded. In the end, he has very good luck, discovering several deserted surf spots next to small fishing villages, where he camps for days or weeks at a time, until forced to return to the larger towns for supplies.

Though his Spanish is rudimentary and halting at best, the native people he meets in these villages are always friendly, helpful, and generous to a fault (considering they are extremely poor, by his standards). They often invite him into their modest homes for a meal, or giving him some of their fish, beans, tortillas or garden vegetables. He tries to return their generosity, to give them some money, at least, in exchange for their kindness, though they often refuse this gesture.

His southerly trek ends some 600 miles south of San Diego, at a place called Punta Pequeña, outside of the tiny village of San Juanico, where he scores many perfect days of righthand, point-break surf in idyllic conditions, while battling the boredom of the barren stretches in between swells with his books and drugs.

Meanwhile, back in the U.S., the Youth International party (or Yippies), along with many other anti-war and civil rights activist groups, stage massive protests at the 1968 Democratic National Convention in Chicago. These demonstrations devolve into riots when they are met with violent police repression, changing the course of the upcoming presidential election. Hubert Humphrey ends up as the compromise candidate, but has lost all credibility and support from progressives during the process.

After the convention, the "New Left" is added to the surveillance list of COINTELPRO, the FBI counterintelligence program designed to neutralize political dissidents. As J. Edgar Hoover, longtime director of the FBI, puts it: "The forces which are most anxious to weaken our internal security are not always easy to identify. Communists have been trained in deceit and secretly work toward the day when they hope to replace our American way of life with a Communist dictatorship. They utilize cleverly camouflaged movements, such as peace groups and civil rights groups to achieve their sinister purposes.… It is important to learn to know the enemies of the American way of life."

Meanwhile, BP is decompressing south of the border, largely unaware of these developments, as his only contact with home is the small, transistorized shortwave radio he sometimes turns on at night to listen to news broadcasts and weather reports. He lives a simple life, surfing, making new foreign friends, getting high, learning Spanish, and trying to educate himself. He rereads the Bible and the Quaker text, *Faith & Practice*, from cover to cover, trying to unravel the mysteries and contradictions of the Christian faith into which he was born and raised. He makes a sincere effort to open his heart to Jesus, as directed in the New Testament, hoping for the light of God to fill his soul, but nothing walks through the open door.

He studies *The Koran*, the sacred text of Islam, and Sufi mysticism as well, reading P.D. Ouspensky's *In Search of the Miraculous* and G.I. Gurdjieff's *Beelzebub's Tales to His Grandson*. A book that he finds extremely interesting was given to him by a friend from school, just before he left town: *The Teachings of Don Juan: A Yaqui Way of Knowledge* by Carlos Castenada. There is something compelling about the way the author speaks of a mysterious realm of *nonordinary reality*, but BP is unsure whether he is reporting it, or fictionalizing.

Near the beginning of September, two other young *gringo* surfers stumble upon the spot he has found. At first he resents the intrusion, having had it alone for so long, but they are both very good surfers and very respectful of his privacy, camping away from him, down the bay, and surfing one of the other lineups at the point, so as not to intrude on his waves.

He quickly realizes how silly his reticence is in the situation, as he probably has more in common with them than anyone else within several hundred miles, so on the second day of surfing together, he paddles up and introduces himself to them in the water. Their names are Jay and John, and they are from Laguna Beach, California. They, too, are on an extended surf expedition, on their way back to the States after beginning the summer in Mazatlan, on the mainland of Mexico, taking the ferry across the Gulf of California to La Paz on the way home. They turn out to be very cool guys, in his estimation, befriending him quickly and effortlessly. He shares some of his LSD with them, and they turn him on to a bag of very strong pot they had scored on the mainland, which they call "Acapulco Gold."

They surf some very fine waves together during an extended southerly swell, and exchange stories. He learns of some of the other great surfbreaks they had visited in Mazatlan and to the south, including one they described as very similar to this one, another "Mexican Malibu," located north of Puerto Vallarta, not to mention several they found at the tip of the Baja peninsula, exposed to the southerly *chubasco* swells wrapping up into the Gulf.

Compared to himself, Jay and John are very well-equipped for their journey, driving a new, four-wheel-drive Dodge Powerwagon with a camper shell in the bed, jerry cans strapped to the sides, along with two spare tires mounted front and back, an electric winch, and a row of night-driving lights attached to the roof of the cab. He is a bit jealous of their rig, but they are basically humble people, not flaunting their wealth in any way. He is very sorry to see them go when they pull out to head north after a couple of weeks. They exchange phone numbers and addresses, and Jay insists that he look them up when he gets back home. "I want you to make me a board like yours," he says. "I like the way it rides. I'll make it worth your while, man, don't worry. Get hold of me, OK?"

After another week by himself, with the swell fading to a dribble, he begins to feel a bit lonely and homesick, where before he had been quite content. At the end of September, with only a week or so left until the beginning of the next school year, he breaks camp and makes the long drive back to the north in three days. Stopping for the last night at K-42, he carefully packs and buries the rest of his drug stash in one of the arroyos there, drawing a cryptic map to remind him of the location, and drives back across the border without any worries about the U.S. Customs officials searching his vehicle for contraband.

Lumumba-Zapata College

As soon as he crosses the border, returning from Mexico to settle back into his place at the farm for the next school year, BP experiences a bit of "culture shock." Beside the obvious differences in the language and the level of development and wealth on the U.S. side, everything seems to be so much more crowded and fast-paced, even frenetic, in a way he had never noticed before spending so much time alone down south. He must acclimate immediately to the greater speed and density of the traffic on the highways, as he has spent most of his time traveling on rutted, washboardy, dirt roads at speeds of less than 25 miles an hour lately. Other impacts are more subtle.

As he drives home towards Del Mar on the relatively new, incredibly wide and smooth, Interstate-5 freeway, he is struck by all the new construction underway everywhere. The rapid growth of San Diego county, which has seen the addition of a half-million new residents in the last ten years, is readily apparent to him. As he gets off the freeway and crosses over to the old Highway 101, he is shocked to see a huge, new condominium development that has sprung up in Carmel Valley since he had left, just below the farm. Driving up Fourth Street to the farm, there are several new houses being framed on what had been vacant lots, adjacent to their property.

He is welcomed home by his surf brothers and regales them with stories of his adventure over a joint or two, listening to the latest Beatles release, the *White Album*, on the stereo. He calls his parents to tell them he is home and doing fine. His mom had been worried about him traveling alone, ever since he told her of his plans, and is relieved to hear that he is well. His dad had mostly been concerned that he get his butt back to school on time.

He settles back into his life, but marvels at how luxurious the comforts of home feel to him now—the simple things like running water, taking a hot shower, instead of dumping tepid water over his head out of a bucket to wash the salt and dirt off his body; using a toilet that flushes to a sewer system, rather than digging a hole with his camping shovel; having a refrigerator rather than a rusty old ice chest to keep things cold; a real stove to cook on, electronic devices to entertain him. He appreciates all the conveniences a modern standard of living offers him, but at the same time, he realizes that he doesn't really *need* them at all—they are not essential, as he has learned from witnessing those who are leading difficult, but contented lives in extreme poverty—and he is liberated by that knowledge. He knows that if he is ever forced, or even *chooses,* to live such a life, he could survive. And the fact that the majority of inhabitants on the planet do not have access to so many conveniences and luxuries seems patently unfair, embarrassing him in a way he never felt previously.

He re-establishes his school routine, enrolling in a full load of philosophy, political science and literature classes, once again enjoying those efforts. His academic achievements the year before had hauled him clear up from near "drop-out" status to making the dean's honor list.

Ronald Reagan's tenure as governor threatens the rapid expansion of the institution, though, as budget cuts loom, and conservatives attack the higher education system. Student activism shoots to even higher levels, with elements of increased participation and organization on all sides.

There are protests against the university's involvement in the war machine, most notably the presence on campus of the Institute for Defense Analysis, which carries out classified research for the government. The administration hurriedly moves all such classified activity and documents down to a small satellite facility of Scripps Institution located on the San Diego bay, the Naval Electronics Laboratory, to protect their security and ensure that federal grant money is not threatened.

Students want to take control of every part of their lives and offer alternatives to the established order. Through the collective effort of a number of hippies on campus, pooling their own money and renting a small, dilapidated commercial building next to the highway in Solana Beach, a "People's Food Cooperative" is created, in order to provide low-cost, unprocessed, natural foods to students. BP contributes some of his own funds and joins the co-op, working a shift at the store once a week, as all members do.

They wrangle with the administration about the lack of public transportation to the north county, where many students live, and manage to win funding for a university-subsidized "Coast Cruiser," an old school bus, which makes continuous runs from campus to Leucadia and back on the coast highway, with a stop in Solana Beach at the food co-op, so students can ride for free and shop there.

Students also want to control aspects of their own education, and by means of an agreement made during the Free Speech movement, they bring the Berkeley-sponsored Sociology 139X course, designed to address special student social concerns, to the San Diego campus. The first lecturer designated for the series is none other than Eldridge Cleaver, the militant Black Panther who is out on bail after the shooting incident in Oakland, and has written a fiery book entitled *Soul on Ice*.

Cleaver's appearance on campus is like throwing salt on an open wound for the conservative San Diego community. His obscenity-laced speech, in the street vernacular of the ghetto, exhorting students to chant "Fuck the war! Fuck Reagan!" over and over again, and reminding them "If you are not part of the solution, you are part of the problem," is not well-received off campus. There are renewed efforts by local groups, including the American Foreign

Legion, to have Dr. Marcuse dismissed from the faculty, as he is still erroneously believed to be a fomenter of student rebellion, though he has never openly participated in campus protests. Merely his ideas are considered dangerous and corrupting.

In November, Richard Nixon is elected president by the slimmest of margins, appealing to what he calls the "Silent Majority" of social conservatives who oppose the counterculture, and promising to bring "peace with honor" to the conflict in Vietnam. The decidedly racist independent candidate, former governor of Alabama George Wallace, carries 5 southern states and receives over 10 million votes in the election, demonstrating the deep resistance to desegregation and affirmative action that exists in the country. In the state election, a bond issue for higher education is defeated, indicating the public's growing distrust of the university system and its reluctance to provide funding, resulting in the first of many increases in tuition and fees for students over the coming years, and cutbacks in the capital program for new construction. The original plan for twelve colleges to be developed at UCSD over 24 years (which had already been extended to a more realistic 36) is scrapped. Expansion will proceed at a much slower pace now, with funding so uncertain.

Later that month, Governor Reagan, attending a meeting of the UC Regents scheduled at UCSD, is greeted by throngs of jeering, shouting students. Hundreds of San Diego Police Department and California Highway Patrol officers are deployed to campus in riot gear to protect and insulate him from the protestors, which only results in further demonstrations by the students over the next several days, focused against the governor, the regents and their own university administrators for allowing this incursion by outside authorities. "PIGS OFF CAMPUS!" is the rallying cry.

While he is not successful in convincing the regents to fire Dr. Marcuse at the meeting, Reagan is able to pressure them into passing a resolution removing the academic credit from Sociology 139X, which is an unprecedented occurrence, as such decisions on curriculum had been delegated to the academic senates at each campus decades earlier.

The students decide it is time to take matters into their own hands. Working with some of the more progressive faculty members, they seek to insinuate themselves into the planning for what will be the third college at UCSD, scheduled to open in 1970. Their ambition is to shape the new college in a way that reflects their goals of universal human rights and equality, their progressive ideals for social change, and most importantly, shared governance.

The BSC had already been working for some time towards having an African-American studies program initiated at the school, and now they join forces with MAYA (soon to affiliate itself with the more militant organization *Movimiento Estudiantil Chicano de Aztlán* or MEChA) to begin drawing up an outline for a new kind of college that would be composed of, and controlled by, mostly minority students, black and brown. Extreme problems require extreme solutions.

During the long Thanksgiving weekend, BP contacts Jay and John and makes a trip up to Laguna Beach to visit them. They surf at Brooks Street, trading boards in the small surf as they had done several times down south, and hang out together, reminiscing over their Mexican adventures. Both Jay and John are impressed with the performance of BP's Zen flyer, even in these junkier waves, and they each ask him to build custom versions for themselves.

They get high on some more of the excellent Acapulco Gold that BP had first tasted with them in Mexico, and hammer out a deal during his stay in their small but comfortable house in Laurel Canyon. It turns out that they are sitting on quite a load of the herb. Apparently, their Powerwagon was packed with more than camping supplies when he had first met them. They reveal to him that they are selling it off for $100 per pound, which is the going retail rate, considering its high quality, general inflation and demand, but would be willing to trade him three kilos for two new surfboards. This seems quite agreeable to BP, and he heads back to Del Mar in his truck the following Monday morning with a brick of the weed, which they have fronted him as a down payment, stopping in Laguna Niguel at the Clark Foam factory to pick up two polyurethane blanks.

Before the Christmas break, he has smoked, given away, and sold off most of the weed in $10 lids, which is highly appreciated in his circles, and shaped and glassed two custom boards for them; a 7'2" for John and a 6'10" for Jay, who is slightly smaller in stature, both of them rounded pintail shapes, similar to his. Though their quality is not quite as perfect as what would be found in a professional shop, he is satisfied with their appearance. As soon as he finishes final exams, he makes another run up to Laguna to deliver them. John and Jay are quite pleased with the outcome, and give him the other two kilos of pot for the boards.

Before he leaves, they ask him if he might be interested in a little LSD. Always curious, especially with his last few hits of the Purple Haze still buried down at K-42, and since Griff has told him that the Bear, Augustus Owsley Stanley III, had been busted in Marin county late last year, drying up that source, he says "Sure!" They give him a bottle with a few hundred little orange pills in it and tell him to try them out, see how he likes them. They're called "Orange Sunshine," he's told, and produced by someone right there in town they call the "Brotherhood," so if he wants more, he can have as many as he can move at 20 cents apiece. BP drives carefully back home, feeling like he is sitting on the mother lode.

Bumper is in Hawaii again, but Skip and Rocky drop the Orange Sunshine acid with him the next weekend. It is good, but seems to be a stronger dose than the Purple Haze. BP suffers from a pretty heavy bout of paranoia in the middle of the trip. Skip and Rocky love it, though, and assure him that they can help him sell tons of it at $2 a hit. True to their word, before BP has to go back to school in January, it is all gone, and he makes another visit to Laguna, buying a thousand more hits for $200 from his friends.

On campus, there is a huge demand for both the acid and the weed he is selling. Cautioned by the pot busts that occurred in the campus dorms at the end of the last year, and rumors of undercover police and FBI agents being inserted on campuses to investigate student activities, he sells drugs only to his close friends and people he has known for several years, usually in larger quantities and at a discount, so that they can make some money on it and keep some free dope for themselves.

He enjoys his studies and still works hard in his classes, at the expense of surf time. A short story he reads in his literature class by the Argentinean writer and poet Jorge Luis Borges, titled "*The Aleph*," especially catches his imagination. The Aleph is a point in space that contains all other points, allowing anyone who views it to see everything in the universe from every angle at once. In the story, it is located in the basement of a house owned by a friend of the main character, who is a fictionalized version of Borges himself. BP is sure he must have taken some acid to come up with some of the compelling descriptions he had written of this infinite singularity.

He is also introduced to the writings of Franz Kafka, which he finds a bit bizarre and impenetrable at first, and Bertolt Brecht, whose work is more obviously political. Brecht uses a concept in his plays which BP finds very intriguing—*Verfremdungseffekt*, a distancing or alienation effect, as it is explained to him by his professor, a German immigrant named Reinhardt Lettau. This technique is designed to provoke rational self-reflection and not just complacent catharsis in the audience, by reminding them constantly that what they are viewing on the stage is just a representation of reality and not reality itself. Brecht's intention was to empower them, to try to make them identify the problems in their own world, and after the play, go out and solve them. BP wonders what Brecht would have thought if he had dropped a little acid, and reality itself appeared as a representation, as it often has in his own experience.

In his political science class, he studies the theory and practice of politics and political systems in a rigorous way that he finds eye-opening. Although he is not enamored of the Communist system, it is obvious to him that American democracy has its own set of problems. While he is not convinced that it actually contains "the seeds of its own destruction," as espoused by Marxist theory, he does believe strongly in one tenet of political theory that he learns: "As any political system grows larger, it tends to become more corrupt."

There is plenty of evidence he can identify of such corruption in our capitalistic system, with corporate welfare and the rule of the rich driving policy. He admires greatly the principles of participatory democracy, of freedom of religion, and the free market, but can see that protections are needed against their abuse, especially when those who control the mass media use it to shape and influence public opinion for selfish and nefarious purposes. He fears the "tyranny of the majority" when it is intolerant and misinformed. He can see that unbridled capitalism brought monopolies and "robber barons" in the past, and that greed can ultimately result in an evil system—domination over resources by a few, oppression of the poor and powerless—without checks, balances and regulation by the government to limit the power of the rich, and equally powerful unions to allow workers to bargain collectively.

Meanwhile, he sees the trend towards concentration of wealth into the hands of a few continuing, as well as governmental regulation gone wrong, such as the rules against recreational drug use. He is convinced these laws are just plain stupid, as had been the prohibition of alcohol in the '20s, driving a portion of the economy underground in an attempt to legislate morality, and turning people like himself into outlaws. There are no easy answers, in such a complex society.

While he is proud to be an American, and feels lucky to have been born in this country, with all that it has accomplished, he thinks the system definitely needs a swift kick (or two!) in the ass. Not a Communist revolution, just an evolution towards some sort of enlightened, tolerant, democratic socialism. Instead of a division between "haves" and "have-nots," he hopes for a future of "enoughs" everywhere, though he sees little possibility of that happening in the near future.

On Mar. 20, 1969, eight activists are indicted by a Chicago grand jury after an extensive investigation into the events of the 1968 Democratic convention. Though it will be many months before they are brought to trial (becoming the "Chicago Seven" in the process, when one of them, Black Panther Bobby Seale, is bound and gagged in the courtroom for outbursts against the judge at the beginning of the trial, and then sentenced to 4 years in prison for contempt, the longest sentence for that offense ever seen in an American court), many people nationwide are outraged over their arrests.

Around the same time, the coalition of activists who had been working on detailed planning for the third college at UCSD issue their formal set of demands to the administration. They are comprehensive and unilateral, containing some bits of Marxist rhetoric that are sure to cause consternation among the powers-that-be.

Recognizing that access to higher education has been systematically denied to members of minority populations, they insist that the third college must admit 35% Black and 35% Mexican-American students, on the basis of a student-controlled admissions committee, ignoring the usual UC admissions requirements as necessary to achieve this goal—"in order to compensate for past and present injustices and to serve those most affected by white racism and economic exploitation."

Beyond this, they demand that the school be "devoted to relevant education for minority youths and to the study of the contemporary social problems of all people;" that student representatives have an equal voice in the governance of the college, including the selection of the provost and the hiring and firing of faculty and staff; and even that the bonds for financing construction of the college be held by minority financial institutions, and the architects and contractors involved must come from the minority community. In a move that is sure to cause heartburn for Ronald Reagan and the regents, they propose that it be named "Lumumba-Zapata College" in honor of those leaders of the African nationalist and Mexican revolutionary movements.

This sets off an intense campus debate, tumultuous negotiations, and a power struggle within the university that will continue for years, while igniting an uproar in the outside community. Nothing could have represented a greater threat to the status quo of the university.

When BP hears the "Lumumba-Zapata demands" for the first time, read by Angela Davis at a large student rally in the Revelle cafeteria, they sound perfectly reasonable to him. There is no doubt about the fact that enrollments of black and brown kids in the university system are far below their proportion in the general population, and it is not because they are stupid. Judging by the overwhelming support the demands receive from many of his peers, he is not alone. In these heady days of change, anything seems possible. What they all underestimate is the massive inertia of the greater society at large, its resistance to change, and the power of the forces arrayed against them.

PEOPLE'S PARK

During the last quarter of his senior year, BP is called to the Revelle Provost's Office for a "degree check." This procedure determines a student's eligibility for graduation, by checking the courses they have completed against the degree requirements. He is mildly surprised to hear from his academic adviser that he is not yet eligible for a B.A. degree from Revelle College, though he must admit that he has never diligently studied the degree requirements in the general catalog. He is informed that he has not yet completed the foreign language proficiency testing necessary for graduation, and that while he has passed a sufficient number of courses for a philosophy major, the hodge-podge of classes he has taken in political science and literature are insufficient to constitute a minor course of study in either one. The upshot of the meeting is that he will not be graduating with the rest of his class in June. His options are to either transfer to Muir College, and convince some professor there to accept his political science and literature classes as some kind of interdisciplinary minor, which he may be able to do over the summer (or perhaps during a single quarter of the next term), or to continue at Revelle for at least the first two quarters of the next school year, in order to earn a minor degree and pass the language proficiency test.

The latter seems the best course of action to him, since as long as he is enrolled as a fulltime student he is not eligible for the draft. He even considers going for the full year, and completing enough courses for a double major, but when he tells his father that he is going to need to stay for a fifth year to earn his degree, his father goes ballistic. In a tense phone call, he denigrates BP for not paying attention to the degree requirements and failing to graduate on schedule. His rant expands itself into other areas of contention between them, sources of alienation over the last few years of which BP had never quite realized the full extent, including his decision to study social science instead of a "hard" science, and his participation in campus activism.

"What are you trying to do, son, ruin your life?" his father virtually screams at him. "You're never going to get a good job and be successful enough to take care of a family the way you're going! Who would even hire you with the way you look now—hair down to your shoulders and beard down to your chest? I'm ashamed for my friends to even see you these days, looking like a damned hippie! I'm not going to put up with your laziness and undisciplined behavior any more. You're going to be 21 this year, and its time for you to grow up and act like an adult. If you expect me to go on supporting your education, you better knuckle down and get serious about it—either shave that beard and cut your hair, stop messing around with these campus protests, or you are on your own. No more money from me, son. It's for your own good," his father declares.

BP is a little shocked by how far apart he has grown from his father, but he is not ashamed of his life or threatened by the idea of independence. He is as convinced of the failure of his father's generation to address the ills of the world as his father is of his apparent waywardness. Though his father isn't aware of it, he has plenty of money to pay for school and live well enough for the coming year without the $75 per quarter his father has been giving him. "That's fine, Dad," he answers, in a bit of a huff, "I can get by on my own, don't worry." It is the last time he speaks to his father for many years.

While it is true that BP does not know exactly what he is going to do with his life, he is young and strong, and the possibilities seem endless. He knows that he does not want to follow the conventional path of career and family, though, as his father expects. He has a strong feeling that his destiny lies elsewhere, and he is prepared to forge ahead bravely into the unknown by himself, under his own power.

On May 7, angered by what they perceive as stalling tactics by the UCSD Academic Senate in approving the Lumumba-Zapata demands, the student coalition members storm out of a meeting with them and gather in Revelle plaza, attracting a larger crowd with their protest, exhorting them to take some further action to insure their demands are met. Somehow, late in the afternoon, it is decided that occupying a campus building will draw more attention to their cause, and put pressure on the administration and senate to accelerate progress. About 400 students march to the Registrar's Office, which is already closed for the day, and one of them kicks in the locked door. Only around fifty people go inside, as it is a fairly small office, while the others stand outside and make plans for how to support the occupiers if it becomes a long siege, or the police show up.

Luckily, word filters back to the senate meeting about the occupation, and a compromise proposal is passed which is acceptable to the students, and quickly communicated to them in the barricaded building. Within ninety minutes, just as the SDPD arrives on the scene to assist the overwhelmed campus police, the occupation ends and the students leave the building, blending into the crowd outside. Only the person who kicked in the office door is identified and arrested, for destruction of public property.

At the same time the Lumumba-Zapata controversy is raging at UCSD, an issue that has been building on the UC Berkeley campus for several months comes to a head. The university had acquired a piece of off-campus property on Telegraph Avenue for a future parking lot and playing field, but it had been abandoned during development for lack of funding. Local activists decided that it should become a public park. University officials never agreed to such a plan, but the community moved ahead and cleared the neglected 2.8 acre plot, installing landscaping and playground equipment over several months time, essentially "commandeering" it for public use, naming it "People's Park." The university administration insisted that their plan for a sports field would continue, but began negotiating with the People's Park committee over a compromise, eventually allowing them to retain at least one-quarter of the parcel for public use when development proceeded.

Ronald Reagan had already called the Berkeley campus "a haven for Communist sympathizers, protestors and sex deviants," reflecting the views of his friend, J. Edgar Hoover, and he considered the university's mild response to the People's Park controversy as "pandering to anarchists who would appropriate state property."

On May 15, seeing a chance to make good on his campaign promises to bring law and order to the state colleges, and ignoring the promises made by the university administration to the park committee, Reagan orders hundreds of California Highway Patrol and Berkeley police officers into the city. They cordon off an eight-block area around People's Park to prevent any interference, and proceed to install an 8' tall chain-link fence around the property to keep people out, while destroying much of the landscaping the community had painstakingly installed.

This move touches off a protest by thousands of students and community activists, who march on the park and overcome the officers left to guard it, throwing rocks and bottles at them, trying to tear down the fence. Police respond with tear gas, but they are unable to control the crowd, and the scene turns into a full-fledged riot. Hundreds more police are called in from surrounding cities and counties, under the direction of Reagan's chief of staff, Edwin Meese III. They wade into the crowd in full riot gear with batons swinging, some using shotguns for crowd control. Hundreds of protestors are injured, and one young man, James Rector, who was not even participating in the riot, merely watching it from the roof of the Telegraph Repertory Cinema, is killed by a shotgun blast.

Governor Reagan declares a state of emergency and sends thousands of National Guard troops into the city, placing it under martial law, arresting nearly a thousand protestors, barricading the streets with barbed wire and armored personnel carriers, and denying any public assembly of more than five people at a time with tear gas attacks from military helicopters, even though the Berkeley City Council objects vehemently to the occupation of their city.

"Holy shit!" BP says when he hears the news. "It's not just the Panthers anymore, now they're shooting white kids!" These are prophetic words, as it turns out.

Kent State

The summer of 1969 continues to be as chaotic, fast-paced, and stimulating for BP as the last school year had been. Surfing becomes his focus again, along with women, who have become a major attraction in his life. The "shortboard revolution" is well underway in California, as it is in the rest of the world. No longer are he and his friends in the minority at most spots, as surfers abandon their traditional longboards in droves. Instead, they are ahead of the curve and in the vanguard of a new movement, leading a sea change in the spirit and nature of surfing, of "total involvement" with the waves.

The major manufacturers in the surfing industry are thrown into a shambles by this development, not having foreseen the scope of it and unable to respond to its rapidity. Thousands of brand new longboards gather dust in the inventories of surf shops nationwide, as new shortboard designs evolve on a daily basis in garages and backyards everywhere.

BP and his crew continue to develop and build their own boards, with the small shop on the farm becoming a hotbed of creativity, attracting other local surfers to try their hand at "home-brewed" shaping as well. They experiment with a number of new concepts and features, including a short, wide, twin-finned, split-tailed, "fish" design that Bumper favors from his kneeboarding experience. BP builds one of these for himself at 6'4", a natural length for him, he figures, as it is as long as he is tall. It is fun and fast, working very well in smaller waves, but he feels it is a little squirrely and unstable for bigger surf. The idea of having a "quiver" of different boards for different conditions becomes perfectly logical and attainable for him now, whereas in the past, owning just a single board had been sufficient.

On July 16, the Apollo 11 mission blasts off from Cape Canaveral, Florida, and four days later, a man walks on the moon for the first time. This is one of the few times that the small black-and-white television set at the farm is turned on. They all hold their collective breath with the rest of the country as the Saturn rocket rises from the launch pad, feel the same giddy wonder and pride while watching the grainy pictures from space of Neil Armstrong and Buzz Aldrin climbing down out of the lunar module to plant the American flag on the moon's surface, and sigh in relief when the crew splashes back down to earth safely.

As impressed as BP is by this monumental technical achievement, as inspiring as it is for the country to reach this seemingly impossible goal that JFK had set nine years earlier, he can't help but feel that somehow it is a showy but empty achievement. The "space race" is rooted in the cold war with the Soviets, after all, the same heedless competition that landed us in the quagmire of Vietnam. He is sure that the government would never have tolerated the immense cost of the space program except for the fact that it represents the new military high ground, a place for the deployment of weapons and surveillance equipment to maintain U.S. superiority.

He wonders what might have been accomplished if we had not spent these billions of dollars on war and the space race, but instead had focused our resources on something else—an end to poverty and hunger in America, perhaps, as Dr. Martin Luther King, Jr. had advocated, with a college education for every child in the country thrown in as well?

Though he is sure that there will be some technological spin-offs from the space program that will advance science, he reckons they will most likely be used for military purposes, or to feed the insatiable materialism of the country with new products and gadgets to consume. What kind of prize does the moon represent, in reality? It looks to him to be just as expected—a rocky, desolate wasteland, totally inhospitable to human life. In terms of space exploration, it is a mere baby step, anyway, the closest heavenly body in our solar system. Compared to the vast reaches of the Milky Way, not to mention the billions of other galaxies many light years beyond, we have merely fallen out of the crib onto the floor, not made a "giant leap." And why this outward focus—what about inner exploration, the secrets of the mind? Is it possible that he has traveled further on acid in his own mind already, in relative terms, without ever leaving the earth?

For him, the most meaningful images from the Apollo missions are the ones he sees published in magazines, the crystal-clear color photographs that show our tiny blue planet rising above the lunar surface in the distance. It reminds him of the fact that we are all trapped together on this spaceship called earth—that life is fragile, and we need to take care of the planet and each other.

Making a run up to Laguna Beach for more "supplies" from John and Jay in late July, he shows them the "fish" board he has made. They take it out in some small surf and like it, commissioning him to build two more for them, a 6'2" and a 5'10". They have sold all of the Acapulco Gold by now, but they have made a local connection for large quantities of some fine Columbian weed, and tell him that their smuggling days are probably over. With people bringing pot into the country by the ton, it doesn't make any sense for them to do it anymore, they allow, when it is easier and safer to just act as middlemen. They hook him up with a kilo of the Columbian as a down payment on the new surfboards, and throw in 100 hits of the latest LSD from the Brotherhood, which are little barrel-shaped orange tablets. "These things are a bunch stronger than the Sunshine," they caution him. "We call them the Orange Crush. They're at least a double dose—maybe 800 micrograms. You can split each one with someone easily."

Life on the farm turns into the usual, perpetual, summertime party, at an even more frenzied pace, approaching bacchanalian proportions at times. Friends and acquaintances of Bumper's from far-flung places show up and stay for days at a time, as well as the usual local crowd of fun lovers, which has only grown in magnitude (and altitude) over the last few years. They hold afternoon barbeques in an open rock pit in the back yard, cooking food for everyone to offset the effects of the copious quantities of beer, wine, acid and pot consumed, winding up with a big bonfire in the pit to accompany the evening's entertainment, which is usually singing and dancing to rock music piped out of the stereo into large speakers on the back porch. People are often camping overnight all over the property, and young women sunbathe topless during the day. Inhibitions are thrown to the wind, and the sense of community and togetherness are high.

BP has come to adore women, enjoying a string of intimate relationships with liberated young females for the last year who find him interesting and require no commitment, other than sharing a mutual passion for exploring each other's bodies and creating pleasure. This summer is filled with many such exciting encounters. Some of these casual romances last for only a night, and some for as long as a week or two, but never with any thought of permanence. They each move on to someone else in the end, with no hurt feelings or regret, as he is always clear about his intentions, and they neither ask nor expect more from him.

When he drops one of the Orange Crush barrels for the first time, he finds the experience overwhelmingly intense, not the more delightful, insightful thrill of his earlier trips. Ignoring John and Jay's advice regarding their strength, he takes a whole tablet and comes on to it fast and hard, barely able to maintain a semblance of normal functioning for many hours. He can scarcely talk, and finds even the simplest things like standing and walking around difficult under the barrage of bizarre sensory input. He suffers another bout of extreme paranoia, certain that anyone who sees him will know immediately how fucked-up he is.

He has made the mistake of taking it alone, and wishes he had the support and guidance of a friend. Luckily, he is at the beach at Torrey Pines for the day, with very few people around, but nonetheless, he laboriously climbs halfway up the bluff and sits in the middle of a clump of bushes, peering out at the ocean and the beach below occasionally, making sure no one is following him—hiding out of anyone's sight until he comes down from the worst of the acid rush.

One of the strangest and most frightening aspects of this daunting mental ordeal for him is a baffling and persistent sense of déjà vu—that he is not experiencing anything that happens for the first time. Everything has a disagreeable familiarity to it, even though he is certain, in his more lucid moments, that his memory contains no trace of such an absurd situation in the past—huddling in a bush on the side of a cliff, peaking on acid, avoiding human contact. He suffers repeated and disturbing visions of a beautiful woman in a flowing, red robe who beckons to him, but then transforms into a horrible monster, fading away as he mentally turns and flees from her, only to pop back into his mind again later.

What had started out to be a stimulating day at the beach turns into a nightmare of paranoid thoughts, imagining himself as a puppet being jerked around by the invisible strings of some malevolent, time-shifting force that is causing him to repeat this unsettling experience over and over again, perhaps never to come down from it. Though the drug wears off after a few hours, as usual, and he returns to normalcy, it is a decidedly unpleasant trip. The prospect of remaining so high forever is frightening, and he wonders if that might be what it is like for people who suffer from mental illness. Is taking LSD actually just "going crazy" for awhile, he wonders? Do the brains of the insane manufacture some chemical that renders them similarly, but permanently, "tripping-out?"

When he returns home, he gives the rest of the Orange Crush to Skip and Rocky, telling them about his bum trip and warning them that each barrel probably contains about four doses, and that under no circumstances should they or anyone else take more than half a pill. As for himself, he is done with LSD and vows not to take it again. It never occurs to him to look any closer into the nature of his latest hallucinations.

Though he sheds this one vice, he soon picks up another—smoking cigarettes. Though his initial experimentation with cigarettes at a very young age had inoculated him somewhat against this temptation, leading him to avoid tobacco use, it is ubiquitous in his immediate social circle, and society at large. Many people, including all of his roommates, smoke cigarettes constantly. Due to lapses in his memory regarding the negative aspects of his childhood experience, he is eventually led to try them again—sparingly at first, usually only borrowing one or two while intoxicated during an evening of partying, especially if a woman in whom he is interested is also a smoker.

Though he had affected an image as a pipe-smoker when he had first entered college, he had never actually inhaled the tobacco smoke. Now, after several years of inhaling pot smoke religiously, it seems a much less noxious practice, and he falls into it easily, quickly becoming addicted to them. He buys large cans of Top cigarette tobacco and carries a pouch of it everywhere, along with Zig-Zag cigarette papers, and rolls his own, spurning the ready-made brands popular with his friends. He figures this is also good camouflage for public dope smoking, as it is impossible to tell the difference between a hand-rolled cigarette and a joint from a distance, except by the odor of the smoke. It also gives him an excuse for carrying rolling papers, which the cops have begun to label as "drug paraphernalia" in field interrogations.

On August 15–18, the Woodstock Music and Art Fair is held in Bethel, New York. Though it is very distant, and no one he knows attends, when he hears reports about it, he is heartened by the fact that hundreds of thousands of like-minded people had gathered for a celebration of music, peace, love, and freedom. It validates the counterculture of which he has become a part in an important way, giving him hope for the future—that this movement will continue to grow and sweep away the constrictions of existing cultural norms, establishing an alternative style of living outside the corporate system.

As he begins his fifth year at UCSD, everything seems to be moving in a positive direction. President Nixon actually appears to be seeking an end to the Vietnam War (while secretly approving the bombing of Laos and Cambodia in an effort to destroy the headquarters and supply lines for the insurgents, until Congress finds out and cuts his funding). In a surprising move, considering his anti-communist stance, Nixon approaches Communist China in an effort to leverage the Sino-Soviet split, forcing the USSR to come to the table for strategic arms limitation talks, while hoping to negotiate a settlement of the conflict in Southeast Asia that is acceptable to all three parties. None of his positive steps are enough for BP to overlook his violent excesses, however, and he will never forgive Nixon for setting up his "Western Whitehouse" at Cotton's Point, causing an increase in security which makes it more difficult for surfers to access the surfbreak there, and at Trestles, just to the south.

The negotiations over the proposed Lumumba-Zapata college at UCSD continue, nudged along, perhaps, by a bit of fear engendered in the faculty by the violence at Berkeley. Gaining more support for the idea in the academic senate, the members of the student coalition attend countless meetings, and committees are formed to establish an appropriate admissions policy and curriculum. The UCSD chancellor, William McGill, steps into the fray himself, though, when he perceives that the senate is capitulating to student pressure, allowing excessive student participation in the governance of the college. This is akin to letting the inmates run the asylum, in his eyes.

To drive a wedge between the militant Marxists and the more moderate students in the coalition, McGill accedes to some of the demands for greater minority representation at the third college, hoping to garner support from the less belligerent BSC and MAYA members, who are working only for greater access to higher education for the underprivileged, while rejecting the more radical demands of those who want nothing short of a proletarian revolution. In particular, he dismisses the idea of the college being built and funded by minority firms, which is impractical for a state institution, and objects to it being named "Lumumba-Zapata," stating that a hyphenated name is repugnant to him.

Early on in its planning, there had been a movement to name the college for the fallen civil rights leader, Martin Luther King, Jr., but his widow would not agree to the use of his name at UCSD. In the end, although the name "Third" had only designated its order in the planning process and architectural documents, students come to accept it as paying homage to the "Third World" somehow, and are hoodwinked into letting the college open with no new designation, as simply "Third College." Clever administrators know that students move on, and once the people who remember its beginnings are gone, the college can easily be renamed.

Amazingly enough, by means of some tweaking of admissions policy and procedures, which is never fully revealed to the regents, the college will open in the next year with a 70% minority population, and greater student governance than any other at the university. Though blunted somewhat by compromises, the activist thrust of the last year hasn't come to naught.

BP enrolls in a minimum course load of three classes, including a conversational Spanish course (which he finds much easier than the courses in German he had taken previously), to help him pass the language proficiency requirement. Perhaps it is the time he has spent in Mexico, or the fact that many of the place and street names in San Diego, that he has been pronouncing since he was very young, are Spanish, but it is much easier for him to read, write and speak than German. This lighter class load leaves him more free time than ever before during his college career, which is fortunate—not only because of his increasing participation in political activism, but because the winter of 1969 brings a series of large swells, due to unusual storm activity in the north Pacific, culminating in the "swell of the century" in December.

During the first of these swells in November, BP finds his smaller boards inadequate in the bigger surf, and hurriedly shapes a couple of longer, narrower single-fins from one of Bumper's Hawaiian "mini-gun" templates, to give him more paddling power and stability. He ends up successfully surfing the largest waves of his life so far (at times, over 20' high on the face) off La Jolla Cove during the first week in December, under dreamy, warm, Santa-Ana weather conditions. While it is definitely an exhilarating experience, it is fraught with as much fear as pleasure for him. One does not dominate such waves, at least at his level of experience in big surf, one simply rides to survive.

He hears later in an excited, trans-Pacific telephone call from Bumper that he had flown to Maui during the swell and ridden perfect, 15'–18' Honolua Bay. It had been 50' on the north shore of Oahu, completely unrideable and out of control, with the huge surf flooding the Kamehameha Highway during the storm surge, actually washing away buildings which were too close to the shoreline. He had been lucky to get to the airport and fly out to a more sheltered spot.

At the same time this giant swell is running, the west coast equivalent of the Woodstock festival is held at the Altamont Speedway outside of San

Francisco. Though he is engrossed in surf fever at the time and pays little attention to it, 300,000 people are reported to have attended the free concert by the Rolling Stones and other bands, but the scene is marred by disorganization and some violence. A man who brandished a gun in the crowd around the stage was beaten and stabbed by a Hell's Angel member (hired by the Stones to handle security) and died from his wounds. Though the concert goes on, with many people unaware of the incident until afterwards, it is a reality check for the hippie movement in the aftermath.

BP's biggest hope for a reprieve from the threat of being drafted comes on December 1, 1969, when the first lottery is held by the Selective Service, purportedly to insure a more fair and even-handed method of conscripting young men into the armed forces. This is accomplished by drawing days of the year at random out of a glass jar and assigning them a priority number. Your date of birth determines your priority for service. Unfortunately, December 21, BP's birthday, is chosen seventieth, about midrange of the 150 days (minimum) which are sure to be "selected" during the coming year.

In January of 1970, after beginning his final quarter at UCSD (provided he can pass the language proficiency exam after one more Spanish class), his old friend Donny returns from his tour of duty in Vietnam. BP gets a call from him out of the blue, announcing that he is back in town on leave for a few days, visiting his parents. BP invites him up to the farm for a party, but Donny declines. "Nah, I don't want to put you and your friends out, Beep. Can you come down here?" They make plans to meet for dinner at Bully's Restaurant in Bird Rock that evening instead. BP is happy and excited to hear that Donny is OK, and chides him for not writing him at all in the last year. "Well, Beep, I've been pretty busy," he answers awkwardly. "I'll tell you about it tonight."

They meet for steaks and cocktails at Bully's, but it is not the joyous reunion BP had anticipated. Donny seems stiff and reserved, though he gives him a smile and a big hug when they meet. "Look at you, Beep! You're a full-on hippie now, huh?" BP has to admit that they are quite the contrasting pair—he with his long hair, beard, resin-stained t-shirt, cargo shorts and *huarache* sandals, Donny with a fresh shave and a buzz-cut, wearing an immaculate Army Ranger uniform with spit-shined boots. They sit down to eat and drink and catch up with each other, but BP cannot help but feel a bit of estrangement from his friend. Donny chooses his words carefully at times, lacking his normal warmth, enthusiasm and openness, even being a bit evasive on some topics.

"So what happened to you after I saw you last?" asks BP. "Did you go to 'Army-mechanic school' like you hoped?"

Donny blushes slightly. "No, you were right about that part, Beep. Once you're in the service, you just follow orders. I never had any choice about what to do. They give you some bullshit aptitude tests after boot camp and then they send you to whatever training they want. Turns out, what they really needed was more LURPs, so that's where I went."

"What's a lurp?" asks BP, unfamiliar with the term.

"Oh, I'm sorry, Beep, I keep forgetting people don't get Army jargon—we go a little crazy with acronyms for all the long names, sometimes. Long Range Reconnaissance Patrol is what LURP stands for. The training was pretty tough, and as soon as we were done, they sent my unit to 'Nam."

"That sounds pretty gnarly. What did you do over there?"

"Aw, Beep, I'm not even supposed to talk about that, you know? Some of it was classified activity. The Army doesn't really want people to know everything that's going down over there. You wouldn't believe it yourself!"

"Were you in combat the whole time?"

"Not the whole time. We were in and out of a lot of places. There were some nasty firefights and ambushes, but there was some downtime in between, and a lot of times we were just going into places and assessing bombing damage and stuff, trying not to be seen, so no one would shoot at us. We tried to have a little fun and relax when we could."

"Did you get high over there?" wonders BP. "Was there any surf?"

"Oh yeah, man. I never got any, but I heard there were waves around Danang—some place called Mye Khe Beach. You wouldn't believe the dope everywhere, though. Locals would sell you pre-rolled, Thai-stick joints by the pack, opium, even smack—some guys had a problem with it, they'd go a little overboard sometimes. My team was cool, though. We'd just smoke a little Thai weed in the downtimes. On a patrol, you wouldn't want to be high, for sure. Shit could happen in a hurry. You never really knew who the enemy was, and where they were going to come from, even in the pacified areas. The charlies would just blend in with the civilians...."

Donny is obviously uncomfortable talking about the war, so BP changes the subject, and they talk about old times together and mutual friends. They finish their meal and BP asks him where he's off to next. "I've got a little leave left, so I'm heading for Vegas in a couple days to meet some of my buddies for a little R&R before we head back to the base," Donny tells him. "Then, I don't know. They'll probably rotate us back in country for another deployment. That seems to be the way things go."

"You don't have to go back if you don't want to," BP suggests, softly. "There are guys in the Army who are quitting and becoming war resisters. There are people around here who will help you, if you want..."

"No, Beep, I gotta go. I can't stay behind if my buddies ship out again. We got really tight over there, and some of them didn't make it back. I could give a shit about the place, really, and I'm not sure what we're fighting for there, but I can't let them down like that."

BP can tell that Donny's mind is set and there is no use in arguing the point. They part ways in front of the restaurant, shaking hands and hugging once more. "I worried about you, bro', and I'm glad you made it back OK," he tells him. "If they send you over there again, stay safe!"

"I will, Beep, and I want you to know that you were right—I never should have joined up. But now that they've got me, I've gotta stick with it to the end. I've never done anything as a soldier to be ashamed of yet, despite what a lot of people seem to think, and I'll try to keep it that way."

Just before Easter, BP finally completes all the requirements for his degree, and is awarded a Bachelor of Arts diploma with a major in philosophy, and a minor in political science. Since it is mid-year when he graduates, there is no ceremony, and no pomp and circumstance. They send the diploma to him in the mail. He celebrates with his friends at the farm, who have watched his progress through school and know what he sacrificed to get to this point, missing many a good day of surf, and studying through quite a few sweet parties. There is the mandatory dope-smoking and the usual merriment and jocularity. They address him as "Dr. Beep," even though it is a B.A. degree and not a Ph.D. They notice that his diploma has Governor Ronald Reagan's signature on it. "I hate that motherfucker," declares BP, "How did we ever elect a B-grade actor as governor?" Together, laughingly, they make a crude frame for the diploma, and hang it upside down over the toilet in the bathroom.

He does not forsake the campus, though, as the political situation is heating up to a boiling point again. Strictly speaking, he might qualify as what some would call an "outside agitator," since he no longer has any official status at the university, but he cannot abandon his classmates now, any more than Donny can abandon his Army buddies.

On April 30, Nixon announces the invasion of Cambodia on television, just when it had seemed that the Vietnam War was winding down. His "Vietnamization" program had been proposed as a way of extracting U.S. troops, substituting South Vietnamese forces, and de-escalating the conflict, but now it appears as if we are expanding it into another country! Widespread protests break out all across the nation.

On May 4, 1970, Ohio National Guard troops, sent in to quell a series of disturbances at Kent State University (including the burning of the abandoned ROTC building, during which fire fighters were pelted with rocks), open fire on a crowd of protestors with high-powered rifles, killing four people and wounding nine others, some of whom had merely been innocent bystanders.

Like Gov. Reagan in California, who had unrepentantly stated only the month before: "If it takes a bloodbath, let's get it over with—no more appeasement," the governor of Ohio, James Rhodes, has a similar view of the war protestors: "They're worse than the brownshirts and the Communist element and also the nightriders and the vigilantes. They're the worst type of people that we harbor in America. I think that we're up against the strongest, well-trained, militant, revolutionary group that has ever assembled in America." In reality, the protestors are nothing more than innocent, idealistic kids. Their own children. How can they fear them so much?

In response to this tragedy, and the government's callous reaction to it, hundreds of college campuses and millions of college students go on strike, the only such collective action by students in the nation's history. Turning their anger on the most obvious manifestation of the military on campus, 30 other ROTC buildings are burned or bombed across the country. There are violent clashes between students and police at many schools, and National Guard units are mobilized in 16 states. On May 8, four days after the killings at Kent State, 150,000 protestors gather in San Francisco and another 100,000 in Washington D.C., with reports of protestors smashing windows, slashing tires, and dragging parked cars into intersections to block police pursuit. Nixon calls out the military to protect government buildings against this "insurrection" and flees to Camp David for a few days to hide out.

The protests at UCSD are non-violent, with eloquent activists like philosophy graduate student, Lowell Bergman, who had recently founded the *San Diego Free Press* newspaper to bring a more progressive journalistic view to the city, urging students to boycott classes and stand in solidarity with their Kent State brothers and sisters who had died. Angela Davis is absent from the scene, going temporarily underground after a clash between county sheriffs and some visiting Black Panthers at her apartment in Del Mar (while she was not home), during which, reportedly, shots were fired.

As word spreads on the UCSD campus of the events at Kent State, even many of the faculty and students who had been on the fence regarding a strike over the incursion in Cambodia join in the protest. The campus is shut down completely. Classes are suspended for five days and students camp out in Revelle plaza, picketing and carrying signs by day, making speeches, holding teach-ins, engaging in discussions, doing theatre, playing music and partying by night.

BP helps some sympathetic machinists at Scripps (who are also surfers he happens to know) fabricate a giant, stainless steel urn on wheels, with an attached propane burner. They dub it the "People's Pot," and haul it up to Revelle plaza in the back of his truck. Making many runs to the food co-op in Solana Beach, they prepare a huge vegetable, rice and bean stew in it to feed the crowd of students in the plaza. BP is glad he can contribute something to the effort, and he is especially delighted when one of his fellow protestors, a thin, stunningly beautiful, sharp-witted, red-haired woman, whom he had noticed playing a part in the guerilla theatre being presented in the evenings, decides to join him in his sleeping bag one night on the grass. The rest of the week is absolutely blissful for him.

When the strike is over, classes resume and the administration extends the term of the quarter for a week, to allow students to complete their classes and prepare for finals. The exceptional sense of community propagated during the strike fades a bit as students return to competing against each other for grades, but many outlooks and attitudes have been changed, many new connections made. Some are very profound, as the campus soon discovers.

At the end of the month of May, a young undergraduate named George, whom BP had never met, enters a deserted Revelle plaza late at night. Despondent and grieving over the suffering being inflicted by the war in Vietnam, he sits down, crosslegged, in the southwest corner of the plaza, with a can of gasoline, and immolates himself, in the manner of the Buddhist monks, who had performed the same act of protest and sacrifice in Vietnam.

DRAFTED

The next time BP goes to UCSD, he visits the spot in the plaza where George had committed suicide. There are vases of flowers and notes and signs left by many other people around the small, smudged, smoky-yellow spot that remains, staining the concrete, bearing mute witness to the horror of his final moments. BP doesn't know what to think about this rash and final deed, but it strikes deep in his heart. There is no denying that he is profoundly moved as he stands there, vacillating between anger and grief. Ritual suicide may have some cultural basis in eastern traditions, but in the short and selfish history of western civilization, there is not much for BP to lean on to grasp the value or meaning of such an act. It seems like a senseless waste, in some ways, but he can't deny the impact it has on him. "What was he thinking?" he wonders. "How could he be sure this was the right thing for him to do? Was he insane? How could he think that his death would do anything to stop this fucking war? Did he really expect it to? Was he stupid or delusional? Or did he know something that I don't?"

Ultimately, in trying to imagine what had led to George's irrevocable decision, waves of empathy wash over him for this person whom he had never even known. He is overcome with emotion and he breaks down and cries, sobbing uncontrollably for a few moments, something he had not done for many years. Although intellectually he knows he will never be certain of all the facts surrounding it, in the cathartic aftermath of these emotions, he realizes that George's sacrifice had not been a waste, that it had been done for those who had been left behind, for the relatively small group of people, like himself, who knew about it, or would learn of it, and be affected by it. It was not an earth-shattering statement, it would not have globe-girdling repercussions in world events, but it was everything this young man could give, in an act of conscience, courage and compassion—of this he is certain now.

He turns to surfing again to soothe his soul, as he always has. When he launches himself into the water with his board, he leaves his mind behind on the beach, or at least the part of it which is in turmoil. It is his own, peculiar, personal form of meditation, though it is neither serene nor still at the ocean's raging edge, in Waveland. It demands unending and constant attention, a moment-by-moment engagement with, and awareness of, his relationship with the immediate environment, to put himself in harmony with the cyclic energy of the waves—thus pushing all other earthly matters into the background.

By now, after many years, this is a practiced, nearly unconscious effort for him. He engages in the hypnotic dance and paddle regime with ease and efficiency by simply eliminating other forms of input to his brain—the rest of the world does not exist there. Except for the occasional lull, taking a breather in the lineup before positioning himself for the next set of waves (when he might look to the shore for some geographical reference), the only solid object drawing his attention is his surfboard, all else is fluid motion and process, ceaseless change and flow. He never fails to feel mentally rejuvenated, though physically exhausted, when he finally returns to the troubled shore.

He is invited to the UCSD commencement ceremonies in June, as all mid-year graduates are, but doesn't attend them. He doesn't see any point in it, as they seem to be more for the parents than the kids themselves, and his parents are beginning a messy divorce process. He is not sure they can be in the same place together without a neutral, third-party referee between them to prevent the spilling of blood. The ceremony doesn't matter to him at all anyway, since he has no desire to stand under a hot sun, sweating in a black robe with a silly little mortarboard on his head, to walk across a stage and receive another copy of his diploma from the provost. He has other fish to fry.

When he failed to enroll in any classes after the spring quarter ended in April, his student deferment expired. His local Selective Service board had noted this fact, apparently, and in the first week of June he receives a new draft card, along with a letter from them announcing that he has been reclassified as 1-A (available for induction). He immediately appeals this classification in writing, claiming that the board had not adequately considered his original request for conscientious objector (1-O) status, which he had made when he first registered for the draft at 18.

The wheels of the bureaucracy seem to move frustratingly slowly, but it is actually only two weeks before he receives their response. A letter arrives informing him that he must appear before the local Selective Service board for a hearing on his appeal. It is scheduled for the first week in July.

Events continue to move at what seems to be an ever-accelerating pace. He feels that he is reaching a cusp in his life—a time of decision, of taking a new direction, but the way is not clear to him at all. This issue of being drafted, though, is of utmost importance, he knows—a matter of life and death, literally. It must be dealt with thoroughly and seriously. He has already begun to formulate a plan, which he knows may have to be modified as events occur down the line, but all he can do is face first things first, he reasons, and find out where it all leads, adjusting as necessary.

He contacts the AFSC (American Friends Service Committee) and asks for a referral to a draft counselor. This is something he could have easily done through his mother, as she has worked for them in the past, but he doesn't want to involve her at all. She is knee-deep in an ugly fight with his father over their mutual assets and he doesn't want to distract her from that. He goes to the library and researches the procedures and codes of the Selective Service System. He meets with the counselor and is introduced to a group of war resisters of many stripes and walks of life. There are quite a few young men about to be drafted, like himself, who are looking for help and advice on alternatives, and a number of anti-war groups are organized to serve their needs. By networking with them and learning as much as possible, he feels reasonably familiar with the process and prepared to face it, when the date for his hearing arrives, though still quite nervous about the possibilities.

On the appointed day, he puts on a clean t-shirt, long pants, and a pair of Adidas tennis shoes, forgoes his usual morning reefer, gathers up the materials he has prepared, and drives downtown to the Selective Service office in the Federal building. He quickly finds himself quaking before the 5-member board, composed of upstanding, elder bureaucrats (all former armed forces personnel) who have gathered to judge him. Though it has great import on his life, it is not considered a legal proceeding, in that he is not allowed any support or representation at this hearing—not a lawyer, or a counselor, a parent or a clergyman. He knows that it can resemble an interrogation, an inquisition, more than anything else.

The five board members take turns asking him questions, in rapid succession, which quickly turn from routine to rather complex:

BM #1: "Your name is Bob B. Pilhaus, is that correct?"

BP: "Yes sir."

BM #1: "And you are 21 years of age, is that right?"

BP: "Yes sir, um—last December, sir."

BM #1: "We are the classification review board, Bob, and we are conducting this interview at your request. We will be making a ruling on your appeal after the conclusion of the interview and you will be notified of our action by mail within thirty days. Is that clear?"

BP: "Yes sir."

BM #1: "You were classified 1-A after your 2-S expired, and you are appealing for a 1-O classification, correct?"

BP: "Yes sir."

BM #1: "On what do you base your claim to conscientious objector status?"

BP: "On the information I submitted when I registered at 18, sir. If you don't have my file in front of you, I have copies of everything here, as well as some additional recent letters of reference which I have obtained. It all documents my belief in pacifism, which I've held for quite some time—since I was old enough to think for myself." BP pushes a large envelope across the table towards them.

BM #2: "Thank you young man, and we will consider the written information in our decision, but the purpose of this interview is to hear in your own words about your beliefs. Are you a member of any religious organization?"

BP: "Um, no sir, not currently. I was raised as a Quaker, in the Religious

Society of Friends, at one time, but I am not an active member of the meeting anymore."

BM #2: "Are you aware that the 1-O classification is reserved for those who object to military service on the basis of religious beliefs only, not philosophical reasons?"

BP: "Isn't all religion essentially philosophical, sir?"

BM #2: "Just answer the question, please. If you are not a member of any religious organization, how can your claim be supported?"

BP: "I don't think that 'organization' is what makes a religion, sir, it is the nature of one's beliefs. I consider myself a 'religion of one,' if you want to split hairs over the semantics. My belief system is very complex and idiosyncratic. I wouldn't force it on anyone else and I expect the same from them."

BM #2: "In this 'religion-of-one,' then, is there a God, a Supreme Being?"

BP: "I suppose so—it really is a matter of semantics—what word you want to choose. I believe in an underlying, fundamental order in the universe, which manifests itself at all levels of creation, which might be called 'God' by some. But I don't believe in a patriarchal, anthropomorphic God who lives in Heaven and rules our lives, in the traditional manner of some religions, no, sir."

BM #3: "Are you a Christian, then? Do you believe in Christ as the Son of God?"

BP: "I believe this 'first principle,' or 'grand order,' manifests itself through everything and every human being. Christ must certainly have been a very effective conduit for the positive side of this principle, or force, whatever you want to call it, for so many people to have proclaimed him the son of God, but I have no literal belief in that notion. Personally, I don't believe that our salvation is to be found outside ourselves—no one else is responsible for our actions. Christ may have lived an exemplary life, one we might all admire and aspire towards, if all the stories I've heard about him are true, but I am not convinced that an immutable principle, order, or force, which is the way I think about God, goes around having kids, so calling Christ his 'son' is simply a metaphor. I am pretty certain, though, that if the man we know from history as Jesus Christ were to come back to our world today, he would be pretty appalled at what we have done in his name over the years. I don't think he would want to be connected with it anymore, in the same way that Karl Marx didn't want to be connected with Communism at the end of his life, when he said: 'I am not a Marxist.' There is always a negative side balancing out everything, don't you think?"

BM #3: "You hold Jesus Christ and Karl Marx in equal regard, then?"

BP: "I didn't say that, did I? It was a simple analogy, I didn't equate the two!"

BM #4: "Are your pacifistic beliefs based in religion, then, or on purely humanistic notions?"

BP: "I believe in the resolution of conflict without violence. I don't believe that the end ever justifies the means. Violent means cannot be justified by a desire for peace, nor will it ever actually achieve a lasting, peaceful outcome, in my view."

BM #4: "That sounds more philosophical than religious to me."

BP: "Well, here we are, back to semantics again. I have studied philosophy, as well as religion, and they both have the same aim in the end, actually, so I don't see how you can distinguish the two. In any case, your own governmental code, by which you are supposed to operate, says right here (taking a piece of paper out of another folder and pointing to it for emphasis): 'A registrant must establish to the satisfaction of the board that his request for exemption from combatant and noncombatant military training and service in the Armed Forces is based upon moral, ethical or religious beliefs which play a significant role in his life....' My objections are certainly based on 'moral' and 'ethical' beliefs, even if you do not believe them to be 'religious.' I should still qualify for this exemption. It says '*or*' there, not '*and*.'"

BM #5: "Will you accept a 1-A-O classification and be inducted into military service as a non-combatant, then?"

BP: "No sir, I have considered that question and have decided that I do not wish to be involved with, or contribute in any way, to the military machinery of our government, especially while we are involved in an undeclared and unjust war. I will only accept an alternative service, in the civilian sphere, to fulfill my obligation to my country."

BM #5: "Then your objections are primarily political? Is it just *this* war you refuse to serve in or *all* wars? As you know, the end of that code you just quoted states that your objection to participation in war not be confined to a *particular* war. If your country was invaded by a foreign nation would you defend it?"

BP: "Yes, I would, but not violently. I would try to oppose such an event by other means."

BM #5: "If a foreign soldier was raping your mother in the street, wouldn't you stop him?"

BP: "Of course I would. That is a very hypothetical and extreme example, and I hope I would be able to control myself in such an outrageous situation, but I would certainly try to restrain him instantly—forcibly if necessary."

BM #5: "Then you *do* believe in the use of force!"

BP: "Certainly, but *force* and *violence* are two different things."

BM #5: "Wars are simply the exercise of governmental force, on a larger scale. When faced with violence, sometimes initiating opposing violence, or the threat of it, is the only counterbalance. A people's willingness to fight and die for their government is an indication of that system's justness."

BP: "I'd say it is more an indication of a system's arrogance and stupidity, sir. Times have changed. This is the nuclear age. We have enough armaments available now to totally annihilate the human race—we can't afford that kind of medieval idiocy any longer in human affairs. We can't keep preparing for and starting wars, we need to prepare for and initiate peace—lasting peace, for everyone on earth!"

BM #5: "That's very idealistic, but totally impractical, given the threats we face in the world situation. I think I've heard enough to make my decision, though. Do the other members of the board agree, or do you have something further to ask?" He looks around, but no one steps in. "Do you have anything further to submit for our consideration, Bob?"

BP: "No sir."

BM #5: "You are dismissed, then, and thank you for coming. We will notify you of our decision, as we mentioned at the beginning."

BP is on pins and needles for the next few weeks. He has no idea what the outcome of his appeal will be, but he prepares for the worst, which might mean that he must flee the country, as some war resisters have been forced to do. He knows he will need money in any case, so he leverages his experience and the capital he has already accumulated in the illicit drug trade to earn more. He begins to move kilos of pot with John and Jay, selling it by the pound to the people who used to buy dime bags of it from him, who are also "upwardly mobile" in the underground, prohibition economy.

To carry greater quantities of the weed safely between Laguna Beach and Del Mar, he modifies the rear of his truck, installing panels of thin, finished, door-skin plywood to the interior framing, which can be removed fairly easily, and will conceal many kilos of pot at a time behind them, at least to any cursory, visual inspection. He tunes up the truck's motor and replaces all the bulbs in the signal lights, just to make sure he does not have any problems during his runs. He cuts his long hair and shaves his beard, for the first time in several years, so as not to wave a red flag in front of any cops who might pull him over for a traffic violation.

He is amazed how pale and white his cheeks and chin are under the beard, compared to the rest of his tanned face, and how much of a darker brown his hair is again at its roots, compared to the sun-bleached blond tone the tips had assumed over time. He hates having to shave regularly, but it fits his current purposes to change his appearance radically, even though he must absorb a lot of good-natured kidding from his friends for looking so "*GQ*." After a week or so, when his face has tanned more uniformly, he has some pictures taken, and along with a notarized copy of his birth certificate, applies for a U.S. passport, something he thinks might come in handy in the future.

John and Jay are equally surprised at his appearance when he shows up at their house to make the pick-up on his first 20-kilo deal. "Look at you," they laugh, "Mr. Clean!"

"Better safe than sorry," says BP. "I'm fully going with the Boy Scout motto, 'Be prepared.'" They invite him into the house and he checks out the goods—20 bricks of Colombian weed wrapped in red cellophane. They roll up a joint and smoke it to test the quality. All is good, so BP explains his other preparations, as he counts out the $2,000 in cash to pay them. "I'd like to stash this stuff behind the new panels I installed in my truck for the drive back south. Could I use your garage for that?"

They agree, and John backs his truck out of the garage so that BP can pull his inside. Within two hours, he has unscrewed the plywood panels, stashed ten kilos behind them on each side, and buttoned the trim back up. He feels much more confident and at ease driving back home than if he had just thrown the load in the back of the panel truck in boxes, suitcases, or duffel bags.

Within a week, he has moved all the pot at $100 per pound, doubling his money with loose weed to spare, and arranges to do it again, before the well runs dry. John and Jay assure him that their Colombian connection is steady and stocked to the rafters when he picks up the next load. "We could do fifty or a hundred kilos at a time for you, if you could handle more volume," they tell him, when he is done packing twenty more bricks into his panel truck.

"Naw, I don't think so. I couldn't really fit any more in my truck at one time, and I can't sell it that fast anyway."

"Well, just let us know if you do," says Jay, "and we can always get more acid for you, if you want."

"Those Orange Crush barrels scared me. I put it down for awhile, maybe forever. I made the mistake of taking a whole one right off the bat and had a really bum trip."

"OK, no problem, I can understand that—we told you that stuff was pretty strong. Do you need any coke?"

"Coke?" asks BP, with a puzzled look.

"Yeah, cocaine, you know—blow, flake, the laughing powder."

"I've never had any of that stuff," admits BP.

"What? You're kidding me!" exclaims Jay. "C'mon, follow me." They go back into the kitchen from the garage. "Just wait here a sec," he says, disappearing for a minute, returning with a plastic baggie containing about a half an ounce of white powder. Taking a mortar and pestle off the shelf in the kitchen, he spoons a small quantity of the powder into it and crushes it up.

"This stuff is pretty chunky, *las piedras de la luna*, as they say down south. You need to make it as fine as possible to whiff it." He scoops a small pile out of the mortar and onto the black Formica kitchen counter, arranging it into three long lines with a playing card, takes a drinking straw out of the upper cabinet, cuts it in two with a pair of scissors from a nearby drawer, and then snorts one line of the powder up his nose, half into each nostril. John follows suit with the second line and then hands the straw to BP, smiling, pinching his nose gently.

"What the hell, why not?" says BP, following their example.

BP is amazed at how high he gets within just a few minutes. It is a very enticing buzz, crystal clear and exciting, euphoric in the extreme, not debilitating in the least. "Hey, I think I like this stuff," he proclaims.

"Everybody does," says John. "If it wasn't so damn expensive, it would take over the whole trade."

"How much does it cost?"

"Retail is usually $80–$100 per gram on the street," says Jay, "but sometimes it's 'stepped on' pretty hard. We can get the pure stuff to you by the ounce for about $1,800 from our guys. There're about 28 grams in an ounce, so you can double your money on it if you cut it by about a third, which is easy to do because it's so pure. And it's a lot more compact to carry around than bricks of weed!"

"It sure is a nice high," observes BP, rushing like a dog in heat, feeling sharp as a tack.

"Wait'll you try sex on it," says Jay, "you won't believe how good it is."

"So your girlfriends really like to do coke with you when you have sex?" asks BP.

Jay and John look at each other for a moment and then burst out into uncontrollable laughter. BP is baffled by this reaction. He doesn't understand the humor in his question, which had seemed quite straightforward to him. "What? What did I say? What's so funny?"

Jay finally recovers from his spasms of mirth sufficiently to talk: "Beep, you can be such a 'babe in the woods' sometimes…"

"Whaddya mean?" asks BP, still confused.

"I thought you would have figured us out by now, Beep," says John, drying his eyes, "you've spent enough time with us over the last few years."

"Figured what out?"

"Well, we don't advertise the fact, certainly, and we're still pretty much deep in the closet about it to strangers, Beep," explains Jay, "but you're a good friend, and I think you can handle this—John and I are homosexuals. We don't sleep with women, we sleep with each other. That's why what you asked us about our 'girlfriends' was so funny."

"No way!" says BP, "You're putting me on! You're bullshitting me—this is a joke, right?"

"No, it's the truth, Beep. Think about it—have you ever seen either one of us with a woman?"

"Well, sure," says BP, thinking back, "at that party you had last year—there were lots of women there…"

"Yeah, there are certainly women in our lives, they're our friends, relatives and neighbors, and we invite them to our parties, for sure, but have you ever seen us really *be with* a woman, like you mean?"

BP's mind is racing over the past, considering these new facts, and has to admit that he hasn't. He does recall that the times he had stayed overnight at their house, they slept in the big bedroom together—but it had two beds in it, and he thought they were just giving him the second bedroom so that he could be comfortable and not have to sleep on the couch. Could this really be true? "But you guys are so *normal*," he protests. "I thought queers were all effeminate and flouncy or whatever. You guys are studs—you're gnarly, you're fearless—I've seen you in action! You're *surfers*, for crying out loud!"

"You are such a Pollyanna, Beep!" says John. "There are gay people of many types, in all walks of life. You're getting hung up in stereotypes and prejudices—not all of them are flagrant drag-queens, cross-dressers or trans-sexuals, flaunting their homosexuality. Some are doctors, bankers and law-yers, some are athletes and surfers, even policeman and soldiers, believe it or not, and you can't tell just by their appearance what their sexual orientation is. Are you that naive?"

"I guess so," BP admits, somewhat flabbergasted at never having come to this realization in the past. "I've never really known any queers before."

"*Gays*, Beep," John corrects him, "don't call us 'queers,' please! There're too many negative connotations to that word. Just gay, or homosexual, is fine."

"I'm sorry," apologizes BP, "this is just so new, and kind of a shock for me…I'm having a hard time getting my head around it."

"You can handle it, can't you?" asks Jay. "We're not trying to shock you, and we're never going to try to seduce you, or anything. We're committed to each other and have been for a long time. Some gay people are promiscuous, just like some straight people, but we're not. We're pretty much an old married couple these days. The times you've stayed overnight with us and partied and stuff, we never tried to hit on you, and we never would. We know you're one of those straight, heterosexual types, probably one of the more promiscuous ones, yourself, eh? We're fine with that. We're still friends, right? John and I are no different than we ever were, but now you know something more about us, is all."

"For sure," says BP. "I like you guys and I always have. You've always been totally cool to me. This doesn't make any difference at all, I'm just a little freaked at how unconscious I've been, I guess." He sincerely means every word he says, and they seem to know it.

"No problem, Beep. It happens all the time. Think about how our parents felt when we told them—talk about freaking out! Here, you want a little hit for the road?" offers Jay. "This shit is great, but the high doesn't last very long, and you always want more."

"Sure!" says BP. Jay dumps the remaining coke left in the mortar onto the counter and they snort another line apiece. Then he scoops what's left of the pile up with the playing card, onto a small piece of paper, folding it into a tight little bindle, and hands it to him.

"A little parting gift for you—just give us a call if you need any more," he says, as BP heads out to his truck to drive home.

"Thanks a lot, you guys," says BP, "I will, for sure. See ya later."

On the 90-minute drive home, beside his usual worries about being pulled over by the cops, he can't help but think that there are a lot of things in this world for him to learn about, still—things of which he is totally oblivious, even though they are right in front of his face. He is high as a kite for most of the way, though, feeling like Superman, and these doubts soon leave his mind.

Though he can't quite get a handle on what it could be like to be attracted to men, rather than women, he cannot condemn John and Jay for their sexual preference. He tries to imagine how they make love to each other, but just can't picture it without feeling queasy and weird. Nonetheless, he knows they are good people—they have always treated him like a brother, and been perfectly straight and honest in all their dealings, so he decides to simply accept them for what they are, and not think about it anymore. He can't help but wonder, though, which of his other friends and acquaintances might be gay, without him ever noticing....

Pulling up at the farm, elated by another successful run, he shares his latest score with his bro's. They like the weed, but they like the coke even better. A lot better. None of them have tried it before, and he is happy that he gets to turn them on to it. "Where the hell did you get this shit?" asks Bumper, after they whiff the last rail of it. "This is very fine! We're going to need some more of it."

"Jay and John said they can get a bunch for me, but it's $1,800 an ounce!"

"Who cares," says Bumper, "I'll buy two!"

Within the next two days, BP is back in Laguna Beach, buying two ounces of coke with Bumper's cash, since most of his is tied up in weed, still. When he gets home, he picks up a used, triple-beam gram scale from Surplus Sales at UCSD, so that they can weigh out small quantities accurately, and they begin using and selling it at a tremendous pace. Actually, BP, Skip and Rocky do most of the selling, and Bumper does most of the using. Parties at the farm kick up another notch, with the blow flowing freely.

BP finds that John and Jay are right. Sex really *is* good on coke, and women seem to dig it. He is especially happy to find that while trying to consummate relations with a hot tuna during a cocaine binge, he never suffers from the performance problems he had occasionally experienced on other drugs.

It is towards the end of July when the decision from the draft board arrives. BP dreads opening the letter, and when he does, his worst fears are confirmed.

His appeal has been denied, and he is ordered to report on August 15 for a pre-induction physical in Los Angeles. He wonders if he might have won the appeal if he had been an active member of some official church, but decides not to second guess the whole fiasco. Just look ahead and keep working the plan, he tells himself. There are always alternatives.

He talks to the draft counselors again, and briefly investigates going to Canada, but that doesn't appeal to him much—too cold, and not enough surf. He talks to other young draftees who have gone to their physicals and been declared 4-F (physically or mentally unfit for duty) for some reason or other (some quite outlandish). He thinks about starving himself like Griff, but doesn't think he can lose enough weight fast enough. He considers cooking up some outrageous stunt to try to get a mental dispensation during the physical, but from what he hears, those types of schemes are dicey and may fail or backfire. He learns as much as he can about the procedures and layout at the induction center, slowly beginning to hatch a strategy.

Meanwhile, the lease is up on the farm, and Bumper tells them that it won't be renewed. Apparently, the land is being purchased for a huge new subdivision to be built on the mesa. They have to be out by the end of August. "We're losing our privacy up here anyway, with all the new houses and condos going up. Pretty soon, we'll have neighbors complaining about us making too much noise or something. It's probably time to move on."

On August 15, BP drives up to L.A. early in the morning, finds the induction center, which is located downtown in a rather seedy area, sharing a building with a cheap hotel, and parks two blocks away. He knows, from speaking with others who have gone through this, that a bus will arrive from San Diego about 10:00 A.M., carrying the load of draftees who reported down there this morning, as instructed. Before it arrives, he walks into the induction center and checks in at the desk. They hand him his file, which he is to carry through the physical, from station to station, and direct him to a room across the hallway, where the orientation is to be held, to wait for the rest of the San Diego group.

There are only a few young men sitting scattered about the room in folding metal chairs when he enters. He takes a seat at the back, next to a door. There are no military uniforms in sight. The young men are all sitting with their heads bowed, not paying any attention to him. He checks the door and it is locked, but he twists the deadbolt knob above the handle and tries again. It opens, and he is surprised to see, when he cracks it slightly, that it leads not to another room or hallway, but to the street! He is looking out onto the sidewalk, and no one is around. Wasting no time, he shoots another glance around the room, stands up slowly, turns around, lifts his shirt and stuffs the file folder under it, opens the door, and slips through it quietly, closing it behind him gently. He walks quickly but calmly away, down the sidewalk, with one hand on his chest, keeping the file from falling out from under his shirt. His heart is pounding as he walks, but he keeps striding forward, looking straight ahead resolutely, while waiting for the sound of rushing footsteps, or someone shouting something out, to come up from behind him.

As he turns the corner at the end of the block and steals a glance back to see that no one is following, he begins to think that this might actually work. When he gets to his car in two more blocks, he is even more confident of his getaway. By the time that he reaches the freeway and heads home, he is thinking it was almost too easy.

He's not sure what he has accomplished, other than buying himself some time, but several of the young men he had talked to, who had been through this already, had told him that the bureaucracy was pretty fouled up, and that it would take a long time for them to realize his file is missing. "Just take it and get out of there somehow," one fellow had told him. "They'll never miss you. They don't check the list of who came in with who goes out in the afternoon. Try to get out before they take you upstairs, though, if you can. Even then, if you can get to the elevator without being noticed, its doors open on both sides—one side serves the induction center and the other side opens into the hotel. Just get on it, ride up or down one floor, and walk out the other side. I haven't heard anything from them for over a year now, and they know where to find me. They haven't even figured out that I'm missing yet."

It had been a vague sort of plan, but one that he thought was worth trying before other, more desperate measures. He can't believe how easy it had been to pull off. He figures if they come looking for him in the next two weeks, it will be at his mother's house, which is the only address that they have for him, or is on any of his IDs. After that, his plan is to just get so lost that they can't find him at all.

When he gets home, he tells his roommates what he has done, and they burn the file that night, in the firepit in the back yard. "Where are you going to go at the end of the month?" Bumper asks him.

"I don't know. I haven't really thought about it yet. I didn't know how this was going to turn out, and I haven't made any solid plans."

"Well, Rocky and Skip are going to get another place in Del Mar and keep their jobs, but I'm just going to head over to the Islands early. Why don't you come with me? You always said you wanted to surf in Hawaii. Here's your chance."

A light bulb flashes on above BP's head. "That sounds really good, Bumper, I think I just might do that!"

The next two weeks are a blur of activity. They liquidate their inventory, selling everything they can't eat, smoke or snort by the end of the month. Rocky and Skip rent a small apartment together and move their stuff to it. BP helps Bumper put his cars and motorcycles into storage in a small U-Rent warehouse, and sells his own truck and motorcycle, along with most of the other belongings that he won't need, including his wetsuit and all his surfboards, except for the 7'8" mini-gun he uses in bigger waves. He takes what belongings he has left to his mother's house and stores them in her garage, telling her briefly of his plans, and that he will send her an address when he gets to Hawaii so that she can continue to forward his mail. Taking his college diploma down from over the toilet, he puts it in a large manila envelope and mails it to his father.

He visits a friend of his in Mission Beach, a leatherworker with a heavy-duty sewing machine, and pays him to make a custom bag for his surfboard, fabricated out of a heavy, waterproofed, nylon material, with zippers along an entire side. He and Bumper buy tickets for a one-way flight to Honolulu, and they schedule a final, end-of-summer bash at the farm for August 31.

On August 30, BP picks up a copy of the *San Diego Union-Tribune* and the front page news is not pretty. The day before, in east Los Angeles, there had been a demonstration called by the National Chicano Moratorium Committee. 30,000 Mexican-Americans had participated in the largest anti-war protest ever to take place in that city, coordinated with demonstrations in twenty other cities throughout the country. Acting on a report of a robbery in a local liquor store, police attacked the crowd of demonstrators with clubs and guns, after declaring an illegal assembly. Three people were killed, including Ruben Salazar, the KMEX news director and a columnist for the *Los Angeles Times*. BP wonders which of his friends from UCSD had been there, and hopes they are OK, but he has his own worries at this point.

Almost everybody they know (and quite a few they don't) show up for the last party at the farm, which rocks the entire mesa with the live band that Bumper has hired. The little farmhouse barely survives the evening, when Bumper mentions to someone that it is going to be torn down for new tract homes pretty soon. A couple of Mac Meda veterans hear this (who remember the origins of that organization at keg parties in condemned homes in Sorrento Valley, dismantling the structures totally over a few beers with MacPherson, Rakestraw, and Shea), and figure they can take care of it right now. The few remaining pieces of furniture get thrown through some of the windows, ending up eventually in the bonfire in the rock pit, and quite a few holes appear in the plaster walls before they can be reined in. Luckily, no one is injured from the broken glass or flying chairs, and a good time is had by all in the end.

The next day, Rocky gives Bumper and BP a ride to the airport. BP has his backpack full of clothes, his one remaining surfboard in its bag, padded by his sleeping bag and a few towels, as well as his passport and nearly $5,000 cash in a money belt around his waist. As they board the plane and take off from Lindbergh Field, he looks back down at the city of San Diego, the place of his birth, and wonders when, and if, he will ever see it again.

Aloha

As soon as BP steps off the plane in Hawaii, it is obvious that he is in a very different place, a tropical paradise. The foliage is riotous—green and lush, everywhere he looks. The muted, spare, tan and brown colors of the southern California hills and plains are gone, and the air is not as smoggy and dry, but moist, and filled with the pungent perfume of flowers. They are everywhere—around peoples necks in leis, in their hair and worn on their clothes, bursting from the trees and bushes which line the streets and surround the buildings.

A gentle, warm, misting rain is falling as they deplane, hardly enough to make things wet, but a welcome cooling influence in the late afternoon heat. They collect their baggage, and BP follows Bumper to the curb at the passenger loading zone, where he is introduced to Bumper's friend Wally, who is waiting to pick them up. As Wally whisks them from the airport towards downtown Honolulu, BP takes in the radical change in scenery and realizes what a leap they have made during a trans-Pacific flight. He feels like Dorothy when she lands in Oz.

"It's so different here," he says to Bumper, aimlessly.

"It may be the fiftieth state in the Union," states Bumper, simply, "but to guys like you and me, this is a foreign country." It will become more obvious to BP how true this is in the coming months.

Trying to orient himself as they drive along, he looks at landmarks and listens to the running conversation between Bumper and his friend, Wally, who he soon finds out is a transplanted Californian, and a surfer as well. Though he must be at least ten years older than Bumper, already sporting a receding hairline, he is well-tanned and looks very fit and energetic. Apparently, he manages the property Bumper owns here, as between smatterings of surf talk, he hears scattered references to maintenance needs at "the apartments" and talk about "vacancy rates."

This all becomes clearer when they pull into a short cul-de-sac surrounded by low-rise buildings at the mouth of the Manoa valley, just north and east of downtown Honolulu, near the University of Hawaii campus (which Wally points out to him as they drive past). "This is gonna be home for awhile for us," announces Bumper as they park the car. "The house on the north shore is booked until November, but there's a vacancy here we can stay in until then."

They unload their bags from the back of the black Jeep Wagoneer, which BP learns also belongs to Bumper, and follow Wally to a furnished, two-bedroom unit at the end of one of the legs of the U-shaped complex. It is airy, modern and comfortable, with two stories—bedrooms and a bath upstairs, living room, dining nook and kitchen downstairs, along with another bathroom, and a nice, fenced patio out the back door, with a shade-cloth ramada over a long picnic table, an outdoor shower to one side, and a brick barbeque pit built into the wooden back fence.

Over the next two months, BP explores Oahu from this base of operations, accompanying Bumper on daily surf trips. Since the island is exposed on all sides, swells come from every direction, from a number of different weather sources, and rideable waves can usually be found somewhere. If not, the crystal-clear, warm, blue, ocean water is always inviting for a swim, paddle or skin-diving. Water temperatures average in the upper 70s on the Fahrenheit scale, and air temperatures in the upper 80s, though the prevailing northeast tradewinds bring in cumulus clouds off the ocean, with an occasional shower to help moderate the heat. It is indeed a waterperson's nirvana.

But there are troubles lurking in the background of paradise. Some arise from the relative size and isolation of the islands. Of the hundreds of islands in the archipelago, only seven are inhabited to any extent, with the greatest density of population on Oahu, the third largest in the chain. It is less than 600 square miles in area, one third the size of San Diego County, and it lies approximately 2,000 miles from any continental landmass, making it one of the most isolated islands in the world. This isolation brings with it logistical problems of supplying modern demands for food and materials, resulting in one of the highest costs of living in the U.S.A.

BP is a little shocked to learn from Wally that their apartment normally rents for $200 per month in the off-season, so he insists on giving him $100 each month as his portion of the rent, even though Bumper, as the former absentee owner of the property, is not concerned about it in the least, and pays nothing. Food is also more expensive, he discovers, as is gasoline and almost every other manufactured commodity. Like San Diego, tourism and the military are the linchpins of the Hawaiian economy.

The total population of all the islands numbers only a little more than 750,000, with three-quarters of that on Oahu, mostly concentrated in Honolulu, giving it a population density higher than anywhere on the mainland. The people are far more diverse than any BP has ever encountered as well. Along with the native Hawaiians and others of Polynesian descent, there is a large Asian presence of Japanese, Filipino and Chinese immigrants, plus many people of Portuguese and Puerto Rican ancestry. For the first time in his life, as a white person, he is in the minority, and an outsider as well. Due to its diversity and history, with the overthrow of the Hawaiian monarchy by American and European interests having taken place only 77 years before, there is an undercurrent of racial tension in island life unlike anything he has ever experienced.

Nowhere is this more evident to him than in the water. Bumper reminds him incessantly of the need to have great respect for the native Hawaiian surfriders, and to give them priority in the waves. BP is introduced first to the breaks at Waikiki, which are besieged by tourists the year 'round, and where the locals are the most tolerant (or the least hostile, it might be said). Sometimes they surf with Wally, but often not, as he is busy with tenants or maintaining the apartments. The beachboys who run the tourist concessions on the beach fronting the major hotels are very friendly, epitomizing the spirit of *aloha* for which the islands are famous, and Wally and Bumper seem to know many of them well. When the surf is small, less suitable for their shortboards, they can bicycle to the beach and borrow longboards from one beachboy or another's rental stash, as long as business is slow enough and there are boards to spare.

When they venture out further, driving to the west side of the island, towards Waianae and Makaha, however, he notices that they are viewed with somewhat greater distrust and resentment by the locals, and must be vigilant and obsequious in the water. Having learned strict surf etiquette at Windansea long ago serves BP well on these occasions, and they have no serious problems. The smaller summer surf does not challenge his abilities much more than the waves he had been accustomed to in California, and the conditions are ideal.

During the summer season, the south shore of Oahu has the most potential for good surf, with storms originating in the Antarctic circumpolar trough breaking out and turning the corner around New Zealand, sending swell northward through Polynesia. They catch several of these seasonal swells and he begins to get a taste of what "Hawaiian juice" really means. The few times the waves climb to over six feet or more, they surf Ala Moana, at the entrance to the Ala Wai Boat Harbor. It is a very hollow lefthand break, with a heaving, tubular bowl section, and the competition for the best waves is fierce. Still, BP manages a few brief but deep, inspiring tuberides there, practicing patience and deference to the locals.

Generally, they keep a low profile, which is unusual for Bumper but suits BP just fine. He rents a P.O. box and writes his mother a letter, giving her the box address to forward his mail, rather than the street address of the apartment. No sense in anyone else knowing where he is living, he figures, and they will be moving to the north shore soon anyway.

Instead of throwing parties, Bumper is content with the club scene downtown, and is much more of a night person than BP. His favorite leisure pursuit is to troll Waikiki for loose, unattached, tourist tuna to wine and dine. BP lets himself be dragged along on many of these missions, though he would just as soon stay home and go to bed early.

Bumper is charming, fun-loving, good-looking and rich, so his expeditions are often fruitful. If he happens to meet a woman who is traveling alone, BP is more than happy to fade into the background and disappear, but it is surprising how many pairs of young women are traveling together to visit Honolulu from all over the world, and are eager for male companionship. They often end up as a foursome, doing the town and seeing the sights, sometimes even bringing the women home, or going back to their hotel rooms, and getting extremely lucky. These relationships are perfect for him, as they are mostly casual and short-lived, as inevitably, their ship or plane leaves town.

Knowing that BP's resources are slim, and enjoying his company, Bumper often generously picks up the tab for these escapades, paying for dinners in nice restaurants, and drinks in the nightclubs, without batting an eye at the expense. Some of the women want to pay their own way, but Bumper won't hear anything of this sort, preferring to act as the magnanimous host.

While the supply of locally grown *pakalolo* and Thai sticks from Southeast Asia is plentiful and fairly cheap, the cocaine with which Bumper has become enamored is scarce and expensive. Though his local contacts are extensive enough, locating good blow is a chore. Whenever he can find it, he buys as large a quantity as is available, and snorts it daily until it is gone, despite the fact that it costs $2,500 per ounce or more. Money is simply not a concern. Though Bumper often shares a few lines with him, BP doesn't even consider such excessive purchases, limiting himself to an occasional small bag of weed.

Within the first week of his arrival, BP had explored the University of Hawaii campus, which is a short walk from their apartment, locating the major library collections among the buildings. When the surf is flat or blown out and he is bored, there are always books and journals available to read. In some ways, he misses the structure and discipline of his college studies and the university atmosphere, which he finds familiar and comfortable.

Browsing the course catalog in the bookstore, he picks out what seems like an interesting class, and begins auditing it three times a week. It is a course on Polynesian culture, teaching about the paths of migration through the south Pacific, and the great voyaging skills involved in the original discovery and settling of the islands, which he finds very intriguing. He also learns a little about how the odd Hawaiian creole, or pidgin English, developed over time—a dialect he finds somewhat baffling, although Bumper is much more familiar and capable with it. Neither of them try to speak it in daily interactions, though, except for a few isolated words, as it is considered an affectation for non-natives to do so, but he finds it helpful to be able to understand it a bit better.

The lecturer in this class is a very engaging, articulate young professor of art history named Dominic Pukui, who BP eventually learns is half-Italian and half-Hawaiian, a former football star for the UH Rainbow Warriors. He cuts an imposing figure in the classroom, tall and broad of stature, with long, wavy dark hair, tied in a pony-tail, and a deep, baritone voice, invariably dressed very casually in open, flower-print shirts and khaki shorts, with a pair of the ubiquitous "slippahs," or thongs, on his feet. He specializes in the arts and crafts of the Pacific basin, but teaches this introductory class in Polynesian culture to undergraduates each year. It is immensely popular, as BP finds, when he attends for the first time and can barely find a seat left in the lecture hall, and for good reason. Dr. Pukui's energetic style is very accessible and informative, making the subject matter interesting and alive, ranging over a broad area of topics in a coherent and fascinating manner, with good measures of humor thrown in as well.

BP is so impressed with the man that he approaches him after the first lecture to introduce himself, and tell him how much he had enjoyed the hour. Dominic is very appreciative and polite, asking to be addressed by his first name, and letting BP know that he is welcome there, even as an auditor.

In order to be a little more independent, BP locates and purchases a used motorcycle, to augment the bicycles which Wally keeps in the garage for tenants. This gives him more freedom to explore the island without depending on Bumper's schedule, while not depleting his funds too terribly. He doesn't bother getting a Hawaiian driver's license, figuring that his old one from California should be good enough, since there are so many transient tourists running around the island. Though it isn't the most convenient transportation in the wet, it is perfectly suited for exploring the dirt roads out in the country.

The differences between the country and town on the island amaze BP. The contrast between the bustling, glaring, concrete jungle of Honolulu and the rest of the island, outside the city limits, couldn't be greater. While riding around the island in a day, he can go from crowded, thriving, modern metropolis to sleepy, laid-back, poverty-stricken farming and fishing villages that seem to be almost from a prior century. In the more desolate areas, he can sense the wildness and beauty of what paradise must have been like when the first humans set foot here.

On November 1, they make the move to the north shore. The house that Bumper owns there is leased from March through October, leaving the prime surf season, from November to February, for his own use. It is an old, ramshackle, plantation house, down a dirt driveway in Haleiwa, surrounded by a veritable jungle of unkempt trees and vegetation, at the southwest end of what has been called the "seven-mile miracle," a stretch of coast revered by surfers worldwide. Between there and Sunset Beach, seven miles to the northeast, are nearly forty surfspots containing the most concentrated abundance and variety of challenging, quality waves to be found anywhere in the world.

It is only thirty miles and about a 45-minute drive from Honolulu, but it is a world apart, BP finds. Bumper tells Wally that he will not be returning to California in March, as usual, and asks him not to rent out the apartment in town, but keep it vacant, as they will be back in it soon enough, and it would also make a useful crash-pad, if they come to town for some nightlife and don't want to drive back out to the country.

For BP, surfing the north shore is much like graduating from high school and going to college had been. The waves are bigger, faster and more power-ful, and the competition for them is more intense, as the best surfers from all over the world show up during these months to ride them. He finds himself in the 50th percentile again, skill-wise, and even further down the totem-pole by virtue of the fact that he is a new *haole* face in the lineups. The native Hawaiians and longtime locals rule with an iron fist here. Threats and even acts of violence are common. He deals with this in the same way he found most effective in the past—by showing the utmost respect and also avoiding the prime-time sessions at the most desirable breaks, especially when pho-tographers gather, and reputations are being made or maintained. He has no desire to be in the limelight, or draw unnecessary attention, good or bad.

Nonetheless, he is able to surf waves that are beyond his expectations, of a level of excellence he has never known. Swells arrive out of the north Pacific on a more regular basis during the winter, generated by Aleutian storms that send waves into the coast unchecked by a continental shelf, heaving them-selves onto volcanic and coral reefs to form the most perfect, peeling barrels he has ever experienced. Even the less popular spots offer fast, challenging rides for him, and the range of wave size exceeds his ability at times. Though it is not as epic a winter as the year before (by Bumper's and anyone else's accounts), there are at least three gigantic swells during the next four months that leave him in awe and shivering on the beach, hairs standing on end, chicken-skinned all over, despite the heat.

When the waves reach 20' in height, he has little desire to challenge them, as the danger-to-fun quotient does not compute well in his estimation. Big-wave surfing requires a commitment, strength of will and bravado that BP finds admirable, and he spends hours watching the best practitioners of this rare art at Waimea Bay (one of the only places that can hold this kind of size), but he has little desire to ride such waves himself. No one is trying to get tubed on these huge waves, they are just trying to survive, and for him, tube-riding is the ultimate thrill and goal in his surfing. [It will be many years, still, until the equipment, abilities and attitudes of surfers evolve sufficiently for anyone to purposefully attempt to get barreled in giant waves.] At times like these, he prefers to go in search of waves wrapping around the west side of the island, where the giant swell is refracted, reduced in size, and is often much cleaner and less angry. Bumper is of the same mind, though he will sometimes take an inter-island flight to Maui to surf Honolua Bay, when conditions warrant it, leaving BP behind on Oahu (since BP doesn't want to spend the money necessary for such a trip).

The north shore is also a hotbed of surfboard design and innovation, merging ideas from all around the globe, and BP and Bumper continue building their own boards. There is a small shaping shed at the Haleiwa house, though it is not as nicely appointed as the one at the farm in Del Mar had been. Taking cues from Dick Brewer's designs, the legendary local shaper they hold in the highest regard, as well as features they notice in boards arriving from Australia, they proceed with refining their designs, and testing the results in varying conditions. Over time, BP builds up a quiver of four boards again, suited for the range of surf he most enjoys, and does some repair work for a little cash income, subcontracting with one of the local surfshops to patch dings and fix broken boards for their customers.

He continues to make the trip into town three times a week to attend his class at UH and check his P.O. box for mail. He sometimes goes alone, but often Bumper tags along, as he is always willing to escape the boredom of the country, where there is an anemic, nearly non-existent, social scene and very little nightlife, unless you consider a movie at the one, old theatre in Haleiwa exciting. They sometimes stay overnight in the apartment, if it has been flat or the Kona winds are blowing, and there is no prospect of good surf the next day; or if they simply stay out too late, or drink too much; or there is some extended errand to take care of, such as car or motorcycle repairs; or if Bumper is trying to score some more coke from someone in town.

Friends of Bumper's drop in at the house in Haleiwa from as far away as South Africa, France, Peru and Australia, some staying for days or weeks at a time. BP does not mind this at all. The house is large, and they are generally very interesting people to meet, offering diversions to the normal surf routine.

Early in January, they enjoy a two-week visit from Rocky and Skip, who fly over from the mainland for a vacation. BP and Bumper are glad to see them, happy to show them around, and their bro's are ecstatic to surf in warm water and party together again, catching up on each other's lives.

It is shortly before they are due to move back into town at the end of February when BP receives some devastating news. In a letter from his mother, he hears that his friend Donny has been killed in Vietnam. She includes a clipping from the *San Diego Union-Tribune* detailing the tragic event. It seems that Donny's unit had been in a forward area, calling in airstrikes on the enemy forces, when a miscommunication or mistake in positioning was made, and the bombs were dropped on his squad instead of the Viet Cong, wiping them all out in an instant. The news hits BP hard and lays him low. Sitting on a bench in front of the post office, where he had sat down to read his mail before jumping back onto his bike to return home, he weeps involuntarily and openly, his head falling into his hands, covering his face, sobbing loudly and not caring if anyone sees him in such distress.

When the first wave of grief passes, he feels only anger for quite awhile. How could this have happened? He reads the article again carefully, which only serves to feed his rage. The incident had taken place over a month previously, it appears, and the truth of the "friendly fire" nature of their deaths had not been reported at first, but covered up by the military instead, until a muckraking journalist had forced an investigation, and the embarrassing details had come out. Not only had his friend died in a stupid, illegal and unjust war, but he had been killed by the idiocy and ineptness of his own countrymen. Then, to top it off, their leaders had tried to suppress and alter the facts, sweeping it under the rug! He feels infuriated and helpless, at the same time.

The final stages of despair, depression, guilt and recrimination play out over the next several weeks, as he thinks about how sad it is that he will never see his friend again, and ponders all the things he might have done to prevent this horrible occurrence. He thinks back to the time in Baja when Donny had announced that he was joining the Army, and wonders whether his friend might still be alive if he had been more forceful in trying to talk him out of such a decision. He thinks about the last time he had seen him at Bully's in Bird Rock, and regrets mightily not having expressed his misgivings about the war more clearly, or been more forceful about his willingness to help Donny with an exit strategy.

Most depressing of all, when he digs deeply into his memory, he recalls thinking, as he had watched Donny leave that evening, that it might be the last time he would ever see him, while discounting such a possibility at the same time, to comfort himself. Now it has all come true, and he can't help but think that he had known it would, even back then....

Maalaea

During the last two weeks in February, it is obvious to Bumper that BP is in a depressed funk over the death of his friend, but he hopes that a liberal application of weed, laughing powder and surf will cure him. He doesn't know what else to try, as BP refuses to talk much about it. When he finally broaches the subject, BP avoids it with an indirect question: "Why didn't you go in the Army, Bumper? I know you told me you were 4-F, but you never said why...."

"That's right, I did say I'd tell you that story one day," answers Bumper. "I've got no beef with the Vietnamese, and I didn't want any part of this war, just like you. Remember I told you about studying *karate* and then *aikido* when I was a teenager? My *sensei* taught me things about marshalling *ki*, the life energy in the body, for both calmness and intensity. While I was at my doctor's one day, just by accident, I found out that these techniques could control my blood pressure. By relaxing and breathing in a certain way, I could lower it, and by tensing my body core, I could raise it. With a little practice, I was able to go to my draft physical and flunk it due to high blood pressure. They measured it many times over several hours, told me I should see a doctor immediately for treatment of my hypertension, and let me go. I think they were afraid I would have a heart attack or stroke right on the spot. It was really a pretty easy 'out' for me."

"Shoot, I should have asked you about that sooner—maybe you could have taught me how to do that, too...or Donny...." With that, BP falls silent again, and Bumper doesn't want to push him to talk any further, so he rolls up a joint and they smoke it, eventually improving the mood with a few lines of coke as well.

The 1970–71 winter season on the north shore goes out with a whimper rather than a bang, with only a single notable swell during this period. They surf Sunset Beach at a solid 6'-8' with a dwindling crowd, as many of the foreign surfers have returned home. A 6' wave on the Hawaiian scale, as BP has come to learn, is twice that of the size scale used in California—it is measured down the back of the wave, which makes the face of the wave 12', or double-overhead, when the trough in front of the wave is included. The crest of an 8' wave, the largest in the sets on this day, can be 16'-18' high, when looking up at it from a bottom turn, which is approaching his comfort limit for high-performance surfing. These sessions have some curative power for BP, as he feels very much in control, as if he has made considerable progress in the last few months. He gets many good set waves from the outside lineup clear through the hollow inside section, including several massive, intense, stand-up tube rides.

The break at Sunset reminds him of Windansea on steroid treatments. They are very similar spots in the way the waves shift and peak before they break, though the scale of the playing field is much larger at Sunset. He is beginning to comprehend the positioning required, and is becoming more accustomed to his equipment as well, trusting that his board will go where he tells it to when asked, feeling confident about the moves and timing necessary to set himself up for the inside barrel section. He makes few mistakes, which is fortunate, as the thickness and power of the lip when it throws out on a large Sunset peak is as deadly as Paul Bunyan's axe—you do *not* want to be in the wrong place when it comes down. The price to be paid for a wipeout is to be rag-dolled mercilessly, followed by a long swim to the beach, hoping that your board is not caught in the rip and swept out to sea while you are coming in with the whitewater.

By the time they move back into town at the beginning of March, BP's psyche is healing. His sense of irretrievable loss is fading with time. He and Bumper fall back into their urban routine, surfing the south shore and chasing women, while getting high with a vengeance. Spring is a transitional season for surf, and quite spotty. There is still a chance for a few weak, late season northwest swells, and they make several day trips to the north shore whenever they hear there are waves, but mostly they are waiting for the southern hemisphere to start ramping up again.

Being back in town makes it much more convenient for BP to finish attending his course at UH, as it is once again within walking distance, and he begins to spend more time on campus. He often stays after class to talk with his professor, Dominic, asking questions about the course material and eventually branching out into other topics, including politics. Spurred on by Donny's death, he begins to participate in more anti-war activism, which is not as widespread or as well-organized on the UH campus as it had been at UCSD, but certainly still prevalent, and passionately expressed.

Dr. Pukui is one of the most outspoken opponents of the war among the faculty, as well as a vocal proponent of the Hawaiian sovereignty movement, which had been born from the growing sense of awareness and outrage over the historical colonization of the islands by the U.S.—how the indigenous people of Hawaii were displaced and disenfranchised for the material benefit of a small, white elite, who claimed to provide their moral salvation. BP admires his stance on these issues, and has many extended conversations with him after class, over coffee or lunch, learning a great deal about the overthrow of the Hawaiian monarchy, which reminds him of the "pacification" and marginalization of the American Indians back on the mainland, a sad tale of blood and tears. At the same time, Dominic appreciates BP's intellectual curiosity and sincere concern over these issues, even though he is not an enrolled student, and a full-blooded *haole* at that, inviting him to attend anti-war rallies and teach-ins, as well as community meetings regarding Hawaiian nationalism, where BP sometimes feels as out of place as when he had attended a James Brown concert in downtown San Diego long ago—one of the only white faces in the crowd.

Becoming caught up and involved in current affairs again, he pays more attention to news reports in the media. In April of 1971, he hears that nearly a half-million people had come together in Washington D.C. to protest the war, including thousands of veterans, who threw their medals on the steps of the Capitol to show their disgust over the course of the nation.

From April 20–May 27, Congress initiates the Fulbright Hearings, concerning U.S. foreign policy and the government's conduct of the war. A representative from the Vietnam Veterans Against the War organization, a young man named John Kerry, testifies before the committee on April 22, and BP reads his words the next day in the newspaper:

"Several months ago in Detroit, we had an investigation at which over 150 honorably discharged and many very highly decorated veterans testified to war crimes committed in Southeast Asia, not isolated incidents but crimes committed on a day-to-day basis with the full awareness of officers at all levels of command. They told the stories at times they had personally raped, cut off ears, cut off heads, taped wires from portable telephones to human genitals and turned up the power, cut off limbs, blown up bodies, randomly shot at civilians, razed villages in fashion reminiscent of Genghis Khan, shot cattle and dogs for fun, poisoned food stocks, and generally ravaged the countryside of South Vietnam in addition to the normal ravage of war, and the normal and very particular ravaging which is done by the applied bombing power of this country."

BP is astounded to read that most of the leaders of our country dismiss this testimony as "collateral damage" and "isolated mistakes made in the heat of combat." If ever there was a time for America to be ashamed, thinks BP, this is it.

As the summer wears on, good waves are still scarce. Swells from the south are small and short-lived. Finally, in late July, Bumper receives an urgent phone call one morning from a friend of his named Chris, who lives on Maui, telling him that a south swell is beginning to show up with just the perfect touch of east in it to light up the fickle break at Maalaea, on the Valley Isle's south shore. "Get your ass over here, right now," is Chris' advice.

"We gotta go!" announces Bumper, as soon as he hangs up the phone. "Pack some clothes and grab your board, we're on our way to Maui. I'm calling the airport for reservations on the next flight."

"But, Bumper, I can't really afford...," begins BP.

"No 'buts' about it!" interrupts Bumper, curtly. "You're going with me this time. You can't miss this—it's a once-in-a-decade event when Maalaea goes off! It's the longest, fastest tuberide in the world when it fires. Get your shit— we're on it! Screw the money. Meatball don't work that way!"

BP knows there is no arguing with Bumper when he uses this expression, which is something he picked up out of his most cherished literary source, the underground Zap Comix. It is his favorite way of ending disagreements—a *non sequitur* supreme, which can mean practically anything from "Life ain't like that," to "We could argue about this all day, but my mind is fuckin'-well made up, so shut your mouth." At any rate, BP is tantalized by his description of the break, and decides that his finances can be damned. If it is that good, it is certainly worth using up some of his stash of cash for it.

They catch an inter-island flight that afternoon, and BP is relieved to find that it is only a $30 fare, which represents a month's food budget for him, but won't totally break the bank. Chris picks them up at the airport and they are surfing Maalaea before the sun goes down. The waves are everything Bumper and Chris said they would be.

When a strong, long-period, south swell lines up perfectly with the eight-mile gap between Kahoolawe island and the southwest tip of Maui, sweeping into Maalaea Bay, held up by stiff offshore tradewinds, it is a sight to behold, and the stuff of which surfing dreams are made. The wave is a freight-train righthand wall, peeling swiftly and relentlessly, nearly unmakeable—a full-speed drive right from the takeoff, pulling in under the curtain and trimming hard down the line, racing the lip as fast as you can go, until you are either swallowed up or spit out. It is not a huge wave, in comparison to spots on the north shore, and the sets can be inconsistent, with big lulls, typical of any southern-hemi swell that has traveled thousands of miles to come ashore, but they are ruler-edged and clean, groomed by the offshore winds. The first day is not as big as the second, when wave heights top out at about 4'-6' (8'-12' on the face), but it is possible to ride for 100–200, even 300 yards at a time inside the tube, if you get lucky in your wave selection, and have enough speed to connect the various sections.

Chris seems to know almost everyone in the water and introduces them to a Hawaiian surfer named "Buddy Boy" as soon as they paddle out. "We just call this place 'Buddy's Bay,'" Chris tells them, "'cause he is the hottest guy out here whenever it breaks." Giving respect and waves to the locals, while proving their skill in the water by riding competently, the three *haole* boys are accepted into the rotation of the lineup without conflict. Riding his 6'8" board, currently the shortest in his quiver, BP gets the most enthralling tube rides of his life, one after another.

These are breakthrough sessions for BP. The waves are almost mechanical in their perfection, with a predictability and length that allows him to experiment with his trim and positioning repeatedly. There is no time for big maneuvers on these waves—as soon as he paddles frantically over the ledge and drops in, trying to keep from being blinded by the spray in his face from the offshore wind, he sets the edge of his inside rail and angles right, trimming up towards the nose with a small shuffle as soon as his turn is completed. From there, it is a full-blast race with the lip, the curtain of blue water falling to his left and enveloping him.

He discovers that it is still possible to turn the board subtly from this forward position, pumping it smoothly up and down the face to gain speed, weighting and un-weighting the inside rail to match the progress of the tube's raveling path. This allows him to stay in the barrel longer, and make it further down the line, increasing the length of his rides as he perfects the technique with practice.

Most amazingly, as he had experienced before, but never to this extent, his perception of the duration of time while in the most critical, barreling portion of the wave is altered drastically. While in the midst of the most frantic, accelerated physical effort, he is able to see things with such clarity and detail—every bump on the curving face as it approaches is accounted for by his feet, each lunge of the lip as it races ahead of him is anticipated and matched easily with his trimming moves, pulling in higher and tighter and then rhythmically releasing the inside rail to skitter down and forward ever faster. The view of the eye of the tube is hypnotizing, a bright elliptical disk framed in whirling water—drawing away from him, as he falls back deeper into the shadows, then rushing towards him, as he increases his speed, willing himself towards the aperture of light—all seeming to happen in slow motion. Even when he can't make the wave and emerge from the barrel, it is such a euphoric experience that he doesn't mind sitting off the back of his board and taking his beating in the "rinse cycle" of the wave's soupy collapse. It is a small price to pay for such ecstasy.

They surf constantly for three days, taking breaks only for food and water to replenish their systems, and to sleep, crashing heavily in exhaustion each night at Chris' house. On the fourth day of their trip, the surf drops off, and by the fifth day the swell is gone. Maalaea returns to its normal state as a tranquil bay next to a boat harbor. As he drops them off at the airport for their flight back to Honolulu, BP and Bumper thank Chris profusely for tipping them off to the swell and putting them up, inviting him to come visit them on Oahu anytime, where they would be happy to return the favor.

On the plane ride home, BP is curious, and asks Bumper if he has ever experienced the same sort of anomaly regarding the passage of time that he had felt while riding in the tube. It is difficult to articulate exactly what he means, but he describes his experiences as best he can. Bumper struggles with the lack of clarity in the question, but finally allows that he, too, had sometimes felt that things were happening in slow-motion while tube-riding. BP decides that this might be a more common effect than he had originally thought.

On his first night back in Honolulu, BP has a strange dream, one that he remembers after waking up, which is unusual for him. Slightly different versions of it repeat several times over the next few months, always resulting in a disturbing feeling when he awakes. The dream may begin differently at different times (this remains a bit fuzzy in his mind) but it invariably ends with him riding deep inside a tube, focusing on the orb of light at the end of the tunnel, representing the route for his escape from the twirling barrel, when suddenly it is transformed into an eye—not a metaphorical eye, but the actual eye of a living organism—complete with white sclera, bright green iris and dark black pupil, staring back at him unblinkingly. The swirling around him slows down noticeably and he is able to study it quite clearly. It is when he notices the shape of the pupil—a distinctly feline, vertical, almond shape, not the round pupil of a human—that he always wakes up. Try as he might, he cannot think of a reason why a cat's eye is in his dreams.

LEILANI

When the next school year starts at UH in September, BP looks through the catalog to find another class taught by his friend, Dominic, and begins auditing an upper-division course of his in Polynesian art, just to keep in touch and provide a little stimulation outside of surfing.

At the same time, he reassesses his financial situation and realizes that despite his very thrifty lifestyle (along with Bumper's generosity), he has already spent $2,000 of the money he had brought from the mainland. Calculating that his remaining funds can only last another eighteen months, at best, he decides he needs to find a source of income—the sooner, the better.

Dealing is not really a possibility in his current situation, as he does not have the contacts for such endeavors on the island. He also doesn't want to be on any company's regular payroll, requiring submission of his Social Security Number, which might raise a flag in the government bureaucracy regarding his whereabouts.

Using a recommendation from one of the north shore surfshops for which he had done repair work during the last winter season, he is able to pick up some patching work at one of the board manufacturers in town, on a cash basis, off the books. This suits him fine, and he applies himself diligently to the job, impressing the owner sufficiently with his fiberglassing skills and diligent attention to detail that he is quickly promoted to glassing new boards on a part-time, piecework basis. He can work whatever schedule suits him, and is paid $10 for each board he laminates, with another $5 for hot-coating and sanding, cash under the table, each Friday. He feels satisfied that he can keep his head above water now, even working as little as ten hours a week.

He and Bumper move back out to the country in November, when the house in Haleiwa is free again, and he spends his second winter season on the north shore, surfing with more confidence and aggression, having become more accustomed to the conditions, as well as reaching a new plateau of ability over the past year.

This season, he finally begins surfing once in awhile at Pipeline, achieving a dream he had held for many years. Pipe is the center of the media circus on the north shore, and thus attracts the most competitive crowd of surfers on its best days. Besides being the most photogenic break in Hawaii, it is also one of the most difficult to master, with a well-established pecking order. He chooses his sessions there carefully, usually paddling out on the lesser swells at dawn, when the spot (and the photographers) suffer from "morning sickness," before the wind is blowing offshore hard enough, and the sun has risen high enough, to create the preferred conditions. He sacrifices some quality by doing this, but otherwise might not get any waves there at all.

Riding this break on his backhand is quite a challenge, as he has never perfected his switch-stance surfing well enough to feel comfortable turning around and facing such a wave going left. Even in small (3'-4') conditions, when it is just beginning to work, the wave is very powerful, with the lip jacking furiously skyward when it hits the shallow, lava shelf and throws out. The takeoff is a heart-stopper, the drop-in is sketchy, and mistakes are punishing, as he finds out when he goes through a double rinse-cycle on his first wipeout, being sucked over the falls twice by the same wave, as it imploded and churned on the rocky reef. Being bounced off the bottom is fairly commonplace, as the number of injuries at the spot each year attests. It is a short but intense ride, and the widest, squarest tube he has ever seen, working best on a more westerly swell later in the season, after some of the sand that accumulates on the reef during the summer is swept away by the early season surf.

When there is a little more north in the swell, it is also possible to ride the other side of the "A-frame" Pipeline peak, which is called Backdoor. BP actually prefers this right-hand tube, as it is on his frontside, like Maalaea, but it is just as dangerous as Pipe, since its end section dumps on a very shallow part of the reef, with prominent, rocky outcroppings. Though he succeeds in getting a few good barrels at both spots, it is only on the smaller days, and never in "prime-time." Overall, the reality of a crowded, perfect day at Pipeline cannot live up to the cinematic expectations of his teenage years, and he enjoys surfing other spots more, out of the limelight and under the radar.

He continues to commute to town at least three times a week for work, and to attend class. His friendship with Dominic develops further, as they seem to have a natural kinship, despite their differences in experience. He is even invited to his home for some parties, beginning with a few weekend barbeques Nic throws before the home football games of the Rainbow Warriors. BP enjoys meeting and talking with many different folks at these gatherings, including Hawaiian intellectuals, artists and athletes, and is very happy to meet his wife, Mari, who is a very contrasting individual from her husband. She is of Japanese-Hawaiian descent, very petite, quiet and reserved, compared to her husband's outgoing, even boisterous, and physically imposing presence. He discovers that Dominic enjoys a bit of *pakalolo* and a beer at these gatherings as much as he does.

Staying very busy, time passes quickly for him, and soon they are moving back to town for the springtime doldrums. Bumper is feeling the effects of "cabin fever," after spending eighteen straight months on these tiny rocks in the middle of the ocean, so he takes off on a three-month sojourn to Australia on the spur of the moment, to visit friends "down under," hoping to score some fine, pointbreak, cyclone surf before the season is over there, leaving BP alone in the apartment.

This interlude is actually very welcome in BP's view, not having to keep up with Bumper's frenetic pace for awhile. He works longer hours at the surf-board factory, and spends more time at the university library, instead of going out to clubs in the evening. He reads more books and magazines, catching up on current literature and cultural events, which helps him feel less isolated and alone. The political situation continues to aggravate and enrage him, and he sometimes thinks that being less informed might actually be a blessing in some ways.

He learns about, and follows the progress of, the Shafer Commission in Washington D.C., charged by President Nixon to study marijuana and drug abuse in the country. This national commission presents its findings to Congress on March 22, 1972, recommending the decriminalization of marijuana, claiming: "The criminal law is too harsh a tool to apply to personal possession even in the effort to discourage use. It implies an overwhelming indictment of the behavior which we believe is not appropriate. The actual and potential harm of use of the drug is not great enough to justify intrusion by the criminal law into private behavior, a step which our society takes only with the greatest reluctance."

BP is heartened to hear such sensible words spoken in the halls of government, and has hope for some reform to public policies.

During May, however, there is a highly publicized report on the growing epidemic of heroin use among U.S. soldiers in Vietnam. President Nixon buries the Shafer Commission's findings, and names drug abuse as "Public Enemy #1" in America, declaring a "War on Drugs" at a press conference, refusing to remove marijuana from the most strict, "Schedule I" category of dangerous drugs in the Controlled Substances Act, while tobacco, beer, wine, and spirits are explicitly exempt from it. BP is furious at the government's continuation of this idiocy.

It is during one of his research sessions in the library that his life takes a sudden turn. As he is rounding the corner of one of the stacks absorbed in thought, he bumps into a young woman, clumsily knocking the books she is carrying out of her hands. He mumbles his apologies and helps her pick up the books. He only looks her in the face as she thanks him, smiles and walks away. He is left paralyzed in her wake. It is as if he is struck by the pro-verbial thunderbolt when he gazes upon her visage—a prototypically-perfect Polynesian beauty with glowing, brown skin, long, dark, brown hair framing wide chestnut eyes, high cheekbones, and perfect white teeth behind the most luscious pair of lips he has ever seen. He is stunned by her attractiveness, and it is several moments before he can breathe again, watching her move grace-fully away, hips swaying under a formless, flower-print muumuu.

Finally coming to his senses, he follows her, watching her sit down at a table, opening one of the books and flipping through it. His pulse is elevated as he takes a place at a nearby table facing her, staring at her covertly, pretending to look through the book he has taken from the shelf, trying to work up the courage to talk to her. There is something so familiar about her face that he racks his brain trying to remember if he has met her before, but he can't recall ever having seen her anywhere.

Her appeal is overpowering, and he is driven to approach her somehow, but he also has a sense of foreboding. What will he say to her? What if she rejects his advances? Where do these strong feelings come from? What do they mean? Is this "love at first sight?" He doesn't even know who she is, or what she is really like—how can he be so deeply affected by simply looking at her? A shiver runs through his body.

While he is having this internal debate, he sees her suddenly close her book, get up from the table and walk away. Is she leaving? He panics. Jumping up from his seat, he rushes back to where he had been sitting previously and collects his knapsack, which he had left laying there. He hurries toward the checkout counter, trying to catch a glimpse of her. He spies her just going out the front door as he approaches the counter. With no time to check out the book he is still carrying, he places it on one of the trolleys sitting next to the counter and hurries past, towards the exit.

As he bursts out the front door of the library into bright sunlight, his eyes have trouble adjusting to the glare. He pulls his sunglasses down from the top of his head, where he had perched them while inside the building, and looks left and right, trying to spot her. She is nowhere to be seen amongst the people walking on the various pathways. He hurries to the right side of the library and looks around the corner to see if she had headed that way, but no luck. He hustles to the other side of the building and checks for her there, but she is nowhere to be found. Frustrated and angry with himself, he wanders around the campus aimlessly for an hour, hoping she is in a class and will reappear afterwards. Finally, he gives up the search and pedals his bike back home, chastising himself for blowing the opportunity to speak to her when he had the chance.

Amazingly, two days later, while he is attending Nic's class in Polynesian art, there is a special presentation of traditional Hawaiian dance as part of the curriculum. A troupe of dancers comes into the lecture hall to perform for the class, and he is stunned to recognize her in the group! He cannot take his eyes off her as she moves artfully to the chanted *mele* in unison with the other dancers, barefooted in a bulky tapa skirt, lei around her neck and crowning her head. He is determined not to let this chance to meet her slip through his fingers, so after class, he joins the others in congratulating the dancers. Ultimately he winds up next to her and introduces himself, complimenting her on her performance.

He finds out that her name is Leilani, and that she is indeed a student at UH, when he mentions having seen her in the library a few days ago. Before she leaves, he says that he would very much like to see her again sometime, and asks if they might meet for lunch, perhaps, when she is back on campus. She seems interested, and they make a date to meet at a coffee shop just down the street the very next day.

BP is on top of the world. The girl of his dreams is within reach. [Although he doesn't recall these dreams whatsoever, at this moment in time.] Over the last two weeks of the school year, he meets her every day on campus, gradually getting to know her, and slowly revealing pieces of his own life. When Bumper returns from Australia towards the end of June, with stories of surfing perfect, 8' Byron Bay, he finds BP quite distracted with his new romance, and unwilling to paint the town, as usual.

Leilani, whose name means "royal child of heaven," as BP discovers, is his only focus. Other women do not exist for him anymore. He finds her utterly fascinating. She is a full-blooded native Hawaiian, a rarity in this state where mixed race is so common, and very much in touch with the land and its people, tracing her ancestry back to the days before the monarchy ended. She had graduated from the prestigious Kamehameha preparatory school before attending UH, and is very intelligent and articulate, with an odd mix of traditional and modern sensibilites. She has studied the ancient Hawaiian language, which had been banned from most schools in 1898 and become almost extinct by 1950, but speaks perfect English and fluent pidgin as well. She paddles canoes for sport, and even *surfs!* During the summer, they spend many days in the water together at Waikiki, and though she is not an accomplished rider, she is very competent and graceful on a longboard, and a strong paddler.

One day, they take a ride on his motorcycle out into the country, to a special place she wants to show him. They park the bike at the end of the road and hike deep into a tropical valley, following a stream up its course. Eventually they come to a deserted clearing, with a deep, freshwater pool fed by a cascading waterfall and surrounded by a rocky shore, holding back the thick vegetation.

They rest and sun themselves on a large flat rock at the head of the pool. Leilani takes off her clothes, baring her brown body to the sun in a most natural way, and BP follows suit, barely able to contain his excitement. Without a hint of self-consciousness she stands before him, totally naked. Her lovely body is breathtaking, and BP cannot bring himself to move or speak, entranced by this vision.

"C'mon, follow me. I know a special place here. It's wonderful," she says softly and turns, walking away from him and diving gracefully into the pool. He watches her swim towards the waterfall, turning back, beckoning him with a wave of her hand.

Without hesitation, he follows her. The water is crystal clear, but much cooler than he expects. He swims towards the waterfall, watching her disappear underneath it.

He ducks and pushes through the foamy, white curtain of bubbles and surfaces behind it, to find her sitting on a shallow ledge, leaning back on her arms, laughing with joy, as the edge of the waterfall rains all over her glorious body in glistening sheets.

The totality of her allure is absolute, and BP cannot stop himself. He struggles awkwardly up onto the ledge next to her and pulls her into an embrace, pressing their wet bodies together and swaying as the water sparkles and beats down on them with a stinging caress. He tries to kiss her, but she pushes him away gently, turning her head. "Please, Beep, can't we just be friends? I like you very much, but I'm not ready to be in love with you in that way, and I don't know if I ever will be."

BP is devastated. This had seemed to him to be the culminating moment toward which their relationship had been building, and an undeniable, rock-hard erection has sprouted between his legs to prove it. "But I truly do love you, Leilani. I want to be with you always, in the worst way."

"You don't understand....You are *haole*, we could never be together like that."

"Why not? If I love you, and you loved me, what could keep us apart?"

"You don't know me, or my family, all that well," Leilani explains, with a pained expression on her face. "They would never accept you as my husband, and out of respect for them, I couldn't marry outside my race, either. I'm so sorry! I've enjoyed your company so very much, and I do want to be your friend, but I can't love you in that way. I didn't mean to lead you on—please don't be angry with me. Maybe I shouldn't have taken my clothes off? Did that inject too much sexuality between us? It's so natural for our people, though... especially in a place like this. Did you know that once upon a time, women danced the hula topless, with just a wrapped skirt, and men and women both surfed naked in the waves together?"

BP is crestfallen and crushed, but he tries not to show it, as he doesn't want her to suffer from any more awkwardness than already exists between them. "I think I understand," he says, despite his disappointment, "or I'll try to, anyway. We better be heading back, it's getting late." He rolls off the ledge and into the pool again. The cool water has a calming effect on the fire in his loins, and he tries not to look at her delectable body again as they swim back to the edge of the pool and get dressed, lest it be reignited.

As they ride back to town on his motorcycle, she wraps her arms around him and hugs his chest tenderly. Several times, he feels her lay her head against his back, pressing her cheek against his spine, making him think that perhaps she, too, feels regret over what might have been today—rather than merely sheltering her face from the whipping wind.

Aloha: Phase Two

BP is confused and depressed again. He doesn't understand how he could have been so mistaken in his feelings for Leilani. They had seemed so clear and powerful. He had been so sure that she was the one he was meant to love forever, yet it is obvious now that she did not feel the same way. He wonders if she might grow into it with time? Surely she had *some* feelings for him, didn't she? Why should it matter that he is white and she is brown? Hell, except for under his boardshorts, his skin is tanned almost as dark as hers!

He has never experienced such feelings of alienation and ostracization before, simply because of his race. Sure, he had been given the occasional "stink-eye" from the Hawaiian braddahs in the water, but giving up a wave is different than giving up the woman he loves! Should he fight for her, somehow, or should he show the deference and respect he has learned to give in the surf? If she doesn't really love him in the same way, is there anything to actually be won? He can't *make* her love him, after all. Maybe he needs to just let it go....

He doesn't understand why he hadn't seen this coming. Thinking back, it is obvious there were signs he should have considered as portentous. For instance, he had never met Leilani's parents, or been to their home. He knew she lived with them still, in a house out towards Diamond Head, but he had never seen it. They had always met at school, or in town, or down at Waikiki for a surf. Was she keeping her relationship with him a secret from them all this time?

It doesn't help that his dreams are often filled with her image. More than once, the scene at the waterfall is replayed in his mind while he is asleep, and even sometimes when awake. The sight of her silken skin, her sinewy, curvaceous body is difficult to put to rest, and it is dredged up from his subconscious often. He finds himself laying next to her again, stroking her softly as the water cascades down on them, and she returns his embrace, kissing him madly, welcoming him, spreading her long legs, wrapping them around him, and just when he is about to enter her he wakes up—with a giant, annoying boner that he must beat into submission.

He finds it extremely odd that every once in awhile, during these erotic dreams, Leilani turns into someone else—a white woman with green eyes, who is also very beautiful, standing naked before him with a towel wrapped around her head like a turban! Where does that come from, he wonders? Is his mind playing some sort of trick on him, or is it a sign, a lesson of some sort, perhaps, telling him he needs to "stick to his own kind?" What the fuck! This is not *West Side Story*. It's not a Hollywood movie—it's my life! Why can't my brain help me figure this stuff out, instead of just confusing the issue, he wonders? Who wrote this script? Who's in charge here?

Bumper can see that his friend is deeply troubled again, and wants to help. He approaches BP one evening, while he is sitting around the apartment, seeming particularly morose. "Hey Beep," he says, "I've got something here that will make you feel better." He takes a paper bindle out of his pocket and puts it on the table between them. "One snort of this, brah, and I guarantee you will be feeling no pain in about five minutes."

"Nah, I don't feel like doing any coke, Bumper," says BP. "Thanks anyway."

"It's not blow, man. This is some 'China White.' Some of me mates from Maroubra, down in Oz, turned me on to it."

"Heroin?" blurts out BP, surprised and repulsed. "You're doing smack now, Bumper? What are you thinking? That shit is deadly! You wanna be an addict? A junkie?"

"It's not that bad," Bumper tries to explain. "I've only been doing a little taste of it, here and there. You know how people blow drug problems all out of proportion. If you don't snort it very often, you won't get a monkey on your back. It feels so good, you won't believe it. C'mon, give it a try."

"No way! I don't want anything to do with it," insists BP, "and you shouldn't either. That stuff isn't like weed, or hash, or even coke—it's highly addictive, and you build up a tolerance for it quickly. You'll just want more and more of it. Pretty soon, you'll be mainlining the stuff. That's how it goes. Don't kid yourself!"

Bumper is offended at his reaction. "Don't get all preachy with me, now," he retorts. "I know what I'm doing. It's just another high—I can handle it! I thought it might help you chill out."

"It may be a nice high on the inside, but from the outside it can get ugly, buddy. I've seen enough junkies to know that, and so have you. They are worse than sloppy drunks—remember those two guys who said they were friends of Griff's, who were camping at the farm, the last summer we were there? They were shooting up smack all the time, stumbling around and slurring their words, throwing up on themselves, pawing chicks at parties and drooling on them. You threw them out yourself! Don't you remember that?"

"Those guys were losers. I'm not like them."

"I don't care how cool you are Bumper, you're playing with fire, here. Listen, I can't handle this right now! I don't even want to be around if you're going to do that shit. I'm going out for a walk, and I hope you just flush it down the toilet by the time I get back." He gets up and heads towards the door.

"Don't tell me what to do!" he hears Bumper yell, as he is closing the front door behind himself. "Meatball don't work that way!"

The summer drags to an end for BP with no relief in sight. He still sees Leilani occasionally, but the magic is gone from their relationship. It is a harsh internal struggle for him to banish his sexual attraction from their interactions and treat her just as a friend, or a sister, though he would like to be able to do that. To some extent, she seems to be aware of how difficult it is for him, too, and tactfully allows their relationship to cool off.

Bumper is a bit sullen after their argument, but then appears to forgive him, and never brings up the subject of heroin again, though there are quite a few nights when he goes out and fails to come home until the next day. BP does not ask where he's been, and hopes that he simply picked up a woman and stayed at her place.

There is no one he can talk to about his recent experiences. He thinks of Nic, who might be particularly helpful to him in explaining Leilani's (and her parent's) feelings about him as a *haole,* but unfortunately, he left in June for a year-long sabbatical in Italy, to study the classical art of the western masters "up close and personal," as he had put it. BP had received a postcard from him recently, giving an address in Rome, and saying he was welcome to visit anytime—but Europe is so very far away. He wonders about calling him on the telephone, but he has no number for him, and he is not sure how he might find it. Would he need to speak Italian to the long-distance information operator? He abandons that idea and struggles along alone.

Checking his P.O. box at the end of August, there is a letter from his mother, with another envelope folded up inside it that she is forwarding to him, still sealed, from the Selective Service System. The letter from his mom is the usual chatty stuff, wishing he is well and telling him about the finalization of her divorce from his father, and that she is enjoying college at San Diego State again, working on her teaching credential. She is content and happy, it seems. In a postscript at the end, she mentions that the letter from the SSS had looked important to her, and that she wanted to get it to him as soon as possible.

His hands tremble slightly as he opens it. Inside is another notice to report for a pre-induction physical in Los Angeles on September 25, 1972, a little over three weeks from now. It is identical to the form letter he had received previously, in 1970, except that he notices the address of the induction center in Los Angeles is different. There is no mention of anything else—no hint that there might be something odd about the fact that they had done this same thing to him two years ago, and that he has been lost and unaccounted for in their system all this time.

He wonders if the SSS might have just caught his status (or lack of it) on some routine review of their files, and simply re-issued the notice, or whether something more sinister might await him if he shows up for it. He imagines that the change in location of the induction center might have something to do with the lack of security at the old center, but it doesn't matter to him, anyway—there is no way in hell he is going there. "Fuck them! If they want me, they can come and find me. I'll just claim I never got the letter—the first one *or* the second one, for that matter. Screw it!"

It is while he is surfing the next day at Popular's in Waikiki that he notices a problem in his left armpit. On windy days, he sometimes wears a simple, light vest made of thin neoprene to protect him from being chilled by evaporation, even though the water is warm. The edges of the vest often cause a rash to develop in his armpits from chafing as he paddles, but something is different this time.

For as long as he can remember, he has had a small mole, high on the inside of his left arm, which can get especially irritated under these circumstances. He has abraded it several times over the years so badly that it bled. It is bleeding now, but when he looks at it in the mirror after showering, it looks quite different to him. It is torn again, but it also looks quite a bit bigger, blotchier and more inflamed than usual. There are tiny, red trails radiating out from it that he had never noticed before.

Thinking that it might be getting infected, he visits the student health clinic at UH the next day. He has no insurance, and his health has always been excellent, so he has not been to a doctor since he came to Hawaii. The one time he had gotten some coral cuts from bouncing off a reef while surfing that had become infected, he had come to this clinic and they had treated him for free, never even asking for his student ID, which was a good thing, since he was not actually enrolled at the school.

This time, a nurse sees him shortly after walking into the clinic, with no questions asked again. BP shows her the mole and asks her if they can just remove it, as it's becoming a nuisance. She examines it and mutters something that sounds like "Wait just a minute," scurrying out of the exam room and returning quickly with a doctor. He scrutinizes the mole under a magnifying eyepiece, with a strong light source focused on it, and grunts.

"Harrrumph!" says the doctor. "I don't like the looks of this. I want you to see a dermatology specialist, son. I'll write you a referral. Do you have your ID card?"

"Umm, no, I don't," answers BP, playing dumb. "Do I need that?"

"Well, you will when you get to his office, if you want to have your student health insurance pay for the visit, but we'll just give you his name and address so you can make the appointment. Don't delay, though, this mole looks suspicious—it may have turned cancerous, and I'm pretty sure he will want to biopsy it." The doctor scribbles something on a pad and gives it to the nurse. "It might be nothing, but it is better to be safe than sorry, young man."

BP follows the nurse back to the front counter, where she shuffles through some drawers, coming up with a business card which she hands to him, along with the piece of paper from the doctor's pad. "Just call Dr. Devin and make an appointment," she tells him. "He's very good—we send all the kids there for dermatology treatments." She flashes him a comforting smile as he leaves the building.

He is feeling anything but comfortable, though, as he walks home. There had been something ominous in the doctor's tone, and he did not like hearing the word "cancerous" at all. His stomach is fluttering and he feels quite nervous. The illegible scribble on the prescription slip tells him nothing.

He phones Dr. Devin's office when he gets home to make an appointment. They can see him at 3:00 the next afternoon. He tells them that would be fine, and asks for directions to the office. He doesn't eat or sleep well that night, smoking a big reefer and drinking three beers (which is a lot, for him) to finally calm down and rest.

Things do not go well when he sees Dr. Devin the next day. With one brief look at the mole, the doctor decides they must do a biopsy. "It is a relatively simple procedure," he explains, "and we can do it right here with a local anesthetic. I will simply remove the mole, and a margin of tissue around it, and we will send it to my lab for analysis. They will be able to tell us within 36 hours what we have here."

BP agrees to the procedure, signs the consent forms, and they lay him on the table, with his arm over his head. After cleaning the area thoroughly, Dr. Devin injects novocaine at several points, then waits ten minutes for the skin to become numb. After some sterile linen is placed over his whole shoulder and against his face, he can no longer see what is being done, but he can feel some tugging and pressing on his arm, and hears the doctor's voice, muffled a bit by the surgical mask he is wearing.

"There does seem to be some growth underlying the mole," he says at one point. "I'm going to excise a little more tissue. You shouldn't feel a thing." This does not sound good to BP.

"We're going to cauterize the incision now to stop any bleeding," Dr. Devin says next, and BP hears a buzzing sound, followed by the smell of burning flesh.

"Now we're going to close the wound, and we'll be done." BP feels some more tugging on his arm, but no real pain whatsoever, so he just lies quietly on the table. After five minutes or so, the doctor declares the procedure finished, and asks the nurse to apply a bandage. "I'm going to take care of another patient in the next room," he says, "but I'll be back to speak with you in a few minutes."

It takes only a short while for the nurse to bandage his arm and he is able to sit up again. "You'll want to change this dressing every day, and don't get it wet for a week. We put in six stitches, and they will come out in seven days. Here is some antiseptic ointment to apply to the wound each time you change the dressing, along with some extra bandages." The nurse hands him a plastic bag with the supplies inside.

"So I guess going surfing is out, huh?" he asks. "Can I take showers OK?"

"Yes, you should not immerse it in water for any length of time, but you should be able to shower carefully, without getting it too wet, then just change the bandage after you dry off. Do you have any other questions about the wound care?"

"No, I don't think so."

"The doctor will be back to talk with you in a few moments then," she says, leaving the room.

BP puts his shirt back on and fidgets in the exam room for what seems like a long time before the doctor returns, although it is actually less than ten minutes.

"Of course we need the results of the biopsy to confirm my suspicions," the doctor begins, "but I am very concerned about what I found on your arm. There was what appears to be a subcutaneous tumor under the mole, and I had to go much deeper than I expected to remove it. There were threads of it going down even further into the muscle tissue, but I didn't want to risk any nerve damage, especially since we don't yet know if it is malignant. We will call you with the results of the biopsy when we receive them, and when you come back to have the stitches removed in a week, we will talk about what further actions may be necessary. Until then, just take care of the incision and watch for any signs of infection. If it gets swollen, red and puffy, call me immediately, OK?"

"Yes sir, thank you," says BP. "The nurse told me how to take care of it."

"Fine, then, we'll phone you within two days, and you can make an appointment for next week at the front desk before you leave."

BP goes to the front desk and pays the bill in cash. It comes to $125, without the lab work—more than he had expected, but since he doesn't have a bank account or credit card, he had been sure to put some extra money in his wallet that morning. He makes an appointment for seven days later, as instructed, and leaves the office in a fairly shaken state.

"What does this mean?" he wonders, as he rides his motorcycle home. He doesn't have a good feeling about it. "Let's see, this is Wednesday, so I should know by Friday, I guess." He is on pins and needles for the next two days.

Dr. Devin calls at 8:00 on Friday morning. BP is sitting by the phone, waiting. "I'm afraid I have some bad news," he says, getting right to the point. "Your biopsy was positive for malignant melanoma, which is a very dangerous form of skin cancer. I would like you to come into the office for some more tests as soon as possible. Are you free this morning?"

"Yes sir," answers BP, "I could be there in less than an hour."

"That would be fine. We just want to take some blood and an X-ray at this point. You don't need an appointment, we'll fit you in as soon as you get here."

BP is in the office in 45 minutes. They draw some blood, take an X-ray of his entire upper torso, and examine the incision from the biopsy, which they say is healing nicely. He never sees Dr. Devin, but is told that his test results should be ready by the time his stitches are removed, and the doctor will talk to him about a course of treatment at that time.

Before he returns on the next Wednesday, he goes to the library to find out everything he can about melanoma. It is not a pretty picture. Malignant melanoma accounts for 75% of all deaths associated with skin cancer, according to the medical books he reads. The risk factors include sun exposure, the age at which it occurs, and the degree of skin pigmentation of the subject. As a young, light-skinned surfer, he is a veritable "poster boy" for the disease, he realizes. The prognosis for recovery involves the stage at which the tumor is detected and whether it has metastasized, spreading cancer cells to other parts of the body. He assumes that this is why the doctor ordered further tests.

He doesn't talk to anyone about his diagnosis, trudging along in a daze until he speaks to the doctor again. He satisfies Bumper's curiosity about the bandage on his upper arm by saying that he had an "infected mole" removed that was hindering his paddling.

It is a complete bummer when he talks to the doctor again. After removing his stitches and poking around in his armpit, Dr. Devin tells him that according to the size of the tumor and his blood markers, it has almost certainly metastasized. Though they didn't find any evidence that it had spread to his lungs or bones, there is some swelling in the adjacent lymph node that is suspect. His recommendation is that BP should submit to an additional surgery by a specialist, which will require admitting him to a hospital. They will excise additional tissue surrounding the site of the tumor to a distance of two centimeters, at least, which will involve removing a portion of his bicep muscle. At the same time, they will examine and biopsy the lymph nodes in his arm, and if they are cancerous, remove them as well.

"What is my prognosis, then?" asks BP.

"It will depend on what stage the cancer has reached," answers Dr. Devin. "We will know more after the surgery. If it is at Stage III, there is a 25–50% survival rate. If it is at Stage IV, with distant metastasis, the prognosis for survival drops to 10–15%. In that case, we would undertake chemotherapy and possibly radiation treatments as well, depending on which organs are involved."

"How much is this going to cost?" wonders BP.

"I imagine the initial surgery, with the anesthesia and follow-up hospitalization, will amount to $5,000 or so. Do you have health insurance?"

"No."

"Well, then, if you can't afford this, there are state social services for indigent patients which can help pay for it. I will give you a referral to the specialist I would recommend to perform the surgery, and you can talk to his office about how to take care of the costs. Just make an appointment as soon as possible and discuss it with them."

BP is devastated. This development is like a bullet out of the blue, striking him right in the heart. His mind is racing over the implications, but he tries to ask a few more questions about best and worst-case scenarios, details of the surgery, recovery time, and subsequent treatments. It is difficult to focus on the answers though, with a strident little voice echoing in his brain, over and over: *"I'm going to die!"*

Finally, he stumbles out to the front desk and pays his bill for the tests and office visit, folds up the receipt and the sheet of paper with the referral and puts them in his pocket, then gets on his motorcycle and rides back through the city. "What am I going to do?" he wonders. "This is insane—it can't be happening to me!"

Automatically, he makes the turn to cruise past Waikiki for a surf check. He sees gentle 2' rollers cresting and breaking offshore, and his immediate course becomes clear. "I have to go surfing," he says to himself.

It has been a week since he has been in the water, but now that the stitches are out, there is nothing stopping him. He pulls over and parks his bike, running down to the beach. He borrows a longboard from Rabbit, his favorite beachboy, and strips off his T-shirt, tennis shoes and the clean pair of walking shorts he had put on for the doctor visit. Underneath, he is wearing a nylon Speedo racing swimsuit, which is the only form of underwear he has used for many years. Though normally he wouldn't be caught dead surfing in anything but a proper pair of tailored boardshorts, this is an emergency! He paddles out to Canoes without caring what anyone thinks of his appearance, and proceeds to take out his anger and frustration on the waves for the next several hours, ripping every wave he can catch to shreds.

He feels better when he comes in, returning the board and putting his clothes back on over the wet Speedos. Realizing he is famished, he rides over to his favorite Chinese restaurant and orders some lunch. While he is eating, he tries to rationally sort out his alternatives.

He knows he does not want to register with any social service agency in order to pay for the surgery, as he has scrupulously avoided making his whereabouts public knowledge for so long now to avoid the draft board, who may soon be breathing down his neck again. But he has only about $3,000 to his name, and the doctor had estimated the cost much higher than that for the initial surgery alone. If there were follow-up procedures and treatment, undoubtedly the costs would go up. How will he be able to afford this and maintain his freedom? The silver lining to this dark cloud might be that the draft board wouldn't want him anymore if he is truly cancer-ridden, but what if they are after him for his past evasions?

He is still wrestling with this quandary as he finishes his meal and breaks open the fortune cookie that is always provided for dessert. He gasps as he reads the sentence on the slip of paper inside it, as a ray of hope lights up in his brain: "Friends will get you through times of no money better than money will get you through times of no friends."

"Of course!" he thinks, as the idea comes to him. "Bumper! He's my friend, and he has money—more than he knows what to do with! Maybe he will lend me what I need, and I can pay him back later. I should explain the whole situation to him and ask. It's worth a try. Oh man, I hope he's not too pissed at me over that smack thing, I really need his help." He throws some bills on the table to pay for the lunch and a nice tip, then rushes out of the restaurant, speeding home.

He burst through the front door of their apartment and calls out Bumper's name. There is no answer. "Bumper," he calls again, shutting the door, "are you here? I need to talk to you." Still nothing.

He walks through the front room to the lanai and checks the back yard. It is empty. He goes upstairs and sees that Bumper's bedroom door is closed, so he knocks on it softly and calls out his name again. Wondering if he might be taking a nap, he cracks the door open and looks inside. He sees his friend sitting up on the bed, his head tilted back against the wall. He knows immediately that something is very wrong.

Rushing into the room, his world comes crashing down around him. Grabbing Bumper's arm to shake him, it is rigid and his skin feels cold. His face is drained and pale, his eyes are closed. Feeling for a pulse in his neck, there is nothing. *His friend is dead!*

Recoiling in shock and horror, BP's legs become wobbly and he falls to his knees beside the bed. "NO! NO! NO! This can't be happening!" screams in his head, silently. But the reality of it is right there in front of his eyes. An empty syringe lies in Bumper's lap. A piece of surgical tubing is still hanging loosely around his left arm. A tablespoon and a candle are on the nightstand next to him, along with two small bindles of white powder, one a little more sparkly than the other.

BP's body melts limply down onto the floor into a fetal position, wracked with convulsions as he sobs, crying his guts out, tears falling like rain. Many minutes pass before he is able to regain some control over himself and his emotions. Eventually, he is left empty and exhausted, lying on the carpet, staring up at the ceiling.

After the grief, just as with Donny's death, comes the anger, guilt and recrimination. He is furious with Bumper for making such a horrible mistake, and wasting such a beautiful life, for such a cheap, momentary thrill. He wonders what he might have done to prevent it. Should he have stood up to his friend's heroin experimentation more fiercely? Would it have made any difference? Should he have arranged some sort of intervention? Surely

Bumper would have resisted and resented any such action on his part, and it would have destroyed their friendship, in all likelihood. But better a resentful ex-friend than a dead one....

Eventually, fear, anxiety and desperation creep into his mind. He feels totally hopeless, abandoned and alone, backed into a corner. There is no easy way out of this situation. His last great hope has vaporized. It occurs to him that the best path out of this mess might just be to follow Bumper to wherever he has gone. The cancer may kill him anyway—why not just get it over with now? It would be an easy matter to simply cook up a hot shot for himself, sit down on the bed with Bumper and check out. All the ingredients are here, and Bumper certainly seems peaceful enough, lying there with his eyes closed and his lips forming a crooked little half-smile. It doesn't look like he suffered much. BP tries to imagine what death is like, but draws a blank. Is it just like going to sleep? Do you simply drift off into nothingness? Does he have the guts to do it?

Finally, the practical aspects of his predicament sink in. He knows that Bumper's death must be reported, and surely there will be an investigation of some sort. Even if it is determined to be an accident, he will certainly be a material witness, and there are probably enough drugs in the house to result in his arrest on multiple felonies. It will be difficult to maintain his anonymity and freedom under such circumstances, to say the least. Suicide is looking better all the time.

Could he possibly claim that he didn't know anything about Bumper's drug use, that he was just his oblivious, law-abiding roommate? If they eventually let him go and don't send him to jail, he will still have to run from the SSS, if they don't catch up with him beforehand, once his name and location become known.

Maybe it would be best to just get a jump on this whole thing and flee right now. He could get in a few good months of living someplace far away, perhaps, before either the cancer or the law catch up with him, one way or another. This idea appeals to him the most. He desperately needs to get away and have some time to think things through more clearly. He figures he can take his own life anytime, if that is what he decides, when circumstances close in on him. When there are no other alternatives, there will be no problem with leaving this cartoon of a life. But right now, he needs some space to think. He has to get off the island.

Once he has made this decision, there is no time to waste. Trying to think as practically as possible, he takes a shower and packs some clothes and travel necessities into his backpack. He unzips the mattress cover on his bed and takes his money belt out from where it is hidden, with his passport and all the cash he has left inside it, strapping it around his waist.

To minimize the possible damages, he flushes the small bag of weed he has in his room down the toilet. He wonders what other drugs Bumper might have stashed in the house, so he goes back into his bedroom and looks around. He doesn't want to mess with the drugs on the nightstand, as that would be considered tampering with evidence, he supposes, but he doesn't want the police to label Bumper as a dealer, either.

He searches quickly through his closet and finds nothing. Looking through his dresser, he finds two plastic bags of white powder, about four or five grams apiece, a bag of weed, and a small chunk of hashish, wrapped in tin foil, in the top drawer. He takes it all into the bathroom and flushes the weed down the toilet. Dipping his finger into each bag of powder and tasting it, he determines that one is cocaine and one is heroin, just as he suspected. Bumper had been injecting speedballs and probably miscalculated the dosage.

He flushes the heroin down the toilet, rinsing out the bag, pushing the lever several times to send everything far downstream. The hash and the four grams of coke he puts in his pocket, figuring it is compact enough to conceal and smuggle easily, and may come in handy in his travels.

Looking back into Bumper's bedroom one last time, he feels another pang of guilt for abandoning him there, but he knows there is nothing more he can do for him now. Heading downstairs with his backpack, he picks up the postcard from Dominic that is lying by the phone, and grabs his address book, stuffing them both into his pack. Leaving the apartment, he jumps on his motorcycle and heads for the airport. He buys a ticket on a flight leaving for San Francisco in an hour, figuring he can make connections from there to anywhere. He will just make up a plan as he goes.

When the plane lifts off the runway, he feels much less like the speedy, carefree Roadrunner of his youth, but rather more like his old nemesis, Wile E. Coyote, who finds himself launched off a cliff and suspended in the air, about to fall a thousand feet into a deep canyon.

As the islands grow smaller in the distance and drop from his view, he thinks of the strange fact that in the Hawaiian language, the greeting word "Aloha" also means "Goodbye."

"Aloha, Bumper," he says to himself, with a sigh, tears filling his eyes again.

ROME

BP paces and smokes, alone with his thoughts and a clay pipe filled with Moroccan hashish. In pacing he seeks solace—his thoughts are feverish and full of the past; in the cannabis he seeks inspiration as well as sedation. He walks mechanically, tracing the rectangular outline of the faded, dusty rug which covers the center of the hardwood floor in the small room, pausing only occasionally to strike a match to the pipe and fill his lungs to the bursting point with acrid smoke before resuming his march, turning smoothly and sharply to the right at each corner.

He is in a moment of crisis in a life which has become crisis-ridden. A mounting rage of frustration and confusion is barely kept under control by his mindless physical activity and the illusion of lucidity, of normalcy, supplied by the hash. If either were taken away from him at this moment, he is certain that some very dreadful images might claw their way up from his subconscious and onto his perceptual screen. He struggles for control with the few poor tools at his disposal, attempting to make sense out of the chaotic mosaic of his experience.

Up to his open doorway walks his host, Dominic, at this most inopportune time. BP does not stop pacing. "What's happening, Beep?" asks Dominic, stopping at the threshold to greet the queerly agitated figure of his pacing friend. "Are you all right? You don't look very well, I must say! We haven't seen much of you the last few days—Mari and I were starting to worry."

BP is embarrassed, but much too stoned and anxious at this point for subterfuge, for an elaborate cover-up. He simply states the facts: "Sorry, Dominic, really, but the truth is I haven't been out of this room for two days. I know it's rude of me, but I've got some problems I've been trying to sort out, and I've been on kind of a binge back here."

"Hey, Beep, you don't need to explain anything to me, but if you want to talk about what's bothering you, I'm ready to listen." Dominic is really concerned. He has never seen BP looking quite so ragged and worn, so nervous, so pale, or so stoned.

BP is grateful for his friend's compassion. He knows he has already stretched his credibility thin by showing up on such short notice, from so far away, and after so long. It has been over three months since Dominic and Mari had left the Islands for a year's sabbatical in Rome, courtesy of the University of Hawaii. When he arrived at their door two days ago, after a curt, telegraphed announcement, they had graciously accommodated him in the guest house of their rented villa, no questions asked, unconditionally. He wants to reciprocate their trust, to explain his situation, but he realizes that from within his frenzy, there is no way he can really discuss his problems without sounding very crazy or very afraid, for the truth is that he has no good handle on them himself.

"I'm just trying to get some stuff figured out," mumbles BP, as he strides along, "I'll be OK. I really do want to talk to you—that's why I came over here in the first place, along with the fact that it was a long way from the Islands and I needed to get away from there for awhile—the pressure was building up on me so bad I thought I was going crazy. But coming here didn't change anything—I'm still going crazy! I've been pacing around back here for two days now, trying to get my shit together, and it's just getting worse by the minute. I don't know what to do. I know I should have at least walked up to the front house and said 'hello' to you guys. I mean, how far is it, a couple hundred feet? I'm so rude, sometimes, and I can't seem to help myself...."

"Well, why don't you sit down and try to tell me about it," offers Dominic, sympathetically, "that's what friends are for, aren't they? Kee-rist, man, you look like you're about to fall down any minute!"

"I can't stop, don't you see? Walking's the only thing keeping me sane—I gotta keep moving to think straight, or else it all starts boiling up in my brain. You don't know...."

"Don't know what, Bob? Are you in some kind of trouble? Have you been smoking too much of that stuff? Did you take something else, any other drugs? Is there something going on here that you're holding back on me?"

"No, brah, it's not that. I'm not an overdose case, if that's what you're think-ing. I mean, I've been doing a little coke, a little hash, but I'm not that messed up. So maybe I haven't had anything to eat, or much sleep, for forty-eight hours—no big deal. I've done that plenty of times before. That still doesn't explain what's been going on inside my head, Dominic. This is stranger than drugs—I think I'm in the fucking 'Twilight Zone,' man! You don't know what it's like. You'd have to be inside my head to see it."

"C'mon, Beep, things go wrong for everyone once in awhile, you can't let it flip you out. I've never seen you like this. Something is seriously bothering you, isn't it? Are the police after you? Are you in trouble with the law? Is that it? C'mon, you can tell me about it. You know I'm on your side. I'm your friend. You know I'll help you any way I can. C'mon, it'll do you good to talk about it."

"Well, if I went back to Hawaii right now, the police would definitely want to talk to me," admits BP, "but that's not the worst of my problems. That's not the ultimate bummer—that's not what's freaking me out. It's the particular *way* everything is happening to me. You wouldn't believe it if I told you, and I don't think I can explain it anyway—it's far too subjective. I don't think I could put it into words that would make any sense to you."

"Why don't you give me a chance, pal? Don't underestimate your friends, or yourself. Let me try to understand—communicate with me, give me something to work with. If you don't talk to me, I can't ever know!" Dominic is beginning to lose patience. "Try to give me the big picture first. What is it that is bothering you the most?"

BP paces several laps around the rug while formulating a response. This is no simple question at any time, but it's especially daunting now. "Some really bad stuff happened to me in the last few weeks, but that's not the worst of it. It's really a matter of control," he says, finally. "I just feel totally out of control, Nic. My life is like a huge, chain-reaction accident on the freeway in L.A.—despite my best attempts to steer this way or that, I always end up crashing. And now lately, it's been like I'm driving in the rain, at night, with my lights out, and every once in a while the windshield wipers stop working, besides! Do you know what I mean? I'm, like, helpless, 'cause what we're talking about here is not really cars and windshield wipers, remember, it's my life and my mind we're talking about. I'm starting to fall apart, man! My mind is playing tricks on me. I can't even trust my basic equipment, anymore—my own body and mind! I may be going crazy, Nic...."

"OK, hold on a minute, Beep, you're losing me. You've made some mistakes, you're running from the law, and now you're having some hallucinations, is that what you're telling me?"

"No, not exactly. I mean, I enjoy a good hallucination as much as the next guy. But this is different. It's some kind of memory lapses and breaks in my concentration that are all tied into my dreams somehow—I've been having some really disturbing dreams! Sometimes they come back to me when I'm wide awake, and sometimes I have trouble recalling them. It's too spooky, man, I'm starting to blow it! It's a lot worse when I straighten up and try to dry out, so I've just been staying stoned, and trying not to think about it. But that doesn't seem to be working either, really...."

BP takes another hit from the pipe, absent-mindedly. Staring down at his feet as he paces, he is surprised to see he has worn what appears to be a path, a track, almost an indentation in the floor around the perimeter of the carpet. He watches his feet smooth the groove as he walks on.

"What is it that you're afraid of, Beep? That drugs have scrambled your brain? That you might be arrested and thrown in jail? Didn't you consider all those possibilities at some time in the past? What's so different now? You've been able to live with those decisions up to this time, so what has changed?"

BP is flustered. "That's just it—nothing has changed. I can't figure it out. It's like some kind of clog in my brain pipes—my mind just refuses to go in certain directions that I point it, sometimes, like a stubborn, barn-sour horse. It just won't be led that way. It won't go there. I feel like there is something really important that I'm supposed to be remembering, but every time I try, my brain just hops around it—sort of sidesteps it."

Even as he speaks, a corner of his mind is drifting, becoming entranced with the peculiar perception he is receiving of the groove in the floor. It seems to him that it is almost ankle-deep now, even though, in another, more rational, corner of his mind, he is perfectly aware that the hardwood could not possibly be wearing down so quickly.

"It's kind of tough to talk about unknown variables, Beep, especially imaginary ones. You've got to give me something a little more solid to go on—and for God's sake, will you stop pacing? You're getting me all hyped-up just watching you! I'm sorry you're depressed and troubled and I'd like to help you, man, but you've got to meet me halfway, here."

BP is lost in his hallucination and fails to respond. Dominic takes this as a signal of rejection. "I think maybe you're wallowing a little too deeply in self-pity, Beep. You've got to snap out of it. 'Life's a bitch, and then you die.' Everyone has problems, everyone has their ups and downs, we just have to struggle through the best way we can. But I'll talk to you again sometime, when you're a little more sober, maybe." He turns from the doorway and begins to walk back across the garden courtyard which separates the main residence from the guest house.

BP is absorbed and doesn't notice his departure until it is too late. When he looks up, Dominic is gone. "No, wait!" he calls out, stopping in mid-pace. Immediately, the groove he has walked into the floor seems to take on the proportions of a trench—he feels himself sinking down. He tries to scramble out of the ditch and get to the door but it is a futile struggle. His feet will not lift, they seem glued to the ground. The more he struggles, the faster he sinks—up to his neck in hardwood quicksand.

"Why did I stop?" he wonders to himself. "I knew this would happen, didn't I?" He quits fighting as he realizes it's useless to resist, while a black, stuporous whirlpool envelopes his senses.

"IT'S BOILING UP!" he screams weakly, just before passing out.

Forked-up Again

It is early morning, still quite dark. Bob Pilhaus opens his eyes, awakening from a fitful dream. Close in his view is the ceiling of a Eurorail car. He is in a private sleeping compartment. The rhythmic vibration of steel wheels rolling on rails penetrates through his back as he lies in the Pullman berth. An occasional sway of the car testifies that the dual rails are not always set perfectly level on their wood ties and gravel bed.

"I've dreamt it then," he mutters to himself, as he recognizes his surroundings. The rather pleasant (and slightly erotic) content of his dream is brutally erased from his consciousness, replaced by the hard facts of waking reality. The more depressing, lonelier aspects of his current situation sink back into his brain with the crushing immediacy of a cannonball obliterating a butterfly.

Rolling over, he reaches out to part the heavy curtains covering the window. The small reading lamp is still burning overhead, so all he sees is his own reflection, pale and hollow-eyed. By switching off the lamp and darkening the compartment, he is able to distinguish some of the passing scenery outside, bathed in moonlight. It looks like farmland—flat fields, pasture, some trees, a fence line running close beside the track.

"We must be in France by now," he computes, checking his watch. "I need some help. I feel terrible!" He has a splitting headache, his stomach is growling, his ears are ringing painfully with the noise of the train, his nose is stuffy, and his eyes feel as though they have been lightly sandblasted.

Wincing as he flips the light back on, he surveys the disarray of his belongings strewn about the tiny compartment. Sitting up and reaching across to his backpack, he retrieves a folded, wrinkled postal envelope from one of its side pockets. Opening it carefully, the small paper bindle containing his last gram of Peruvian cocaine is revealed. He spoons out a couple of grains of the chunky, crystalline powder and begins chopping it methodically.

The tools for this job are close at hand, since he never bothered to put them away after the last twenty-hour binge. A single-edged razor blade and his government-surplus emergency signaling mirror make short work of pulverizing the chunks.

As he works, he sings to himself a folksong he had first heard performed a long time ago by Dave Van Ronk. It has somehow stuck with him, recurring every time he finds himself in this situation: "Cocaine is for horses, not for men. They tell me it will kill me but they won't say when..."

"I may be dying, but I'm gonna have a good time doing it," he says to himself, with conflicting tinges of determination and desperation. A memory, a remembrance of Bumper as he last saw him, sitting up in bed lifelessly, flashes into his brain. It suddenly occurs to him that there is a meaning to this lyric that he has been ignoring for years. While he has taken it mostly as a paean to the glories of the drug, he realizes that it is also a plea for release from its addictive qualities by the artist. He pauses and sits up straight, remembering some of the other lines from the song: "Every time me and my baby go up-town, police come and they knock me down"; "Yeah, baby, come here quick, this old cocaine 'bout to make me sick"; "Well, I reached into my pocket, grabbed my poke, note in my pocket said, 'No more coke.'"

"But that's not me—I'm not an addict," he thinks, trying to convince himself. "That's for people who shoot the drug—junkies! I'm smarter than that. I only snort it. It's not a problem for me, is it?" He is beginning to have doubts. The chilling memory of Bumper won't leave his mind.

"I must have finished that whole liter of wine last night," he remarks to himself, "'cause there's the empty bottle. And over half that gram is gone so I must've whiffed it, unless I just got sloppy and spilled it somewhere." Such a mishap has been known to occur before. His head is pounding from the hangover, and he realizes that he never could have drunk that much wine the night before without the occasional toot of coke to keep him going.

"I've got to get hold of myself, here," he decides. "I have a lot of things to figure out, and I can't be getting this fucked-up, or it'll never get done. I'm just drowning myself in my sorrows, and that's not going to be any help to me now." With an extraordinary burst of willpower, spurred on by these realizations, he picks up the mirror, the coke, the razor blade and the bindle, opens the window in his compartment, and throws it all off the train.

Feeling relieved, he busies himself with repacking his belongings and tidying up the compartment. Getting dressed is no problem, as he had passed out the night before still wearing all his clothes.

Stumbling out into the gently rocking corridor of the train, he makes his way forward to the dining car. He wants some coffee and a cigarette first, then perhaps some food, if his rebellious stomach feels up to the task. By midday, the train should be pulling into Paris, then a short layover and transfer, and he will be on his way to Biarritz. His spirits are buoyed by the prospect that he will soon be surfing on the Basque coast. He is still slightly chagrinned about having fled his friend Dominic's home the morning before with only the briefest explanation of "I've gotta get wet, Nic," but he determines that he will write a note apologizing for his actions and mail it at the next stop.

There are few of his fellow passengers in the dining car at this early hour. He seats himself and orders coffee when the waiter comes around. He lights a cigarette and checks out the other occupants of the car. At the far end, in the very last dinette, is a curiously-dressed young woman sitting alone, facing him. She catches his eye immediately as he looks her way, and he is excited to see her offer him a brief but warm smile in acknowledgement. Even at a distance he can tell that she is strikingly attractive, with long, brown hair rolling off her shoulder and cascading down over her red dress, which appears to be a cross between an evening gown and a robe. It is low-cut in the front, displaying a bountiful bosom, but full-length, covering her legs in folds and draping to the floor, with a large hood attached at the shoulders.

"What a dish!" he thinks to himself. "I wonder if she's alone?" He watches her until his coffee arrives, and since no one has joined her, he picks it up, screws up his courage, and shuffles down the aisle, stopping in front of her table.

"May I join you? Are you alone? Do you speak English? I hope you don't think I'm being too forward, but I couldn't help it—you look very familiar to me. Have we met? Are you an American?"

"Those are very many questions for one breath," the woman replies calmly, "but yes, you may join me if you wish. I do speak English, and I suppose I am also 'American,' if you include the entire North American continent in that definition. I am Canadian by birth." She smiles up at him.

He slides into the seat opposite her, drinking in the vision of alluring, familiar femininity she presents. Though obviously a few years older than himself, she is still within his range, he figures. Her smile is dazzling, her teeth even and white. Her eyes are the clearest, most intense color of green he has ever seen. They absolutely sparkle. "God, she is even more beautiful than I dreamed," he notes to himself in awe, "but what's with this outfit she has on? Man, would I like to see what she's got under that thing...."

He becomes so engrossed in lustful images involving lifting the rich, red velvet fabric of her robe and burying his face in the curvital softness within, that he fails to notice she has not answered all his questions. Worse yet, he does not recognize the truth that he speaks inwardly—he *has* dreamed of this woman often, and as recently as last night.

With his eyes drooping low-liddedly to the luscious valley of her exposed cleavage, he introduces himself. "My name is Bob, but my friends call me BP, or just Beep, for short. Those are my initials—my last name is Pilhaus."

"My name is Esmeralda," says the woman, bringing her hands up from her sides and rummaging through the copious folds of material mounded in her lap, "and I am not exactly traveling alone. This is my cat, Abraxus."

Standing up in her lap and flashing onto his screen, like a preview of a bad movie, is a large, black cat, staring back at him with another colder, wilder, feline pair of green eyes. Except for a certain glazed trace of cruelty and selfishness, and a slightly elongated, almond shape to the black pupils, they could be the same eyes as Esmeralda's. The shade of green is identical, the luminosity equivalent.

BP is startled by this turn of events but tries to maintain his casual demeanor. "You have a cat?" he says, trying to think of why this fact is so disturbing to him. "Don't cats have to ride in cages in the baggage car or something? How did you get to keep him with you?"

"Abraxus is a she, actually," explains Esmeralda serenely. "She hates being in a cage and she's very cooperative, so I usually just carry her in my bag on trips like this." As she speaks, she reaches into the voluminous, woven straw handbag at her side and brings out a small, antique wood-framed hourglass. Shaking it to empty one side of the glass, she turns it over and sets it deliberately on the table between them. The fine, white sand trapped in the upper chamber begins to flow to the one below.

"What are you doing?" asks BP, beginning to lose composure slightly as he follows her words and movements, which seem to him to be strangely disconnected. "Is this how much time you're giving me to talk to you? Are you playing some kind of game with me?" He fidgets in his seat, eyes downcast, paranoia creeping into his brain. His mind races, trying to remember where he has seen her before.

"My friend, Bob, don't be afraid," says Esmeralda soothingly, "I'm just trying to help you remember."

"Remember what? You're trying to make me blow it—lose my cool—aren't you? You probably love to play practical jokes on the men who approach you, right? You're playing with my brain, here! Have you been looking for me, or did someone send you to find me here?" BP fights his paranoid flashes and tries to remain calm.

"No one is after you, Bob," Esmeralda assures him, "and this is not a joke. Please calm down and pay attention! There is no gigantic conspiracy against you except for the one that you have constructed yourself. If you recall, it was *you* who found *me*! It would be a poor conspiracy, indeed, which depended so heavily for its success on the actions of the victim, don't you think?"

BP pulls himself together as her words sink in. He straightens up in his chair and clears his throat. "I'm sorry," he apologizes, "I must be in pretty poor shape to be so paranoid. Things have been going badly for me lately, and I've been worried about a lot of stuff."

"That's unfortunate," replies Esmeralda, "I'm sorry to hear that. Do you want to talk about it?"

"Well, not really. It's very complicated. A whole bunch of things have been coming down on me lately, one after the other. I've got a lot of things to figure out, decisions to make, and its wearing me down, I guess, because I've just been getting awfully stoned lately to forget about it all. I'm going to straighten up and face it, though, I made that decision this morning. I'm stone sober right now and ready to take it all on, straight up, I hope. But what does that have to do with this hourglass? Are you timing our meeting here?"

"The hourglass is an instrument for measuring the passage of time, to be sure," explains Esmeralda, "but I am using it here as a prompt, a symbol to jog your memory. I was hoping you would be able to remember where we have met before. Tell me, Bob, do you dream much when you sleep?"

"No, I don't think so," says BP, defensively. "I mean, I don't know how much other people dream, so how am I supposed to compare myself? Anyway, when I *do* dream, I don't remember it for very long after I wake up." Her question puzzles him, as does her reference to having met him before.

"Do you try?" asks Esmeralda. "Never mind. Try for me now, will you? Look at the hourglass, relax, watch the sand running through its waist, and try to remember if you had a dream last night. What was it about?"

BP is confused and distracted, but he looks at the hourglass and tries to think, thankful for this small respite. "What's going on here?" he asks himself, rhetorically. "Is this woman crazy? Am I? Should I get my butt out of here while the getting's good? Why is she playing with my mind like this? God, she's such a fine-looking lady! I'd really like to get next to her, but she scares the shit out of me...." Her physical attractiveness is undeniable to him. He would like nothing better than to find a way to insinuate himself further into her sphere of attention, perhaps even to what must certainly be the sublime center—the creamy, nougat core....

He is drifting mightily, but he snaps out of this lustful daydream and tries to concentrate on her request. "I can't be thinking with my dick instead of my brain at a time like this!" he says to himself. "Where have I seen her before?" He tries to remember any dream he had the night before, but it is lost in the aftermath of an alcohol-and-cocaine haze. He searches further back in his memory, trying to recall something, anything, that will give him a clue. Was it in Hawaii? He indexes his memories and flies through them in his mind, remembering the people he had met there. No, not Hawaii, he is pretty sure. Before that? The farm? UCSD?

He stares at the hourglass again, at the grains of sand sifting through its narrowing throat and falling into a pyramid in the lower chamber, and something clicks in his brain, coming back to him slowly at first, and then in a rush. He recalls his first acid trip at Black's beach, watching the sand sift through his hand and sparkling. But she wasn't there. That can't be it. Then it hits him. His last acid trip—the Orange Crush, hunkering down in a bush on the side of the bluff at Torrey Pines, the terrible hallucinations that seemed to go on forever, that he had pushed out of his mind! He looks up from the hourglass and straight into Esmeralda's face, his eyes wide, his mouth hanging open in shock and dismay. "OMIGOD! It's her!" screams through his brain. His heart is pounding in his chest as he recognizes her visage unmistakably as the woman who had transformed into the time-shifting monster in his LSD-laced visions, the one who had chased him for hours!

"You *do* remember me, don't you, Bob?" says Esmeralda softly, as he stares at her, dumbfounded and speechless. "I can tell by the look on your face. It's OK. Don't worry. Everything is all right. Take some deep breaths. Relax. We have plenty of time."

"I…I…you…you…" BP gulps great gobs of air, trying to offset a dizzying sense of vertigo. He struggles to maintain the memory he has grasped and express it. Breathing deeply, as she suggests, he calms himself and is able to go on: "I was very stoned once, on some strong LSD, and I had some very strange feelings, some scary hallucinations. You were in right in the middle of it."

"Ah, now we're getting somewhere," Esmeralda says calmly. "What feelings were you having?"

"It was a strong sense of déjà vu—that I had been there before, and done the same thing," BP explains in a rush. "Then I saw you, and you were waving me to come closer, but when I did, your hair turned into snakes, writhing around your head, and I was afraid, and ran away. But every time I looked around, you were still there, and it would happen all over again. I thought it would never end—it was very scary, but the acid finally wore off and I haven't thought about it again until now."

"What do you think that meant? Where do you think that vision might have come from?"

"I never wondered about that," says BP. "It was too frightening—nauseatingly so, in fact. I never wanted to revisit it, and I never took LSD again."

"Will you think about it for me again, now? It is nothing to be afraid of at this point, it's just an old memory, far in the past—it can't hurt you. I'm sure you can remember it all without any fear by now, if you really wish to, don't you think? Take your time, just sit back and remember for me, please.…" Esmeralda reaches out and picks up the hourglass, turning it over.

BP watches the sand in the hourglass flow down into the bottom chamber, and he relaxes, beginning to recall that final LSD incident in more detail, when the same sense of déjà vu suddenly envelops him again, but it is not frightening this time. Esmeralda does not turn into a monster, she remains her serene and beautiful self, gazing back at him. He looks around the railroad car, down at the hourglass, and back at Abraxus the cat, who jumps up on the table and walks across it to settle in his lap. He stares directly into the cat's green eyes and has the strangest epiphany: "I *have* been here before, haven't I?" he asks in wonderment, semi-rhetorically. A blinding light flashes in his eyes and he hears chimes. It passes in an instant and when he looks up, Esmeralda is still there, sitting across from him. The scar tissue over the well-healed wound in his psyche melts away. Isolated neurons and synapses begin to fire in his brain, and memories come flooding out of subconsciousness.

"Yes, you have, Bob," Esmeralda answers.

"This is truly bizarre! And we had this same conversation then, didn't we?"

"Yes, we did. It was twelve years ago, by your reckoning, to be exact."

"Only it went a little differently last time, didn't it? I remember it all now—I asked you to send me back to live my life over again, so that I could fix all the mistakes I had made...."

"That's correct, Bob, and I granted you your wish."

"I can remember it clearly now! I *did* go back, but I couldn't change anything, and here I am, back in the same old mess! And if I asked you to send me back again, right now, you would do it, wouldn't you?" BP is fighting back a strong sense of unreality, of confusion, caused by the persistence of his intellectual conviction that what he now remembers to be true is impossible.

"Yes, I would, Bob."

"And I wouldn't be able to do anything differently once more, would I?"

"Not in any material way, I don't think, not in your current state. Obviously, things were slightly different for you this time. You were able to effect some minor changes on your own, otherwise we wouldn't be having *this* conversation—you would already be playing baseball on a field back in San Diego right now. But things might also have gone worse, and they might still, if you tried to do them over once again. There are no guarantees, and there is some danger involved with these things."

"Worse!?!? How could things be any worse? Look at me—I'm a mess! My life is a smoking crater, and I've had two tries at it now, hard as that is for me to accept. What could be any worse?"

"You made it back here, Bob, you found me again, and we're having a different conversation this time. You should be thankful for that. I can tell you that there are people like you who have walked on by and never even recognized me or spoken a word. At least you have another chance, now. Tell me—are you even certain that this is only the second time you've found me on this train?"

"Holy shit! What am I supposed to do? I can't go back again—I know you're right. I don't understand what's going on at all. I could never make any difference the way I am. Please, *help me!*"

"Ah! That's what I need to hear, my friend. Now that you have asked, I can help you understand a thing or two, but it will take some time. Can you give me a little time, Bob?"

"Of course I can. I've already given you twelve years in order to hear this, haven't I? But I need to know the gist of it right now—the synopsis, the executive summary, the *Cliff Notes* version—just to put me at ease, *please!* What am I supposed to do?"

"I can answer that in two words: Just *live!*" states Esmeralda. "Now, let's order some breakfast, shall we? We've still got a long way to go today, and a few things to take care of before we can get started. You're going to need your strength and all your wits about you."

Paris

For the rest of their journey, Esmeralda makes only small talk with BP, avoiding any more serious discussion about his predicament. She asks him where he's going, and he tells her his only current plan had been to catch some nice autumn surf on the Bay of Biscay, and try to relax. She asks him about his surfing life, his adventures in riding waves, and what it has meant to him. He tries to explain it as best he can, to pass the time amiably until they can get on to the meatier subjects for which he craves answers. She asks him about his drug use, and the details of his experimentation with LSD. He answers her as truthfully as possible, while also recounting his despair over his medical diagnosis.

Eventually, when they are nearing Paris, she asks if he might give up his surf trip to Biarritz. Instead, she suggests he get off with her at the next station and come to her home, so that they can spend more time together and have some extended conversations (which she imagines might last for several days, perhaps more). BP agrees to this immediately, but when he tries to wheedle any additional information out of her regarding these plans, exactly what she has in store for him, nothing more is forthcoming. She brushes aside his pestering questions and tells him to be patient. Her answer is always the same: "You cannot know until you are ready to know." She does not lose her temper with him, but he can tell that he is straining their new relationship with his constant inquiries, so he finally desists.

They get off the train shortly after noon and have lunch in a small bistro near the station. He eats sparingly and speaks little, nervous and anxious to get on with it, to see what his fate will bring. Esmeralda seems merry and chatty, telling him about the wonders of the City of Light and her love for it. His responses are mostly monosyllabic. As he has yet to convert any dollars to francs, Esmeralda pays the bill, and he follows her down the street, like a puppy, without the leash.

She stops at a small street market to buy some fresh bread and groceries. Reaching into her large straw bag, she takes out a smaller, net bag made of string mesh, petting and cooing at Abraxus as she pulls it out, loading the groceries into it and handing it to BP. "Will you carry this for me, please?" she asks. "It's only a short trip to my home from here." He complies willingly, and follows her to the entrance of the underground subway, where they board the Métro for a quick ride to her apartment, located in the Latin Quarter, on the left bank of the Seine, not far from the Sorbonne.

Her flat is fairly large, modern and well-appointed, on the third floor of one of the newer buildings in the neighborhood (which is to say that it is less than 200 years old, and more recently renovated than others). When they finally climb the stairs and enter it (the electric lift is temporarily out of order, apparently), BP is happy to be able to shed the weight of his backpack in the entryway, as Esmeralda deposits her long robe in the hallway on a coat rack, revealing the very chic and smartly tailored outfit she is wearing underneath it for the first time.

She asks him to bring the net bag of groceries he has been carrying into the kitchen. He follows her, admiring her shapely figure from behind. She sets her large handbag on the kitchen counter and reaches into it, withdrawing Abraxus and setting her down on the floor. Picking up two ceramic bowls, she quickly prepares fresh water and food for the cat, as it purrs and rubs itself against her slender ankles and well-muscled calves. "What fine legs she has!" BP can't help but think to himself, as his eyes raise involuntarily from the kitty at her feet, clear up to the elevated hem of her miniskirt, fixating on her trim, ravishing thighs.

Following her into the living room, Esmeralda draws back some heavy drapes and opens a set of dual doors leading to a small balcony, overlooking a courtyard below, with a beautiful view of the city and the Seine River in the distance. She draws more drapes and opens some windows to let in the afternoon sun and fresh air, as the apartment has been closed up for a few days. BP is struck by the number of bookcases lining the walls, from floor to ceiling in many of the rooms. "Have you read all these books?" he asks. "Do you collect them or something?"

"Oh yes, I've read them all, some of them several times. Why?"

"It's just that it looks like a library in here, I guess."

"I love libraries, they're one of my favorite places to spend time, and I love books, don't you? These are the ones that I have bought instead of borrowed, and I suppose it is a collection, but I don't consider myself a collector. They do make this place look a bit like a library, I guess, but I find it comfortable. Now that we're here, let me show you around." She escorts him down the short hallway and points out her bedroom, the guest bedroom (where he will be staying), and the bathroom. "I'm sure you would like to clean up from your travels. Why don't you take the bathroom first, and I'll follow when you're done. I'm going to put the groceries away right now, so just go ahead and have a bath, if you like."

"That sounds really good," says BP. "I do feel a little grungy." He carries his backpack into the guest bedroom, retrieves his toiletries kit from one of its side pockets, grabs a clean t-shirt, and heads into the bathroom. He is feeling a bit exhausted and bedraggled, both emotionally and physically, but soaking for thirty minutes in a hot bath refreshes him somewhat. Toweling off, he shaves his face and looks at himself in the mirror. He can't help but notice the dark circles under his slightly bloodshot eyes from lack of sleep over the last few days. Lifting his left arm over his head, he examines the inch-long scar from his biopsy. It seems to be healing nicely, but he gets a tight little knot in his stomach thinking about what the doctor had told him. "What am I going to do?" he asks himself. "Or rather, what is she going to do with me now? This is all so confusing—I am just totally lost!" After combing his hair, he picks up his things and heads back to his room, calling out to Esmeralda from the hallway, "I'm done in there, now, if you want to use the bathroom."

"Thank you," Esmeralda calls back from the kitchen, "I will."

He is quite tired, and decides to lay down on the bed to rest awhile, but his mind is still too active for sleep, running over the explosive events of the morning and his strange epiphany, trying to make sense of them, just as he had done twelve years ago, sitting in his Little League dugout. "I remember it all so clearly, now" he thinks, "she truly did send me back. I remember thinking then that it was just a dream, or that I was hypnotized or something. This is so unreal. How can I have met her twelve years ago, and then found her again today, yet she has not aged at all in that time? She didn't go back with me, did she? She looks exactly the same still—she couldn't be a day over thirty! Her face does not have a single wrinkle on it, her body is so tight—she is exactly as she was then. And how could I ever have forgotten her? How did I fall asleep so fast, and continue to make all the mistakes I made before once again? Especially when I knew how important it was to keep remembering! I do recall wishing to forget, though. It was just too painful to go on remembering."

His inner dialogue continues for an hour or so, in the same fruitless loops as before, until he is interrupted by a voice at his door. "It's time to begin, Bob," he hears Esmeralda say. Rising on his elbow and turning towards her voice, he sees her standing in the doorway, wearing nothing but a towel on her head. He feels his chest expand quickly as his lips suck in a sharp little breath. On his screen is the most appealing vision of feminine pulchritude that he can imagine, made from all the technicolor dreams and movies of his youth. She is the most beautiful creature he has ever seen, and his heart is filled with lust. His pants are already getting tight in the front when she says: "The first thing we must do, Bob, is to have some sex together."

BP can scarcely believe his ears. This is not what he had expected at all, but certainly what he had hoped for, in his wildest dreams. "W-what?" is all he can stammer out.

"We must get this out of the way before anything else," she says, walking across the room and sitting next to him on the bed, unwrapping the towel and shaking out her hair, still damp. "Otherwise, you will be too distracted. You will not be ready to really hear and understand everything I'm going to tell you."

"I-I don't get it," stutters BP, totally distracted now by her overwhelming proximity—her glistening hair, falling around her shoulders, the dewy bloom of small beads of sweat on her forehead, the piercing flash of her green eyes, the gentle jounce of her full breasts as she runs her fingers through her hair and shakes her head. His eyes continue on down her body, drinking her in.

"See! You're doing it right now, Bob! You are a blatant misogynist, I'm afraid, and you must recognize and admit this to yourself before we can go any further," she scolds him mildly, taking his hand and soothing him at the same time. "It's not your fault, entirely. You are the product of your genes, your hormones, and your upbringing in a patriarchal society. You've lusted after my body since we first met, and to your own detriment. Admit it!"

"Well, of course I have," says BP, watching her sitting next to him so naturally, so unselfconsciously, and so completely, marvelously naked. "How could I not? Look at you! You're incredible!"

"You wanted me so badly the first time we met that you didn't even think about the things I said to you. And in our second meeting, you barely came to your senses in time to listen. I don't know if it was because you were less stoned this morning or what, but you came very close to a rerun of our first encounter, and you know it."

"I suppose so," admits BP, a little embarrassed. He does remember being attracted to her strongly and immediately when they first met, and obsessing over the idea of how to get her into his bed. If he had only known what it would take, how far he would have to go to get to this point—twelve years of living his life again!

"The truth is that you're thinking of me as an object, just as you have all the other desirable women you've known in your life. Until you see me as an equal, someone you respect and trust, you're not going to be able to learn anything from me," she explains, "or truly listen to what I have to say. All you'll be able to hear, as usual, is your little Peter, clamoring constantly for attention, wondering what it would be like to be inside of me. You're allowing outer appearances to rule your attention and judgment. The quickest way to overcome this is to simply satisfy your curiosity, and your desire—so you won't keep wondering what it is you might be missing.

"Understand me now—this will only happen once between us and never again. I'm not trying to be your girlfriend, or your soulmate, or your nurse, your mother, or your whore. I'm none of those things. I am an independent and strong woman, and I have appetites just like you do. I'm attracted to you, as you are to me, and I enjoy sex, but I do not want to be fucked—I want to teach you how to make love, even though I don't want to be your lover. Otherwise, you will never have a satisfying relationship with a woman, as a true partner and mate for life, you will only keep looking for the next thrill, the next receptacle for your more shallow longings."

"I think I understand," says BP, perceiving a tad of shrinkage from "little

Peter," having been called to task by name.

"Women want different things out of sex than men, so you must pay attention to me, and my needs, not just your own." She smiles at him and reaches out to touch his hair, leaning in slowly to kiss him tenderly. For the next hour, she leads him through the most joyous, wonderful, intoxicating and satisfying merging of two bodies that he has ever experienced. It is another revelation for him.

In the afterglow, lying together on the bed, he knows that she is not like any other woman he has ever met. He understands that he will never be hers, she will never be his, but that there must surely be a God in heaven to have let him have this experience. Clasping her in his arms, he asks: "Are you an angel, Esmeralda? Have you been sent from Heaven to save my sorry ass?"

"This is where it begins to get difficult, Bob," laughs Esmeralda, looking into his eyes. "That was the fun part. Now the real work begins. But first, I think you should rest, have a good nap, and try to empty your mind. You're going to need all your faculties keen, and your powers of concentration focused. I'm making a nice dinner for us, and I'll wake you later to eat. After dinner, you may begin to ask me all the questions you want, but none of the answers will be easy for you to grasp, I'm afraid."

La Rive Gauche

BP is as relaxed as he has been in days, possibly weeks. All the tensions seem to have been drained from his body. After falling asleep easily and deeply for a few hours, Esmeralda wakes him gently, and they eat a delicious dinner of simple but nourishing peasant food she has prepared—a chicken stewed with vegetables, a salad, bread and cheese.

As they eat, Esmeralda asks him to tell her how his last twelve years had gone, compared to his previous time living them. "I didn't do any better with my life," says BP. "I made the same mistakes again, but perhaps with slightly different reasoning. I wasn't able to change anything, and I forgot about you and my past, or my future, or whatever it was, almost immediately. I do realize now that I often thought about things slightly differently, though, while still coming to the same decisions. Many times I had these overwhelming feelings that I was forgetting something important, or not properly considering the whole situation—that I knew before I acted that it was the wrong thing to do, yet I did it again anyway.

"I'm still in the same mess, as I told you before—the doctors say I might be terminal, that the cancer has spread, and I may not have long to live; there are several government agencies who probably want to find me right now and put me in jail; I couldn't see that the woman I thought I loved didn't feel the same way about me; and worst of all, two of my best friends are dead, and I didn't do everything I might have done to save them. I still don't know if I can face all this and go on, but you have made me feel much better now, and I thank you for that."

After dinner, Esmeralda pours them each a glass of wine, and they go out on the balcony to watch the sunset and talk some more. BP smokes an after-dinner cigarette. "That reminds me, Bob, of the next two things you are going to have to work on for me. Your smoking is the first. You know that it's bad for you, yet you still do it. This has to stop."

"But I'm dying anyway, what does it matter?" protests BP.

"We are all dying," answers Esmeralda, "it is inevitable. But you will not die now, or anytime in the near future, unless you decide to do so. I want you to live. That is why I'm here—to help you. Would you believe me if I told you that in the future, cigarettes will actually become socially unacceptable and banned in many places?"

BP hears her and puts out his cigarette. "I understand. Thank you! I really do need your help, and I appreciate it very much."

"That brings us to the second thing" she continues, lifting her glass and pointing at it. "Your substance abuse must cease. I gave you this one glass of wine tonight, and that's all you should allow yourself from now on—one glass of wine or beer per day, nothing more. No other artificial stimulants, no other drugs of any kind. Agreed?"

"Yes, ma'am," answers BP, sarcastically. "Can I smoke a joint instead?"

"You don't have to call me ma'am, Bob, we are friends, now. You can call me Alda. And there is nothing intrinsically worse about using marijuana in moderation, except that it is illegal, and you don't need any more trouble with the law at this point, do you?"

"No, ma'am, I mean, Alda, and you can call me Beep, by the way," answers BP, graciously. "I thought you were going to let me ask you some questions, though, and not just lay down the laws."

"I did say that," says Alda. "Feel free to ask."

"I've got to know who you are, or what you are," begins BP. "You seem superhuman to me—totally unreal! I've thought at different times you were an angel, or a witch, or a magician, or a hypnotist. You are not like any person I have ever met."

"I am a human being, Beep, just like you, but also different. We are each unique, don't you think? But we're all of the same species, even though we have different traits. I have some traits you will find very difficult to understand, and they bring with them certain skills."

"How did you get them? I want those skills."

"You can develop some of them, Beep, but some are the result of my genetic makeup, and one must be born to that. That is what evolution is all about. It is an agent of change. I told you once that I am just an 'evolved human being,' and that's the way I think about myself. I believe I was born with a part of my brain active in a way that most people's are not. You will never be exactly like me, if that's what you are wondering. But you can learn more about how to be yourself. That's what's important here. It takes all kinds to make up the world, and we each need to be who we are, to the best of our abilities, and become what we may."

"What is different about your brain?"

"The best way I can put it to you is that I have an ability to sense time in a way that most people do not. I sense it in the same way that you see, feel, hear, smell and taste things. Time and space form a continuum, as I'm sure you have heard. I can 'see' that continuum, the fabric of space and time, as well as you can see the normal three-dimensional reality, when I 'look' for it. For you, the three-dimensional mileau is marching through the fourth dimension of time, moment by moment. For me, I can experience time in its totality—I can see the beginning and the end, the alpha and omega points, if I pay attention in the right way, and I have sensed what is beyond, the other dimensions, in the same way that you sense time."

"I'm not sure I totally understand that," says BP, bewildered.

"Ah, that's where we come to the difficulties in this, Beep—the limitations of our language in describing it, the inability of words to express it. We can only hint of it in speech and express it by our actions, to some extent, as an artist might. Mathematics can describe it, but no one can render another dimension sensible for you, make it real, so that you can feel and manipulate it—you must be born with that trait, or be blessed with unusual insight. There's nothing stopping you from understanding what it means, though, if you try. The brain is an incredible organ, and it actually changes according to how we use it. We know so little about our brain, and use only a fraction of its capacity, but this can be altered over time—as we learn more, as our experiences and knowledge change the way we think, and as we evolve, physically."

"How many people are there like you?" wonders BP.

"Not many living at the moment, I don't believe, but there have been more than a few throughout history, I'm sure, as I've seen where they left their marks. If you look back in history, you can spot the actions of a few who have changed the course of the world. Many ordinary people have been able to see and understand such things as well, I'm positive, but they haven't talked or written about it, so history has ignored them. I'm not sure if they sensed things in exactly the same way I have, but they often came to the same conclusions. Both knowledge and evolution are cumulative, passed through generations, but not everything of this nature has been recorded.

"Evolution is a spiraling tree with many branches. Events occur in cycles, to be sure, but we are not going in concentric circles. On each turn of the wheel, we are further down the road, the branches reach further into the sky. There will be more born like me in the future, I am sure, because the survival of our species depends on it, and there will be others, like you, who learn or guess something of these gifts without actually possessing them fully, to help humanity turn the corner."

"What corner?" asks BP.

"The corner that turns us away from our rush to extinction."

"I'm not sure I understand completely, but that certainly sounds heavy."

"I wish I could demonstrate it to you as clearly as I know it, but there are difficulties, as I said. Not only the limitations of my words, causing me to speak to you in allegories and metaphors, but also your inability to fully hear the truth. You can only know and understand things which are similar to what you have known before. Something that is too different, in another category entirely, will always remain a mystery to you."

"But I want to know these things. I have searched for such answers all my life! I know I have been distracted at times, but I have longed for the truth, always. You must teach me, please! Can't I stay with you now until I learn it all?" pleads BP.

"I'm sorry, my friend, that's not possible, as I've told you," answers Alda.

"You're not completely ready to understand, still, and there are other reasons why this can't be. I don't have the time, for one thing, and you are not my only concern. I'm not perfect, Beep, I am a human being, and we all have our limitations. I don't know everything—I'm still learning as well. There are aspects of my gifts that I don't understand fully yet, myself. If I could just touch you and turn on the part of your brain that would transform you, I would do it—but I can't. I am not God, or an angel, and I'm not a magician. But you have the perfect starting point upon which to build. You know, now, that you can assume nothing. You know that you must question all your previous ideas about the nature of existence, as they have been turned upside down. Such a rampant skepticism is a healthy attitude.

"And even if I could just give you everything you wish, you wouldn't know what to do with it all. A person can only be given that which they can use. If they don't recognize a gift for what it is, they will not remember it for long, or just discard it, as it will seem to be of no use to them. You'll need to find out for yourself, along your way. It will take time, perhaps your whole life, and beyond. Sacrifices will be involved, for people do not value things for which they have given up nothing.

"Knowledge is like a vast ladder, Beep. You're standing on its rungs some-where in the middle. There are quite a few people with you on your rung, some on the rungs above you, and many more below you. If I were to pull you up to the rung upon which I'm standing, in your current state, the view would only seem strange to you, completely unintelligible, and you would be unable to do anything with your knowledge of it, to effect any real changes in yourself or the world. I'm trying to help you take just a single step right now, a more manageable one, and the rest will be up to you.

"But here is the key: In order to ascend the ladder, you must help someone else, who is on a rung below you, to take *their* next step. That is how things are, and always have been: 'As above, so below.' This is where sacrifice and hard work, over a long period of time, come in. The ultimate truth does not abide laziness or selfishness in its pursuit. That's been part of your problem in understanding things—your selfishness, your cravings, your need to gratify every impulse and desire quickly and easily."

"So this is why you're helping me—to further your own knowledge?" asks BP.

"Yes, in a way, and to save your life, of course, though you seem to be determined to throw it away."

"But how did you choose me, of all people?"

"It happens that your particular situation, your mindset, is perfectly suited to my gifts. A great thinker in the future will say: 'When thinking changes your mind, that's philosophy. When God changes your mind, that's faith. When facts change your mind, that's science.' Whether you realize it or not, Beep, you are a scientist at heart. You are also a bit of a philosopher, but without the direct experience of some seemingly miraculous facts, which I conveyed to you through my particular ability to manipulate time, you would never have come to the realizations you've already made, and you would not be able to progress much further in the future—toward recognizing the beauty and perfection of your existence, despite the mistakes you've made. As hard as it is for you to accept, as badly as you think your life has gone, it *is* what it *is*, and the only way things will change is if you focus your attention differently from now on.

"Also, you needed to hear this from a woman, due to your propensity to discount the female of our species—to help you actually come to see us, to recognize that women hold up half the sky. As nurturers, not warriors, we have something very valuable to contribute, if given a chance. Women may not be so inclined to conquer everything in sight, as you are, but they don't want to be dominated either, and their time is coming. This is another key aspect of the lessons you're learning."

BP listens to her words and feels astonished, humbled and grateful—yet confused, as he is attracted mightily to her at this moment, like a moth to a flame. A great passion rises in him and he reaches out to her, touching her arm, looking at her with longing, wanting to draw her to him and experience the oneness he had known with her once more.

"I know what you're thinking," she tells him, putting her hand on his and looking into his eyes, "but it is not going to happen, Bob, as I told you before. We're not meant to be lovers, though I do love you. Our time together is limited, and it would be wiser to spend it in other ways."

"Can you read my mind?" he asks.

"Some things are more obvious than others, and that one is written all over your face right now—no need to go into your mind!" she says, laughing. "It is getting late, though, and you need to rest. I want you to go to your room and sleep now, digest what I've told you, and ask me more questions in the morning. I will tell you all I can, as truthfully as possible, as much as you can take in, and the rest will be up to you to do alone, by your own effort. You will find your path, but it will not be with me—we are not meant to be together. You will leave soon, to rebuild your life on your own. That is simply how it is. You have many other things to do, still."

EMPIRICAL MYSTICISM

On his first morning in Paris, BP awakens feeling refreshed and alive. All thoughts of suicide have been banished from his brain. They seem now to have been frivolous, pitiful and selfish ideas, in his new frame of mind. Esmeralda, his lovely Alda, has given him new hope, and a desire to live. How can he thank her enough for that? It is impossible, he knows, just as he knows that there is no chance in this world that she would ever be 'his,' forever. He can do nothing but listen to her now, try to understand what she tells him, and act accordingly, as best he can. There is no other way.

It is a fantastic autumn day on the Left Bank, so after breakfast, they stroll together around the *arrondissement* and talk, taking in the sights. The fall foliage is on fire, the wind is calm, and the air is crisp and cool. Anyone watching them would think they are a pair of tourists on their honeymoon—the way they walk and talk, going from place to place together, drinking in the scenery, the weather, the monuments, the buildings, the people, but always absorbed in each other and their own, personal dialogue.

BP holds her hand, as she allows him this familiarity—she even takes his arm at times, clasping his elbow to her bosom and leaning against him as they walk, but he knows this is as physically intimate as they will ever be again, merely as close friends, or brother and sister, and he is fine with that. What is important to him, at this point, is to find a way to ask her the right questions, and hope that he can understand her answers.

"Were you always like this?" he asks, at one point. "I'm curious. Did you grow up knowing that you could read minds and see the future, or was it something you realized along the way? What were you like when you were young?"

"My gifts aren't exactly like that, Beep. I can't really 'read minds and see the future' in the way that you think, but I knew I was 'different' from the time I was a small child, growing up in Montreal. And apparently, so did everyone else," Esmeralda laughs. "My mother and father say that I always asked the strangest questions when I was a child, many of which they could not answer or even understand. When I was about eight years old, I realized that I sometimes embarrassed them with my inappropriate questions to friends and neighbors, and I became more guarded, talking less openly about the things I could see that no one else seemed to know or care about. They even put me in a sanitarium once for 'observation,' on a doctor's advice. Since he couldn't find any organic problem with me, he suspected that I might be developing a mental disorder. I quickly learned how to pay attention to the same things that other people do, and not reveal the others, in order to maintain my freedom.

This remains one of my worst fears, Beep, and it's the reason why you must never betray me, or try to find me again, once you leave."

"I can't believe you are worried about that," says BP. "You seem fearless to me."

"Not true, and this proves how human I am. I have no desire to be a martyr for anyone or any cause. You know what they did to Jesus, don't you? And Socrates, and Gandhi, and Dr. Martin Luther King, Jr., and many others—humans tend to kill people who are different, with certain gifts or insights which create fear in them."

"That sounds a lot like what my friend Bumper used to say: 'Let the wrong person know who you are and they'll eat you.' But can't you just look into your future to see what will happen to you, and change it, if necessary?"

"'Looking into the future,' as you call it, doesn't quite work that way," explains Alda, "and changing things is even more difficult. There are trillions of different possible futures, probably more, depending on the choices each of us make, and nudging certain possibilities towards actualizing can depend on altering the decisions and actions of more than a single person. It is very overwhelming and confusing at first—very difficult to focus in on any single possibility, or to make a given one happen. Infinity is bigger than you think, Beep, and can be very disturbing to contemplate and behold. It took me years of struggle and practice to understand and master only parts of my sense of it. And it seems to be a particular limitation of my gift that my own future is not fully accessible to me, try as I might. It appears to be a matter of perspective, and the fact that I have free will, just as you do, to choose my path and change it. All is not foretold, everything is not pre-determined. But I digress—where were we?

"Oh yes, I was telling you about my early years. My family moved to Seattle when I was about ten years old and I became very 'Americanized.' Hoping to be accepted and admired by my peers, I paid attention only to those things which they did. It was much later, after I came to the Sorbonne and studied science, philosophy and mathematics deeply, that I began to re-discover my hidden gifts and explore them again, exercising them carefully, in private moments, and slowly developing some skill with them.

"After college, I worked as a model for awhile, to make a living, but the fashion industry did not appeal to me. At one point, I realized that by scanning all the possible futures in a certain way, I could perceive some trends and facts that weren't obvious to others. I took my earnings from modeling and invested them wisely, and now I have time to do the work that most interests me, that I think is important."

"I remember I had thoughts when you first sent me back in my life, while I still remembered my future, that I should invest in the stock market and get rich," confesses BP.

"Money is a tool," declares Alda. "It's important to have enough of it to keep body and soul together, and care for your loved ones, but greed is evil, Bob. Many people work for money alone, or for power over others. Materialism is not happiness. Having lots of nice things is not success, especially when many others have little or nothing. Using what you know and what you have to obtain dominion over other people is even worse. Tyranny is not an aphrodisiac, it's a curse."

As they walk down a narrow street, they encounter the dead body of a small dog in the middle of the road, flattened so horribly by traffic that it is nearly unrecognizable. Alda stops in her tracks and clutches his arm when she sees it. "Oh, that is so sad!" she exclaims. "This is why I never allow Abraxus out of the house, unless I'm with her." They begin to walk again, hurrying past the scene as she averts her eyes.

"Tell me, Beep," she asks, as they reach the end of the block, "why do you think it is that so many animals are run over and killed by our cars and motorcycles, buses and trains? Don't you think that is odd? Animals are generally so wary, and so nimble and quick, you would think they could avoid such accidents entirely."

"I've never really thought about that much."

"Well, I believe it's because they don't have the same sense of causality that we do. Their brains and sensory organs are arranged and wired differently, and while they seem to see and react to the same things as we do, they don't perceive them in the same way."

"Don't they just lack our powers of reasoning?"

"That may be, although they seem to be able to deduce other things, and sense things that we do not. Could it be that they perceive time differently? While they function in the same four-dimensional space-plus-time as humans do, mechanical motion is as mysterious and unpredictable to them as the ends of the universe are to us. It appears chaotic and instills fear, which can cost them their lives when they do not react properly. We humans seem to have a built-in sense of motion they lack—we look automatically for its cause. We're able to predict mechanical motion, using our skills of deduction, logic and reason, according to our understanding of physics. But time is an important element in those Newtonian laws, and I don't think animals integrate time in the same way in their brains.

"We overcome our fears and take advantage of our mechanical devices, even though they can still represent a danger to us. We ride in our cars and planes, though some of us still crash and die, because we understand them, we've developed rational rules for them. We know the risk is small, so we don't fear them in such a way that it disturbs our normal functioning, like a deer or rabbit, caught in the headlights, who freezes and doesn't run away in time. There are many other ways we have created havoc for the other forms of life on earth during the course of human development as well, wouldn't you say?"

"I suppose so, although there are some who say that insects will outlive us in the future," answers BP.

"When we humans look out into the vastness of the universe, we sense the same possibilities of chaos and insignificance as a small animal facing a hurtling locomotive. We are filled with the same fears, caused by the same lack of understanding, only on a different level," continues Alda. "Let me tell you a story—sort of a science-fiction parable. Bear with me, please, for it's quite a long tale.

"Imagine that there is a race of evolved, cheerful, trans-dimensional beings—or call them space aliens from another planet, if that's easier for you to picture—who seeded the earth with the first humans, and have watched over our development for all these years, like farmers watching over their crops. Suppose that they are much more advanced than ourselves, very powerful, nearly eternal, on our scale of life, and are able to move among us, without being noticed, because they're able to transform themselves in such a way as to fool us and appear human.

"Though they act as good farmers in tending and watching over their seedlings, they have no intention of ever 'harvesting' us. They do these things with no ill-intentions, simply as a pastime, an entertaining experiment, as they are a fun-loving bunch. They're not able to endow us with their power to understand and manipulate other dimensions of being, but they instill in us the very elegant process of evolution, which they've found present in all forms of life. They know it will allow us to adapt and change, over many generations, and hope that this will bring us eventually to their own level of development.

"The first problem they note with their 'crop,' after dropping us onto a forbidding planet in a spiraling arm of a huge galaxy in this corner of the universe, is that humans are afraid of almost everything in their surroundings—the way the sun comes and goes, light turning into dark, heat into cold, the way the seasons change, the fierceness of some of the other animals on the earth, all of which hamper our development. The aliens invent methods to ameliorate the fear of the unknown in us and spread them about, like a calming, protective mulch, among all the colony.

"Over time, they introduce powerful, comforting ideas, and support them with seemingly magical or miraculous acts which convince us they are true, either acting directly, disguised as humans, or through surrogates. They create these first myths so that humans will grasp some kind of predictable order in the universe and not be afraid. They help us discover tools, to manipulate the environment and domesticate the beasts. Their interventions influence the course of events and the direction of human development in desired ways, enhancing the yield, so to speak.

"As the tribes grow and separate, spreading across the earth, the situation becomes more complex, so the aliens adapt the original myths and knowledge further, propagating new ideas through many more discreet interactions, in order to point us in a more favorable direction and increase our productivity.

"Some of these experiments are more successful than others, but the aliens learn as they go along, realizing that perhaps they weren't as 'all-knowing' as they had originally thought, when they began this experiment. Unfortunately, they endowed their creatures with free will and the ability to reason, qualities which are cherished in their own culture, so humans tend to take some of the ideas that are cultivated and go off on tangents, having minds of their own, after all.

"Eventually, many diverse tribes with their own unique religions develop, each evolved to perform optimally in different areas of the planet, offering unprecedented success and growth. But the aliens realize that humans are taking their beliefs to extremes, in unproductive ways. The ideals of mutual love, respect and tolerance for all life which were originally instilled are lost. The distance between the tribes becomes too great. Their languages, customs and beliefs alter, over time, in such a way that miscommunication and misunderstanding become common, fostered in part by opportunists and charlatans who manipulate the original creeds for their own benefit. Wars constantly break out, destroying much of the progress that has been made.

"The aliens decide to take a different tack, and introduce a new age of reason, through the vehicle of science, to wean us away from the more destructive elements of our religious past. They propagate new ideals of logic and reason, based on examination of our sensory experience, along with the scientific method of research, leading us to powerful discoveries through empiricism. They hope this will get things back on track, by promoting a new universalism among humans, giving us a common platform from which to build unity among all people. They help us develop more efficient means of communication between the tribes, to spread this knowledge more quickly over long distances.

"To some extent they are successful, but the increased size and geographic scope of their human colonies make it difficult to plant these ideas evenly, and they take root more rapidly in some areas than others, resulting in an imbalance of power that causes some groups to dominate others. Though religious groupings are replaced with secular nationalism in many areas, the influence of individual organized religions runs deep in defining these new boundaries, and there's still much conflict and destruction of life involved in the process, to their consternation.

"Despite the taking of many lives by needless violence, the growth of the human colony on the planet, which had always been increasing exponentially, begins to stretch the earth's resources to the breaking point. Humans use science to develop technologies that increase their lifespan and survival rate, but at the same time they develop weapons of mass destruction, devour resources, and pollute the entire planet with the waste products of their civilization, threatening the entire race with extinction. It's getting to be quite a mess on earth. What do the aliens do now?"

"I have absolutely no idea," admits BP. "but I'm sure they'll think of something. Are you making this up, or is that what's really happening? It sounds eerily familiar. You aren't one of these space aliens, are you?"

"No, it's just a story, Beep. I'm simply telling you another myth to explain life on earth, purely for purposes of illustration. Anyway, when the aliens realize the extent of the destructive course humans have taken, they conclude that the root of the problem has been their own dishonesty. The myths they instilled have been distorted and modified over time. The science they introduced to clarify the myths and unite the tribes did not succeed in doing so, but instead, had brought on a whole new set of problems. There are still great arguments among the people regarding the proper way to live, and a sad propensity to kill their neighbors if they don't agree.

"The aliens decide to reveal themselves to all earthlings and tell them the whole truth about their past, in person, undisguised. They appear across the earth, all together, at one time, and admit their role in initiating, guiding and manipulating human history since the very beginning. They explain that it was their intention that we all cooperate and thrive, as we sprang from the same source—not that we should compete for resources greedily, misunderstand, hate and destroy each other, while despoiling the planet.

"They confess their errors, apologize for their condescension, and inform us that from now on they are done meddling in our affairs. We are free and on our own. Now that we know the reality of the situation, no longer suffering from the delusions they cultivated previously, they're confident that we will be able to sort things out and develop as they intended. They can do no more. Telling us that they look forward to the time when we will meet again, they withdraw to their own dimension. Once we have fulfilled our purpose, they announce, as they leave the earth, we will know where and how to find them."

"Whew," says BP, "that's quite a tale. Does it have a happy ending?"

"I hope it will, Beep. The jury is still out. The end of that story, as well as our own history, hasn't yet been written."

"What is it supposed to tell me, then?"

"What did the aliens leave us with, when they departed?" asks Alda, answering his question with another.

BP has to think about this for a moment. "They left us with a lot of confusion, I imagine, over the validity of our knowledge and history. But we still had our experiences, our religions, and our science, along with the new goal to ultimately find them, I guess."

"That's a very good answer. There are, by our nature, two ways for humans to know things: through our bodies and through our minds. Our religions are a construct of our minds, and science is based in our senses. The entire history of human endeavor is composed of this duality, of thought and of sensory experience—a constant, progressive, dialectical synthesis of these two modes of knowing, throughout time.

"The 'confusion' you spoke of corresponds to skepticism, or doubt, which should be a constant companion to our pursuit of what is true. By revealing themselves, the aliens stripped us down to that state, destroying all our preconceived notions about ourselves and our knowledge.

"'Finding the aliens,' as you put it, represents our ultimate goal and purpose, which is to develop our potential and find the truth of our existence, through self-awareness, in order to live well and good.

"The essence of religion, or faith, is born in pure mind, and leads us to conclusions of cohesiveness, of connections to all things, of unity. Science is born in the senses and their reductionism, and leads us to conclusions of separateness, of rampant individualism. What is needed for the future is a new synthesis of these two modes of knowing, a birth of what I would call a 'sensible mysticism,' or a 'mystical empiricism,' which will bring them together, allowing each to inform the other in ways that are essential to our survival, if we do not destroy the planet and ourselves in the meantime, which is still a distinct possibility.

"This synthesis will require an upheaval in our world view of a larger magnitude than the Copernican revolution, however, and will not happen easily. Scientists will insist on physical proof, and those who simply believe in a creed will continue to ignore the settled facts of our sensible reality. What is needed are new methods for us to bind matter and consciousness in ways we have never known. The observer cannot be separated from the observed. The effect of our consciousness on material things must be taken into account. All of our beliefs must be challenged, and these two ways of knowing must be melded."

"But how could this come about?" wonders BP. "Those two ways seem so far apart."

"More than anything, what's needed is a new perspective on time. Both faith and science suffer from problems with the element of time, but in different ways," Alda explains. "In our religions, it's the *duration* of time which causes confusion. The original words and meaning of the founding prophets were not always understood well, even by those who sat at their knees. Once these words were passed on through generations, translated and interpreted in many languages, and applied in different cultures, with evolving social structures and changing needs, the original meanings and messages became subverted or ignored. We must not cling rigidly to obsolete, historical myths which separate us from each other. We must strip the fallacious doctrine and dogma from our views and arrive at the core tenet of our faith—the personal, overwhelming experience of unity that reveals and convinces us of our connections to all things. This is the true *kerygma*, the kernal of all religious teachings. True faith comes from a personal experience of the timeless ideals contained in the original *logos*, the true, transcendent revelation of the Word, not from blindly following a creed by rote.

"What people call God is but the Grand Idea in which everything participates and from which all things come—the supreme, collective intelligence—which is also supremely oblivious and ambivalent. This magnificent idea is in place, and it is unfolding all around us, but it does not meddle directly in our affairs, telling one thing to one person and something else to another, putting them in conflict. It is universal and immutable. Only a false god would allow humans to abdicate responsibility for their worst actions. God does not choose sides, and can't be used as an excuse.

"The problem *science* has with time is that while it underlies all theories and measurements, we have no clear sense of what it actually *is*—it is accepted as a given, entwined with the spatial dimensions, without further scrutiny. Science has illuminated much concerning the nature of the visible universe, facts which I have no doubt are true, but it tells us little of what it is all *about*. Its techniques can approach the beginning and end of our universe, but have failed to tell anyone what is beyond them, where it all came from, and why we are here.

"Scientists must not deny the reality of our spiritual nature and of mystical experience, but rather seek it out, investigate it, and achieve it. In some ways, the methods of science—of doubt, of objectivity, investigation and historical analysis—can be useful in preparing us for true spiritual experience, and might even be capable of explaining it more fully, when reflecting upon it afterward.

"The conceit of science is in its rejection of the truth of subjective, mystical or spiritual experience—of the direct, personal revelation of truth that has been found in pure mind by many people throughout our history, including those without formal education, in so-called 'primitive' cultures. These insights are timeless in nature, and can instill an ethical morality in us without depending on any objective proof, or a written language, or system of mathematics to justify them. The proper ethics to guide its development are what science has often lacked, leading us to horribly destructive discoveries and inventions.

"There are many truths to be found in religious or spiritual activity, and they need not and *should* not conflict with the truth of science—insights must evolve along with our factual knowledge, to lead us eventually to the ultimate good, the Grand Idea. We each must continue our personal, individual quest for direct experience of the transcendent truth, regardless of the organization, society or tradition with which we affiliate ourselves, while we continue to investigate the natural laws of our visible reality. But most importantly, we must develop a new ability to understand and appreciate time, in its fullness, within these quests, for this limitation keeps us from perceiving and understanding the other dimensions of life, where the Grand Idea abides, threatening the survival of the human race in the same way that cars threaten our pets.

"If everyone could know what I know, and see what I've seen, they would understand that there is no conflict between these two paths, and that they can lead us together to the same, right place in the end—if they cooperate, through their own strengths, without one dominating the other. Each tradition has accomplished much, and at the same time, done many shameful things. As Einstein said: 'Science without religion is lame; religion without science is blind.'

"*Science* is something we can learn, and its business is to reveal natural law. *Faith* is something we must experience, and its business is individual enlightenment, the revelation of truth. Both can inspire love and joy, and alleviate fear—the absence of love—in their own way. We can either *learn* to love, or *experience* it directly.

"Unfortunately, at this time in our history, true faith is as rare as enlightened science. Organized religions have often been reduced to cultism, and science has largely been subverted by corporate greed and militarism."

"How do you know all these things, Alda?"

"I believe it's my heightened sense of time that has revealed them to me."

"So I'll never understand? Or be exactly like you and achieve the same insights?"

"Perhaps not exactly in the same way, but if you can grasp these ideas even partially, you will understand that there is no reason for you to fear the death of your physical body at all. That's why I'm here, and what I want most to impart to you, Beep, before we're done."

"That I should not be afraid to die?"

"Yes, that," answers Alda, "and also its corollary—that there are so many wonderful reasons to live, and there is no reason to hasten one's death needlessly. Our dying is the final adventure, but we should not embark upon it before our time has come."

"Oh, you mean my ideas about taking my own life? Don't worry, Alda, you have already helped me realize how stupid that was. I have put such thoughts out of my mind forever, believe me."

"That's good, Beep," says Alda, squeezing his hand. "That's the first step I hoped you would take. I can assure you that death is no more difficult a transition than the one I have already put you through. You must know that

I will be with you then, whenever it comes, as we are linked together forever. All you have to do is remember me and I'll be there, but we will not be in these bodies, and we will not know each other in the same way."

"I will never forget you again, Alda," declares BP, with the most fervent intent.

Approaching her home, as they climb the steps to the front door, she stops and turns to him. "Next, Beep, now that you've decided to live, we must work on what you need to do from here."

"You really *can* read my mind," says BP.

All and Everything

BP and Alda prepare a fine lunch together in her kitchen, and take it out on the patio to eat, while enjoying the crisp weather and the view of the city. The food tastes fabulous to BP and he is ravenous, but his mind is whirling over the information she has offered him—the implications it has for his future. There are so many ideas to consider, but there are unexplainable facets of his recent experience that he cannot let go of yet.

"Can you explain exactly what you did to me, Alda—how you transported me into my own past?" he asks, when he can no longer contain his curiosity. "I don't understand what happened, or even how it could be possible—what the mechanics of such an event could be like. Was it what people call a miracle?"

"Not if your definition of a miracle includes a supernatural cause, because as I've told you, I am not a supernatural being. But it definitely defies the laws of physics, as you know them. All things happen according to natural laws, but all laws of nature have not yet been fully discovered, or clearly known and understood by many. This is where my explanations may become more murky and less helpful, for you can only relate to them through the things that you already know, as I have told you. The simplest explanation would be to tell you that time is like a river, and you are in a small canoe, anchored in that river, as it flows past. All I did was pluck your canoe out of the river and deposit you back at a point downstream, where you would see the same water flowing past you again. Is that a sufficient explanation?"

"Not really," says BP. "That's a massive over-simplification, isn't it? I think I can handle more. I'm in no position to demand it, certainly, and I'll never deny the truth of what you did to me again, but won't you give me a little more information about how you accomplished it, in a way that I can understand? It simply defies all my reasoning that I could be in one place at one moment, and then be many thousands of miles away and a dozen years in my past the next. I desperately want to understand how that happened. Please, please, help me!"

"I can try to be more precise, but it may not allow you to understand any better, until you can see things as I do. In truth, Beep, there are many of these rivers and they are vast and intertwined. You exist in all of them, but there's only one canoe, your consciousness, for you to sit in at any given moment. When you are in the canoe, the electromagnetic milieu of the world is filtered through your body and you share that reality with all the others, floating in their own boats, anchored at the same point on the river. But there are other realities that exist in other dimensions, and you are in them as well, at the same time, you just cannot perceive them in the same way, as you must step off your boat for them to be revealed."

"That makes me wonder, then," says BP, pausing to formulate the words to his query as precisely as possible, "if you sent me to another world, and there's another 'me' out there in another dimension, what is *he* doing right now?"

"He's doing whatever you're doing here, just a fraction of a nanosecond later," answers Alda. "Your consciousness can only be in one place or the other, Beep, you cannot yet be aware of yourself in both worlds at once, as I can. Either *you* are riding in the canoe at any one moment, or *he* is. It is not big enough for both of you. Whatever is happening here will be communicated there in an instant, and he will know it, just as you did when he was here and you were there."

"I think I'm going to need a bigger boat!" laughs BP. After thinking about her words for a moment, he wonders further: "But what is it like for you to be so aware that you can be in two worlds at once, and how do you go there?"

"In some ways, my experiences resemble those told of by mystics and spiritual seekers throughout history, yet different. It's all done in my mind. I usually start by forming an idea of whatever object is grabbing my attention at the time, in its ultimate 'form'—as Socrates would have put it—the true archetype of the thing, both its appearance, including its development over its whole cycle, from birth to death, not just how it appears in the current moment, and its purpose. This gets me going in a certain way of thinking, and as I get to the essence of the idea, my thinking about it stops. I *become one* with the form instead, merge with it, and I take flight. Everything after that happens in the blink of an eye, but I can't really describe to you how far I go, and what wonders I see—the connections and interweaving of things and events—everything is there at once! In some ways, it's very unreal and dreamlike, quite baffling. I can spend hours or even days there, it seems, and sometimes I can even reach out and 'touch' things, though not in the normal sense, and they change. Before anyone even notices I've been gone, I am back in this world.

"What I did to you happened in a similar way, Bob. This will be hard for you to understand, but what you just experienced as the last 12 years of your life recurring over again all happened in an instant, just now, since you've been sitting here with me. Everything you recently experienced, though it seemed to endure for years, happened in the blink of an eye in this world, in this reality we are sharing now. Here, we have only actually met this one time, and between the moment you first saw the bright light, you lived those twelve years going 'sideways,' so to speak, in relation to this shared river of time. It all happened and was over before the chimes stopped ringing in your ears. I helped you to see and experience time in its totality, and you were back in less than a second. Nothing has changed but your mind."

"Omigod...how can that be? I saw and felt it all! It took *forever*...or at least it fully *seemed* like 12 years, in every way," says BP, grappling with this paradoxical tidbit. "But you know, I think I felt the same sort of thing on acid once—I thought I saw a cliff in terms of its whole life, milleniums happened in a few seconds, and the cliff rose up, turned into a giant earthen wave and scared me to death when I thought it was going to dump on top of me."

"That's never happened to me," says Alda, laughing. "Your experimentation with hallucinogens may have given you some clues about this, Bob, and there are certainly such cultural traditions dating far back into the past, but in general, that can be a very dangerous path, and may not bring the results that you hope."

"I thought I could see all the connections between everything while on LSD, too, and I've also felt it sometimes when I was surfing—like I was just such a natural organism, connecting to the ocean and its energy. The porpoises were my brothers."

"That's a much safer and healthier way for you to experience it."

"So you can see these other dimensions?" BP asks.

"It is not 'seeing' in the way you mean, of looking at things with your eyes," answers Alda, "but yes, I sense them, and to some extent I can interact with them, but I must leave my body behind to do it, and with it goes my normal sensory perception as well."

"How can I experience these other connections? I want to know them, too."

"You already do, to some extent, Beep, through your thoughts, or the absence of thought, your dreams, your memories, and your subconscious mind. You can even see evidence of the gateways to them with your physical eyes, now that scientists have developed such powerful astronomical instruments. You know about the 'black holes' in space, no?"

"Yes, of course. They're super-massive points throughout the universe, possibly collapsed stars, that are so dense, with such large gravitational fields, that even light can't escape them. They're said to be warping space-time into a whirlpool effect, sucking nearby matter into them, never to be seen again."

"Ah, yes, never seen again from our little boats on this river," says Alda, "but in truth, space, time and matter come out the other side of these black holes and into other dimensions, in another phase of their existence. This very same transition is happening in the realm of the very small, below the sub-atomic level. There are minute gateways there also, which some physicists call 'wormholes,' that connect to other dimensions as well. These portals, or gateways, can never be observed and known fully from within our sensible reality, as they equal zero and infinity, which mark the beginning and end of our normal perception, and of space and time as we know them. As scientists probe the depths of high-energy physics and the heights of astronomy, they bump up against the limits of their sensory knowledge, but continue to see hints of the truth—that the totality of all that exists is more complex and be-wildering than their wildest speculations. These are areas beyond the scope of their current theories, experiments and instruments. In sub-atomic physics, for instance, they've seen that fundamental particles appear to make *choices*, and can actually move *backwards* in time. What could be more incredible? Matter seems to actually be participating in *mind!*"

"How many of these other dimensions are there?" BP asks in wonder.

"I have sensed at least ten, but I'm not sure how many there are. They are vast—underlying and surrounding our visible universe—and contain all things, past, present, future and beyond. There are other versions of our present world within them, which exist in another phase, another 'polarity', if you will. This is where I put your consciousness when I sent you back—into one of these 'alternate universes', which contains a world so similar to the one you were previously in that you were unable to detect any difference in it, but there, the river of time flowed 'perpendicular' to ours."

"You put me somewhere else, but you said I never left this world. Is this the same world now where I met you the first time? I'm getting so confused."

"It is, but it isn't. You are here now, but you are also there. Didn't I tell you how difficult this would be to describe? It all depends on your definition of 'world.' Such terms are more relative than you imagine."

After pondering this for a few minutes, BP offers a conclusion: "What you are saying seems to me to confirm the 'Many Worlds' interpretation of quantum physics, doesn't it? You should tell the scientific community what you know..."

This causes such a sudden outburst of laughter from Alda that she nearly chokes on the piece of bread she is chewing. "Oh, I tried that at university, Beep, believe me, but they didn't want to hear such things from a 'crazy' young woman, and I never seemed to have quite the knack for higher mathematics to prove it to them in a way they could understand. What would you have me do? Send them all back together in their lives to convince them? That would cause quite a stir! It would be difficult to stay out of the public eye under those circumstances, don't you think? And anyway, at that time I didn't have the same control over these things that I have now. I decided I didn't want to deal with a bunch of stuffy, male chauvinists at any rate, so I struck out on my own—to work anonymously and develop my skills alone, revealing them to a single person at a time, who might be in need of my help. For me, it is the only way to go."

"But if your goal is to change this world, wouldn't it be faster to let more people know?"

"Faster, perhaps, but certainly not safer. Do not underestimate the resistance to change in most humans, Bob, nor the power of a few individuals and ideas to influence the course of events over time. I am in no hurry, and I also want to survive, to pass my genes along to the next generation. If you wish to take this experience and work on the mathematics to justify and prove the reality of it to others during your future life, so be it. More power to you! We need more scientists like that. Just don't come looking for me to demonstrate and confirm your proofs to the world. You must do it on your own, if that is your desire.

"Frankly, I think it will take an extraordinary merging of mathematics, physics, neuroscience and philosophy to convince most people of the existence of alternate realities, or other dimensions, but perhaps it's your destiny to do so. I do believe it will happen sometime. Perhaps not through your efforts or mine, or those of our children, or our children's children, but eventually—as our instruments and communication systems improve, as more people are educated, and their capacities evolve, it will come. Would you have believed it yourself, if I hadn't helped lead you to the conclusion?

"But you'll spend your time better at this point by thinking about your immediate future in this world, at this moment—about the choices you have to make, and not about these highly complex, provocative concepts, which I've so inadequately communicated to you."

"But what could be more important than knowing what reality truly is?" asks BP. "I *so* want to know what the universe is like for you—what these other dimensions consist of and where they are."

"I can try to describe them to you, using the terms of the physics you know, but again, these are just inadequate words to describe the indescribable. Without direct experience, as I have had, this may sound like the stark ravings of a lunatic. It will require a certain amount of faith on your part to accept them, but in the tradition of many prophets in the past, I've given you a small 'miracle' to back it up, so that you will listen well."

"Tell me, then, and I'll try to understand."

"These other dimensions are everywhere, Beep. Some are infinitesimal, and inhabit the same space-time as our current, shared reality, beneath and within the smallest sub-atomic particles we are able to detect. Some are right alongside us, running roughly parallel, immersed in the same river of time, along with our past and all our possible futures. Other dimensions are un-imaginably large, outside our visible universe, which is itself many billions of light years across. They spiral out and around from the ends of our universe, surrounding it totally, and even seep back into, and through, our space-time. Many of the dimensions which are beyond our physical sight are beyond our river of time as well, though they contain it. They can create force waves running through ours, such as the one we call 'gravity.' The reason that gravity is a much weaker force than electromagnetism, or the strong and weak nuclear forces, is because the gravity wave exists primarily in another dimension. It has stronger aspects there, equal to that of the other forces, but interacts within our world on a different scale. I told that to my professor once and he laughed at me! And I could not come up with the mathematical proof of it, so I had to stay quiet."

"I suppose if Einstein couldn't do it, it would be a lot to ask from you," jokes BP.

"You're welcome to give it a try, smarty-mouth," teases Alda back at him. "The mathematics to create a Unified Field Theory are certainly non-trivial, and always make my head spin. Our current science can only go so far in explaining everything that is, for it is tethered to our senses and anchored in the river of time with us. It cannot yet speak to what is beyond the beginning and the end of our visible, physical universe—what is outside the familiar space-time continuum.

"Our world is only sensible to us because of the river of time which is bound to our spatial dimensions. But just as gravity moves through our sensible reality from another dimension, in other dimensions, the river of time as we know it neither appears, nor acts in the same way. It is transformed, and becomes an ocean instead. In the beyond, the reality of these other dimensions is not grasped through the normal senses. All our logic and the most sophisticated instruments of science cannot explore this ocean yet. How does one measure the energy, position or velocity of an *idea*?

"Time is the bedrock of all scientific theory, because without time, there would be no order in which things happen. Even in Einstein's theory of special relativity, which allows for fluctuations in time according to relative velocity, we, as humans, can never experience the physical condition of moving near the speed of light, where time would slow down and stop, as it would take an infinite amount of energy to do this. Thus, our bodies do not have the same direct sense of time as we have of the other three spatial dimensions. This incomplete notion of time has not hindered the success of science, but is its main limiting factor. It constrains us in that we, as observers, can describe only the natural world we can see, the one that supports our existence. In reality, there is much more to be found beyond the visible universe, and we exist in more ways than simply our physical aspect, so science has yet to explain all that truly *is*."

"What is it that truly *is*, then, Alda?"

"There is only *Unity*, in the end, Beep—All, and Everything, is *One*," she answers.

This is a puzzling statement, and BP considers it. "I don't know if I understand what that means, completely."

"I'll try to help you," says Alda, "for if you can grasp it, you will know all that you need in order to live your life well. It is the key to understanding that something did not come from nothing, who you are, why you are here, and what this thing is we call the world, questions which are at the heart of any philosophy or religion.

"Just as this planet of ours is but a tiny speck in the universe, so the entire universe is but a small frogpond in comparison to the ocean that is beyond it—beyond space and time as we know it.

"You must begin by trying to understand time in its fullness, and grasp its true nature and purpose. But to understand anything fully, you must look at what there would be in its *absence*. This is the difficult part, and where most people, and science itself, are unable to go yet. Some people can make this step partially, and actually experience the absence of time through dreams, meditation, prayer, and devotions of all sorts. For you, Beep, this is one of the things that surfing is teaching you, perhaps, through the dilation of your sense of time, which you told me you have experienced when riding waves. But this is just the beginning of experiencing Unity. There is much further to go, still, to understand how everything that exists is One."

"Then you are a monist?"

"Philosophically speaking, yes, but though everything springs from the same everlasting source, this does not preclude the duality that permeates our world. Everything we see is ephemeral and transient—it comes and goes, it lives and dies. Duality is a primary fact of our earthly existence, and we must come to grips with it. Within our universe, there is a tendency toward maximum diversity, and opposites exist simultaneously in all things, in different measures, morphing into new combinations all the time.

"The greatest difficulty in perceiving Unity, is that when *time* is transformed, things do not have to make the same sense anymore. In these other dimensions, anything and everything is possible, because time does not exist there in the same way! Things have no beginning and end, no clear cause and effect, as in our sensible world. There is only All, and it is One and Eternal. Everything that *is* has *always been* and *always will be*. In Unity, there is no creation and no death, there is only Everything—time does not pass, and there is nothing but constant transformation, change and flow, the grand dialectic of opposites. It is impossible to give a clear picture of it with words.

"It is in our minds that we are connected to this eternity, and you can find it, touch it and know it through your consciousness. Our best ideas are what link us to the Grand Idea, the ultimate truth, the collective mind, the One. It is our minds that can join us to all things and bring us to the truth—that we are all related to each other, and to all other things, no matter what our bodies and senses may tell us. Separateness does not exist where there is no time. What we do to others, we do to ourselves.

"The concept of unity creating diversity is not so far away from the current model of the origin of our universe, is it? We are all built out of the elementary particles which came into being from the 'Big Bang.' A singularity produced everything."

"I can see that, similarity," says BP, "and what you've told me will be useful as I learn more about the world, which I certainly intend to do, but there's still the question of *why* it all came about?"

"Simply because within the Grand Idea is Everything, and it must *know itself*. The creation of our physical universe came in a spontaneous explosion of energy, though I would more accurately call it an *implosion* within the All, which always existed. In the first breathtaking moment of this implosion, which was actually the mixing, or collision of two other worlds, very unlike our own, both time and space were born, proceeding at an immeasurable rate in the beginning, stretching out in a way we have never seen since, creating energies, heat and velocities of seemingly impossible proportions. Ultimately, when this expansion slowed down sufficiently for light to exist, it resulted in the totality of all matter being created, similar to what you have learned, except that beyond the edges of our known universe, there is not *nothing*, there is *Everything else*, still feeding and containing our expanding universe.

"From matter, ultimately, came all life, and we evolved finally as human beings, after billions of years, with our minds and our consciousness—giving us the capacity to reflect on our world and ourselves. This is the link that enables us to know from whence we came—our self-awareness—and our awareness completes the great circle—it allows the Grand Idea to know itself. This is what is meant by the saying about God having created us in his own image. It's not that God resembles a man, physically. If God were to assume a body, I prefer to think it would be a woman's, anyway! But the whole idea of an anthropomorphic God is simply a myth, a comforting mental creation that served a purpose in an earlier time. It allows humans to avoid facing the true complexity and multi-dimensional aspects of our existence. It is a travesty, honestly, and it is now obsolete, given our developing knowledge of the world and our current situation within it. This is sad, really, as the full, immense, understanding and experience of Unity can be equally comforting and inspiring, and so much more relevant, realistic and utilitarian in the end, than a God as Man, or Man as God.

"We will never govern ourselves rightly here on earth without recognizing and honoring our connections to all things, the unity of our being. Our leaders, especially, must know and understand these things and act accordingly in guiding human affairs. Would you believe it, Beep, if I told you that in the near future, there will be other wars like the one your country wages in Southeast Asia, but this time in the Middle East, caused by the same persistent ignorance, conceit, misunderstanding and fear that has plagued humans for centuries? Will we never learn that we cannot have peace without tolerance and respect? How could we forget that Jews, Christians and Muslims are all sons of Abraham? Do you understand what I am trying to say?"

""Whew! You warned me this would be dense, but I think I'm beginning to, get it," says BP. "I wish I had a tape recorder, though, and could go over it again tomorrow. This is as difficult as any lecture I ever heard in my philosophy classes!"

"I hope you at least took notes," she laughs, "because we don't have much more time together. It is such a simple idea, and a great insight, but it is also quite complex, and its massive scale is very difficult to capture and communicate. It is even harder to internalize the idea and apply it to daily life. I don't expect you to accept this unquestioningly, but I do hope that you'll contemplate the possibilities further, and try not to forget this. When faced with the complexities of everyday life, especially when being assaulted with absurdities, contradictions, and evilness, that's the most difficult thing to do—to *remember*."

"It's a tall order, I know, especially considering how easily I seem to forget! But when I look at how far the rest of the world has to go to be in harmony with such an idea of Unity, it is very discouraging and frightening. Do we really have a chance to succeed, Alda?"

"There are many possible futures, as I said, and I can't pay attention to them all, but there's reason for hope. Human frailties and fears may never be banished completely from this world—they are in each of us, in a balancing act with our positive aspects. Ultimately, they cannot be fought outwardly and restrained in others, they must be overcome in our own consciousness. Our enemy is ourself. We each must promote love and Unity through the choices we make and how we cast our attention, for the good to prevail.

"I have great faith in the potential intelligence, inventiveness, creativity and resilience of the human race. There are breakthrough events which could come from many quarters in human affairs and tip the balance—by the expansion of our knowledge and understanding; through the process of evolution changing our capabilities; by individuals of conscience, who challenge the inertia of the community and struggle against untruths, injustice and corruption, often at great personal risk; and by science, which can help eliminate competition for resources and the fouling of our environment, possibly even coming to demonstrate the existence of the other dimensions of being.

"Perhaps a scientist in the future will invent a machine which makes the experience of eternity, timelessness, and oneness accessible to all, through a particular physical stimulation of our brains—an 'Ecstasy Machine'—who knows? I certainly don't, but I do know that we have to be guided in all our endeavors by the development and expression of our power to love, according to the principle of Unity, difficult as that may be.

"Most people do not realize the totality of what Unity means until they die, and are not prepared to comprehend it, even though they have called it 'God' their whole lives. When their time here ends, there they are—smack in the middle of it all, without their bodies and their familiar river of time to guide them, and God is not the white-haired, benevolent father-figure they had imagined or were taught. God is actually Everything, and everywhere.

"There is something of Everything in everyone. We each have a seed of it within us, that we can find, nourish and grow while we are here, and that persists beyond our death, when we leave the earthly dimension of time. It is contained within our minds, part of our consciousness. Most people call it our 'soul.' That's why it is said that 'The kingdom of God is within you.' But this is not a supernatural phenomenon, it is another function of our brains which is simply not well understood at this point in our evolution."

"Whoa, I think I know what you mean now—about words not being adequate." At this point, BP is certain that in comparison with Alda's perception of the universe, his own is on a level with the poor, little, squashed dog they had seen earlier.

"Don't worry, Beep, just take whatever you can from these words and think about their relationship to your life. Go to bed now and dream about them, and what you need to do, where you need to go. Let your subconscious mind wrestle with it all while you rest your body, and in the morning we'll deal with the practical application of what you might glean from this experience. Just remember that no one can be happy who acts against their better judgment. You can only be wise when you *are* what you *know.* And you must also be aware of what it is that you do *not* know, for it is this ignorance of the Unity of being which is the source of all evil in our natural world."

A New Day

BP is awakened the next morning by Abraxus, who has come through the open guest room door and climbed onto his chest, purring and digging her claws into the blanket, kneading it rhythmically with her paws. As his fuzzy morning vision focuses, he is greeted with the sight of her emerald eyes, staring back at him, and is reminded of when this happened before, long ago on the train, just before the blinding white light and the ringing of bells in his brain. He shudders at the memory.

"What do you want, kitty?" he asks, without expecting any response. Looking around, he can see that he has slept quite late, as the room is already filled with the glow of morning light, streaming in through the thin, gauzy curtains on the windows. "I better get up," he thinks, lifting the cat off his chest and rolling over, dropping her gently to the floor.

He dresses and wanders down the hall, noticing that Alda's bedroom door is open, but she is not there, nor is she in the bathroom, which is his first stop. He continues into the kitchen, but doesn't find her, so he calls out her name. No one answers. "That's strange," he mutters to himself, putting the kettle on the stove to make some coffee. The cat is circling at his feet, rubbing against his legs, and he notices that her bowl is empty. As he waits for the water to boil, he fills it with the dry food from the large jar on the counter, as he had seen Alda do, and refreshes the water in the other bowl. This seems to satisfy the cat, and she pays him no more attention as she gobbles her kibbles. He finishes making coffee and takes a cup out onto the balcony.

"I wonder where she is? I have so much more I want to talk to her about. This has all been so strange, and so complicated. And I still don't know what I should do, exactly...." Just then, he hears the front door open and shut, and footsteps in the hallway. "Is that you, Alda?" he calls out. "I'm out here on the deck."

"Yes, I'm back," she answers. "Just wait a minute and I'll join you."

He hears some rustling in the kitchen, and soon she appears with a tray of pastries and fruit. "I had some errands to run and you were sleeping so soundly that I didn't want to wake you. I got us some breakfast while I was out. Thanks for feeding Abraxus—she seems quite happy."

As he munches the delicious pastry and sips his coffee, looking out over the city, he is filled with a sense of well-being and peace. Some thoughts fall into place. "I realize now why I ran away from Hawaii, Alda—or at least one of the main reasons. I was so afraid of my cancer, and of dying, that I couldn't face it. I was in denial. When they told me that they needed to cut out a large portion of my upper bicep, and that I wouldn't be able to surf again for many months, and that I might need chemotherapy afterwards, which would be very debilitating, also, and that the cancer may have spread and I could still die anyway, I didn't feel it was worth it. I just wanted to get away—maybe even check out for good. I didn't think I could live without surfing...."

"Surfing has been a big part of your life, Beep, and represents much of your identity," Alda says softly. "I can understand how you felt. Surfing taught you many important things, and helped you manage your life. It developed your body and made it strong. From it, you learned discipline early on, that it would take constant effort and much practice to ride the waves successfully. It gave you courage, to face the frightening and powerful forces of the ocean and to respect and deal with them, while recognizing your own insignificance in its vastness, which brought you humility. It taught you how to focus your awareness and depend on your instincts at times, and to never stop learning from your experiences. It allowed you to express yourself as an artist does, through its medium, and it even unchained your mind from the grip of time, in your tube-riding. It's no wonder you didn't want it taken away from you. It's a huge part of who you are, and what you are to become in the future.

"But it certainly doesn't have to be an 'either/or' situation. It may be required that you leave it for a time, and that you have an extended rehabilitation before taking it up again, but that would not be the end of that world for you, even if you never recover sufficiently to perform at the level to which you aspire. You might still participate in it in other ways, even if you're physically limited, I'm sure—you could become a photographer or filmmaker and document the sport, or write about it for others, or coach young children and beginners in its basics."

"I know you're right. I've sometimes thought if I was unable to surf anymore, I could still build boards for people."

"That would be a worthy occupation. People tend to discount craftspeople in this modern age, but they must be forgetting that Jesus was a carpenter at one time. Did you know the word 'craft' comes from the German root meaning 'magic?'"

"No, I didn't," admits BP. "That's interesting. It does seem like magic when you make a board that rides well. OK, maybe that answers that question, but what should I do about all my other problems?"

"I think you already know what you need to do there too, Beep, if you only think about it and trust your instincts, your knowledge, and your judgment. Remember what I told you when we first met: 'You knew it all before.'"

"What I've really learned here is how little I truly know, and how selfish and ego-centric my life has been up to now...."

"That's a good beginning," says Alda. "True insight has to come from within, from your own understanding. I cannot tell you what to do. You will find, though, that you know enough to do the right thing, if you just think about it, and feel it. We all have the capacity to know right from wrong, if we haven't been too damaged by the circumstances of our lives. However, the power of the moment, the urgency of events and our emotional, conditioned responses to them, often shape our actions and destiny more than truth, or understanding. We must be forgiven, and forgive others, for this tendency, as it is our nature, at this point in human development. But change will come. It will come internally, from within each of us, by the choices we make as we overcome our fears, until it becomes a groundswell of change—a tsunami!"

He sits in silence for awhile, thinking back, reviewing events. He ponders the guilt and grief he feels over Donny's death, and Bumper's, but he realizes that their passing doesn't seem as formidable and confusing to him now, as he is coming to grips with the fear of his own death. He thinks about his possible troubles with the police, and with the Selective Service System. They seem less daunting, too, given his current perspective. "I'm going to go back to Hawaii and have the surgery," he announces, suddenly.

"That's good," says Alda.

"If they have to cut off my whole arm, I'll learn to paddle and surf again with only one," he states, emphatically. "If the cops want to come and arrest me, I will do my time, if need be, and pay my debt to society, but I'm going to fight against that result every step of the way, as I don't feel I've done anything really wrong. If I recover from the cancer, and they still want to draft me into the Army, I'll refuse to serve in war, but I will work for two years in a veteren's hospital emptying bedpans, if that's what it takes, and do it gladly, to serve my brothers who're being wounded and maimed overseas. If the government finds this unacceptable, they can throw me in jail for that, too."

"You are making progress, now!" claims Alda. "That'll address your current dilemmas, but what will you do in the long term?"

BP considers this question for a few moments. "I'm going to find a woman who not only excites me with her body, but stimulates me with her mind, and believes in things the same way I do. I'm going to marry her and spend the rest of my life with her. If she wants, we'll have children. We'll educate and raise them carefully, and when they are old enough, I'll tell them stories about you, and hope that they might develop your gifts.

"Ultimately, I think I'll continue to study science and philosophy, until I can understand all the ideas you have given me in a broader way, and possibly try to make a contribution that might help others, somehow."

"It sounds like you are cured, my friend! Those are brilliant ideas. As Goethe said: 'He who cannot draw from 3,000 years is living hand to mouth.' But do not forget about art, and its ability to communicate our feelings and insights about what is true. You may find someday that the art of surfing may not be the only medium through which you can express yourself. Something else may just spill out, sometime. That's the way that art works."

BP gets up off the chaise lounge in which he has been semi-reclining, and walks around the table to Alda, joining her where she sits on a wooden loveseat, giving her a hug and kissing her on the cheek. "I couldn't have done it without you," he confesses, "I would have just gone nuts alone, or done something irretrievable." Sitting down next to her, he feels like a weight has been lifted from his shoulders.

Alda reaches out to the table, raises the tray of food and withdraws a large manila envelope from underneath it. Leaning back, she says: "I've been waiting to give this to you until now." Opening it and pulling two smaller, white envelopes out from within, she hands one to BP.

"What is this?" he asks, taking the envelope from her.

"Look for yourself." Tearing it open, BP is surprised to find a one-way airline ticket from Paris to Honolulu, departing the next morning.

"What's in the other one?"

"This one is a train ticket for me," Alda says, holding it up. "I have someone to meet tomorrow."

The idea of parting with her brings a stab of sorrow to his heart, but he knows it must be. "Thank you," he says humbly, hanging his head. "You knew what I was going to decide before I did, didn't you?"

"I had a feeling about it, yes, so I just took care of things when I went out this morning. You are ready to move on, now. Don't worry, you know everything you need to know, told to you already by the great teachers throughout history. And you knew in your gut all along that they were right: Do unto others as you would have them do unto you; Love thy neighbor as thyself; Thou shalt not kill; To whom much is given, much is expected; and my favorite, the Great Law of the Iroquois nation: 'In every deliberation we must consider the impact on the seventh generation...even if it requires having skin as thick as the bark of a pine.'

"You probably learned everything you needed to know before you reached puberty—it is just too easy to forget or push it aside out of fear, or in the selfishness of the moment. Don't ever forget that you are connected to all things, and the true nature of time. It is not about *you*, Beep, it is about *us*. If you want the short form, in my own words, here it is: *The only things that are important in this life are love, compassion, service and ideas.*

"By *love*, I mean all forms of it—the love of yourself must be foremost, along with the love of doing right things. Take care of your canoe, and steer it to the best of your ability, or all other forms of love become impossible. That is why you must heal your body first, and accept whatever treatment is necessary to restore your health, otherwise there will be no 'you' to experience and share the love to come—of your mate, your children, your parents, and your extended family of friends—the love for everyone and everything in the world, along with the awe and wonder over your chance to experience it all and be aware of your connection to it.

"In *compassion*, I include *empathy*—that you must strive to sense the feelings of others and recognize the plight of the less fortunate. Never forget or ignore their suffering, and consider well the impact of your actions. If you make a mistake, despite your best efforts, when you realize it, just pick yourself up, apologize to those you may have harmed, do your best to repair the damage, and go on.

"By *service*, I mean that everyone must hold up their piece of the sky, maintaining their portion of this reality through constructive works. Take responsibility for yourself, and do whatever you can to take care of others as well. Everyone and everything has a purpose to fulfill, and something to contribute, even those who are born to do nothing but struggle and die. Those who inherit more fortunate circumstances are required to sacrifice more greatly.

"By *ideas*, I mean you must seek, respect and use your human ability to think, reason, learn, and be aware of yourself, to develop your best judgment. Use your imagination and energy to achieve good things, and not to cause harm. Share your ideas with others, and use them to fly into other dimensions if you can. Ponder time in its totality and in its absence, and who knows how far you will go?

"It may help you to remember these things by equating them with the energy fields of physics that you learned in school. In human affairs, *Love* is a form of the strong nuclear force, binding us closely together with the people we know well. *Compassion* is a form of the weak nuclear force, allowing us to feel the sorrow and joys of others, tying us to the people we might know less well, or have not yet met. *Service* is gravity, the weaker but essential force that keeps the fabric of society from flying apart, and binds humankind together over great distances. Electromagnetism is the *Idea* field, the medium and vehicle for human enlightenment, interaction and unity across all boundaries.

"It's in the way we focus our attention that things become real to us, and that change is possible, both in ourselves and the world. If you can internalize these insights and act accordingly, you'll always know what to do, even if it's to deal with such a seemingly complex and contradictory act as laying down your life to save that of a stranger. If it is truly the time for such selflessness, you will know it, and have nothing to fear."

"I think I'm beginning to get it, now. Thank you so much, Alda. I will try to remember every word of this and practice those principles in my life, from now forward."

"That's all I have hoped for, Beep."

"Can I ask you one more thing?"

"Certainly."

"What are you going to do now, when I leave?"

"Do you mean in the short or long term?"

"Both, I suppose."

"Well, in the short term, I'm meeting someone tomorrow whom I first encountered ten months ago. And just so you don't get your little jealousy hackles up, she's a Spanish woman I met in my travels. Her problems stemmed from the death of her firstborn in childbirth. We have a rendezvous I must not miss.

"In the long term, I will continue my struggle for a new paradigm, acting like a space alien from my parable, only on a lesser scale. I'll attempt, in my own small way, to abolish people's delusions and fear, much as Plato's cave-dweller did when he was freed and realized that what others in the cave believed to be real were merely shadows cast on the wall. I'll encourage them to not look outside themselves for their salvation any longer, not to depend on myths, but to seize the *truth* instead. All we need to know is within us, if we only use the powers with which we are endowed, in our minds. I know this is true, and although I am not willing or able to announce it to the whole world at once, I will continue to reveal it to one person at a time, in a way that may bring them to accept it.

"Our evolution is changing the situation all the time, by means of alterations in our genes and by the accumulation of our knowledge. One day we will all have the insights, objective facts, plus the neurological equipment, to enlighten us fully. These things will be accessible to everyone, or at least to a critical mass of people, who will then be able to save the world for the generations to come, and we'll have no need for distorted myths or hatred any longer.

"We'll reach this truth eventually—individually and spontaneously, and be able to feel it, touch it, and dwell in it, as I do, without resorting to any outside intervention. Until then, I am going to continue prodding things along, one suitable human being at a time."

The next day, before the sun rises very high in the sky, BP boards a plane bound for Hawaii, and Esmeralda catches a train for Madrid.

ABOUT THE AUTHOR

Little is known about Stewart Parks, and he seems to like it that way, having refused to submit to his editor either a photo or biography for inclusion in this publication. We have been able to establish that he is a fourth-generation native of San Diego, a UCSD graduate, a member of the WindanSea Surf Club, and a lifelong student of physics, philosophy, and cosmology, who can often be found prowling the beaches of southern California.

He claims that his consciousness is frequently involved in inter-dimensional time travel, but his wife tells us that when this happens, it just appears to her that he is napping in his well-stuffed, black leather Barcalounger®.

—Ed.